SHARKS WITH LIPSTICK

SHARKS WITH LIPSTICK

Hinemura Ellison
&
Ted Hughes

BACH DOCTOR PRESS

This first edition 1.0 published in 2018 Bach Doctor Press

ISBN: 978-0-473-45613-9

Cover design by: Artistic Studio

Dedication:

The utmost thanks to our loving whānau without whose tireless support this mahi would not have been possible. Like the cycle of life, the seasons in time, it has evolved from Te Pū, to Te Pō. Tihei, Mauri Ora

Acknowledgements:

To our fabulous Beta Readers, you know who you are,
keep shining.

Ko te kāhui mauka, tū tonu, tū tonu, ko te kāhui takata
karo noa, karo noa ka haere

The people will perish but the mountains shall remain.

He mahi kai takata, he mahi kai hōaka

It is work that consumes people, as greenstone
consumes sandstone.

Ngāi Tahu whakataukī

Contents

PART 1

THE WEEKEND BEGINS AND ENDS
with a twist, but business as usual

PART 2

MONDAY MORNING
Meetings and more meetings

PART 3

MONDAY AFTERNOON
Meetings and even more meetings!

PART 4

LATE MONDAY AFTERNOON
All is revealed, or is it?

PART 5

NEWS FLASH, THE BS HAS HIT THE HEADLINES
At last!

PART 1

THE WEEKEND BEGINS AND ENDS

With a twist, but business as usual

Prologue

With blood dripping from a nasty gash across her forehead, the woman slips in and out of consciousness as images flash through her mind. She can see them as vivid as life and she asks herself, *Is this series of events what you see before or after death? Or am I already dead?*

Horrified at what she sees and hears, the fear of rejection along with disappointment surges through her.

The poor woman cannot bear the flash of lights, mixing in with the loud and disturbing voices. Screaming into her vision come people from her life, previous school principals, classmates, friends, colleagues, bosses past and present…even her shrink! It is too much for her and she blacks out, hitting her head severely against the toilet cubicle door, slamming it shut when someone tries to push it open.

She comes to again, the voices in her head become raucous slipping from her sub-consciousness with a force that abruptly startles her awake. Her head throbbing, she tries to stand but is now far too weak. She surrenders to her exhaustion and sits back on the toilet, swaying in time with the gentle rocking of the train. It is almost soothing to just go with the flow. The slow, repetitive motion of the train sending her back into a stupor. She sees a flash of faces and not one of them has anything nice to say. They all blur into one before a couple of them stand out as if they were the 'passed over' souls who appear at psychic readings raising their voices above the others queuing up, clamouring to get their message across to their loved ones still residing on Earth.

She recognises the face of Nigel and hears him spit out "I've never met such a nasty piece of work before. You should be ashamed of yourself. You are meant to be using your position to empower women, to encourage their voices to be heard. Instead you suppress them, and you deflate them. I feel sorry for your children, *if* you have any…or perhaps your mother..." his voice peters out and the next one promptly comes in.

Carmen flashes into her mind. "How could you take advantage of people's weaknesses and exploit them the way you have? Why did you bother with that engagement survey and oversell it to everyone spouting that all answers would be treated with utmost discretion and confidence and then crucify those who gave you constructive feedback by performance managing them out of their roles?"

It's like a 'death by PowerPoint' slide show, with images that just keep playing over and over in her mind.

Stephanie appears, but louder, more confident and articulate than in real life. "I was here to help you. I accepted you were the better person for the role and I stepped down graciously. Only to be humiliated by your cruel words of 'how could I have ever thought I was a worthy enough contender for the HR Director role, let alone someone's ideal partner.'"

Bernard's voice booms out over Stephanie's, with the words and tone of a former school principal. "I'm sorry. I can no longer support you. I understand you have been going through a tough time, but I must take into consideration the safety and wellbeing of everyone else here. You just can't treat people this way. I had hoped for better. I'm so disappointed."

Other faces appear all with a similar theme. The woman says to herself, *Oh my god, what is the point?*

Chris is worst of all laughing out loud like a demon possessed, pointing his finger in her face and smiling like the cat that had just scored the cream. "I told you, your day would come. You were wrong, we are not peas in a pod. We may have been brought up on the same side of the tracks, but unlike you, I'm not all smoke and mirrors. You are about as real as your fake imitation Gucci watch, all show and no substance…"

The train rattles on into the night towards its destination, the woman finally losing her battle with consciousness.

Chapter 1

Friday evening, close of business, 'It's a wrap'

With a tinge of narcissism crossing her lips, Cat smugly finishes her memo and tightly packs her highly confidential papers into her deep, designer laptop bag.

In her mind, she reviews the memo she has written. Smirking and cruelly saying to herself, *same time of the year, same topic, just different people.* Pushing herself contently away from the desk she decides against engaging the send button to an email she has been excitedly working on. Her brain ticking over, *No, let them suffer a bit longer,* the HR Director sniggers to herself. They are mostly deadwood anyway and it's high time for them to wake up and realise they all have cushy numbers. She is over their personal grievances and the union with their ranting that they're 'working too hard' or it is 'not in their job description'. She decides she's doing them a favour, they need to go out and experience the real world, and realise how lucky they had it. Some may even see later with hindsight that the pitiful lives they have led have been boring, monotonous and heading in one direction, towards a DEAD end.

With that done she throws her slinky, long leopard print overcoat over her shoulders and heads out from her cubical with her laptop and todays' shopping, charging full steam ahead. Her bearing set, she passes through the open-plan office, around the sterile rows of half empty pods where the rest of her minions sit day after day.

Each part of the pod layout within the huge open-plan office is a mirror reflection of each other, neat orderly uniformed rows of white flat pack minimalistic desks, three in a row, each spying on one another from close quarters. A bit of privacy being allowed for with low white plastic partitions, giving each pod user a smidgeon of wall space to hang up some corny corporate statement to show they are on board the Big Super Ministry journey. The problem that no one knows what the destination is or how to get there, is a minor detail.

Scattered over the entire floor one can see sterile clusters of whiteness, broken up into two very definite compartments, a bit like the inside of an aeroplane. The end of each compartment features a communal 'break out' area, each of these configured differently and decorated by a person who was obviously colour blind or a plane spotter tripping from psychedelic drugs. With each floor differentiated by colour, the sixth floor purple to represent Thai Airways and another floor teal to represent Air New Zealand, with another decorated in orange to represent EasyJet or Jetstar, depending on which continent you resonate with.

Cat walks past the multi-coloured area ignoring the remaining staff, her stride purposeful with her mind scheming on the devastating blow she will deliver to the public servant plodders on Monday. She smiles while gazing at the faces looking on, wondering how many tears she will generate with her devious announcement. Perhaps she might even break her own record of twenty-three tearful outbursts from the last time she initiated such a structural change to the wimps at her previous employment.

*****

Cat worms her way past another set of pods, her departing shadow causing another pair of smouldering eyes to cut daggers. *Damn that merciless woman! The sanctimonious self-styled Queen of slicing and dicing. Just wait until I've finished with you, you nasty piece of work,* Carmen thinks to herself. The Senior HR Advisor quickly reapplies her thick, black mascara. Snatching her handbag from the desk top, she purposely but discreetly follows Cat out from the floor.

Suddenly, the silence is shattered as a conversation takes off in the middle of the floor.

"Oh, I know it's just sooo unfair, darling! You know how it is, Ernest, I have to be seen to be putting in the hours, or that pitiless prude will have me out on the street faster than you can mix a cocktail sweetie!" Nigel, Head of Recruiting tries to explain to his much loved partner. "That malicious bitch will come a cropper one day and I think I know just how to do it..."

There is silence once more, but just for a moment while Nigel reviews his plan in his mind. "What's that?

Sorry, I was away with the fairies…I know it's a poor pun darling…Yes, yes I'll be there as soon as I can…but put the bottle of Bolly in the fridge, we will need to celebrate once I've finished…"

Half listening to Ernest at the other end of the line, he watches Cat nearing the exit and sees Carmen not far behind, her face set and hard. *Cat really has got herself quite a fan club,* Nigel thinks to himself. *If she tries much harder she'll be carried out in a coffin before the end of the month, although no one would want to give her the satisfaction of carrying such a heavy item, she would probably just slide out on her own slime.*

"...see dear I heard you, no I wasn't somewhere else... anyway, who says us men can't multi-task?"

*****

Raising her head above her pod, Sven, the Big Super Ministry's new lifestyle coach watches the women stride away from her, Cat firstly with Carmen following closely behind. *Wow, if Carmen's looks could kill, Cat would be history!* Samantha Ann Svensson is relieved that Cat has finally left so she can stop playing the silly game of being seen to be putting in the hours, she's thankful that there's still enough time to get to the train and meet the girls. Half listening to Nigel's phone conversation, she packs her handbag to comply with the latest 'clean desk' policy – a management directive meaning each time she leaves her desk (even to go to the toilet), she must de-clutter like a good spring clean and have the surface free of paper, folders, and all secret confidential material, especially if she is lucky enough to have a 'Red Folder'.

Sven sits in one of these spartan, open-plan, spiritless, replicated areas. Unlike her last position where she was surrounded by colour, pictures and highly expressive and articulate fun people.

Sadly, she finds the BS Ministry the opposite of the above where creativity and innovation in the true sense must be inhibited at all costs. However, like with most rules, they have made an exception with Christmas. Each pod has a competition to dress or jam-pack their pod with as many tacky $2 shop Christmas ornaments as possible to win a surprise prize. Sven has timed it well. With only weeks before Christmas, each pod has suddenly taken on a unique personality and any resemblance of sheep mentality is temporarily put on hold.

This is the one time of the year people can express their individuality, where they can tap into that latent creativity and burst out with innovative ideas. Unfortunately, it is not that spontaneous or random; there must be meetings to discuss the contents that come in from home and the 'Xmas pod decoration' committee must agree with each idea. Anything too radical will be intercepted and not allowed through the front door, and if it does somehow slip through the security channels, then the offending merchandise must be kept tightly packed away and taken home at the first opportunity, to comply with the 'clean desk' policy. Sven is still struggling with the absurdity of the inconsistency of it all.

Coming from the private sector after being head-hunted by the Departmental Chief Executive (DCE) Bernard 'BJ' Johnson, while working in her Grandfather's native Sweden, Sven finds the public service similar to visiting a foreign country, where you don't know the language, acronyms, customs and wonder if you're even on the same planet.

With ninety per cent of the BS Ministry's occupants filling their days with non-existent job descriptions, no big picture purposes and sitting around in danger of catching piles, Sven finds herself and her role misunderstood. Enduring boring stuffy meetings which end with no real outcomes, but she has been given free rein by the DCE and that means there are two ways to tackle this beast.

One option is to sit around bored surfing the internet, drinking copious cups of tea and the acceptable quota of coffee, reading a book and self-destruct. Or two, treat the experience as an adventure and explore this brave new world of Public Service land, Wellington city, and break the day into little projects and endeavour to keep to her mantra of doing her best (no matter what).

One of her official projects being tasked by Bernard is to attend the multitude of tedious meetings and report back to him their content and outcomes. Most meetings, alas, are beyond boring and in order to keep sane, she makes notes, brushes up on her te reo Māori (one of New Zealand's official languages) and vents through writing poetry.

Another effective way of whiling away the time in her new office besides collecting her weekly pay cheque is to exercise. On returning to the Land of the Long White Cloud, Aotearoa, she noticed some colleagues were now sporting different coloured plastic wrist bands, another twenty-first century digital invention, the Fitbit. She straight away copied some of the smarter clones and invested in this new wearable device-cum-accessory. This new toy has been a godsend, and has basically given Sven a whole host of non-work related challenges she can strive for during the working day. Syncing her steps to an app on her smartphone and comparing steps with her bestie Clara at the end of each day. A wonderful way of doing her exercise during work hours, a bit like the Defence Force where Clara is currently contracted to.

Fortunately, as Sven is promoting and advocating for health and wellbeing, she could claim reimbursement for her new trusty Fitbit for it is classified as a tool of the trade and just wearing it and putting it to good use reinforces to her fellow colleagues that she is practising what she is preaching: the Hauora (health and wellbeing) of her colleagues.

After working a little too hard while abroad and having to actually put in at least ten-hour days, coming home and truly working only a smidgeon of those hours, Sven is in her element, having found something she can do that adds value during the working day. Naturally, while multi-tasking with the above, she manages to reflect on where she could make the most impact with her coaching skills within the four solid Art Deco walls of BS Castle (as their building is so fondly known).

Sadly, the office interior and décor does not coincide with the classical architectural exterior of the 1930s. With the exception of the bright, vivacious interior colours in the break out rooms, and the odd innovative tall poppy specimen of the human kind, the majority of the floors and its inhabitants blend into one mass of unoriginal black dress attire and the uninspired whiteness of the pods. The people, their papers, and pasty face complexions blend into one. In HR, in particular, no one figure really stands out from the crowd screaming 'innovation and creativity' like the much talked-about polished and revised yearly Mission statement.

Each of the nine floors are filled to capacity with clones glued to the latest LED screens, or those who were 'hot-desking' attached to their laptops or tablets. However, they have something else in common, all tightly holding smaller, slimmer digital devices that appear surgically attached to their palms, another amazing twenty-first century must-have toy created to make people's minds more fragmented and busier – the smartphone!

****

Chapter 2

Reception, the front window to the Super Ministry

Her office receding behind her, Cat, or Cathryn Ann Tennyson which her father used to yell at her, and now more importantly known as THE HR Director at the Big Super Ministry, heads briskly towards the lifts, her padded shoulders moving confidently in sync with her stride.

For almost a year she has been working at the Big Super Ministry, the Ministry of all ministries, located in the heritage building in downtown Wellington. Locally it is known affectionately as BS Castle – yes, BS and brimming full of Bull Shit. It has been a Wellington tradition that the largest government department should always be located at BS Castle, churning out similar folders and projects for similar looking ministers since Wellington was crowned the public service capital of New Zealand in 1865.

One day four years ago, coincidentally on April Fools'

Day, a group of crusty old long serving ministers decided to do something unheard of and create something new. Over a few too many expensive Scottish single malt whiskies at the parliamentary restaurant Bellamys, they randomly grabbed a table napkin out of a waste paper basket and scribbled furiously, carrying on over the back of a fag packet, writing down the names of five ministries. These five ministries would be lucky enough to merge and become one happy family. And voilà, on that very day, the BS Ministry was innovatively and strategically created.

One could ask why these random departments?

The purpose of the liquid lunch was to address how to cover up their own huge incompetency while running the five ministries, Labour, Employment, Immigration, Science and Children's welfare that they were each held accountable for. Cleverly, they could pass the new ministry onto a junior upstart MP and watch him fail spectacularly from the side-lines. A brilliant plan and hey presto, the newly conceived entity was nicknamed quite aptly the Big Super Ministry.

A star was born, although little did anyone realise that it was a shooting star, one huge fireball about to crash and burn.

Emerging from the lift, Cat drops an envelope off to the reliable Aileen at the reception area. "Please get this on tonight's courier – it must be delivered first thing Monday morning to the Minister. I'm off to catch the train."

"Oh, it's Friday, it's Kiwi Con's Happy Hour, Cat. Enjoy a wine or two," Aileen greases, knowing full well she must do whatever it takes to keep her job. She, like too many of the building's occupants, has a mortgage for life and is aiming to have it paid off by the ripe old age of seventy. *Only ten years to go*, she thinks proudly to herself. She and her husband had to buy the biggest house in the worst street, in order to show it off to her friends. It was the standard thing to do when she first got married to her husband Jim, four decades ago. Though she has been paying for this error of judgement ever since by having to front up to the Department of Labour and every other government department across town and pretend to be nice to everyone as the department's official face to the public.

Those she needed to show off to have moved on and are no longer her friends. The street they bought in has never gone places, even though the real estate agent at the time had insisted in her over-used cliché, 'This suburb, especially this street, is up-and-coming', and sadly the reverse happened with all sorts of undesirables moving in. She has tried to sell her marital home several times to downsize since the children have left home, to no avail. Chained to the house, she must stay on at BS well after her retirement age of sixty-five and suck it up, and one of those things she must 'suck up' to is the young Cathryn Tennyson. The woman makes Aileen's blood boil, but she puts up with it, and she continues to repeat her mantra of 'Fake it till you make it' to herself each time she must be pleasant to the likes of Cat.

Passing through Security Cat gives off another 'shark with lipstick' fake smile to one of the good-looking security guards Dave, who gives her the eye, shamelessly taking in her feminine curves from top to toe. Passing through the doors to the outside world, she lets out a huge sigh of relief, turns and races off with great strides in the direction of the railway station near the end of Featherston Street, one of the many prominent one-way streets in downtown

Wellington.

Depending on what time of the day it is the street transforms itself into a sea of waddling, hunched men and women dressed in black and grey. They look bedraggled and windswept on the best of Wellington days in gale force winds. It's the only time the men can be distinguished from the women. The women's pasty faces are concealed by their skirts lifting generously into the air like parasols mimicking Mary Poppins, flying at great speed out of control towards their destination, or worse still, depending on the direction of the wind, towards the harbour's edge.

Cat, very short in stature, with signature bright red lipstick, sporting a short black bob hairstyle with deep green eyes contrasting with the grey-clad zombies. The difference markedly apparent being a tailor-made top to accentuate her cleavage, with a mid-length flowing skirt.

Stalking down the pavement in her bright red high-heeled shoes making her look three inches taller than she actually is, she joins and merges with the masses of people and together they march as if they were trotting down the Mall in London. Instead of trees and a park, they pass the now derelict office buildings which stare out forlornly, wondering what they have done to be left waiting for another city engineer to sign off an edict to transform them into a pile of rubble.

Wellington's large earthquake a month earlier has resulted in a few of the office buildings now being classified 'condemned' and many a public servant is now homeless, meaning more than usual are now supposedly working from home. Who would know? Although there is no nosey fellow pod worker or CCTV towering over them clocking their 'working' hours from home, there is Big Brother in the form of a little green light that shows everyone that is logged into their Outlook mail account.

Cat, feeling the wind up her skirt turns a shade of scarlet red to match her lipstick for like her fellow female walking companions, she finds her skirt lifted by the gale force winds, its form flying over her shoulders to display her skimpy lacy red lingerie to the delight of the three homeless men begging with open beanies lining the route to the station while her fellow commuting companions who pretend not to notice and continue to stare blankly straight ahead.

From the full view of windows and protruding balconies from high-rise buildings and fellow government departments, down below is a mass of grey, swirling and battling against the strong Friday evening winds.

Most Fridays around 5pm, the weather changes – the winds come up, the rain pours horizontally in and the working city's inhabitants evacuate. Everyone heads as far as public transport will allow them into the surrounding suburban hills to hibernate for another two days, returning on Monday rested and rejuvenated; well that's the theory.

*****

With Cat's recent departure from BS Castle, Aileen lets out her own sigh of relief, turns to her workmate Sally and raises her eyebrows. It's always Sally and Aileen who are rostered on and the last to leave the building on Friday evenings. The young ones have lives of the social kind and need to get going on Fridays, while the older ones stay on to 'hold the fort'. Aileen taps away on her keyboard with nicotine-stained fingers from her youthful days being a heavy smoker. She has never ventured into Botox but her younger colleagues at Reception have felt the need. Today Botox is compulsory, like a ritual of smoking Pall Mall filters from bygone days; costing just as much and in the long term probably doing the same amount of damage.

Aileen believes in the good old-fashioned business dress etiquette and still wears her frilly laced white shirt with black imitation tie and bright orange lipstick which accentuates those lovely lines around her mouth that most people of her age have from inhaling cigarettes religiously over the last five decades. The bright orange lipstick is a classic, Rimmel from back in the swinging sixties – 1963 to be precise; she ordered boxes of it when it was on end-of-line special at the make-up counter of DIC, another old historical building which housed a department store back in the sixties.

Aileen jokes with her old-time workmate. "Sally, you have to keep in her good books or you'll be down the road before you know it. That Cat operates in a devious way, being lovely and sweet to those she knows can make a difference to her career, and scratching and clawing out at others when things don't go her own way. She has a reputation for being a survivor, a cat with nine or should I make it *ten* lives.

As for her work colleagues, they scurry and run for cover whenever they see her, scattering in polar directions if they get the chance. However, like all good cats, she has great eyesight and can spot someone a mile off, leaving the person she is stalking very little time, if any at all, to run for cover."

To be fair, Sally hasn't had a lot to do with Cat, but she is a good judge of character and keeps her ear close to the ground – her modus operandi to stay beneath the radar, collect her pay cheque and do the minimum required. "I hear Cat has shafted people over countless other organisations and sadly this ministry will not be the last. Evidently she casts aside anyone standing in her way, and then she sets out to empire-build by surrounding herself with her favourite brown-nosing 'Yes' people," Sally replies.

"Aye, Cat's specialty – nepotism; the more the merrier, surrounding herself with those who worship her – fellow smiling basking sharks whose bright, velvet red lipstick matches, revelling in the discord they cause," Aileen continues. "No one lasts very long as 'everyone has a use-by date', and if they don't dance to her tune, then it's out the door before the ink has dried on their termination letter!"

"With today's employment law, you would think she wouldn't be able to bully and dismiss people the way she does," Sally queries.

"Unfortunately most people do not have the financial or emotional capacity, let alone the balls to hire a lawyer and fight their battles, even if they do have a fair case of constructive dismissal and belong to the good old union," Aileen comments.

"Oh, I know! Each place she has gone to Cat has done the same, by restructuring, downsizing and casting off people like they are poor pathetic rag dolls in some hideous pantomime, happily chirping as she pounces on from one place to another. 'Time to slice and dice again', how does she sleep at night?" Sally laments.

Aileen gazes back to Sally and nods in agreement; she has heard rumours already surfacing about the next chop. Her thoughts are interrupted as a furious Carmen stalks by. She hears Aileen say farewell and smiles too, but Sally already knows from what she has heard that Carmen could be the one Cat cuts off at the knees next.

*****

Chapter 3

On the train

Cat's march is brisk pounding the pavement on her way to the railway station, her matching laptop and phone case in one hand and a large bag full of the latest fashions purchased in between meetings and coffee catch-ups in the other. She awkwardly keeps her skirt down beneath her hips running for shelter away from the Wellington winds. She looks forward to trying on the new black number with extra high matching heels; a real power outfit to make her look even more intimidating when she makes the announcement on Monday, not to mention giving her tits a standout performance more than usual. *Now* that *will get his attention, she thinks to herself.*

It's exactly one minute after the stroke of five and public servants are spilling out from buildings all over town, heading towards bars, shops, parking buildings, bus stops and the train station.

Approaching the Kiwi Connection, Cat admires the

grand old lady as one of the few trains still owned and run by KiwiRail. The luxurious seven-carriage train that whisks the Wellington workers to and from the capital each weekday is a thing of beauty recalling the bygone era when rail was king.

The journey of this plush steel machine starts in the mornings from Palmerston North, a small satellite city just over two hours' train ride away from Wellington. Its quest to satisfy those willing to grace its compartments begins each weekday around 6am. It parks up in the railway yards in Wellington from 9am until 4.30pm each day and then makes the comfortable passage home north again, most of her passengers still looking as frazzled as they were when they got off the train eight hours earlier. The Kiwi Connection, or KC as it is affectionately known, leaves at 5.10pm from the capital, stopping at the main stations of Paraparaumu and Waikanae on the Kapiti Coast before stopping at three more stations en route – Ōtaki, Levin and Shannon, arriving at its destination of Palmerston North at around 7.10pm.

On board the KC, there are five to eight carriages depending on demand, including a buffet car and fully-stocked bar, the seats sumptuous and comfortable and strategically centred around shiny white plastic tables. This way the commuters can stare into their screens, or each other's eyes if they dare to make eye contact, eat, drink, or be merry, whatever takes their fancy.

The fare is well priced and only a couple of dollars more than the foreign-made and operated commuter trains which stop at every station imaginable, where there is no space at all to sit, let alone stand, and certainly no conveniences. While the KC sports a bar and food menu, not forgetting the power points to recharge one's important twenty-first century accessories – phone, vibrator, laptop and the like. These commonly used devices are glued to various parts of the body, like a permanent appendage. Whatever happened to the old-fashioned briefcase and newspaper to go with it? Not to mention the coat, hat and umbrella. The umbrella in Wellington is a complete waste of time, due to the overbearing southerlies. Often numerous discarded umbrellas can be seen afloat in the harbour or stuffed unceremoniously in umbrella-type cemeteries.

Cat likes to consider herself classy and is on the highest salary she has ever been on. What's splashing out on twenty bucks more a week in return for sitting in magnificence and reducing the journey time in and out of the capital each day? In Cat's opinion, it's also a status symbol to be seen riding the more superior train, like first class, as opposed to the regular trains which are designated for the menial and lowly paid.

Cat confidently places her heel onto the first step of the carriage, and holding the rail, pulls herself up off the platform and onto the next step. She wobbles a little as she balances herself, only to get the heel of her two-day-old stilettos stuck in the step. She wobbles again as she tries to retain her balance, lifts her foot and attempts to proceed into the compartment. She slips, banging her forehead and shoulder against the corner of the door's edge, her shoe still firmly on but the heel now lodged within the groove of the step.

"Damn, what sort of dickhead created a step like that? Hardly user-friendly for women with high heels – clearly a man designed this train!" she says out loud, exasperated. Focusing once more, she tries to remove the now firmly lodged heel from the groove of the step, but is unsuccessful, snapping the heel from the shoe, resulting in almost falling headfirst back down onto the platform, while still balancing all her accessories – bag, phone and shopping in one hand and holding onto the train rail with the other. She gives up leaving her heel behind and tries to proceed as elegantly as possible, hopping lopsidedly down the aisle to her usual carriage four. Almost in tears she grits her teeth, she had spent at least five-hundred dollars on those pair of heels. "KiwiRail is going to pay for this inconvenience, big time!" She shouts to the stunned passengers. Her mind already working on the letter she will send in the morning, she can see it now: *'KiwiRail, I'll serve you one on social media, watch and stand aside for the fallout and female customer backlash!'*

Most of the passengers have already settled nicely into the regular Friday night ritual, having obviously left work the second their bosses' backs had been turned. In their frivolity, they are raising and clanging beer bottles and wine glasses to celebrate the beginning of another weekend. *Oh, they really are so simple-minded and so easy to please, you would think they had never experienced a Friday before,* Cat angrily thinks as she pushes her way past the masses down the narrow aisle of her regular carriage.

"Hi Cat. What time is your announcement on Monday?" Bernard asks, while Cat brushes past her boss.

"I can't talk now, I have just been highly humiliated, that pig of a step grabbed the heel off my shoe and now I am lopsided. You haven't got a spare heel in your man bag by any chance, have you?" She rummages around in her shopping bag and pulls out her new pair of shoes and puts these on instead.

Bernard is left speechless, not sure what to say. Trying not to laugh from embarrassment, eventually he finds the words. "Look, I am sorry about that Cat. Let me buy you a drink."

"It's FINE," she exclaims. Now she has her brand-new shoes on, she feels complete. Knowing she is naturally very short, she can't allow anyone to see how short she really is, otherwise she would unnecessarily blend in and she can't be having that. She composes herself and replies to his original question.

"Right, Monday morning, of course, how could I forget? It will be starting at eight-thirty sharp, a stand-up in 101, Bernie dear, don't be late." Cat smiles wickedly. "Off to the bach this weekend then?" she says rhetorically, moving off down the carriage, not bothering to wait for a reply.

"How do you put up with her disrespect, Sir?" asks Stephanie, after Cat has moved out of earshot. Stephanie, the mousey Assistant HR Director, who was passed over for Cat, is still licking her wounds from not getting the role and their last nasty conversation. She believed it was a natural progression for her to be awarded the new HR Director role, but this time round, it was not meant to be.

Bernard, the relatively new DCE of the BS Ministry responds. "Well, she came with good references from the corporate sector and made quite a presentation at the Rotorua conference, so I thought it would be a good move politically with the Minister to bring in a more corporate dynamic as there could be relevant synergies with the size of the BS Ministry. Damn the Minister for such a poor acronym!" Bernard expands with frustration over the 'BS' brand. Stephanie puts on her professional hat and nods her head to insinuate she is in full agreement with Bernard.

Clearly, Bernard had forgotten that Stephanie had applied for the job, or had been awarded it in all but name, but like a last minute decision on a US Bachelor programme, she was stood down as soon as she stood up. Left out in the cold, only to see the crown given over to an unknown candidate, one from outside the Ministry. Worse still someone from that forbidden city up north that everyone in the rest of the country loves to hate, Auckland, where its inhabitants are known colloquially as 'JAFAs', or more aptly 'Just Another Fucking Aucklander'.

Being just two weeks before Christmas and everyone's spirits even higher than a usual Friday evening, most have been whiling away their working hours at pre-Christmas parties dotted along the Quay and up on the Terrace. The BS Ministry's veranda on the seventh floor has been particularly busy and has been booked out solidly for the last few weeks with end of year departmental gatherings.

Cat lands at the last table in carriage four, her usual place, and dumping her stuff down, one of her train buddies offers her a drink. "Hey Cat, I'm just getting in a round, great timing. What do you fancy, the usual?" Claudia screams over the loud voices.

"Yes, please, that would be great. I so deserve a drink or two this evening, it's been a very busy day."

Claudia responds, "Busy, ha, when is it not busy for you?"

"I know, BAU!" says Cat and the gang burst into haughty-taught laughter at their insider joke.

Never one to have many friends, Cat is quite content to have Claudia and Debbie as train companions, people she can share the latest business developments with and only that. They both sit in awe of Cat, who laps it all up like the feline she is, loving the attention of her little fan club. Claudia and Debbie, both public servants, are patiently hoping that one day soon Cat will ask them to join her expanding and mighty empire at BS. They are living in fantasy land and if they were really being true to themselves they would know that is never going to happen; well not on Cat's watch. Like mice, they are good to play with, but only until the next catch comes along and falls into her neat little trap.

Claudia pushes her way forward to the bar, only to see there are crowds of people trying to order drinks. She can see the regulars but there are also a few fresh faces.

The train has been packed to capacity recently for there have been huge roadworks' repairs going on up and down the Kapiti Expressway, the changes causing huge hold-ups in the morning. With the zero tolerance to drink and drive policy being introduced just in time for the pre-Christmas parties, no one wants to risk bringing their car into work and getting caught in traffic or being done for drink-driving.

Drinks finally in hand and with help from the ever-friendly men milling around the bar, Claudia makes her way back to her seat. Claudia, Debbie and Cat all get into the Friday night spirit of drinking and gossiping, and start swigging away, unaware of the train's unusually late departure as it pulls out from the capital.

"I passed Bernie on the way through, he must be heading up to the bach for the weekend," comments Cat. Cat has a habit of giving people pet names, especially men. This gives her a feeling of superiority over them. She remembers her father doing the same and in particular with her, even when she became an adult, he insisted on calling her Katie as opposed to Cathryn. It annoyed her immensely. Therefore, if she can abbreviate men's names to make them sound like an adolescent boy, more the better.

"Bach! Ha! It's more like a palatial weekender!" Claudia screams with laughter, nearly spilling her drink. "I love how you get away with calling your DCE Bernie. It's kinda cute, a real term of endearment. I wish we could give our DCE a pet name and get away with it. However, Margaret Johnson is the bitch from hell."

Debbie butts in. "Cat, what's your DCE's surname? They're not related, are they?"

Claudia carries on, ignoring Debbie. "She does remind me of Margaret Thatcher, a real, stern iron lady. Some of us call her Maggs behind her back, but never to her face and some call her Naggs, because she does nag and go on a bit. Another typical narcistic management executive who does a lot of talking, but when you translate the conversation there is little or nothing of substance behind the endless words. You are still just as confused if not more when she has finished, and you never dare to question her and ask her for clarification – that sends her into convulsions. It's hilarious to see, it's like watching someone trying to throw up. You are lucky with your boss; dear old Bernie seems like a really nice guy. Anyhow, I love good old Kiwi baches."

"Baches, aye? Gone are the days of the good old one or two-bedroom cottage with bunkhouse. Nowadays a bach is inverted snobbery for a modern grandiose over-the-top five-bedroom house with built-in sauna, pool and movie theatre, only used a couple of weekends a year all to show off to business associates or so-called friends how much money people have!" adds Debbie, as she fondly remembers whiling away her happy childhood days at her granddad's bach at Waitarere Beach.

Her family bach still stands today, which is remarkable as it had no foundations. Built like a typical prefab, a small fibrolite glorified shed that her granddad dumped onto a cheap piece of land he had bought.

Debbie, a good born and bred Horowhenua girl, used to love sunbathing at her favourite surf beach. Unfortunately, her face today is a living Levin legacy of the strong UV rays she used to endure, topped up every sunny day with baby oil to ensure she got maximum rays and maximum suntan coverage. Today, translated to well-covered facial wall-to-wall lines, and not of the minimalistic kind either.

"Half these so-called baches are not freehold, the bank owns ninety-nine per cent of these holiday houses in most cases," Cat chips in. "I can never quite work that out, as houses down here compared with Auckland are such a steal. I saw a bach went at your Waitarere Beach the other day for three-hundred K, Deb. Now up in Auckland, you can multiply that figure by at least five, especially on Waiheke Island." Cat goes off reminiscing about her wine-filled weekends on the island, a commuter island within thirty-five minutes of downtown Auckland city, known for its million-dollar-plus beach houses and vineyards.

"Hey, and don't forget the compulsory accessories that come with the baches, such as the latest Porsche 911 coupe in the garage, so they can potter into the nearest village for a paper," Claudia pipes in, clearly showing her age of fifty-plus by making reference to a non-digital accessory such as a newspaper.

*****

Throughout the carriages, conversation is flowing fast like the food and beverage consumption. Robert, the buffet car bar manager, is rushed off his feet as nearly everyone on the seven-carriage train is getting stuck into the pre-Christmas celebrations by downing a beer or wine or two in true Kiwi fashion – true excess, nothing in moderation, just like the infamous 'six o'clock swill' of last century. Get as many drinks in under the belt as possible, you never know when and where your next one is coming from!

Carriage four is more packed than usual and passengers are milling up and down along the aisle; not everyone has managed to find a seat tonight and the overfills are sitting on armrests and flowing over into the buffet car. Fortunately, the Health and Safety Gestapo have finished work for the week, otherwise they would be having a field day offloading passengers and writing in triplicate Hazard Identification (ID) forms like there was no tomorrow.

At the other end of the carriage Sven, the new BS lifestyle coach, rushes to board the train. Being 178 cm in height, blonde hair, brown eyes with olive skin, she attracts quite a few admiring glances from the male passengers as she takes her seat with friends. A relatively new addition to the Big Super Ministry, she has been taken on as part of a pilot, by Bernard.

Sven has loved working in her grandfather's native country of Sweden for large multi-national banks, gaining an impressive track record of making a positive difference coaching teams and their respective managers. Her friend Clara, 'Flat White', is high up in the public service having spent most of her life working for them – she knows everyone and everything around town. Unlike Freya their alternative friend, who is relatively new to the public service in Wellington and struggles with different contracts around town.

Flat White is tall, slim and like her name implies, her skin is white, in fact pure porcelain white. Always classily dressed she looks like butter wouldn't melt in her mouth, but is quite the opposite. Flat White plays the 'corporate game' very well and knows what to say, when and more importantly when not to say it. Her self-confidence and assurance only recently dented, but landing back on her feet with the help of her friends. Sven has always been a tad jealous, for she tends to not just think the words, but say them out loud for all to hear. No filters, no pauses, just out at the speed of sound and too late to retract anything, which usually lands her in a pile of trouble.

Sven has this amazing ability to work out who is real and authentic and who isn't quite what they appear to be. Cat is high up on her bullshit radar; 'Warning! Warning! Keep ALL contact to a minimum, but Keep Clear and Deal with Caution'.

The screech of female voices grows higher, Cat's Kiwi accent booming out above them all. Sven can hear the whole chain of events, detail by detail, of the proposed restructure being relayed, yet again, to Claudia and Debbie.

"That woman never knows when to shut her mouth; she has the emotional intelligence of a gnat. She gives all of HR a bad name. Why doesn't someone try to stop her?" Sven mutters to Flat White and Freya.

Freya, like Flat White, has known Sven since their school days and is also half Swedish and half Kiwi. It's great to have real friends from back in the day, where you can talk about anything without having to watch your p's and q's. This is one of the few times one can be highly inappropriate and not be judged or condemned for it.

Sven keeps talking and is on a roll. "You know, getting paid to spend most of the week watching and listening to that woman is bad enough and takes every ounce of patience and diplomacy to do so, but now on a Friday, in my own time, I have to listen to her all over again. I draw the line here. She is one of those true sharks with lipstick."

Flat White looks down the carriage at Cat in full swing, showing off her latest fashion purchases. "I would say a shark is too nice, I would say more of a Rottweiler with tooth decay and red raw lips from too much Botox!" Flat White is onto her second glass, her Monday to Friday 'PC radar' is down and she is not holding back. Amazing what a couple of glasses can do to the most conservative play-it-by-the-rule-book public servant. The three of them shriek with laughter, the 'oh too true' visions of Cat as a Rottweiler dancing around in their heads.

The next hour is full of vibrant chat, a lot of shop talk, and the screeching high-pitched chorus of women's voices. The sort of irritating voices and cackle you often hear when too many women get together at a party or pub, each one trying to raise their voices above each other and the music, just to be heard.

Sven at first cringes internally at the sound of the females with their Kiwi drawl shrieking above each other. Working in the UK and Sweden exposed her to the British 'toffy' accent of the European bankers and yuppies; ultimately it had clouded her judgement of her own Kiwi accent, though she notices now she is back in New Zealand she finds the raucousness oddly endearing and comforting.

"I'm checking out the new retro shop in Foxton this weekend, what are you guys up to?" Freya asks.

"Groovy baby, do you want a ride up there in my Capri? I need to take her for a spin, can't keep her locked away looking pretty in the garage forever!" Sven replies. "After all, everything cool, groovy and funky from the sixties and seventies is now back in and called 'retro' so maybe the same cool words, music, fashion, and office memorabilia like the old tea trolley may come back in, just like the 'blackboard' or my classic Ford Capri," she adds nostalgically.

Sven's dad bought her a 1978 Strato Silver Mk III Ford Capri as a welcome home present, a bit of enticement to get her back to New Zealand – a successful ploy to get his grown-up daughter to settle down. Sven's grandfather Olof was born and bred in Umeå, a town in the north of Sweden. Sven had fallen in love with her grandfather's red summerhouse in Skeppsvik, a seaside village just out of Umeå and had spent the last couple of summers holidaying there. Five years away, this time around was well long enough to get the travel bug out of her system. Kurt, her father, loved Sweden and her mother Hana, a New Zealand Māori, had fallen in love with it as well.

However, at the end of the day, New Zealand was their home, and this is where her family had raised her. Of course they wanted their grandchildren to be raised here too, with the bonus option of them travelling to the northern hemisphere if they so wished. The Svenssons were true Vikings, having wanderlust in their blood. Sven's twin brother Stefan was no different – he was still working in London with no intention of coming home any time soon; he wasn't so easily manipulated. The idea of having a classic Capri was exactly the right carrot to hook Sven and bring her back home.

Sven reminisces with her cronies and starts talking about the good ol' days.

"I remember my first job was with the good ol' public service, back in the late eighties. I was a shorthand typist, working in a typing pool. You know the BS Ministry is really no different from the old Post Office days. Sure, the furniture and accessories have changed, but the mentality and the slowness of anything happening, let alone getting actioned and signed off is still the same. Everyone still runs around with pieces of paper in their hands, pretending to look busy, which is funny as now everything is digital and online. The carrying a piece of paper around the entire floor and up and down the stairwell is really dated. However, managers still fall for it, don't they?"

"Oh well, some things never change," says Freya. "That must be a good thing – same mentality, same inefficiency, just a different day, decade, or in this case, a different century, a different millennium. Oh, and some of the characters have changed. Wow, just think, last decade, century, millennium, we were working in the UK and Sweden, all together."

"Though at least now some smart people have another purpose for carrying around those pieces of paper; they can multitask while checking their step count they've clocked up on their Fitbit while pausing for breath in the traverse of the stairs," laughs Flat White, looking at Sven pointedly, "I'm sure that's how you beat me most days."

Sven has made many trips to Europe over the years, but the longest she has stayed away was the last five. She has spent more time abroad working than she has in her own native country of New Zealand.

"Yeah, those were the days. They really are a lot more

ahead over there up north, aren't they? I mean northern hemisphere, not Auckland," laughs Flat White, reminiscing and changing subjects.

"Yeah, which is great, as they are ready for in-house lifestyle coaches. No one is afraid of asking for help and taking advantage of the free mentoring and coaching service that companies provide. After all, if it can save the increasing number of burnouts and breakdowns, then it's a win-win for everyone – the employer, employee, and their family. I do find it frustrating and ever so slow over here. Look, I am a Kiwi and a proud Kiwi, but is it something to do with the Kiwi psyche, are we just too afraid to ask for help, is it a sign of weakness or something?" shrieks Sven passionately, looking far too serious for a Friday night. She's a little too loud, as usual, purposely showing off to a group of good-looking guys at the neighbouring table who are busily talking about the final victorious test match where the All Blacks won against England at Twickenham.

Unfortunately she has attracted the attention of the wrong audience; two highly conservative public servants dressed in grey pants and suit jackets which have clearly been dry cleaned too many times. They gaze on slightly taken aback, their white crinkled shirts displaying hues of pink from being subjected to the same wash as their wives' coloured knickers. The men with their receding and diminishing hairlines twitch slightly at Sven's words. Slouched and bent over in their usual seats, a symptom of having spent decades walking bent by the windy Wellington weather and crouched over non-ergonomic desks, they look older than their years.

Sven surveys them closely, watching their body language and realises she has spoken far too loudly. She backs up a little and takes note. She should think a little more before she lets out her thoughts so loudly, but a couple of glasses of bubbles can do that. Laughing to herself, she espies an unusual shaped birthmark resembling a turd on one of the men's foreheads, accentuated by his receding hairline and sniggers out loud. *How unfortunate,* she thinks.

Sven continues her conversation with the girls. "However, I love being back here. I actually love the slowness, that kind of quaint laid-back style us Kiwis exude. I know our accent can make us sound a little naïve at times, especially to our dear cousins from Mother England, but I know each time I come back home after being away, I feel like kissing the ground when the plane touches down on dear old Aotearoa. The great feeling going through customs and some true-blue Kiwi chick or cute bloke at the border greets you, 'Kia ora, welcome home Ms Svensson', especially if it's one of my good-looking Māori cuzzies. Man, those hunky Māori customs officers are pretty easy on the eye and I love hearing te reo roll off their tongues. Have you noticed they have more bros in customs and immigration nowadays, especially at the Auckland International airport? I do miss our Kiwi accent and I am proud of mine, it does make us unique when we are overseas."

"Even if we do get mistaken for Aussies sometimes," Flat White says, butting in and nodding at Sven's comments. "Oh, and by the way, sis, which Māori customs officer are you not related to? You seem to whakapapa back to just about every iwi! I can't keep up with all your tribe and hapū affiliations!"

"Anyhow, I think it's funny being mistaken for an Aussie. Nothing like a bit of mistaken identity so you can play up even more. That was a good thing sometimes, especially if we had had a few too many wines and got into a spot of bother," Freya winks. "Remember when..." and she is off on another tale of misadventure.

However, to be fair, since Sven had been attending and delivering the latest courses on emotional intelligence, mindfulness and social awareness for good measure, she had improved with restraining herself before she went off on a tangent with her vocal cords. She would now take advantage of those pregnant pauses, and take the time to reflect or wait for the other person and think before responding. She had realised these pauses were good for both parties. It gave her clients plenty of time to consider their thoughts before coming back with an answer, and it gave her time to change down a gear or two, thinking mindfully of what her next probing question or reply would be. Sven had grown a lot since working in different countries. Not the same girl who, much to her parents' dismay and embarrassment, had been expelled from the highly prestigious, not to mention highly expensive boarding school, for being too loud and outspoken and setting the still unbroken school record for a boarder breaking the most rules in one term.

Freya finishes her story and they laugh loudly, spilling their drinks, the excess flowing and splattering across the floor, blending together like some good old-fashioned trifle laced with grandmother's short-sighted liberal douse of sherry and brandy.

Gazing on, Clara and Freya sometimes wonder if their old rebellious mate has permanently disappeared, but then usually on the Friday night train over a drink or two, good old Sven comes rolling back in and in top form. They can't put their finger on it, but Sven isn't always the good old 'free spirit' like she had been back in the day. They put it down to having to grow up and try not to think about it too much. Sven has also been getting in touch with her Māori roots, doing a part-time course on Rongoā Māori (Māori health and wellbeing) held every couple of weekends on a local marae. She takes it seriously and enjoys connecting with new whānau and getting in touch with her Māori ancestry and customs. However, when she isn't doing her weekend courses, she parties up on the Friday evenings, making Fridays a great time and excuse to enjoy a good quality hour or so of the old Sven.

Suddenly dominating carriage four's conversations, Cat's voice has switched up from third gear, skipped fourth and gone straight into overdrive. Her tone, pitch and pace and that Auckland nasal-like twang has also gone up more than a notch or two.

Disgusted with Cat's complete lack of emotional savviness, Sven abruptly heads off to the bar for another round of drinks, where she can hear the odd word drifting down through the carriages each time the adjoining glass carriage door slides open. "Oh my god, that woman is definitely my worst nightmare," she gasps, realising she has spoken her thoughts out loud before she has had time to bite her tongue.

Leaning against the bar, she subconsciously rolls her eyes lost in her own thoughts, when a man in the crowded bar responds. "Yes, I think I know what you mean. That female voice back there is really grating, JAFA accent isn't it? In fact, that's why I've come down here, to find some peace and quiet."

Sven turns to see who has just spoken, as she doesn't recognise the voice. She glimpses a vaguely familiar face, however, all too soon more people push in and shove themselves against the bar, and she never gets a chance to eyeball him again. Well, not that evening. A little taken aback by his refreshing outspokenness, she realises this is the beauty of alcohol; no matter what country you are in, everyone loosens up on their PC and appropriate lark and becomes human again. Filters down and saying it how it is.

She just wishes humans could be more forthcoming, without the need for her constant coaxing with questions or alcohol to get them to open up. If they were brave enough to have courageous conversations, imagine the issues, time and money they would save. Not to mention reducing the rapidly increasing disease and dilemma of mental health. That's what she enjoyed about her Rongoā Māori course; a large component of it was based on the Māori Health model, Te Whare Tapa Whā, where all four areas of a patient's life were assessed – emotional, physical, family and spiritual. The root of the problem was addressed, and a treatment plan designed around all these areas as opposed to prescribing a drug that would fix the symptoms, not the cause. However, bringing a lifestyle coach into a government department was radical enough, let alone bringing in another health model such as the Māori Health model. That was for another day, another campaign to sell to the managers, who weren't ready for too much change, quite yet.

After a long wait and now with three glasses of bubbles, accompanied with the mandatory bags of toasted cashew nuts and salt and vinegar crisps – stuffed under her arms and down her bra, Sven stumbles through the carriages. She gently allows her body to sway with the rhythm and flow of the carriages as they wind through the tunnels and out along the coast, high above the ocean's breaking waves below.

She marvels at what a wonderful part of the world this is, grateful to have the opportunity to live in this little piece of paradise. Sure, people are on edge at the moment with the recent earthquakes, and they are sooo over the weather, the wind, the rain, the flooding and the like. But this is Mother Nature, Papatūānuku shouting out for the ninety-eight thousandth time, 'Don't forget me, slow down, enjoy and stop abusing everything and everyone and we will all get along just fine'.

Lost in her thoughts, she enters the fourth carriage where her merry party sits in their usual seats and is relieved to hear just the banter of the blokes close by. "Wow, what a pleasant change. All I can hear are the dulcet tones of a couple of quietly spoken women and a few of the rugby blokes grunting and laughing. Cat must have run out of conversation. Now that's never happened before!" she shares with her mates, plonking the wines down unceremoniously on the table.

"I don't think that would ever happen, would it? She loves the sound of her own pompous voice far too much," laughs Freya. "Don't tell me she's enjoying a reflective pause after an hour nonstop on the train, allowing someone else to have a turn?"

"Sorry to repeat that awful phrase, yet again. Now that's never happened before," Flat White says, trying to wind Sven up. She knows how much that expression really annoys Sven.

Each time Sven would ring customer services, or deal with a tradesman or IT guru, they would usually respond with, 'Oh your email account just doesn't want to work, now *that's never happened before*. Must be something to do with your phone, or how you are using it, *I've never come across that before,* probably best we completely replace this, it's far too old to fix', or words to that effect.

This has triggered Sven, since her mother first started responding to her experiences with, 'Oh Samantha, *that's never happened before* to me, it's clearly you. This doesn't happen to Stefan, he never talks like this. Can't you see it's all to do with *you?!*'

This line is tattooed inside Sven's head, and she recalls her mother's words each time a tradesman or colleague says the same. She knows that people are using this line as a cop-out, but she still emotionally can't help feeling hurt and annoyed by it.

Sven shares with her mates what just happened back in the bar. "Hey, I just had this guy speak to me at the bar. I didn't really get a chance to eyeball him, but I think I know him from somewhere. He said something like he had to get away from the carriage because some JAFA woman just wouldn't stop talking. I assume he meant ol' madam down there. So, you see, it's not just me, she even annoys blokes. We could even hear her when the carriage doors slid open!"

"So, someone else can see past those false eyelashes, bright red 'come hither' lipstick and big fake tits, seeing the deep, hollow, soulless pit beneath?" Flat White says, spouting her opinion firmly. She may not voice it often, but when she does she certainly makes up for lost time.

"Don't hold back!" Freya laughs.

The guard, Humphrey's voice, comes booming across the intercom politely articulating, "Good evening folks – whoops, I mean kia ora, to all our passengers bound for Paraparaumu. We will be pulling into the station in a couple of minutes. Please make your way to the doors, and mind the gap on the way out. Thank you for travelling with us this great Friday evening and we look forward to being of service to you again on Monday morning, bright-eyed and bushy-tailed. Ka kite."

"Huh, he's obviously been sharing some of that lolly water from the bar, he's not usually that friendly at seven in the morning. I might remind him of that when he puts on his grumpy voice first thing Monday," says Sven, looking at her watch. "It's just coming up to six o'clock. You have to love KiwiRail – since they took over this train again I actually get to work and home on time. Just like the trains in Europe, everyone and everything works almost like clockwork."

"Just like a team at BS Castle," Freya laughs sarcastically.

The train pulls into the seaside town's station. On the platform several people weighed down with Christmas shopping start shuffling towards the respective carriages. They groan in frustration as they see the train is packed, clearly concerned they may miss out on a seat. They start chasing the train up the tracks to the various moving carriage doors, faces set in determination. Sparks start triggering off like skyrockets from one of the steps and suddenly wide-eyed, those closest back off, their faces changing to surprise as a red stiletto heel pops out from the step like a cork from a bottle of bubbly. Through the windows of the carriage doors, a cloud of grey and black rises from the seats, the suits ready to depart with their coats and devices in hand.

The lights flicker for a moment with the halt of the

carriages, the suits pressing and pushing while waiting in line to alight.

In the ladies' cubicle of carriage four, a passenger lies bruised and bleeding, slumped against the wall, drifting in and out of consciousness. Her mind blurred and dimmed, while outside the sound of chatter and smartphones obliviously passes her by.

*****

Chapter 4

Mondayitis and rigor mortis

Kiwi Con (KC) is on time as it pulls into Waikanae on Monday morning, and Sven jumps on board at 7.30am sharp, the usual time. The train still has that lingering smell of stale alcohol from Friday night. Clearly, the staff didn't do a clean of the train on Friday evening, let alone the deep clean they usually do on the weekend. Sven finds her gang's regular seats and can see some of the remnants of the crisps and cashew nuts she was scoffing down on Friday night. She remembers dropping a handful down the back of the seat as the train took off out of Paraparaumu. "Well that's proof in itself that no one cleaned this carriage, I can see the remains of my Friday night dinner. Perhaps I could finish where I left off on Friday night and down them for breakfast – I didn't have time for brekkie this morning," she says half seriously to Freya and Clara as they settle in for their one-hour journey south towards the capital.

"Thanks for securing our patch Sven, it's almost tribal us all marking out our territory," Freya acknowledges, as she spies the rugby boys already aboard. Noticing the tables are still sticky and not the type of surface you want to place your coffee cup, let alone rest your arms on. The windows are smeared with alcohol and the lingering smell of stale cigarettes and something much worse. Clearly someone got so pissed they lit up a cigarette in the loo and the smell has seeped into the carriage," comments Freya repulsively.

Clara responds. "The carpet has an unusual patchwork pattern with the remains of crushed crisps and other unrecognisable morsels of food stamped into it. Perhaps this little trademark is from where Bernard was doing his impression of the cha-cha-chá up and down the aisle with you, young Sven!"

Clara volunteers to go and get a round of coffees and notes that the buffet car looks a little rough as well. There are still empty plastic water bottles in the rubbish bags that clearly weren't emptied on Friday night. Empty beer and wine bottles are strewn along the side of the bar and spilling out over onto nearby tables. She wonders if they're short-staffed.

"What happened to the cleaners on Friday night, Robert?" she asks the friendly guy serving behind the counter.

"Don't ask," he says, lifting a hand up as if to say 'stop'. "I have been trying to clean up this brothel since clocking in at five this morning in Palmy. Something is going down with the cleaners, they aren't allowed to do overtime unless it's signed off by their supervisor. But Joseph the head cleaner went west with the last restructure and hasn't been replaced. So if we're late into Palmy like last Friday night, then the train doesn't get cleaned until the next shift, which is tonight. I know," Robert explains to Clara, "the efficiencies of the free market…tell me about it!"

Clara returns to the carriage to give her mates the update. "Oh my god, the buffet car is still in a mess – it's something to do with the cleaners not being able to clean it all up due to their minimum wages clearly being too costly."

Sven responds. "Bloody SMT and HR, cost-cutting, restructuring, lean manufacturing, continuous improvement, outsourcing, contracting out this and that, so-called best practice, whatever other words you want to throw at it. What ever happened to good old-fashioned personnel management, a service ethic and treating humans with respect and empathy? What we end up with are those meaningless, shallow policies, visions, values, mission statements – they are as hollow and senseless as the Cats of the world who design them. Oh, and the latest line they will be using, I can just hear it now, is: 'We as the Senior Management Team need double digit exponential growth in this next financial quarter so let's do away with all the unnecessary departments and to achieve our KPIs, we need this done almost immediately for this financial quarter and next.'" This is the new catch phrase that all the suits took away from the Rotorua HR/Leadership conference Bernard and Cat attended that Sven over heard in a meeting. She is peeved and infuriated at these corny lines being repetitively used like an old forty-five record being played over and over again, or to be more current, an MP3 on repeat.

Sven pipes up, "It's not fair, the cleaners are on minimum wages as it is – what would it matter if they gave them a bit of overtime? At least it would take their pay up to almost a normal hourly rate and besides, where has the good will to all man*kind* and Christmas lark gone? Whoops, not allowed to say 'mankind' anymore, either!"

"That's our Sven, always fighting for the underdog, and anyone out there who is being taken advantage of, our Sven is on the case," laughs Freya endearingly, nudging Sven in the ribs.

Sven stands up in the aisle to shake her skirt free of crumbs as she can feel the leftover crisps starting to lodge between her legs; not a good feeling on a Monday morning, least of all a good look when marching into the office trying to look professional for the first meeting of the day – Cat's HUGE announcement.

"The announcement of the century is going to be so big I wonder if they've put it on the huge reception board downstairs that reads like an airport departures and arrival screen? The Privacy Act is out the window well and truly when it comes to this board flashing like some neon street sign for all to see. Anyone off the street can come and read it and you can quite clearly see who and what is going on in each designated meeting room and at what time. If you wanted to pop someone off, just come and have a squiz at this board, it will tell you everything. As for gaining entry into any of the rooms, it's not a problem, just wait a couple of seconds for someone to walk through the main doors off Reception and follow in close behind. And hey presto, there you are sitting side by side with a minister or the like. Take your pick, the board is like a restaurant menu, choose a topic, a person, a room and you can be there in seconds, security or no security. You have a free pass, you can pass go and you can collect..." Sven bitches.

"Wow, did the neighbours' security light wake you up too early again, Sven? You are on a serious gripe there," Clara laughs.

"That insensitive wanker left at 4 am this morning! Why does he have to have an aircraft search light strength security light?" Sven moans.

"That's boys with their toys for you," Clara fires back winking at Freya.

With Sven about to go into a serious meltdown, Freya tries to divert the conversation. "Man, I am digging this warm weather. Yeah, with summer well on its way, there's no need for stockings. Amazing, even in the cold, windy capital city, we can expose our bare, white winter legs." Freya had just moved back down from Auckland where the climate is sub-tropical, supposedly warmer and had missed wearing skimpy summer clothes for most of the year. "It's great to feel the fresh air swirl between your legs, not to mention air your private parts. Everything needs a good airing, nickers and bras are so over-rated. We spend half our life strapped up, everything is pulled in and covered, why can't we be like Papatūānuku, or Mother Sweden and just flop it out and all about?" She does a little twirl, imitating what it is like to be free and let it all go.

Clara, always the one to be more conservative and go with the flow, says, "But not so much when you can feel the texture of the sticky vinyl seat beneath you."

Sven laughs as it takes her back down memory lane. "Oh yes, and remember those vinyl bench seats in the front of cars back in the day, where on a hot summer's day or night, your thighs would stick to the vinyl and you needed to manhandle yourself off the seat as you were almost permanently stuck. Man, I loved those old classic cars. Remember the Zephyr and the Holden and Falcon, all with seating in the front for three? I used to love going cruising in those. An ex of mine – well, his father, had a Zephyr Mark II, then he progressed to a Mark III, and I used to love riding with him in the front seat, sitting right up against him and feeling his arm against mine, when changing the gears. It was a column change, and the gears were on the wheel, left-hand side. Wicked."

Sven goes off on her memory lane tangent about how cool the cars were back in the day, but then brings herself back to the present moment, in the twenty-first century.

Still having problems dislodging the crisps out from between her legs, Sven ends up smearing the grease from them right across the front panel of her white skirt. With Sven, everything must be perfect, bordering on obsessive. Sven suffers from a mild case of obsessive-compulsive disorder (OCD), which her mates keep reminding her of since some random shrink in Stockholm diagnosed her with it. She had been suffering from a lack of sunlight after having several summers in a row over there without a glimpse of sunshine, and had caught a bad dose of seasonal affective disorder (SAD). Her Swedish doctor had recommended a local Polish psychiatrist and he had been struggling with where to put her on his DSM V (Diagnostic and Statistical Manual of mental disorders used by mental health professionals) chart. After toying with every label from bipolar to narcissism, he came up with a mild case of OCD. At the end of the day she was just a good old Kiwi girl who had been brought up on the beach with plenty of outdoor space to play in and sunshine to absorb, but needing to find a box to put her in, he had given her the OCD label. Her friends would never let her live this down now.

At the end of the day, what Sven was really suffering from was a dose of undiagnosed Kiwi homesickness with a dollop of high standards and expectations, not forgetting a little eccentricity, and passion for all sorts of worthwhile causes. However, the Polish psychiatrist – who suffered from transvestic disorder (TD) and took to cross-dressing between appointments, had misinterpreted it. A few other antipodeans, fellow Aussies and Kiwis had also been referred to the same shrink and had returned to work with a Smörgåsbord of over-used labels: bipolar disorder, borderline personality disorder, obsessive compulsive disorder, society anxiety/phobia, body dysmorphic disorder (BDD), post-traumatic stress disorder (PTSD), agoraphobia, generalised panic disorder (GAD), and panic attacks, you name it. Not forgetting a much-needed introduction and insight into TD.

As a result of this traumatic experience, Sven had decided she would stay away from the health professionals and instead of seeking external help when feeling down or at a crossroads, she would work on herself. As a result, over the year she collected her own set of self-help and self-care tools for her kete. That is part of the reason why she made such a good coach. Young Sven was on her own hīkoi, searching for what made her feel good and in return by healing herself she could help and inspire others.

However, on this Monday morning it was becoming more and more evident to her friends on the train that Sven liked everything and everyone to be in order and for communal areas to resemble some level of order, hygiene and cleanliness. The KC was not showing any of these qualities and Sven was venting and displaying a full range of expletives while becoming more and more obsessed with feeling the grime, the wine and the remains of the Friday night snacks on her legs. Beside herself, she hurries off in disgust towards the loos to clean herself up.

"Gross, I can't spend all day in this white skirt when I know I have greasy, Friday night crisps stuck to my clothes and worse still, my legs!" Sven whinges. "If I hadn't had that leg wax over the weekend and was still as hairy as I had been on Friday, then these gross leftovers would be sticking to my ten-foot hairs and not my skin and I could have combed them out."

Freya, joining her in the aisle, has a dig. "Not like back in the day, aye Sven? It was very normal for you to turn up to work the next day, or on the same day, or to an appointment with the remains of the party food on you. Remember what your optometrist said about you the other day at that family gathering? That you used to turn up to his rooms on Saturday morning, straight from the party with your hair standing up like one of those female singers from the B-52s and your eyeliner resembling something a make-up artist would do on Alice Cooper before going on stage, and…"

But Sven was a little older, a little wiser now and she knew that it wasn't so much what she could offer the BS Ministry that mattered, it was how she was perceived that really counted to the masses, unfortunately. Therefore, as she needed the money to fulfil her lifetime dream, she was determined, as hard as it was, to bloody well see out this contract. Making her dream come true would make her parents happy; it was a surprise, a risky venture, but she believed the return on the investment would pay big dividends for all of her family.

Besides, the money was particularly good and in the interim, 'Doyle' her baby, the 1978 Ford Capri Mk III, needed some serious repairs and maintenance and the BS money would help pay that off without having to dig into her own precious savings for her venture. The good thing about working for overseas banks is they had taught her a lot of savvy ways of how to make her money go further and how to save and invest. Sven had always been very good with money due to her dad's accountancy and auditing background. It was a generational thing as well; both her parents were children growing up through the Second World War and her grandparents through the depression and she had seen how tough they had had it and how they were very frugal with their money.

She needed to see this contract through to a successful completion, hence jumping on the long train journey each way every day. She had managed to negotiate with Bernard a few extra privileges like working from home, flexible hours and extra professional development (PD) and conferences that were only happening in Aussie. Unlike her other friends, she, like Cat, only needed to go into the office three to four times a week and enjoyed taking advantage of the flexible working conditions policy, the WFH (working from home) privilege. After all, the BS Ministry prided itself on being accommodating to its employees by offering the flexibility, not to mention generosity of working from home. BS loved branding itself as the 'best (little) employer in town'. They would quote this in all their recruiting ads and marketing material.

Meanwhile, Sven continues to attempt to get into the train's WC, and after using a different carriage's washroom as carriage four's door is still stuck or occupied, returns to her mates a little calmer and chats away about her cool weekend visit with Freya to Foxton's retro shops and how she's not looking forward to going into work.

"I could easily take a rain check on today's pantomime at work. Today is the day Cat is making her big announcement that has been all hush-hush, top secret. No one is meant to know the details, even though Cat was clearly overheard several times referring to it on this very train for the last few weeks, and in particular early Friday evening. However, I've been doing one-to-one coaching sessions with a few of the top HR people who have been under huge undue stress as they don't like all this 'slicing and dicing', as Cat calls it. And they don't want to be part of the 'lean (keep you mean)' project when Cat starts implementing it. So, you see, she hasn't managed to get *all* her so-called HR loyal, royal followers on board. It will be very interesting to see how it all pans out today. I have a feeling though that it is not going to turn out how we all suspect, so watch this space! Make sure you gals keep your phones switched on so I can update you as news comes to hand."

Freya adds in, "Yes, and wasn't Bernard spending the weekend out here on the coast? So no doubt they got together with the sole purpose of smoothing off any finishing touches and wrapping it all up nicely in a pretty bow, representing the BS colours to serve sweetly to everyone hot off the press, in the best possible taste." She turns around. "I'm surprised I haven't seen him on the train this morning. Maybe he came back with his wife instead by car on Sunday night to avoid the rush hour traffic. Or possibly he is so over you, Sven, he can't bear being in the same carriage as you again. I mean, accusing him of having an affair with Cat, while you two were trying to cha-cha down carriage four – it wasn't a great career move. Speaking of Cat, where is madam this morning?"

Clara pipes in, "Maybe all three got cosy over the weekend. Bernard, his wife and Cat are now all best friends after their ménage à trois and commuted happily in together by car. Now that's cosy!"

The girls roar with laughter. "Oh, gross Flat White, don't freak me out! Oh no, now I have hideous visions in my head, and when I see Cat or BJ later I won't be able to take either of them seriously."

"Hmm, Sven, when have you ever taken that woman seriously?" Freya questions her friend.

Sven's thoughts move on and she opens up a bit more about her worst nightmare, Cat, and putting on her philosophical hat. "I don't know what motivates Cat, in fact I don't think she has one good bone in her body. Man, she must've had a rough childhood, and she's taken that baggage into her so-called 'adult' life, no wonder she doesn't have a ring on her finger; who would want to be tied down to a control freak like that? I mean a bloke tying her down physically to a grotty hotel's bed post is different to being tied down to her legally on a life sentence."

"Never dismiss the idea of being tied to a bed Sven, it's wonderfully exhilarating," Clara intervenes.

She takes a pause as all three laugh and then she continues on a more serious note. "I see how she works the floor at functions and in meetings, she smiles ever so sweetly and most of the blokes who are new to the game, – her game, fall for it. But like she said to me once, 'Samantha, everyone and everything has a use-by date, disagree with me and step out of line and your time here will be short-lived.' She smiled ever so sweetly while she said this with special emphasis on 'use-by date' and 'short-lived'. As if she is the one that signs my pay cheque. I think that's half the problem, she knows I report to Bernard, even though the organisational staff chart says through the dotted line I report to her. But BJ just did that so I can keep an eye on her for him. However, I definitely wouldn't want to cross her, but then I'm not going to pander to her either, like all the rest of the sheep, including Bernard. Those two really have got too close for comfort for my liking."

"You really don't like this woman, do you? Maybe we need to get a contract in HR and see for ourselves?" Clara suggests.

Sven screams with delight. "No, how about getting a contract on *her?* Hey, one of you could come and work at BS. That would be fabulous, please at least one of you come and work at BS. Oh yes, please, I need an ally or two. But seriously, that's not as silly as it sounds – one of our senior HR advisors walked out last week because she doesn't want to see the latest strategy implemented. She has values and doesn't want to see people's heads on the chopping board, especially just before Christmas," Sven explains.

The girls nod as they sip their coffees listening to Sven's offer.

"Oh, please let me pass on your CVs to our ever-efficient Recruiting team. Nigel is just aching to be able to do his job and take his team back off the chopping block. Everyone like me gets recruited through the back door and he is feeling a little redundant, so to speak. Oh god, there's that 'r' word again. Look, seriously, they are desperate for staff, skilled staff, and you would piss in with your talent. Freya, they are not clever enough to delve down and work out why you had three jobs in one year. Just say they were all contracts. It's not lying, at the end of the day that's how you saw them – as just short-term roles while you were moving around in Auckland, getting ready to make your escape down here. Flat White, how about you, can we tempt you to jump ship and into another sinking one?"

Sven realises she just opened her big mouth again and quickly tries to back up and cover up what she has said. "I didn't mean you had a wicked past, Freya, and that they were desperate, I meant your contract here in Wellington is almost up and this would be a fantastic opportunity for us to work together again. I know you are a great asset for a company, with the right boss, right conditions. Let's make it happen."

"I know what you meant,' Freya chips in. "It's not a silly idea, I will think about it. It's just that you know all the agencies around town are crying out for contractors, and from what you keep telling us I would rather go and work anywhere else than the BS. Even though others not in the know think it is the biggest and best ministry that a pack of shifty ministers created, and they are the forerunners in anything innovative and creative. We all know that's bullshit, like their name, and that their values were written by some outsourced marketing team in Asia that use the same one-liners for everyone else. Everyone likes to see themselves as innovative, creative, challenging the status quo, and love using such words in their visions, but at the end of the day, we know they are at the other end of the spectrum with those meanings," she exclaims, making her case.

"Great," Sven replies, "Anyhow, I will put on that poker face when she makes the announcement today that another restructure is coming up this side of Christmas. The timing is always absolutely amazing. I mean, as if there isn't enough going on in people's lives leading up to Christmas – unreasonable deadlines, in-laws coming to stay, buying presents, parties and the like."

The train reaches the end of the line – well, the end of the line for the north island at Wellington's grand railway station. In New Zealand terms, Wellington has a huge railway station with ten platforms. At certain peak hour times of the day, the platforms are a hive of swarming activity: huge clusters of people spilling out of carriages, streaming out across platforms in huge droves, heading for the many exits, invading the streets of Wellington. As the clusters of clones move further and further away from the railway station, they thin out, but most have disappeared off into old buildings in and around Lambton Quay and The Terrace, the centre of Public 'Serviceville'.

"You girls go on, I've dropped my phone and I'll text you for a coffee after the meeting," Sven is a little slow to leave the train, dragging her feet, suffering from a serious bout of Mondayitis. She is also a little angry as after retrieving her phone, she still couldn't get into carriage four's rest room which delayed her further. "Oh my god, have they done anything to this train since I got off three days ago? Clearly not!" She looks back to see a couple of characters with Hi-Vis vests and uniforms with the old Kiwi Railway logo; they board the carriage she has just jumped off. Thinking they looked far too well dressed to be cleaners, she stops outside the carriage to fossick in her handbag for her lipstick.

Bert and Ernie board the train with their tool boxes ready to open the toilet door that has been firmly locked since Friday night. "I don't know what all the fuss is about, it's only a loo door. Passengers are so picky and precious, there are six other lavatories on the train, why couldn't they just use the other ones? It's not as if it is like the normal commuter trains that have no loos," Bernie exclaims, and his mate nods his head in agreement. It appears these two are suffering from Mondayitis as well, as they drag themselves heavily off the platform.

"It's a bit whiffy though, Ernie," comments Bert. "Come on then, let's get this door sorted."

"Just what we need on a Monday morning – three-day-old jobbies! Right you are, Bert," Ernie agrees.

With a bit of manhandling between the two of them they finally wrench the door open. "Oh my god…"

Shock sweeps across the two men's faces. It is hard to read what they have just seen as their hands fly to their faces to cover their noses and eyes.

Ernie turns to Bert. "I've never seen that before!"

Sven, overhearing them, thinks it's a bit of a strong overreaction to a toilet that hasn't been cleaned for three days and wonders how they would react to the toilets on the trains in Egypt or India.

*****

Chapter 5

HR Stand-up – Take 1

"Where the hell is the HR Director today? We made an effort to be on time at 8.30ish, why the hell can't she be, and practise what she preaches? She's kept us waiting in suspense all weekend, and now she can't even have the decency to put us out of our misery and turn up on time. She really is a piece of work!" mutters Carmen, the Senior HR Advisor.

Carmen, now well in her fifties, is suffering from Mondayitis, along with many of the others in the HR team. However, her suffering goes a bit deeper than this. She has been trying to escape the clutches of the BS Ministry but due to this new epidemic, 'ageism', has been unable to. She feels like the invisible woman, hence the leopard print tights, shirt, skirt and coat, with overly bright eye shadow and lipstick that would appear was glued on twenty-four seven.

Carmen must have the most polished CV in all

of Wellington, always adding her latest skills and achievements, while permanently logged on to the online job board constantly checking all job alerts that ping throughout the day to her. When she receives a notification every time a suitably matched job appears, Carmen hastily sends out her fabulously laid out CV and matching accessory: the cover letter. Nine times out of ten she never hears back or receives an acknowledgement. On the rare occasion she does and scores an even rarer interview, she finds herself confronted by an interview panel of millennials and middle-aged men who pass her over, after making very little eye contact with her throughout the one-hour clipboard, cognitive behavioural-based questioning ordeal, known as today's interview. All sentences start with 'Tell me a time when you had to deal with conflict, what did you do? Tell me a time when...' as they scribble her answers furiously on their interview notes, following today's 'best practice'. She feels she answers the questions very well and is convinced her dress sense and presentation skills are impeccable and appropriate for today's job market, but alas, she ends up with the usual results of, 'We felt you weren't quite the right fit' or 'We had such a high calibre of applicants'.

Poor Carmen, stuck in the same job, feeling invisible to the outside world and to the inside world of the BS where Cat continuously ignores all her ideas and suggestions. Friday afternoon's HRLT (Human Resources Leadership Team) meeting was no different; Cat completely ignored Carmen's case for saving her staff from being the latest to join the ranks of the unemployed.

Other HR members are also disgruntled with all the waiting around for Monday's HR meeting to start and similar words of disillusionment can be heard resonating from one person's lips to another. A sea of staff can now be seen standing impatiently in a huge group like a flock of sheep waiting for their next feed – their weekly HR stand-up.

Candy, a more junior HR Advisor can be heard explaining to a group of perplexed looking newbies, backfills and contractors, "Yes, we no longer call our meetings 'meetings' even though in effect they are meetings. Instead we call them a 'stand-up', as it is a quick catch-up on the run as opposed to sitting down and having time to digest what is being said and having the ability to ask questions for clarification. Time is of the essence and we must use the time effectively, as 'time' is another cost to the business."

Candy continues to rabbit on to some of the newbies, feeling she is being helpful. "If you all turn to the back four pages of your Induction Book – 'Welcome to the Big Super Ministry', you will see a handy glossary. There you will find the meanings for some of the more commonly used 'public servant speak' words, acronyms and phrases, like 'stand-up' and 'words on a page'." Then trying out a joke on the attentive audience, she goes on to explain that a 'stand-up' is nothing like the stand-up comedy that one can attend if looking for some light relief after a busy week working. No one laughs so she continues to follow the induction trainer notes and doesn't go off script again.

As people bundle together for the big HR stand-up, they complain bitterly about having to jam-pack more into their already frantically busy days and still more and more meetings crop up on their radar. Even though ministries and companies are constantly downsizing, they are also continuously outsourcing, paying for outsiders to do 'business as usual' or a 'piece of work' and due to limited resources – time and space, they have stand-ups, a bit like having lunch on the run. If they don't formally book a meeting room the size of Africa, which most offices don't have the luxury of leasing, they get everyone to gather around like a gaggle of geese, standing room only and then someone heads the meeting from the other side of the floor. Usually the person who is meant to be running the meeting is far too busy at another meeting, double booking themselves or working from home and someone else at the last minute, who clearly can't think on their feet, let alone articulate to accommodate for the short attention span of the fragmented listeners, fills in and nervously reads from a sheet the latest goings-on over the last week and what's on the horizon. This type of communication is what passes today for 'blue-sky thinking' in the public service.

Stephanie, the second in command, looking a little worse for wear after the weekend, opens the 9am stand-up apologising, "Good morning ladies and g-g-gent, thank you for taking the time to attend this morning. Now there is no time to go through everything I have been working on, and I'm about to go into a v-v-very important ELT meeting but I will give you a quick snapshot as follows. Please listen up..." She directs the last sentence to the usual group in the back row who haven't stopped to take breath since entering the room fifteen minutes earlier and haven't even noticed the meeting has started.

Stephanie, not a natural speaker in public, always gets incredibly nervous when she needs to speak at meetings or in public and tries to avoid it like the plague. She has a highly obvious nervous twitch and in public situations like this her left eyeball goes off on a tangent, twitching embarrassingly for all to see. She often puts glasses on when this happens to divert attention, but today she has forgotten her glasses and her left eye has a mind of its own. Rumour has it that when she was a child she was trapped in a building and couldn't get out and as a result she is now suffering from post-traumatic stress disorder.

Stephanie continues making her speech while her eye is now twitching in full force. "Susan went to China to build relationships with the HR team over there, Adrienne went to India to build cultural awareness, Bernard, our lovely CEO returned to his wife's parents' home country, the UK to catch up with family, whoops, I mean he went over there to build relationships with our office, and not to escape the New Zealand winter…"

As Stephanie drones on Sven is beside herself; with her attention span failing rapidly she gets out her ipad and starts writing, pretending as usual that she is hanging onto every word that is said. Instead, she starts jotting down her observations of Stephanie, writing her private thoughts down in her favourite rhyming verse.

Stephanie, a real introvert

Playing the game as a great expert

Staying below the PS radar

In BS she'll go far

She's been around 15 years

Never one to discuss her fears

Very quiet, likes to be on her own

Following her path all alone

Not sure what makes her tick

For some reason, we just don't click.

Sven stops writing and scans the room. Stephanie still has the centre stage and is updating everyone on the latest justifications for blowing the travel expenditure, "Susan, the Head of the Chinese Capability Engagement team (CCE) and Adrienne the DDCE (Deputy Departmental Chief Executive) are key stakeholders in anything to do with cultural capability, which means they know how to talk with people from other cultures and ethnicities."

Clearly there is a 'special' way to talk to some people, but Sven's view is that all people should be spoken to the same way, with kindness and respect unless of course they are complete tossers.

Stephanie is fluffing around with her lines and shuffling her papers when suddenly her file of notes drops to the floor. There is a long, awkward pause. With no one coming to her rescue, she picks them up herself, reshuffles the papers yet again and tries to continue. Meanwhile, time ticks on and the level of impatience and annoyance starts to go through the roof; staff have had enough, and naturally the conversation leads to how busy they all are. While Stephanie checks with her offsider who is to get up and talk next, Sven listens into the eclectic array of random conversations starting up around the room. The threads of conversation range from anything on trivia to sheer scandal happening in town right now, and most of it is all outrageously true.

One conversation in particular takes Sven's attention

and she pushes the send button on her latest text to the girls, 'BORING!' "So, I pulled the 'unsafe' card on him today as I saw on Facebook that his car had a small oil leak in his garage, so his home where he has had my boys staying is now considered an 'unsafe environment' for him to have the kids. There go his visitation rights. I'm surprised you didn't hear him going off from Upper Hutt once he heard the news!"

"If you keep this up he'll have a heart attack! Either that or he will be spending his last few dollars on lawyer's fees to get access restored and all because he..."

"Well he wouldn't help out with some more money for the kids to have a new computer, so that's the price he must pay to fuck with me."

"I thought he got you a computer last year?"

"He did, but I wanted the latest one. The cheek of it! Everything that bastard Evan Mitchell buys for the boys is from op shops, he is so stingy. I'm not having someone's hand-me-downs all over my place."

"How deliciously evil. Oh, you are a *real* bitch!" And both HR Advisors fall around the floor laughing. "The good old adage, if you can't have him, then no one else can have him. Therefore, you are going to make him mentally and financially exhausted so he has nowhere else to go but be put out to pasture in a caravan park where he suffers for the entirety of his life, and no woman worth their weight in gold is going to want him then, is she? Even if there is a man shortage in this country!"

Sven continues to listen in fascination. Another lose-lose situation in the making. She suffers, her ex suffers, the kids suffer and everyone else who has to listen suffers. Even the taxpayer must suffer, as they pay good money for public servants to fill up their day, to talk such trivia. Then the Social Welfare department must pay her x amount for being a solo mother working part time, and then hardship because she doesn't declare she gets a generous under-the-table allowance from her ex, but as a private arrangement, not through Welfare. Not to mention generous hand-outs from her elderly parents, and her new fancy man. That way she can double and triple dip and still be ungrateful and live unhappily ever after.

Sven admits to herself that 'piece of work' and her sermon was almost worth coming in for, just to listen to that tragic bit of gossip. She figured the woman had broken up with her husband, as she has been even shittier than usual. Sven would love to meet him some day, and tell him the good news, that he doesn't realise how lucky he is to have escaped, even if it did cost him a laptop and x years of his life. What a lucky break, if she's half the bitch she is at work as she is at home, no wonder he ran for the hills. He dodged a bullet, and Sven tells herself she must congratulate him if she gets to meet him and hopefully hear that he did live happily ever after with the new Mrs Right. Sven makes a mental note to remember his name – Evan, Evan Mitchell. She also notices that his ex, Leanne, still keeps his surname. Clearly he doesn't pay her enough to change her married name back to her maiden name. If Sven disliked an ex-husband that much, that would be the first thing she would do – disassociate from him in every way, including changing her surname back to her maiden name.

Not being able to help herself, Sven then turns her ear to another couple of advisors who are deep in the flow of another conversation, but a lot more contrite. Theirs just can't compete with the last conversation.

"I'm far too busy to stand around waiting. Can't she just send us an email about what is so important that we have to stand around waiting for her like we did last week and the week before, when Cat was far too busy to remember to attend?" another self-inflated HR person screeches.

"Yes, I am so busy I don't know how I am going to finish this piece of work this side of Christmas, and then I've got the in-laws coming and my oldest one is having their graduation this week. I haven't even had time to shop for a new dress to wear to the ceremony, let alone take advantage of the David Jones' and Farmers' pre-xmas sales going on at the moment."

The conversation continues amongst the little cliques that have started forming on the sixth floor.

Sven continues to listen on from the corner of the room, like a fly on the wall. Quality, happiness, and letting the good times roll don't seem to be part of people's daily lives today, everyone is so obsessed with how much they can pack into a day and how much they can take from this and that. And no one seems to take time out to gauge how stressed-out they actually are, or look at seriously doing something about a real work-life balance. The number of 'off the record' potential burnouts, meltdowns, not coping based conversations she has had with this lot, not to mention depression, bullying, anxiety and anger bubbling away, is just staggering.

Sven continues to ponder on the huge epidemic that society is facing today and looks at the faces and the body language in the room and counts how few of the many that have been to see her about their concerns. Most of them feel they are just going through the motions and living life's dream of 'get the house, get the job promotion, get the kids, get the ring, get the mortgage to pay for the wedding, get the divorce, but in no particular order'. All of those 'tall order' boxes to tick, just to keep up with everyone, so they can say they are busy at work, busy at home, busy on holiday, busy sleeping, busy being busy, living their life the twenty-first century way, living 'The Dream'!

Of course the 'D' word, Depression, not forgetting its close cousins of anxiety and burnouts, must not be openly mentioned as we are far too busy playing stiff upper lip. However, statistics have shown all these good twenty-first century by-products are couched in such terms as 'chronic fatigue syndrome' or 'myalgic encephalomyelitis' or ME for short. They are on the increase and therefore must be addressed before the world completely melts down along with global warming, and that is where Sven comes into it. The results of a recent survey show today there is a lack of happiness and contentment, an increase in depression, anxiety and marriage break-ups. Not to mention Aotearoa having one of the world's highest suicide rates today.

Sven is glad for this delay in the announcement. Like most news, it is now old fish and chip paper. She knows the HR news won't affect her, but will undoubtedly affect her workload, as even more people will be queuing up to see her secretly and stressed to breaking point. That is the whole reason why most people prefer permanent, full-time work, as they believe that way they are guaranteed an income every week, regardless of how busy or how present or absent or effective they are. She takes the time to reflect on her notes and research, and starts compiling her weekly report to Bernard along with justifications for the proposed extension of another three months' work to outline how her role is making a real difference. The number of people wanting to make an appointment with her has increased, however, the demand and number she sees is still spasmodic and fluctuates day by day.

Bernard had been privy to some employee engagement survey results, where the following information had become prevalent. Working mothers were finding it increasingly hard to find and sustain the ideal work-home life balance and as the BS Ministry, and especially HR portrayed an incredibly high percentage of women, a solution needed to be worked on. Voilà, Bernard and his SMT decided to hire a lifestyle coach as part of an All of Government health wellness pilot. All part of implementing the BS's safety and wellbeing policy. So, enter Samantha Svensson into the mix.

Sven, a contractor, with her own highly successful online coaching business had been headhunted and has especially come over from Sweden to run the new Hauora wellness pilot. Sven had been working incredibly hard over in Europe off and on for the last decade or two. She had learnt the hard way, from personal experience what price one must pay if they insist on burning the candle at both ends. Feeling like she was once a superwoman and indispensable Sven worked long hours in both London and Stockholm for the bank and celebrated by playing hard. She would take her work home with her and make herself available to clients online twenty-four seven through Skype calls and responding to emails. She also socialised a lot with the bank employees, never having a real break from work. She ended up double booking her appointments and spiralling out of control, and was advised by the bank's Swedish HR Personalchef (Director) to take time off. She had reached a turning point; her body and mind could not sustain the heavy workload. As a result, she has learnt from this ordeal and now, practising what she preaches, works effectively as opposed to every hour god sends and with her clients, she stresses the importance of a happy work and home-life balance. Sven's brand now clearly demonstrates that in order for human beings to sustain the number of hours and projects they balance, in the long term they must take time out for themselves to self-care, because no one else is going to look after them and therefore the buck starts and stops with them.

Sven is happy to be back in New Zealand with a slower pace of life thanks to Bernard finding her again on LinkedIn, as well as her father, Kurt, dangling the carrot of purchasing a classic Ford Capri for her. Sven took these all as signposts to come home. A coaching role and a classic car, how could she resist? Sven, being superstitious and loving the symbology of numbers with her numerology wondered about all the c's – didn't they say that things come in threes? What would the third 'c' be? Classic car, coaching career and c…?

Sven abruptly stops daydreaming and returns to the present when she sees a movement from the corner of her eyes. She looks up to see Stephanie back on the soapbox again with her papers. She seems to have them in order now after the false start. "Excuse me everyone, thanks for your patience. Look, I am sorry, there has been a delay and I'm not at liberty to make the announcement after all. We will need to postpone now until 10am."

Everyone sighs and the moaning and groaning sweeps through the room like a Mexican wave. "Are you serious? We have been delayed already starting with the trains this morning, and now this! What a way to start the week," exclaims one of the HR ladies.

Sven takes this as a cue to exit and turns around to leave the room. She's had enough of all the rescheduling and the roller coaster of timetabling, nothing ever going according to plan. Everything at BS always seems to be so last minute and reactive as opposed to planned and proactive. Then taking a leaf from her own book, she flips the situation in her head and turns the inconvenience into a positive. Feeling inspired by the interruption she makes her way back to her cubicle deep in thought and flies through the report she needs to hand in by the end of the day.

*****

PART 2

MONDAY MORNING

Meetings and more meetings

Chapter 6

Recruiting, Comms and HR – Take 2

Tapping her pencil on her workstation, she thinks about how this coaching role is right down her alley. She decides she needs to be more patient and not get too hung up with the constant delays and resistance. She realises that people are doing their best – they are not capable of any more or less.

Sven heads to the breakout room to grab herself another coffee. The huge break out room being open-plan and equipped with a small kitchen is a terrific way of networking and discovering who is meeting who. Or as they would say in the old days, 'Who is up who?'. On the whole, those shenanigans of the old days, office affairs are a thing of the past. Well, except for downstairs. Sven takes advantage of one of the small break out cubicles separated by a ghastly bright purple partition and starts typing away on her laptop. She strategically places herself in front of the large glass doors that open into the lift and stairwell area. This way she can keep her eye on everyone who comes and goes.

With her HR colleagues sitting in nearby booths having informal meetings she listens in to the idle chatter when she gets bored with people-watching. The good thing about the Ministry is spotting a daily new face, a visitor, a backfill, someone she hasn't seen before. The hilarious thing about working in HR, where everything must be treated in the strictest confidence and every email and document is classified to the highest security level, is working in an open-plan office or having a meeting in a break out area, where there is zilch privacy and conversations are easily heard, especially when certain voices get heated and their conversations carry.

She gets up to cross the room to get a glass of water when she overhears a conversation, quite by chance. Two of the HR ladies and one gent are deep in conversation about 'coaching'. Sven's ears naturally prick up and she sits back down behind the adjoining partition and pretends to continue to type to mask the fact she is listening in.

"Look, I don't know what planet Bernard is on, but we don't do in-house coaching. He, the CEO of all people should know that we outsource everything to do with Learning and Development, and that includes coaching. This is not best practice having someone in-house, and how did she get the job? I don't remember the job being advertised, let alone a recruitment panel being set up for the role. I didn't see it internally advertised; if it had been I would have applied, and I certainly didn't see it on an external website, like Seek or Trade Me. Why wasn't it passed by me?" Nigel blurts out, flamboyantly waving his arms about and pouting. "After all, I am the Head of Recruiting, or is that a figment of my imagination nowadays? Has someone updated one of those out-of-date JDs and not informed me that my role has changed? I really wish SLT had consulted with me about this. I can't believe all the jobs that have gone over my head for approval. Where did all those backfills come from? I didn't approve those either. What the hell does the CEO think he is doing?" Nigel is a real scream and the girls love being around him as a lot of the time he exaggerates everything and pumps up the most boring meeting and topic into a West End stage show. He is as gay as they come, but the girls love him for it. However, recently his fun, peacockish ways have turned more into a passive-aggressive bitch session flavoured with plenty of sarcasm, and the jokes and dry sense of humour are drying up.

Vanessa from HR reassures Nigel. "Look, I hear where you are coming from – you should have been consulted about this coaching role. But I do have it on good authority that Samantha is very good at her job and she comes highly recommended. She's not some upstart. She's all for helping people, especially women, to increase their confidence, distribute their workload and get the ideal balance between work and home, and she's right into promoting and encouraging women to get out there and make a positive difference in all facets of their life. Her main goal is to show women that they don't have to gauge their sense of self-worth based on how many hours they beaver away at work on endless tasks and forever increasing unrealistic deadlines with limited resources."

Nigel responds back. "Still, I don't like being the

invisible man. Considering I am the only man here, you would have thought he could have consulted me. Besides, why couldn't a man be chosen for the role, they are just as in touch with their feelings as women, aren't they? Maybe he's homophobic and can't bear being in the same room as a poof."

"Well, I couldn't possibly comment on that as I don't want to sound like a sexist pig," Vanessa replies. "But seriously, welcome to my world, I am over fifty and I feel like the invisible woman. Look, you remember the policy that was passed a few months ago, regarding increasing the number of Pasifika and Māori employees we recruit here. Well Samantha Svensson is Māori. She is tangata whenua."

"Don't give me that, she's blonde and from one of those countries up in the northern hemisphere, where they run around naked in and out of saunas and roll around in the snow. Isn't it Switzerland or something where that pop band was from back in the day? My parents used to listen to them and get down on a Saturday night with all their swinging friends, downing Pimm's and shandies like they were going out of fashion."

Vanessa laughs again. "Nigel, you really are a scream. Yes, you're right, it does begin with 'Sw' and it is in the northern hemisphere, but it is Sweden, which is part of Scandinavia, and the pop band was ABBA as you would well know being a rainbow-coloured card-carrying LGBT member! I've seen you getting on down to 'Dancing Queen', you Priscilla of the Desert! Look, you know full well that Kiwis come in all shapes, colours and nationalities today. Show me a full-blooded Pākehā, or a full-blooded Māori. You can't, because percentages don't count, they never have and never will. The Brits were constantly invaded and diluted by Celts, Romans, Vikings, you name it! We Kiwis are a rich diverse fruit salad. We are a bit of Dutch, British, German, Scandi, Māori, Samoan, you name it. So don't give her a hard time, she is the first person we have recruited in two years who ticked our ethnicity box, NZ Māori. Believe me, leave it well alone Nigel, it looks good to anyone out there looking at our ethnicity statistics and as a result we are complying and engaging with one of our requirements, respecting the Treaty of Waitangi. Plus it saves jumping through hoops later when we are audited!"

Sven listens on, deep in thought. She had suspected that the Recruiting team had a bit of a problem with her.

Looking around the room, all she can see on the HR floor are a sea of mainly white faces. Clearly the token Pasifika and Māori employed each year must be hidden away on another floor. There are quite a few HR consultants of the Indian and Asian persuasion, so the BS must be ticking the boxes in that ethnicity field instead.

She makes a mental note about it and remembers that they are now about to go out to tender to get a te reo Māori language provider in and laughs to herself. Another waste of taxpayers' money, yes, put that on the GETS tendering system, take up five full-timers' pay while looking for the best provider outside, and 'Kia ora, here I am, already in-house'. She has no idea what GETS stands for, but another over-used acronym referring to the online tendering submission one must make if wanting to be in with a chance to become a preferred government supplier. It looks like no new people get a look-in, as it is the same suppliers each round that get back in.

Sven, after overhearing the conversation, walks back to her desk, again deep in thought. Her Fitbit goes off telling her she has already clocked up her ten thousand steps for the day. It's not even lunch time and she's already reached her step goal for the day. Checking her phone app, she sees that Clara has still to reach even half of that, so sends her a quick text, 'Get moving girl, or you'll never catch me today'.

It's true, Sven's philosophy is getting women to put themselves first, have some 'me time', whether that be physical exercise, time to reflect, set goals, meditate, try mindfulness, basically anything to do with emotional and social intelligence. Her overall goal is to get these 'health and wellbeing' areas implemented into the BS Ministry and then ideally all other government departments could follow suit, BS being the trailblazer as usual with yet another initiative, that once tested and proven could be taken up by the other smaller ministries.

Sven had initially experienced a lot of resistance trying to introduce her coaching sessions, as most of the employees said they were 'fine' and were 'too busy' to take advantage of this complimentary, in-house service. Not to mention the reluctance to enquire or take part in the free mindfulness classes being run in the organisation, onsite and during work hours. It couldn't get more enticing than that. Get paid to meditate and alleviate stress and anxiety and go back to work feeling rejuvenated and refreshed and being able to work more productively and with more energy and enthusiasm. Not forgetting if they take part in these initiatives, it can go towards their required annual professional development and ticks that box as part of their half-yearly performance appraisal.

As part of this new wellness initiative, she was also introducing well-known speakers around town and trying to brand and tailor these into HR as another way of enhancing their professional development and enhancing their health and wellbeing plan. So far, the majority of employees were just too busy to take time out to attend these talks, even when Sven brought them to work and the sessions were actually held in the building over lunch time, once a fortnight. All the staff needed to do was manage their time, block out one hour in their Outlook calendar and take the lift down six flights of stairs. They would be rewarded with seeing a new face and learning something new and possibly even networking, or for those who were wanting to escape, it could be their ticket out of there to another job or vocation.

There were also BS-wide seminars being organised by the greater BS and their popularity and attendance was just as poor. Sven tried not to take it personally. As Bernard would always say, "It is what it is, Sven, don't take it personally. Remember, we are not in Europe now; we are in NZ and in the public service. Remember, baby steps, small changes, slowly but surely. Change doesn't happen overnight; especially lasting change." With Sven replying, "I will be collecting my pension. I don't have another twenty-five years to wait – my contract expires in three months."

However, there was a marginal amount of success. She managed to persuade Cat into allowing her to get a ten-minute segment into the monthly HR half-day 'sit-down' meetings. Nevertheless, Cat cunningly had Sven's slot always tacked onto the end of other speakers and due to their poor time management and love of hearing their own voices, they all had a tendency to go over time, pushing her slot out and off the agenda. "Never mind, Sven, I'm sure we can do something at the next meeting if we have time," Cat would smile sweetly with that shimmering shark-like lipstick. Naturally next time never came. It was all smoke and mirrors.

Sven would bounce back quite quickly after each initiative was brick-walled or delayed for some reason, remembering that the DCE had rated her work in Sweden, and this was a vote of confidence for her, that Bernard had believed in her enough to bring her home. When she did have those moments of self-doubt and underestimated herself she thought of that. And who is true to their word nowadays anyway? She recalls his parting shot at the bank, Handelsbanken in Mäster Samuelsgatan in Stockholm: "I am going back home now, Sven, back to NZ. I admired the difference you have made here; I have seen the results, the difference in our people. If I ever need someone with your skills, you can be sure I will track you down. I have already met my new crew down under and I have a feeling one of my first goals back home will be to employ an in-house coach, counsellor, whatever you like to call yourself. I am sold, I am a believer. However, I must admit I was the first one to be sceptical when you first came into the bank. But I've seen the hugely positive differences with the staff's morale and motivation, not to mention the confidence levels of employees, both men and women, go through the roof. They are embracing the fact that they can now have courageous conversations without risking being sacked or getting into a situation involving conflict. You know how much the Swedes will avoid conflict at all costs, so this is a real turnaround in behaviour and attitude. The whole culture has changed and for the better. If you are keen, I will be in touch."

Sven is very thankful and vows not to let him or more importantly herself down. She then goes forward in time, reflecting on her first meeting with Cat and Bernard. Cat had believed that Sven's new proposed role was a load of nonsense, but Cat had smiled sweetly to Bernard, brown-nosing with "Of course, Bernard, you know me, I'm up for anything that will make a difference to my staff, especially my female leaders beneath me. I see it as 'succession planning', these capable women can lead the future of our business, the more we invest in them and believe in them the better we will all be."

This was the dream job for Sven back in New Zealand. She knew it was risky and that government did not have in-house coaches, and she would be breaking glass ceilings and many fragile egos along the way. But like her Swedish mentor Anna-Greta had told her once: 'Sven, what other people think of you is none of your business. That's their problem, that's saying more about them than you. You dance to your own tune. No regrets, remember, my dear.'. Anna-Greta was not one to tolerate fools, and she and Sven had hit it off famously, learning buckets of wisdom and great one-liners from this very upfront elegantly dressed woman.

Yeah, bugger them, Sven had thought to herself. She knew her intentions were all good, she would make a real difference in these overworked women's lives, and any future brick walls she would flip around. She wondered which Head of Department would be the best place to get an easy win, and then at their next SMT meeting they could sell her to the rest of their colleagues; Labour, Immigration, Pasifika and Māori…ah, of course Pasifika and Māori. She jumped onto BS's intranet and looked up who oversaw

Pasifika and Māori. Then cleverly in Sven's wordsmith ways, she composed an email to the Head of Department, Julia. How fitting that she was from Western Samoa, Mt Vaea, Tusitala – a place Sven loved.

Sven excitedly sent off the email to Julia and felt better for trying something different instead of waiting for HR to promote her. She had written a spiel about herself and posted it online but had got into trouble with the Communications team. As everything must go through them initially, and due to being short-staffed, there was a delay in getting anything up on the intranet. Besides, Comms needed Cat's permission and a special form to be filled in before anything could be posted. The Communications Policy outlined they needed to interview Sven and write the piece themselves.

"Ve can't allow someone else to, how do you say, pen this and vith due respect Svedish being your language, ve require Native English speaker to pen article," the cocky little Bulgarian Comms Advisor Dubravka barked out to Sven.

Whoops, that went down like a cup of cold sick with Sven and as calmly as possible (with a large dose of sarcasm dropped in for good measure) rebuked, "Excuse me, I am a New Zealander born and bred in Dannevirke, and English is my first language followed closely by te reo – E mōhio ana koe? No, I thought not. Therefore, as English is the language of choice for your media, I am quite capable of writing a piece in English. I do have a degree in Journalism, and I believe the Comms team are not qualified journalists, even though their subject matter expertise is in writing, which does confuse me a little. However, I am sure this is all best practice and as this is only going to be used for 'internal communications', not externally or for the *Capital News*, I thought this would be okay. I was just trying to save your team time, as I appreciate you are short-staffed. However, if you believe you have it all covered then fill your boots, I am happy for you to write it for me. Aroha mai – my apologies."

Sonya, the Head of Communications had just walked in at the tail end of this conversation, and quickly took over. "My apologies Sven, my Comms Advisor is relatively new. I will deal with this," she added as she whisked her away. Ms Bulgaria looked Sven up and down and decided possibly for once in her life it was best to remain speechless.

Before the upstart Comms specialist disappeared through the floorboards, Sven had taken the liberty to continue. "It appears the HR Director has gone missing but as soon as she is back, I will ensure she can provide the necessary triplicate paperwork to request for one of your team to profile the coaching role I am currently doing and promote this free service BS ministry-wide. Again, my apologies for overstepping my mark. Ka kite anō au i a koe, see you again soon."

Sven loved killing people with kindness and being deadly sarcastic when she needed to. For god's sake, here was a free service saying, 'I know all you idiots are stressed to the max, but don't fret, you don't have to look any further, here I am, a qualified multi-lingual counsellor , not to mention journalist, who can assist you with anything you desire, all within the building, and for free'. But of course it is just not best practice…*Give me a break!*

Dubravka, the Comms woman whose name at the time she couldn't catch, was completely naïve, out of her depth and couldn't understand what Sven was saying. She could hardly grasp English, let alone the country's official language of te reo Māori. Dubravka was one of the many recent imported editions that the downstairs' Immigration department had been giving working visas and in-house jobs further frustrating Nigel in Recruiting. Now that's an effective government department, giving visas *and* Kiwi jobs away, not to mention missing out the middle person, the in-house Recruiting team. Sven later discovered that this woman had just arrived from Bulgaria and not understanding English well enough to be able to communicate, was given the job in Communications *and* as Senior Communications Advisor. *Now what a perfect fit,* Sven had thought to herself. Sven took the liberty as usual to investigate through the HR files to find that Dubravka had been the Senior Advisor for the Communist party in Bulgaria and immigration had confused the word 'communist' for 'communications' because the abbreviation for both words is 'Comms.' So sometimes even the public service trip over their own long list of acronyms and can't see the wood for the trees.

However, Sven had to stay focused and on areas that she could control. What the Recruiting and Immigration teams did was out of her control and there was no point wasting valuable energy in those areas. With Cat sharpening her pencil constantly to improve the bottom line by downsizing yet again, staff would find themselves under even more intense pressure, it was important her services were advertised.

At this time of the year – the 'silly season' – nearly every year, the permanent staff were on tenterhooks wondering if this was the year they would be down the road. That was the only way to save money in a lot of managers' minds – to reduce the number of employees or worse still disestablish their positions, and make them reapply for another similar position but with twice the workload, and on less money. They would then need to compete for the role along with their colleagues and mates within the business and of course wait a bit longer while the role was advertised out in the open market, giving more immigrants ample time to polish their CVs and apply.

During a restructure, the first area that was scrutinised and done away with was the Learning and Development team, as most managers believed that training was unnecessary.

However, enlightened managers and Sven agreed; if money was put into upskilling people, these people would be more loyal, motivated and engaged and they would work more effectively and productively which was a far better alternative to pushing the 'restructure' button each time the accountant raised his concerns about the bottom line of his spreadsheets.

Even if an upskilled employee leaves then another company benefits by recruiting them. That person will tell others how their previous company treated them, naturally promoting the progressive nature of the company, instead of spreading the word of 'Hey, don't ever work for…they treat their staff like shit'. But managers don't seem to see the big picture, especially those who class themselves as 'blue-sky thinkers'.

The week previously, Cat had warned Sven that "Some of the usual whingers will probably come knocking on your door for a moan once I make the announcement. I have given those people plenty of opportunity to buck up and fuck up or fuck off, so don't invest any more time in them, because I want them to leave. I mean how long does someone have to work here to see that while working for me it is my way or the highway?" This line had become Cat's catch phrase.

A squeaky voice comes through the office intercom, "Kia ora, talofa, kia orana...ladies and gentlemen, the rescheduled HR stand-up is now being reconvened. Please make your way to the sixth floor."

Speaking of being 'stood up', people are now once again swarming around the HR pod for a rescheduled fifteen minutes' stand-up and the gossip and idle chatter begins yet again as people start congregating around the central row of pods.

Sven stops daydreaming and her thoughts quickly return to the present.

Stephanie, yet again, stands up, clearing her throat several times to get everyone's attention but failing on each occasion. Finally, the Senior HR Advisor, Carmen, does her favourite sheep whistle showing her farming background – shuddering the heritage glass windows as violently as the recent earthquake, and suddenly there is complete silence. Some people look on horrified as they seriously believe the next earthquake is upon them and some start dropping to the ground as they had been told at the last HR stand-up: 'In the case of an earthquake, Drop, Cover, Hold.'

A number of Christchurch people traumatised by the huge earthquakes in Canterbury a few years before, had moved up to Wellington to get away from the aftershocks and living in constant fear of yet another earthquake. Many Cantabrians had been diagnosed with post-traumatic stress disorder and were thankful to leave the shaky isles of Te Waipounamu, the South Island behind, only to experience another huge earthquake, this time in the capital city and affecting many of the tall apartments they had moved into in the CBD. The new and current inhabitants of Wellington were in dire need of finding psychologists, psychotherapists, counsellors, psychiatrists, anyone trained to help them deal with their heightened anxiety and hyper-vigilant states of being on high alert twenty-four seven. Many were constantly on the lookout for any signs that may indicate another big quake was coming.

Sven stands in the middle of a sea of terrified faces, observing everyone. Then as an icebreaker – clearly an unplanned one – Stephanie trips and falls off the platform again, sending everyone into hysterics. Sven stares on in amazement, trying to contain herself, amused at people's reactions and the huge release of tension as it spread around the room like a Mexican wave. Those who didn't know Stephanie would believe it was a well-rehearsed move to get everyone's attention before the announcement.

Stephanie, composing herself, gingerly makes her way back up onto the step, and yet again tries to get everyone's attention for the right reasons. Failing miserably, she tries to talk into the microphone in an assertive manner, tripping over her words. Her voice is drowned out as the microphone squeaks and crackles, piercing the audience's ears.

Stephanie mumbles on, with the audience unengaged with what she is saying. This is a senior leader who should know how to inspire her audience and how to attract and command respect. If only HR knew this basic principle when they were dealing with people. It's not the string of overused, corporatised words 'strategy, synergy, words on a page' that come pouring out of their mouths like a burst sewer pipe that is important; it's the way they deliver this, their non-verbal language that speaks a thousand words.

If the actions don't match the words, then the 'words on a page' or the 'words at a stand-up' fall on deaf ears.

No wonder they need heaps of contractors, commonly known in Public Service land as 'backfills', and no wonder they do the best work, because they have more of an open mind, they have come from the outside with a fresh set of eyes and ideas and have seen how the world operates in a real sense.

Stephanie, to look at and to listen to, comes across very unassuming and non-threatening. She has an unusually round face, puffed up like one of those puffer fish one sees when snorkelling in the Pacific Islands. Her complexion is anaemic with acne scars that still plague her from her teens, and her mousey-grey, straight, greasy hair is chopped severely into a bob style, imitating her leader's no less, Cat. Her body blends in nicely with her face – blobby and pasty, devoid of decades of sun.

The Assistant HR Director does not bat an eyelid – well, not that anyone can see, as her eye is still twitching furiously from Carmen's piercing whistle. In fact Stephanie looks semi-relieved and nods to Carmen, thanking her for her assistance in getting the meeting started. Although clearly thinking it inappropriate for an HR meeting to start this way, she obviously realises her introverted ways won't kick it off.

Carmen, on the other hand is everything Stephanie is not, dressed most days in leopard print. Thankfully her entire leopard collection is never worn at the same time. She is still seething that Cat had the audacity to wear a leopard print coat on Friday.

Carmen favours bright pink lipstick, matching pink eye shadow and blusher. Her platinum blonde bleached hair is perfectly kept in place by the many cans of hairspray she goes through, making a bigger dent in the New Zealand's ozone layer by the week. The empty canisters can be found in the washroom wastepaper baskets or often in one of the recycle bins in the break out room. To be fair, with the amount of time and money Carmen puts into her appearance, not to mention her CV, she should be highly visible, alas Carmen suffers from the 'Invisible Woman Syndrome' aka ageism. Accordingly, Sven has duly noted that ageism is another area that needs to be addressed and has already organised a speaker to come in and present about this topic. The speaker Anita is a contemporary of Sven's, and she will be doing a piece on her specialist topic, Unconscious Bias Training. UBT is the latest buzz word, and Anita will cover everything from people unconsciously treating people differently due to their age, sex, orientation or colour of their skin.

*****

The HR team are definitely an eclectic bunch of females. In fact, HR seems to pride themselves, or more precisely 'label' themselves in two camps: they are either introverts or extroverts.

L & D (Learning and Development), the ones always the first for the chopping board or Cat's guillotine, are branded openly as the poor brothers to the greater HR team.

Sarita leads the team of Learning and Development Advisors and after running several psychometric, state-of-the-art, best practice tests, has suddenly realised that her small team of non-performers, 'Learning and Developers' are mainly introverts. Sarita then makes the huge discovery that this is why her weekly team morale boosting meetings are constantly weak on both conversation and content. In fact, the meetings are pretty quiet, except for the one extrovert who used to constantly feel the need to fill the silences with noises. Kirsty, god bless her bright pink stockings, did not realise that the pauses were necessary for the introverts to go further inside themselves to reflect before they could offer their comments. Instead she took the reflective silences as a cue to crack another ridiculous joke, ensuring everyone remembered she was there.

Kirsty the extrovert – a short, fun-type girl with blonde streaked hair, colourful clothes and different coloured stockings for each day of the week, had the unfortunate mannerism like Stephanie of a twitching eye. Kirsty's eye would twitch more than usual when she had just cracked a joke and was waiting for the reaction, hoping like mad it would be applause or laughter and she would finally gain social acceptance into the team. Being an extrovert, she was quite happy to get up and present in public; in fact she thrived on it.

Kirsty, for all her talking and cracking jokes at the wrong time and place, was a kind soul and did have quite a bit to add even though most of her jokes were hilarious, they were clearly wasted on the audience who simply did not get her humour.

However, a couple of the introverts enjoyed the refreshing difference and dynamics Kirsty brought to the team and tried to find the jokes hilarious. The rest of the team who didn't get them were incapable of initiating anything and were still stuck inside themselves reflecting on the last few meetings. Within the hour they never seemed to come out of their shells to say anything at all.

*****

With Stephanie from time to time, like today, being at the helm and being one of those fellow introverts surrounded by introverts, she was also constantly reflecting on why she had been given the senior position she had. She always dreaded it when Cat was away, even though the other half of her strongly believed she should have got the 'top dog' position that Cat currently held. Stephanie was having one of those moments of self-doubt now and her thoughts stuck like a groove on a well-played record from the seventies.

With a nudge from Carmen, she finally breaks out and speaks. "Good morning ladies. I mean tēnā koe ladies and one gent." Most of the brown-nosers up the front laugh nervously as usual at the reference to the one token male, Nigel the 'nag' in the room full of forty-six women. "I hope you all had a good weekend? All over too soon, unfortunately for some of us! Thank you for turning up today." A few sighs can be heard around the room and people murmuring about not having much choice, if they want to get paid.

Anastasia hastily responds. "Please, we've heard that weak joke before, can you at least be original with your opening? We all know there is only one gent, and he's hardly a 'gent', he's a raving…"

Stephanie fidgets more nervously than usual as the two women, Gabrielle and Anastasia up the back continue to groan and moan and have now started up a conversation about the unfairness of the stingy sick leave and how they as mothers should get more than the singles in the team. Joanna from ER (Employment Relations) taps them on the shoulder to remind them where they are and that smoko is just around the corner.

"I'm sorry that you have been so patiently waiting for our HR leader to arrive. It's not like her and I'm sorry, I'm not sure what's happened," Stephanie continues.

Surely you can do better than this, thinks Sven. Couldn't she just make up a story, that she's just running late, and we will reschedule for later, or she has laddered her one hundred dollar stockings and had to run into David Jones to replace them and got stuck in the lift there with the Director and...

Sven is gagging for a caffeine fix, and could better use her time downstairs over a coffee reading her first client for the day's notes.

Stephanie tries to go on, but everyone is moaning now about how they have waited all this time just to find out that Cat has still not shown up.

Stephanie tries to get some law and order in the room but fails dismally yet again. Carmen takes it on board to be third in charge and rings the silver bell she has on her desk rather loudly.

After a quick few words with Stephanie Carmen takes over, "Okay everyone, we apologise for the inconvenience. I know you are all busy, well not half as busy as I am. Let's reschedule for later in the day, keep your computers and phones switched on and I will send through an instant message and updated calendar invite on when we will reconvene. Thank you and have a good day."

Oh my... They are joking, aren't they? Do they really need to reschedule, reschedule and reschedule what in reality is a pointless meeting, and hardly news, five thousand times during the day?

Carmen, clearly an extrovert and very proud of the

way she took over the meeting, twirls around and flicks her bleached blonde hair back, revealing her face which is going on sixty or seventy despite her hair, which is going on twenty-one. She suddenly no longer feels invisible as all those beady eyes were on her while she replaced Stephanie on the stand.

Since the earlier meeting she has changed from her standard leopard print into her Friday night outfit – skin tight black leather pants and matching shoes, with a black slinky top. This was after having an unfortunate incontinence 'accident' while having a laugh with her team once too often; one of the joys of menopause. Being caught short before, Carmen always comes to work prepared with a spare set of clothes and knickers in her gym locker downstairs.

However, Lloyd, the mail man enjoys whatever Carmen is wearing immensely and makes as many detours as possible during the day to bring up her mail personally.

Now with the much awaited, much talked about HR stand-up rescheduled, all the HR women bar one, Nigel the Recruiting Manager, waddle back to their little white cubicles.

"Damn, that's another half an hour out of my day already. I hadn't counted on that. I'm off for a coffee. Who wants a coffee, give me your orders and I will put them through my app now and go and collect them," says Kirsty kindly. "Hard night last night, I just can't get to sleep because of these earthquakes."

Her workmate and partner in crime, Casey, replies, "But we haven't had any earthquakes of late. Or have we? I'm so stressed with my constant headaches, the floor is permanently moving, I can't distinguish between the floor moving or not and each time I look out the window it is snowing."

"Oh, I must be suffering from those phantom earthquakes they talk about, you know the ones where you imagine the floor is moving, but it's not really, like when you look hard enough and you think there is a ghost in the room, but there isn't," replies Kirsty.

"I heard that too. They say you suffer from phantom earthquakes after the real ones, and they are just as stressful!" Casey joins in.

Kirsty comes back in with, "Snow, yes, that was funny when you thought you saw snowflakes in the meeting room the other day. I think it is due to those drugs you are on to help reduce your stress and endless headaches. Do they actually work or are you just permanently hallucinating now? After today, I wonder if I could have a bit of what you are on? Is it available across the counter from the pharmacy on the Quay? I would love to be able to be away with the fairies at this time of year, it would be a fantastic way to float through the in-law's visit over Christmas."

With that her phone beeps, the coffees are ready and she heads downstairs for her third coffee of the morning. Her mind is buzzing on a caffeine high doing overtime, ruminating over everything that has already happened and lunch time is still miles off. Two cans of diet coke before morning tea just don't do it for her now either. After giving up smoking, those double shots in the Home and Away café every few hours are what get her through her nicotine withdrawal.

Slightly irritated Sven heads off to get her Fitbit steps up to keep ahead of Clara, and on a whim decides to go off to the railway station to see what developments have been made. She has always fancied herself being a detective, but switched to Journalism instead of Police college after her ex police trainee boyfriend proposed. The skills of knowing who the right people are to talk to, to kick-start investigations into an alleged suspicious incident are very similar.

*****

Meanwhile, in their first post training course meeting on the third floor at BS Castle, the newly trained Incident Managers are freaking out big time, wondering if an incident like an earthquake, tsunami, breach of security happened, just what would they do? They are now hurriedly looking for the Incident Management course hand-out materials.

"If you guys are this flustered when there isn't an incident, how are you going to cope when the real deal unexpectedly creeps up and bites you on the bum?" asks Sheena, who had been involved with all the logistics of getting an outsider in to facilitate the recently held incident controlling course.

"What are the chances of another earthquake happening this close to the last one? She'll be right. We can get all this sorted after Christmas," Rupert, the Incident Manager from Immigration tries to say confidently, but clearly to everyone else in the room, he is bluffing.

"Ah, but they do say things come in threes, so there should be another two earthquakes just around the corner," Sheena replies a bit too enthusiastically.

"Great, that makes me feel so much better. I can always rely on you to make me feel worse than I already feel, Sheena. Okay, how's this for an idea, team? Let's all head home now and reconvene on a Skype conference call, that way if an incident happens we won't all be in the same room when it happens!" Rupert puts forward.

The Incident Management team choruses: "Super idea!"

"Fantastic, let's scram!"

"How's the surf conditions?" Brady asks quietly, sweeping back his corkscrew golden locks into a pony tail, as they all eagerly depart the building.

****

Chapter 7

Wellington Railway Station

"CAll the police, we have a…" Bert blurts out, but his voice trails off, drowned by the noise of another train that slides in on the platform opposite. A piercing voice can be heard through the intercom announcing the next departing train: "The train for Porirua leaves on platform four at…"

Once it quietens down and the intercom falls silent, Ernie having time to think responds, "No, wait! This is serious, we must tell the boss first. We got that HR email last week – I didn't bother reading it all, but Kev reckoned it was about how we must never talk with anyone outside – the media, the police or the public until it goes through Comms first. You know how paranoid they are about any of us public servants putting our ministers at risk of appearing on the front page of the *Capital News.*"

Among the many fears any public servant has there is one above all else that makes them quiver in their patent leather shoes. You may think this would be something like not getting paid and the house mortgage payment not being met, or getting caught having an affair in the stationery cupboard with a junior colleague. No, it's far worse than that! Their greatest fear is being the cause of their ministry appearing on the front page of the Capital News!

Hence, no one ever goes beyond the call of duty or eagerly wants to try anything new and innovative, let alone real and authentic in case it finds its way to the front page for all to see. This could be extremely career limiting as it would demonstrate to Johanna Bloggs or Jo Blow out there, the citizen, that a public servant was caught going beyond the call of duty, challenging the status quo, taking risks and improving the broken systems that management take pride in restructuring. A passionate, dedicated public service would work so well that the taxpayer would actually get the public service that they were paying for, rather than the public businesses they have become, that continue to fatten the managers' salaries, asset strip the ministries and layoff specialist staff so that the public service becomes one big homogenised family that has no real purpose.

Bert, being in charge, steps up and offers to run back to the office to spill the beans while Ernie reluctantly stays back, staring wide-eyed at the body that is now lying slumped awkwardly against the toilet cubicle wall. The most prominent feature is the bright red lipstick smeared over the toilet cubicle wall and the remaining lipstick still plastered on those huge lips, looking slightly disjointed with her mouth wide open showing in full 3-D scale a woman's set of teeth. It looks like a scene out of an old Jaws movie, a huge mouth ready to swallow its intended target at the flip of an eyelid.

"Oh my god, just what I want on a Monday, a cold case," Ernie exclaims. Clearly he has been watching too much of that TV programme *Cold Case* where the team go and fish out the files and names of people from the past who can help them with a body that was found dead back in the day.

However this experience has made him realise that some TV programmes really only belong in one place, and that is on the screen and not transformed into reality. Reality can be grimmer than fiction. Isn't that always the (cold) case?

The news of the death on the train was starting to get around the railway yard, getting more out of context and turning into an Agatha Christie murder mystery on the Orient Express. The office jungle telegraph was in full swing at every office cubicle at the railway station, while another drama was brewing up the road at the BS Ministry.

*****

Sven, now back at BS HQ, is listening and observing – her favourite pastime. This time she's up on the seventh-floor balcony, waiting for her first appointment of the day, taking in the incredibly amazing bird's-eye view of most of the prominent landmarks of town. From the neighbouring streets, down Featherston Street to the railway station, other government offices and the harbour, topping off with the glistening waters of Oriental Bay and her golden sands in the distance. It is one of those out-of-the-box gorgeous Wellington days and Sven, like the seagulls swarming above her, can see for miles. Everything looks so serene, the buildings and people oblivious to the storm that is brewing downstairs and down at the station.

A couple of young HR consultants have found Sven's meeting area; not the sixth-floor one but the outside seventh-floor balcony, and are so deeply involved in their conversation they don't notice Sven coming out onto the balcony. They busily carry on with their talkfest, oblivious as Sven slips into the nearby table behind them. One pauses to take a breath, takes a quick glance at her and mistaking her for some no-name backfill glued to her phone, they continue chatting. Unbeknown to them, Sven is not on the phone talking, but is eavesdropping on what they are saying.

"You know what they are all saying at Railways, don't you?"

"Yes, my friend Ingrid in Accounts said that someone took a passenger out on the Kiwi Con on the way home on Friday night," says the tall, slim blonde with a know-it-all tone. Sven remembers meeting her on her first day and tries to remember her name. Looking pretty rough for a Monday morning, without make-up, she looks more like a man than a woman. Her name did rhyme with 'man' coincidentally…yes, it's Jan.

"And Karen in Marketing was saying that Comms are in a real tizz as they don't know if they should call the Minister, the CEO or the police first!"

"I mean what do you make of it?"

"Well Ingrid said that there was a BS lanyard found on the body."

"OMG, Beth! Have they moved the body already? The police won't like that!"

"I'm not sure, but I bet a murder on the KC has never happened before!"

Just as she finishes speaking, they both realise they are talking at the top of their voices in the middle of a public place and look around to notice Sven still sitting there. Somewhat taken aback, they close off their conversation and go to move on, but stop at the veranda rails to lean over. There is more noise and commotion going on out in the street than usual, especially for a Monday morning.

Sven, hearing the sirens of cop cars, joins them and looks over the bannisters to see a fleet of police cars pulling up in front of the railway station. Some have pulled up downstairs at BS's main entrance too.

"OMG, how come our alarms are not going off? There must be an incident. Oh no, I don't know if the Incident team are in today – I think I saw them all leaving through reception earlier."

Sven thinks how impractical this is. The Incident Management team really need to be onsite in case an unexpected emergency happens, and most emergencies are not expected and planned. Just then her phone beeps at her with a declined meeting invitation from her first client of the day. Typical!

The two young girls race back inside and down the stairs to see what's happening. Nothing in their four years has been this exciting and it's all unfolding on a Monday. "Now if work was usually like this, we would come in more often on a Monday."

Sven is suddenly feeling incredibly nervous and her gut feeling is doing overtime. She is certain there is more to this than meets the eye and wonders what the hell Stephanie is not telling everyone. *Comms are so pathetic they wouldn't know if their arse was on fire.* Clearly she is going to have to go outside to find out. She has a quick look at the news app on her phone, but nothing has come up yet. She wonders if what those guys saw in the loo on the train this morning has anything to do with this.

She recalls that some murder did happen many years ago on one of the trains. She remembers her parents telling her about it, some name to do with Captain James Cook, Adventurer. No, the En…Endeavour, that's what it was. A large blue train, with similar carriages to the Kiwi Con. She has a flashback of the old VHS video clip her father had shown her. Realising the Endeavour was very similar in layout and size to the Kiwi Con. Sven looks through some old footage of the Endeavour on her phone and recognises the exact lettering and font size of the letter M – it is the old carriage where the unresolved murder took place. *Oh my god, that is the very same carriage from back in the day. Is this history repeating itself? That's where the murder happened! That's right – Dad said that everyone got superstitious about the train murder happening in carriage M of all carriages. And from then on, that carriage was decommissioned and left like a redundant office chair in the railway yard as people believed it was jinxed. Moreover, the local iwi needed to come on board after it happened and do a blessing to get rid of the tapu, the negative energy it now held.* Sven remembers watching an old film clip with her parents, the kaumātua doing several karakia and other prayers. And then came the recommendation to withdraw the carriage from service due to the grim events that had taken place.

After the murder on the Endeavour, Dad reckoned that everyone was up in arms and after too many misadventures and weird happenings, no one wished to ride her anymore. The service was no longer financially viable, so the powers that be shut the whole train service down and all of the carriages went into early retirement. Most of the carriages were left in the yard or were reduced to scrap. However, over time, people forgot about the history and a new train came on board – the Kiwi Con, and with the increased patronage, the original three carriages grew to seven carriages and the railways needed to expand. With the drama of importing the foreign train carriages resulting in the closure of the Ōtāhuhu Rail Yards up in Auckland with the subsequent loss of KiwiRail engineers' jobs and the Chinese/French carriage asbestos scandal, KiwiRail resorted to doing up some of the older Endeavour carriages and changing the branding, adding them to the Kiwi Con. As the murder had happened well over fifteen years ago and with a facelift to the carriage interior, the present-day passengers were oblivious to its sordid history. Just like the rebrand of a company or government department, so within time, people forgot what it was originally.

However, Sven being Sven, always perceptive, heads towards her pod as her gut feeling tells her something big is about to happen.

*****

Chapter 8

The Announcement

Meetings have been rescheduled left right and centre today, no one knows where they are meant to be and everyone suddenly has more than the usual back-to-back meetings. They are now having parallel meetings and some public servants are meant to be in two or three places at the same time. Thank goodness Sven must only attend the selected ones as a guest speaker or observer as part of her brief from Bernard, just popping in for a quick slot instead of staying for the entire one-hour drawn-out duration.

Back on the sixth floor all is humming even more than usual; there is suddenly an unusually large number of visitors from other floors roaming the pods. Sven sits back and watches from her pod. Where she sits she has a bird's-eye view, observing people as they come and go, all with the prescriptive public service pad and standard unbranded pen in their hand. She wonders if they are just casing the joint out of curiosity or whether suddenly the face-to-face visits have increased and the old-fashioned email communication has reduced. To be fair, it could be because the system is intermittently off and on today with the extra surge of emails and correspondence with the outside world and tittle-tattle going back and forth within the four walls. Suddenly, the HR department is of huge interest to the occupants of the other floors who usually never venture far away from their home floor.

Downstairs on the ground floor where the café is situated along with the meeting rooms for outsiders to book, the entire floor is chock-full. The floor is a constant flurry of people, walking in and around the café, the reception area, mingling outside meeting rooms and hovering at the front entrance. An incredible amount of activity especially for a Monday, when most public servants are away from the office on a combination of sick leave, AWOL (absent without leave), tangi leave, TOIL (time off in lieu), annual leave and the usual 'best practice' working from home, stress leave, earthquake leave, you name it type of leave. It's like a good traditional Swedish smörgåsbord, plenty of options to choose from. Just tick the box and submit it through the online pay system and it is approved by fragmented and distracted team leaders and managers unaware of what they have just put their signature to.

Nevertheless, the momentum and atmosphere today are of the unusual kind, a mixture of excitement, uncertainty and business as usual (BAU).

There are sub meetings, meetings to discuss meetings and an array of parallel meetings. The biggest outcome from one of the ongoing meetings is a decision has been finally made. As a way of increasing the Ministry's profile, they have decided they will pay an exorbitant fee to gain exclusive naming rights for the building. A swanky world-wide advertising agency was engaged in the dizzyingly costly branding exercise, the result being that due to the type of font size, from a distance all you can see are the large letters of B and S, and the remaining letters 'ig' and 'uper' fade into the fashionably bland beige wishy-washy colour of the heritage building.

The EEO commission and the Health and Safety gestapo are up in arms as the Ministry has spent mega bucks on all the latest branding, but have not made the building accessible for those who are physically challenged, e.g. in wheelchairs. Ernest Ragbottom, the Ministerial Undersecretary to the Minister responsible for BS, has temporarily ended up in a wheelchair due to some embarrassingly unexplainable incident involving a marmite jar after hours. To be fair, he is accident-prone. It could be something to do with his outrageous, flamboyant character as he is always taking centre stage to mimic or display his opinions. The upshot being, with the grand entrance to the building only being accessible by a steep flight of stairs, he can no longer gain access into the building. The back entrance which he is habitually accustomed to using, is also only accessible by stairs. Clearly when the building was designed and renovated to suit twenty-first century living, physically challenged people did not exist, or possibly it was one of those 'senior moments' or generally unaware moments where those disabled patrons were not considered to be part of the equation. Either that, or more likely the EEO alterations were conveniently removed when the true costs were shown to the Minister, to keep the renovations within the budget.

Fortunately, unbeknown to many people except those high up in the Ministry and from the government's HQ, the Beehive, there is a secret tunnel that leads between the Beehive and BS Castle and this is how Ernest now needs to access the building. His boyfriend Nigel, Head of Recruiting, usually meets Ernest to assist him from the basement tunnel into the lifts as they can only be operated with certain access cards with the correct clearance and the form-filling involved in acquiring these services can be very lengthy. At times it can be highly nonsensical and always in the required 'best practice' triplicate manner.

Since the Incident Management training, the Incident Management Controllers are now all aware of this escape route and in case of another natural disaster, this has been assigned as the Hub Headquarters where they should meet to communicate how they are going to deal with the next natural disaster. The IC team are still waiting for IT to clear their backlog before they can start loading the clearance onto their security cards. After all, what is the likelihood of another earthquake striking, and so soon?

The excessive amount of wasted money spent on the BS naming rights, having the biggest, glitziest reception area in town along with their very own in-house café has caused the Ministry to hit the front-page headlines of the Capital News, and one time too many. A great deal of unnecessary taxpayers' money has been going down the pan and this is half the reason why the previous DCE 'retired early' under suspicious financial circumstances and why Bernard, a qualified Accountant and Chief Financial Officer for Handelsbanken was brought in as the new DCE to rectify all these exorbitant costs. His role is to get the BS Ministry back into the black and this is half the reason why he was attracted to Cat's portfolio and brought her in, as she too has a reputation for severely cutting costs (while being insensitive to all the backlash this causes). Like a true Iron Lady she storms every building she goes into and whips the bottom line into shape no matter what the true cost to the business or people's health and wellbeing is. Rumour has it that Bernard's wife, Margaret, has similar Iron Lady tendencies. Possibly that was the attraction for Bernard, having someone around the office like his wife; or perhaps it was payback time. Instead of having the Iron Lady at home wearing the big girl pants and telling him what to do, the roles are reversed at work, where he tells the Iron Lady, Cat what to do.

*****

Speaking of facades and grand front entrances, not all public servants are positioned at their weekly office podiums yet as some are taking advantage of the generously expansive glide time and flexitime. This privilege can extend to coming in as late as midday on a Monday, as some poor souls have had to commute from as far away as Auckland and Dunedin, some now as far as downtown Calcutta and the countryside of Bulgaria. Therefore, due consideration and exceptions to the rules must be given for those who need to travel these lengthy distances. As they spend the bulk of the week living away from home, compensation is given to allow them to stay in accommodation that is almost equivalent if not better than what they are accustomed to back home, along with generous meal allowances and extra time off work. After all, they are away from their loved ones for at least four evenings a week and that time must be clocked up as TOIL at a later stage, hence most of these people get a very generous two months paid leave over the summer holidays so they can get to know their absent families yet again. This especially applies to those having affairs of the extra-curricular kind and in some cases even having a double life involving a completely separate relationship.

The other remaining stragglers, who don't have nearly as good an excuse as the above, are known as the 'Monday latecomers' and they enjoy taking advantage of their generous glide time. They now spill out of the grand Art Deco railway station doors and glide on up to their respective offices, most of them filing through the exceptionally grand sixteen million dollar BS entrance. Only the best products have been used for this grand state-of-the-art fixture. Italian marble is positioned nicely over the neon lights shining brightly with the words 'Reception'. Right inside the front doors in the foyer is the highest quality wood panelling (recycled West Coast rimu and kauri imported from Fiji as there is no kauri available for logging in New Zealand; ironically it's okay to fell another country's resource) which has been carved carefully by local iwi into the largest waka ever seen in a government building in the southern hemisphere. The waka and the story beneath written in Māori, represents the journey the five ministries took to merge into one big happy ministerial family, The Big Super Ministry. The one ministry everyone is begging and bribing to work for.

As with most big projects, the planners and All-of-Government purchasing project managers underestimated how much the imported marble pillars and wood-carved waka was going to cost and there were disagreements and cost cutting along the way. If one looks closely they can see a slight split in the waka, a legacy from the tohunga whakairo or master carver, when he found that his fee would be only partly paid, which is ironic as the waka is meant to represent the building's occupants as one. However, like a scene out of the *Titanic,* it is splitting into two and possibly with a few more Wellington dry northerlies, a few more cracks will start to reveal themselves as time ticks on. There were such time pressures put on all and sundry to complete the entrance by a highly important date that some of the finer designs were rushed through and now parts of the reception area are looking like parts of the Kapiti Expressway, ready to be smoothed over and redone further adding extra costs to all taxpayers.

However, due to these budget overruns and the timing for the big opening of the revamp of the building, the waka was not strategically placed where it was meant to be, and the splitting or 'separation of the ways' is not obvious to the naked eye and most people on first entering the building. However, from the opposite direction, all is revealed – the symbology that the split represents – and local iwi matakite (tribal seer) have predicted doom and gloom, an unhappy passage, and there is widespread doubt on whether those who sail in her will reach their destination in one piece.

The main thing is the opening went ahead on time, so the Minister looked good for his by-election, and in good PC fashion the building was blessed by a kaumātua from the local iwi.

Sven, being incredibly proud of her Swedish and Māori ancestry, has been researching and delving deeper into her Māori whakapapa, the history and wellbeing of her Māori people, through her Rongoā Māori studies. She is aware of the impact this lack of respect and honouring agreements means and is embarrassed each time she passes through the entrance. To protect herself, she does a karakia quietly each time she walks in and out of the building, singing quietly to herself her favourite karakia, *'Te aroha, te whakapono, me te rangimārie, tātou, tātou e.'*

*****

The stragglers, forming orderly lines, march up the street, clock in and then exit almost as soon as they have entered the building, off to take part in the daily networking ritual of the coffee circuit. Some pop outside to have their third cigarette or 'Vape' for the day, while others queue up downstairs in the in-house café to begin their daily medication of caffeine.

Like a scene scripted out of the classic UK comedy *Reginald Perrin* who was religiously late every morning due to the usual BritRail technical failures, the Wellington public servants come up with similar excuses. One is heard telling his team leader, "There have been delays on the railway tracks as usual due to some technicality and they needed to repair the tracks then and there. We were stuck in a tunnel with no cell phone coverage, so this is the first opportunity I have had to let you know. All trains were backed up in and out of the city." The team leader must be over hearing these trite excuses, but he looks semi interested, like he has never heard this before and it is news to his ears.

Other just as unoriginal excuses are, "Sheep crossed the line near Featherston today and due to Health and Safety, the driver was not allowed to leave his cabin and had to wait for them to cross. One of them decided to sit down and have a nap before he – whoops, she – I mean 'it' finished crossing."

These sorts of excuses go on for some time, and the clock keeps ticking.

The first meeting for the hour, like the first cab off the rank, is the Ministry's Health and Safety meeting. Each department has their own Health and Safety (H & S) meeting but once a month, H & S representatives from each department represent their teams and speak on their behalf. This Health and Safety meeting is slotted in to replace the HR meeting, as someone believes it is something light and will at least keep people occupied while the big black cloud looms overhead of the missing HR Director and her delayed big announcement.

Bad move. The meeting is anything but light – in fact completely the opposite. It becomes quite intense as every H & S rep fronts up which isn't usual, and as everyone feels on edge, the participants go off on tangents several times and the agenda is not strictly adhered to.

Stephen, the Head of Health and Safety, Diana from Recruiting, Veronica from L & D, Julia the Head of Pasifika and Māori, Toni, Letitia and Pat from god knows where, are present and as usual the ratio of women far outweighs the men. Stephen, being the token male, clearly doesn't have a shit show of keeping the women in line and keeping each topic down to their allotted amount of time.

The above committee members including random fire wardens squeeze themselves into the spare meeting room that in line with meeting Health and Safety regulations should only take three to four at a push, so the door has to be left open or otherwise, according to Stephen, it would be a breach of another Health and Safety policy, namely a Health and Safety fire risk.

All the timetabling of meeting rooms has gone to the dogs. People are in the wrong rooms, the meetings are taking longer than the prescribed time the room is booked for and there is absolute chaos. A bit like Wellington's railway station at rush hour, when due to technical failures the trains are unable to run and there is no backup transport, like good old-fashioned buses to get the commuters out of town. Every spare nook and cranny on all floors is fully occupied. There are people in the stationery alcoves, the stationery cupboards, even the chair cemetery room which is usually unofficially reserved for Security and Reception to get their wicked way in.

Spare conference rooms that have been blocked out for refurbishment or considered unsafe and stickered out of bounds since the last earthquake, suddenly become safe enough to use. All junk rooms are now being used and people are shocked to learn that there are in fact a lot more rooms to use than they were originally led to believe all these years. There are redundant mobile whiteboards, redundant computers, and screens scattered around rooms that haven't been used in the last four years since BS was created. People have placed themselves anywhere, just so they can have a bit of privacy and stay out of the firing line. The vibes out on the floor are not flash and everyone is running for cover.

The timetable Gestapo Ursula has given up trying to evict people from meeting rooms that they haven't rightfully booked via the online meeting room management system. She is complaining of a headache and is threatening to go home sick from all the stress and chaos.

*****

Sven, after looking out over the seventh-floor balcony to see the hoard of cop cars doing kamikaze runs on the surrounding roads and leading up to the railway station, couldn't help herself. She had sneaked in a quick brisk walk down to the station between meetings, justifying it by saying she needed to take her prescribed Health and Safety micro pause break, but really to get more steps up on her Fitbit to stay well ahead of Clara, rather than sitting around waiting for meetings to kick off all day.

While down at the station, she could see a sea of blue uniforms darting in through the side door reserved just for staff, up the stairs to the railway station offices. The KC had been cordoned off with cones and no one was allowed to walk down that platform at all. The only way to have a good look at what was happening was to catch a train out of the station, but no trains were leaving from that platform. With the roof of the station blocking the entire view of the train from above, unless you were wearing the right security badge you could not get past the cordoned-off area. Yes, Security did work in some places. As tempted as she was to pop on up to the police taped-off area and chat up the cops, she knew she would be sent away.

Just as she was about to walk away, she saw what looked like her ex in the distance. She couldn't see his face, but recognised the way he walked. Charlie, her ex-fiancé no less, had a very distinctive way of walking and she was sure this was him. Oh my god, no way, I can't see him. I can't let him see me. No! Feeling more uptight and stressed than she bargained for, she scarpered back off to work. No matter how curious she was, she was not ready to see Charlie Rogers again. It had been far too long and too much water under the bridge since they tragically parted. Firing off a quick text to her girlfriends asking if they knew Charlie was in town.

*****

Meanwhile, the Health and Safety meeting continues in full swing and those attending have temporarily forgotten what their purpose is of being there. They have suddenly focused their attention on something that is of far more importance: Why the Learning and Development department exists. Veronica from L & D and Julia the Head of Pasifika and Māori are in a heated discussion, and for the first few minutes no one seems to notice as everyone else is in full discussion amongst themselves. However, as the others finish talking, Julia and Veronica continue, their voices getting louder and louder, oblivious to where they are and not stopping to think that this isn't really the time or place to throw their toys out of the cot.

"Look!" screeches Julia, raising her tone of voice, "I have been here for the full four years and not once during that time did I know that we had our own BS Learning and Development team. Our little P & M team are hanging on by the skin of our teeth to survive, as each year we get less and less funding. If I had known you had existed and had spare resources we would have come to you and your team of ten and asked one of you to help assist our vital workshops we have been running nationally to increase the awareness of Pasifika and Māori!"

Veronica pipes up, "What do you mean you are running educational workshops, and nationally? You have no right to be doing this!"

"What do you mean I have no right to be doing this? There are only two of us now, being down two more staff members since the last restructure. How do you expect us to increase our profile and get the word of our important work out there if we are not allowed to go out and do our own road show and advertising campaign?"

Veronica steps up the decibels, articulating in a louder voice, "Duh, because all L & D is outsourced, anything to do with Learning and Development cannot be done by one of our ten advisors. You come to us, tell us what you need and then we look at our AOG – that's 'All of Government' list of preferred training providers, and give you the names of three suitable ones and you make the choice from there."

Julia, who is beside herself by this stage, snaps back, "And so you give me the phone number of three providers and I am meant to take my time to interview them and choose which one I think is best? If you have never seen them in action, how do you know that the three you have given me are any good?"

Veronica, popping a chill pill, explains at a slower pace this time, "Because we have been through a robust tendering process where we collect the best suppliers, so you and others here don't have to hunt down the best one because we have already done your homework for you."

"Who pays for these people, if we do choose one of them? I assume it comes out of your L & D budget?" Julia asks.

"Oh no, it comes out of your budget, but we have never been asked to look for Pasifika and Māori providers before, so I'm not sure what we would do in this case."

Julia calmly says, "That's my point. How does anyone

in your team know what we want, especially when you didn't even know BS had their very own P & M team before today? And if my team must pay for outsourced contractors at probably triple my salary, my colleague and I would be out of a job as there would be no budget left over for our salary! That's my point, I have presented my case and the jury is still out. I have no idea what your team of TEN upstairs do and if I had been asked to be part of the review panel who decided whether you should stay or go, I would have said the latter, because I can't see how you add value. You are just glorified middlemen. Okay, maybe I am being too hasty. How about this question: 'Who do you recommend is the best facilitator or provider to run a cultural awareness programme? We need to make people more aware of the challenges tangata whenua, our people face when coming into a corporate-type culture like this."

Veronica is now getting highly agitated. "Culture? What do you mean? No, we don't have anything to do with culture, you would have to go and find your own people for that."

Julia attacks back. "Well, there's my case all wrapped. What is the point, yet again of having an L & D team if you don't even have 101 training to meet the needs of our Pasifika and Māori brothers and sisters?"

Veronica comes back swiftly like she is backhanding on a tennis court and it is vital she wins this round, no matter what. "What's this 101 stuff?"

Julia volleys just as quickly with her reply. "101, my dear, is the most basic, elementary, introductory level of any topic; it is like kindergarten learning, and that is where you and your team need to take yourselves. Back to kindergarten to start your Level 101 initiation on the 'facts of life'."

Stephen, the H & S head honcho who has been listening to most of the conversation, can see that this is escalating into a serious cat fight and interrupts like a good umpire. "Ladies, I think we are off topic here, let's stick to the agenda in hand. We have a very important topic to start the meeting with. You have all had time to enjoy refreshments – let's all thank Toni for bringing in the homemade gluten-free, sugar-free, fat-free vegan brownies with a quick round of applause…also, it is very rare that we have such a great turnout and today has been exceptional."

Stephen kick-starts the official opening of the first topic off the agenda by saying, "I have something of significant importance to bring up and – Letitia, eyes on me please. Can you please refrain from looking out the window? I assure you that nothing out there will be as important as what we have to discuss in here."

Just then Nigel from Recruiting pops in waving a piece of paper and interrupts Stephen in his flamboyant way, but today even more exaggerated and pronounced than usual, "I have an *extremely* important item to add to your *boring* little agenda today. In fact, I think it should be given tippity top priority and moved to the very beginning of the queue!"

Stephen interjects. "With all due respect Nigel, I am chairing this meeting and our first item is 'Nails'. We have had to omit this from the last agenda due to untimely interruptions, such as the one you have just created now. However, as usual I am happy to take all points on board. Could you just give me one sentence on what this pressing matter is all about? And perhaps everyone in the room can take a vote on whether it should appear on the agenda for this meeting or the next. I think that is a fair compromise."

Stephen loves the 'Fuck you' he has just served, right royally to Nigel. *Little upstart, who does he think he is?* Stephen despises Nigel's constant moaning and groaning about how his official staff numbers are not in line with actual staff numbers as everyone keeps taking the law into their own hands and recruiting backfills here and there behind his back.

Nigel backs up his bus just temporarily. "Well, kind sir, I would *really* appreciate that."

Stephen comes back with a swift serve. "Why, I thank you, *kind sir,* for giving me what I asked for; a one-sentence answer and such a lovely, short, concise one. You see, Recruiting can give short answers when they want to. You are in great need after all, Viva La Recruiting."

Nigel interjects. "Excuse me, b-but I haven't given you the subject of the item that needs to be added."

Stephen jumps back in again. "Oh, I am sorry; I thought you had – you had followed instructions and given us the one sentence. Now everyone, please vote if this should be put on the agenda. Push your buttons now," he says, turning the event into a comical TV Quiz show where everyone should be at the ready to push a button.

Nigel is getting heated around the collar, literally, and interrupts. "The sixth-floor break out area's balustrade glass panelling has finally given way and there is NO safety protection in that part of the area, meaning some poor soul could fall through very easily and meet with an unfortunate untimely end on the ground floor landing amongst the cappuccinos in the Home and Away café! I have managed to find one teeny orange party hat that looks like a hazard cone from the Recruiting party box and have placed it strategically there to isolate the hazard, but I would consider this a Level 1 hazard. The glass has been cracked since the last earthquake but within time the crack has got bigger and finally split in half."

Veronica interjects. "Is Level 1 the same as Level 101?"

Julia rolls her big brown eyes and starts doodling on the page with her pen, instead of using it to stab Veronica between the eyes, straight into the right part of her stagnant brain where all creativity and sense has ceased to work.

Stephen, not wanting to get off track yet again, replies to Nigel, "Thank you Nigel, for bringing this to our attention. Does everyone in the room vote this item should be put on our agenda?"

A chorus of 'Ayes' is heard.

"Right, we have added this to our agenda. Can we move on with more pressing business?"

They are only fifteen minutes into the meeting, people are already starting to doze off, and Letitia is still looking out the window to see what all the chaos is outside. It has got very hot as the air conditioning has gone off due to a power surge and even though the door is wide open to fit everyone in, it is like being passengers packed into trains in rush hour on the London underground in the middle of summer. They are in one of the 'fish bowl' floor to ceiling glass windowed meeting rooms and most of the reps are either staring out into the open-plan office or out the window at the paparazzi who are now in full force roaming the street beneath.

Just then there is an almighty crash outside. One of the paparazzi is so busy taking photos she rear-ends the Minister's chauffeur-driven car parked up temporarily outside the front doors. Oh, and who is the other passenger in the back seat?

*****

Sven's mind is ticking like a time bomb. She is trying to concentrate but her heart rate has doubled and she can feel a panic attack coming on. Doubting herself, she checks her Fitbit and yes, her heart rate is going through the roof. She thinks about the last time she saw Charlie, in Courtenay Place, that evening all those years ago when she saw her then-fiancé with another woman. Instantly in her mind she is back there, reliving that gut-wrenching moment. Blinking back tears, she tells herself she can't sit here – she has to go back downstairs. But what's her excuse? Oh my god, I can't think...she despairs. *Oh god, I need...I need...I need...Freya.*

She frantically texts Freya, pausing momentarily for an answer, then texts Flat White, waiting nervously for a reply. She panics, wondering why the people she needs are not glued to their cell phones like everyone else when she had told them to be on standby today so she could update them.

*****

Nigel has stayed on at the meeting as there are leftover gluten-free cookies and he hasn't had breakfast due to the spat he had earlier that morning with his man. He self-medicates by chowing down the remains of the food. With the huge crash outside, he chokes on the coconut icing on the complete square of cake he has just thrown down his mouth. Looking outside, he sees his man –Ernest, trying to scramble out of the now half-squashed parliamentary car. He is trying desperately to open the door of the Minister's car from the inside, so he can get out. He looks like he has Nigel's orange and purple lunchbox in his hand. His high-pitched screams can be heard from upstairs through the heritage single-glazed glass windows. "Quick, the engine may catch on fire at any stage. I've got to get the fuck out of here, get my wheelchair out and open the damn door, you plonker!"

Stephen is not convinced that Nigel's choking or the Minister's totalled car outside is enough reason to postpone the meeting and tend to the crisis now taking place inside and outside the building.

Clearly Nigel has brought his private life to work and this is a definite no-no. After all, the last great managerial one-liner given to staff was 'Leave your home life at home, and bring your *full* self to work'. Besides, at the best of times, Nigel is an attention seeker and Stephen is not convinced that this choking fit is entirely legit. All Nigel can do is stare on in horror from six floors above at the uncontrollable incident unfolding downstairs in full view of anyone who has a front row seat at the windows.

Veronica cannot contain herself anymore; she needs to bolt for the door. The room has got far too claustrophobic and she is not feeling comfortable about the confrontation with Julia. She wonders what will happen if she tells her boss about their conversation.

*****

Veronica has also been recently diagnosed with a mild case of attention deficit hyperactivity disorder and is very proud of the recent label her doctor has given her; she just can't help daydreaming at the best of times. She needs to keep occupied in an interesting way, have plenty of variety and a lot of stimulating projects on the go all at once. For some reason, her boss Sarita, the Head of Learning and Development thought it was a clever idea to put her on the Health and Safety committee as the representative for L & D. It was sold to her as an ideal way of utilising her latent great relationship building skills and to mingle with others, plus she could use the meeting to L & D's advantage and promote her team and what they do. Unfortunately, she suspects with all good intentions, she may have put the L & D team in disrepute. Promoting the team clearly didn't work – well, not in the Head of Pasifika and Māori's case. However, Julia was not alone. It had become increasingly apparent that most of the building had no idea that they in fact had an L & D team at all, as there have been so many restructures and so many different Comms people, that each article on the intranet contradicts the other and no one can work out what is relevant and up-to-date.

Veronica leaves the room, makes her mumbled apologies and heads for Sarita's desk. "Sarita, could I have a word? I have just been highly humiliated at the monthly Ministry H & S meeting. No one has heard of us or knows we even exist and that is why we never have anything to do. As a result the rest of the business goes directly to the outside to source external training providers to get in facilitators and trainers, or due to continued budgetary cuts, some do the training themselves. Now that is surely against policy! And definitely not best practice."

Sarita is severely distracted as she is trying to work out how to get started on writing an L & D strategy and she can't work out what the difference is between an L & D *Approach* and an L & D *Strategy*. English is her second language and she is still grappling with everyday English, let alone Kiwi colloquial English, let alone Business English, let alone BS acronyms. On top of the 'lost in translation' side, she's just not sure what SMT agreed to and where to from here. She is too embarrassed to ask for clarification as that may make her look stupid, and then SMT may not think she is up for the job. Sarita has got away with bluffing her way through for four years, and would rather get away with it for another four or five. She mumbles some sort of acknowledgement to Veronica but, missing the non-verbal cues, Veronica continues rambling.

"It's a very sad state of affairs. If only the rest of the Ministry knew we were a highly efficient team ready and waiting for an assignment, we could then go off and find the best people, best solutions and for the best prices. I just had an altercation with Julia, Head of Pasifika and Māori. I think I may be responsible for the Ministry saving ten one-hundred K salaries over the next year, not counting your salary, as we may now just be without work. I don't think I made a good case at all." Veronica bursts into tears.

Sarita pipes in, "Veronica, you are making no sense. We don't have a Pasifika and Māori team, what are you talking about?" And the nonsensical conversation goes on.

*****

Back at the H & S meeting, Stephen can be heard from outside in the recruiting pod piping up again as he is sick of his precious H & S meetings being hijacked. This time he takes full control. "Okay Letitia, you had a very important item, please take it away?"

Twenty minutes have been wasted already and there

are only ten minutes left to get through nine agenda items. Nigel is absolutely beside himself after being subjected to Letitia performing her version of the Heimlich manoeuvre on him, and followed Veronica's lead and tore out of the meeting room, flying down the stairs to save his lover who he imagines is now trapped, probably burning to death in the street below and no one seems to care, let alone the Health and Safety committee, who ironically should.

Letitia reads from the agenda. "Okay, point 1: Nails." Everyone looks at each other in that confused, raised eyebrow way as much to say why on earth are 'Nails' on the agenda?

Joan, one of the committee members, replies to rectify the awkward expressions on everyone's faces, "Obviously the builders, when strengthening the heritage glass windows from the recent earthquake, have left their nails lying around, creating a hazard as staff could trip on them?"

"No, that's the not the case at all!" One of the guys from the Science Health and Information Technology team (SHIT) has been doing a lot of overtime in the evenings and the head cleaner has come to him and said the following: "It has come to my attention over the last couple of weeks that each time I clean under a particular desk, there are a number of nails lying haphazardly across the carpet."

Stephen is beside himself by this stage. "Nails? What are you talking about, and is this really relevant in the big scheme of things regarding Health and Safety? We are meant to be talking about hazards, incidents, near misses, lost time injuries, near deaths."

Well, the word 'death' is definitely not a good choice of words, as it gets everyone refocusing back on the pending rumour that has been circulating all morning about the 'incident' on the KC. HR and Comms are not working together and due to no open communication, speculation, gossip and the old trusty informal communication link 'the grapevine' is spreading like Australian wildfire.

Felicity, another H & S rep, a mousey, very quiet nondescript girl now pipes up. "Can we get back to the nails please, or we are never going to get through this agenda? What type of nails do you mean – the rusty variety that keeps this heritage building together?"

"No," exclaims Letitia. "The toenail kind. Someone has been cutting their nails and leaving them under the desk. I will just finish reading from the memo I have been given from the HOS. And unless anyone believes nails (of the toenail variety) have any nutritional value and can add value to our core business, then I suggest the person who owns them disposes of them in the usual hygienic manner, in the correct recycle bin in the kitchen or down the loo. The cleaner has pointed out that it is not part of his job description to have to clean up people's toenails and in future he will be leaving them where he finds them."

Everyone roars with laughter. One of the fire wardens, Larry, speaks up for the first time. "Well I do believe we need to fill out a Hazard ID sheet for this and add it to our monthly Hazard Register, and follow this up," he announces, slapping his thigh as he sets off laughing again.

"Really," says Cecily, recovering and wiping the dribble from her chin that had escaped when she burst into laughter, "and how is this a hazard?" Cecily, the backfill from Comms has become so relaxed she has forgotten her rightful station and for the first time since starting her short-lived career at BS is starting to feel at home. She has found her tribe, these H & S people are her long-lost family, whānau. Anything to do with Health and Safety thrills her and she can't get enough of these meetings.

"It is either a biological or environmental hazard and it could lead to a psychological hazard as the cleaner will get stressed from having to collect and dispose of these nails." As the laughter subsides, the meeting is interrupted yet again and only one topic, 'Nails' has been discussed. Stephen is clearly agitated by this stage and is thinking of adjourning it for another month, or worst-case scenario resigning from his thankless position forever.

Felicity adds again, "Wow, that was painful. You would think we were having an English class in here today. Now I know this is very rare but most of us in the room are native English speakers and we were having difficulties. Imagine how our Senior Comms lady, Dubravka would manage – English is her *third* language!"

Stephen adds, "Well, it's just as well then that we don't have her as an H & S Rep, isn't it?"

The intercom blurts out something no one can understand and then the clearer voice of Aileen resounds throughout the building, "The HR meeting has been rescheduled and is due to start in five minutes, it's an HR stand-up…oh, I mean it's an HR stand-down, on the ground floor in 101. Oh, and take your chair, we have a shortage of them and are expecting many to attend."

Stephen irately splutters, "We are not taking our chairs down six flights of stairs. That would be a serious fire risk." No one is listening to Stephen, which has been the case throughout most of the meeting. The attendees all pile out faster than an evacuation, picking up spare chairs along the way as they head for the lifts.

The floor is full of idle chatter, and Stephen can hear

the usual crowd in HR having a good moan. "Oh, a stand-down, now that's more serious. Usually Cat just has a quickie on the fly, but a stand-down – ooh, she must have a real agenda."

Another voice in the crowd can be heard. "What planet are you on? Cat is not showing today; in fact she is not showing *ever again."*

HR, Recruiting, Employment Relations, L & D, OD, Payroll and Finance all suddenly appear from various parts of the building. Some start filing down the stairs awkwardly with chairs in hand while others can be seen waiting patiently for one of the six lifts, also with chairs. The lifts are overloaded today due to all the extra traffic in the building, and more and more people start taking the stairs, the main ones and the back ones. It's like a disorganised evacuation procedure with people filing out from all over the building in a rush to get downstairs, and all 'roads out' so to speak are like an accident waiting to happen. It's one big 'hazard' of a nightmare for the frazzled-looking Head of H & S. Stephen shakes his head and with pen and paper joins the flock of sheep and starts walking at a snail's pace down the back stairs, trying not to be hit from behind by random chairs being awkwardly carried by fellow employees.

*****

Belinda, the OD Manager, is heard saying to her second in command, "We really must have a refresher on evacuation procedures. The earthquake showed we have no idea what we are doing, the Incident Management training we had was such high level, we never filtered down our new systems to the plebs. The over-the-top terminology did not help. And now today is a typical example of how we in HR don't even know how to get down a couple of flights of stairs in an orderly way, let alone evacuate the building in a rush!"

Now that more people know about the chair cemetery and the stationery room, they innocently start finding their way into these areas to grab chairs for the stand-down.

Veronica grabs a chair that looks the most comfortable and screams, "Oh gross, what is that gooey muck? Oh my god, it is under my fingernails, what is this?"

Now feeling embarrassed after drawing unnecessary attention to herself, she changes the subject. "I thought this room was never used? What could it be? It's too far away from the glue and stationery items." No one responds, as they too are equally as mortified as they watch her wipe whatever the off-white sticky substance is onto two chairs nearby. They empty the room of all the chairs, but wisely decide not to take those two particular chairs into the meeting room.

*****

Chapter 9

The Science meeting

In another part of the heritage building, the Science (SHIT) team with their new British captain at the helm is running their top-secret simulations downstairs, solely focusing on the timing and level of the next predicted earthquake. The team are working with huge urgency, as their new manager will shortly be attending an ELT meeting with ministerial observers, and he is under pressure to produce conclusive results to report back on, make his mark so to speak and then be granted with an upgrade from holiday visa to permanent resident in the colonies.

In the wake of the last earthquake only a month ago being a record 8.1 on the Richter scale, dutifully recorded on the much read 'Geonet' website, people are still shaken by the resulting aftershocks and are very nervous of the likelihood of another imminent earthquake. Alexander Goldsworthy (aka Alex), the new Head of Science suddenly appointed to replace Trusty Ted (who had been there since Adam was an ant and rumour has it was sacked by Cat because he couldn't predict the last earthquake), has got himself the latest cutting-edge software which he believes can predict the next big one. Making up for lost time, he is diligently on a mission Cat has given him and is determined to come up with the goods and not disappoint her.

Alex is bragging to his staff. "This software, it's even better than what EQC (Earthquake Commission) have for Geonet which everyone checks constantly to find out when the last earthquake hit, which part of New Zealand it was centred in and where it scores on the scale. That's well and good, but it's not as reliable as this little baby. What do you think guys?" he asks his staff.

Sanjay, new to New Zealand and new to the Ministry, is not used to earthquakes and wasn't in town for the last one. He asks for clarification. "So anything below a five on the Richter scale can usually not be felt without too much of a thump in Wellington, if it has started off in the South Island, which is where most of them have been, is that right?" He has a very strong Indian accent and can be difficult to understand at times. Though Alex originates from the multi-ethnic, cosmopolitan city of London in the UK, even he has some trouble with Sanjay's accent. However, thankfully due to being a big fan of the once BBC Indian comedic drama hit, *The Kumars at No. 42* based in Wembley, London, he has a good grasp of the Indian accent.

"Yes, Sanjay, something like that. Look, if you don't mind, just stick to the task at hand for now." Alex is getting rather anxious about the meeting and convincing the audience of his findings. He is still in the honeymoon phase of being made the new Head of Science so soon after coming to New Zealand from the UK where they rarely have any sizable earthquakes. "More and more earthquakes are likely to start in Wellington or surrounding areas and will therefore, for us, be of a higher power and intensity. I can safely predict that they will be well above five!"

It is this kind of information that has started leaking from the lab and the office grapevine disseminates the disturbing news. Unfortunately, it is only a matter of time before the *Capital News* gets wind of this.

They finish off their analysis and Alex types up the findings into the required BS report template, as his secretary is still away on sick leave. This template must always be used when reporting, but the backfill's filing system was so complex he spent half the day finding it which has annoyed him profusely and delayed him even more. The computer system is particularly slow today and this adds to his frustration as he tries copious times to download the report template but to no avail.

*****

In another part of the BS building, Rachel from Recruiting is swearing and cursing about how yet another new permanent full-timer has been recruited and slipped in the back door without her knowing about it. "How did this new Head of Science get appointed? Why did I not know about this? Has he been reference checked, security checked? Where his is CV?"

Her colleague Sandra replies, "Oh, another backdoor job and one that Cat happily appointed a couple of weeks ago, and yes, some 'no-name' that no one has ever heard of; well in HR they haven't. Somehow he slipped through the cracks. He's a bit of a dark horse, no one knows where he came from and Nigel, of all people, our Head of Recruiting, was not consulted yet again. He is having kittens as he still has not seen any sign of a CV, let alone interview notes. Clearly there was no robust formal interview process and there is no security clearance for him on his file, let alone referee notes. I'm not even sure if he has a work visa! You are right though, another one that slipped through the cracks. You know it really gets to me just how many foreigners we are employing – they far outweigh us Kiwis. I wonder how many Kiwis are falling by the wayside, out of work, and put out to pasture while still in their prime. It seems to me that they are constantly overlooked for all the newbies entering the country by the masses daily, especially through Auckland. I mean we oversee immigration and are issuing visas and passports left right and centre. If they downstairs in Immigration can't do their work right, then there's no hope for us up here in little old Recruiting. Imagine what other rejects we are getting?"

Nigel enters the room through the back stairs after seeing Ernest off in an ambulance, and overhearing the tail end of the conversation blurts out, "Chris is another one, that newbie from IT." He starts his own rant. "There was never an employment purchase order raised for this person and if there is no sign-off, an employee number designated and an EPO number, then theoretically that person doesn't exist. I have a good mind not to approve his employee number, which will mean he will not get onto the payroll system," he exclaims viciously. "Rachel, have you got anything on this computer Chris?"

She responds *tout de suite.* "No, there are no notes in our shared drive: X for Recruiting Records. However, not all is lost; he did come through an agency and it is not the usual practice to vet contractors from agencies as the agencies evidently have their own robust best practice system where they have naturally checked contractors out for references and security, resident status, plus of course the usual psychometric testing. No worries there. That is the perk of using an agency," Rachel spouts off. "Good old backfills, aye? Just filling in on contract until the day we get permission to make it a permanent full-time position, and then their visa hurriedly follows. Then suddenly they leave for a better job, or Aussie. Maybe with a new government, we can then go back to getting a higher number of permanent full-timers and do away with this fiddle by putting them under the contractor/casual heading. At the end of the day it is still costing the taxpayer the same amount in salaries, if not more. It's just this way it looks less as one set of figures appears under salaries and one comes out under contractors."

"Yes, backfills are great, aren't they?" Nigel nods in agreement and adds, "However, it still irks me that no one bothers to tell us when anyone is starting or leaving. I must create a new employment form for backfills, maybe that way we can monitor them. Now what colour shall I use for this type of form?"

*****

Delia coughs to indicate that someone is standing behind her, but Veronica doesn't pick up on the obvious hint. "A bit low in the emotional intelligence field," she continues to blurt. "We just concentrate on our permanent staff and take extra time with getting them upskilled – well, so I believe."

Sven, standing behind her, amused by the conversation adds in brightly, "That's a good theory. I like it." She smiles and carries on walking as she is on her way to the Science meeting with trusty pen and paper in hand. *Low in EQ?* That's rich coming from her! She thinks to herself as she takes the stairs, her mind boggling over Delia's way of justifying all the unnecessary spending. The woman thinks she's so clever and so smart, but how did Sven get in here? Not through the trusty, robust, NOT Recruiting department, nor the agent's robust vetting system, but through her own contact, and with a casual coffee with her old boss from Sweden. No wonder they can't get her contract sorted, they only need to put her employment contract through, with the correct personal details. Sign it off and put it through to Finance for a special purchase order number and then maybe, just maybe, she could get paid this side of Christmas. She makes a mental note to have a word to Bernard and see what he can do to hasten the laborious process.

Sven recalls some of the previous employment battles. How her contract had come out after she had started her job and it hadn't been proofread and was clearly the template used from another contractor as in places it still had another person's details such as their personal address and hugely inflated hourly rate. Again, due to the privacy act, and HR working with private and confidential information, and knowing how sensitive people's pay is, they could have at least got the contract right, as it took so long to send it out. Plus, they had forgotten to reference check, security check, and validate the qualifications. However, to be fair, they had made a request for Sven's company bank details in order for her to get paid. And even then, in the first few months of her employment, the payroll division (tacked onto the HR department like a nightmarish building extension not in keeping with the original building's architecture) had been unable to pay Sven her first two months' invoices. And no, it wasn't because they had entered the wrong bank account details, it was because they hadn't raised a purchase order number internally and put the required funds against the purchase order to enable her to be paid. It was very embarrassing for Bernard to learn of this as he was the one who had gloated about the 'state-of-the-art' Finance and HR systems BS had. They may have the latest systems, but the team were still working with the antiquated systems, as the old staff had not been upskilled to use the new technology. No training had taken place as there was no training budget, and L & D were unaware of that particular training need as no one knew of their department.

These experiences about the lack of security and vetting did make Sven nervous, wondering how many people who walked around the building had slipped in without security checks, and Alex, this Head of Science was only one of the many. Alex, an interesting character – tall, slim and incredibly pale – clearly the UK had gone without a summer for at least three years in a row as he was so white you could almost see through him. He had short well-cropped black greasy hair, and a small strip of hair that resembled a moustache to mask his baby face. His eyes were far too close to each other and he had a pen permanently placed behind his left ear and a cigarette behind his right ear. Most days he could be seen at the kitchen sink wearing the same striped shirt, helping himself to the peppermint Earl Grey tea bags.

Sven was just not that sure about him. It was his eyes. He was unable to make eye contact and he always brushed off stuff he couldn't answer with his arrogant English airs of superiority and laughter. His usual line was, 'Oh yes, you colonials have not got that yet, we in Mother England have had that for years. One day you will catch up with us.' This used to really annoy Sven who had been working in the UK for years and had seen just how antiquated their banking systems were.

Sven gets to the Science meeting just in time to hear Alex, the chair, share his findings with everyone. "As you will know I have been employed to do a particular 'piece of work' and that is to be able to predict when the next big earthquake is coming. After our biggie last month, the people of Wellington are a little anxious and it is my job to relieve them of their anxiety. Cat has asked me to report on when I believe the next one will happen. If we know this vital piece of information in advance, we can let our people know not to come into work that day. Cat is all for the how-oh-ray, health, safety and wellbeing of our staff which is wonderful. You don't get many HR HODs who are genuinely concerned about the health and welfare of their staff." Alex, attempting to be PC, tries to pronounce the Māori word Hauora, but fails dismally.

Sven tries not to throw up as she listens to Alex's Māori pronunciation and sickening words when referring to 'Caring Cat'. She is yet to see that side of Cat, although she admits that the average bloke does seem to suffer from high degrees of change blindness when it comes to that woman, perhaps it is those pushup bras she wears with the plunging neckline tops.

He then refers to her as 'caring' again and Sven squirms, almost unable to contain herself, but she knows she must. In order to keep her emotions anchored and in check, she does what she always does when in meetings or situations she can't bear. She starts writing poetry and makes it look like she is diligently making lots of notes. Sven starts typing into her iPad, taking her frustrations out on the keys, tapping much harder than usual.

Jerk with a capital J. Give me a break

I'm not sure how much more I can take?

I want to put him in his place

That smug, arrogant, s.o.b. face...

Hah, Cat cares about her staff?

Please don't make me laugh...

She stops typing and says to herself, *She's got you tightly wrapped around her little finger, or possibly another part of her body is wrapped around your shifty little d...* That little burst on the keyboard has calmed her down and she parks that image of Cat and Alex and daydreams onto another theory. They have been spending a lot of time together lately and Sven wonders if he's the new beau that she has been wearing those industrial strength push-up bras for. Cat really is all the words she can think of beginning with C; calculating, careless and above all callous. But definitely *not* caring.

Alex continues. "I don't want to alarm anyone but

after burning the candle at both ends over several evenings along with our new temp, I can safely predict – or envisage, if you would prefer that choice of words – the next big earthquake to happen very soon, in fact…"

Sven, losing focus, starts scribbling again. She is finding it really hard to stay focused, suffering from Meeting Overload Syndrome (MOS). She doesn't know what's worse – sitting in an HR Personality meeting or a Science meeting with the SHIT team; they both end up at the same place. Alex is a slime ball and she wonders what on earth Cat sees in him. She then continues to type and quietly reads what she has written about Alex.

ALEX

Alex the upstart and arrogant prick

Never mistaken him though for being thick

He will rapidly put you in your place

I can't stand his oily hair or pasty face

Crunching numbers and printing spreadsheets

In meetings, on and on he happily bleats

Don't challenge him, just smile and wave

Just let him go off and rave and rave

A recent import from London no less

He's here empire-building and to impress.

Sven looks up from her pad and checks back mentally into the room. No one seems to have noticed; obviously they all think she is focused on the meeting, believing she is making notes.

She then glances out of the fish bowl window and catches a glimpse of Charlie Rogers striding purposefully into Reception, looking extremely hot in a well-tailored black suit and tie. Sven starts to feel the sweat beading on her forehead. She is starting to lose her composure. She suddenly wishes she had checked her lipstick before she came in. Did he notice her? Anxious to get out of there, she wonders where he's going. The heart rate reading on her Fitbit goes through the roof and she tries to breathe calmly and compose herself, attempting some mindfulness breathing exercises.

Her eyes follow his tall, taut body into the next-door meeting room shaking hands with Bernard and ELT. She starts to panic – Charlie, here inside the same building as her, on the same floor and with Bernard. She can't stay in here a minute longer; she needs to find out what's happening next door. She frantically tries to come up with an excuse to interrupt them. *Oh, where's Freya when I need her? Or Flat White? Oh my god I feel a panic attack coming on. Breathe, come on now Sven, breathe.*

Sven doesn't have to spend long making up an excuse. Alex is stopped mid-sentence by a sudden commotion outside the meeting room as a woman runs out of the room next door screaming and disappears into the unisex loos outside the HAA café.

Sven tries to leave the meeting room in a calm, poised way, even as her mind is rapidly trying to figure out why all those cops are out there, and just what Charlie has been talking to Bernard and ELT about.

Alex, feeling that no one is listening to his announcement as he can't hear himself talking over the commotion, decides to abruptly finish the meeting. Another meeting cut short by distractions elsewhere.

Exiting the meeting room, Sven overhears the two ELT members complaining about their colleague's demonstrative departure as they too leave the meeting room. "Adrienne shows far too much emotion in public for an ELT manager. She should know better, being in a position of that stature. One mustn't wear their emotions on their sleeve. One must keep a firm stiff upper lip at times like this."

Thinking this is a rather callous statement, Sven wonders more importantly what on earth is going on next door with Charlie.

One busybody is heard saying, "What's with all these cops arriving? There are all these other public servants from other ministries using our meeting rooms and the public accessing the Home and Away café, it's like a film set. One with a steady flow of random extras milling about the place, hoping their talents will get recognised by the latest producer or director while on the set. Maybe Peter Jackson is in town and Comms forgot to inform us."

The former EA of Science, Wilma, who has been brought back to cover for the backfill on sick leave, catches up with Sven and anxiously asks, "I wonder what Alex meant by the next earthquake is going to happen *now?* Does that mean now, today, tomorrow, or when? I need to know!"

"No, he didn't say now, he said very soon," answers Sven and walks off distractedly leaving her to her own paranoid thoughts as she scans the area for Charlie. Sven, after texting the girls quickly, is now on full alert, acting like a meerkat suffering from elevated degrees of hypervigilance.

These conversations out in the foyer peter out, but not soon enough. A Capital News reporter had managed to slip into the building through the good old back door. Kiwis, being polite and ever so helpful, have been holding the doors open behind them for all and sundry to enter the building. And on this occasion some innocent employee had held the door open for just a little too long and Juliette, the journalist, taking advantage of his kindness, has clawed her way in.

Juliette had only got as far as the ground floor, but that was enough. She had been hovering outside the fish bowl meeting room, where she had a VIP front row view and had jumped on the chance of racing after the distraught ELT manager, Adrienne, all the way to the ladies' room to see what she could glean out of her. Not being as successful as she had hoped, she had sauntered back to the meeting room where she overheard the tail end of the random conversation the EA had had with Sven about the next big earthquake. 'Even bigger than the last and centred in Wellington – it could be happening any moment now. Stand by for more!' Juliette taps onto her ipad. Sven had figured her out, and this was one of the reasons why she had walked away, as Sven wasn't going to be part of the 'biggest breaking news BS had ever leaked to the CN in a long time'. Besides, more importantly she couldn't spot Charlie anywhere and decided to track down Freya.

Juliette, licking her purple, glossy lips like the cat that scored the cream, hurriedly emailed these two pieces of hot news through to her editor to hit the front page of the *Capital News.*

*****

Chapter 10

HR Announcement

Informal and formal meetings are being held randomly in every square inch of available space both within the BS Ministry and in the surrounding Wellington downtown cafés, indoors and outdoors. This is the one time that the BS public servants are being creative, and thinking outside the square by being innovative enough to make up random, temporary meeting places as their all-important business as usual (BAU) meetings simply must go ahead. All sorts of spaces are commandeered for these essential meetings taking place in redundant meeting rooms (now junk rooms for retired furniture and pieces of outdated IT equipment). They are making use of the basement, the ladies' rest rooms, the kitchen break out areas, the stationery alcoves, the foyer downstairs, the in-house café, the park. They are lined up along the streets, in the foyer of adjoining government department buildings, in cars, and even in the chair cemetery cupboards.

They have no choice as commercial space is limited all over Wellington right now, due to several large office buildings being condemned because of the recent earthquakes. And on top of this, with today's events, the rooms at BS and Railway House, the Police HQ and other government departments getting involved are starting to fill up with their Comms staff and the local constabulary who are preparing for the next phase of their investigation.

The first couple of blocks between the railway station and the BS Ministry are full of people. Many identifiable by the name badges most of them have swinging from their ministerial coloured lanyards hanging from their necks, another essential PS fashion staple. The weather outside is still perfect and surreal. It is a gorgeous Wellington day, one of those lovely days where the sun is shining and the harbour waters are still and glistening. It is almost eerie, like the calm before the storm, or possibly before the mother of all earthquakes.

Public servants are aimlessly walking around with pieces of paper and pen in one hand and smartphones and/or coffee balanced in the other, roaming up and down the stairs, streets, coffee bars and the like. People are rudderless, not quite sure where they should be and what they are meant to be doing; some are lost, trying to find the latest impromptu meeting room so they can crawl in to attend and appear busy. There is no job description on what to do on days like this, no one to turn to in senior positions who know either.

"Surely this must've been covered in one of the many Management training courses the senior managers are always attending. Why aren't we getting any direction on what to do while we stand around waiting for news? We have been waiting all day for the HR announcement, now we are waiting around for some other news from HR that seems to be more important than Cat's announcement of all announcements," one rather agitated public servant is heard muttering to anyone who will listen.

"Yes, I know what you mean. I am so nervous and anxious. I've just been over to the pharmacy and they have run out of Rescue Remedy. Evidently, since the earthquake, the demand has exceeded the supply and they can't get any more in because the factory has run out of stock," Melissa from ER responds.

"Wow. Well I thought we were already one of the highest nations to self-medicate. You know us Kiwis are known for our high consumption of booze over the weekend or any excuse to celebrate or commiserate. I guess the alcohol and cigarette sales have increased as well during this time," responds Shelley, one of the brighter ER consultants. "I believe all of the advisors working in our Social Welfare department, Child Support and the like are self-medicating during the week now, as the phone calls they need to make to clients while keeping their British stiff upper lip is getting too much for them. They know they need to follow box-ticking scripts or the tree of call centre answers when talking to these poor people due to the constraints of policy, and they rapidly find that they just can't help these people. So, they just get pissed most nights as a way of supressing the depressing lack of control they have in making decisions and creating solutions, as they realise that they are not helping but instead are breaking up those fragile families, causing further damage."

"That must be so disheartening for them, god that is so dismal; I don't think I can take that on board," Melissa slowly processes, changing the subject quickly. "We used to just get by on a few joints, but clearly marijuana is small time now compared to the other drugs of choice you can readily purchase nowadays," she says, hinting for more information, as she really has no idea what she was on about. Melissa's brain has been fried from too many joints and tabs of acid from back in the day, her teenage beach parties now starting to play havoc with her remaining brain cells.

Shelley pipes up again. "Do you know the Ministry of Health have just completed their lengthy research on what will be the biggest disease in NZ in the next few years? Depression, it will be the biggest twenty-first century killer. Our minds are just getting far too busy, fragmented, scattered and stressed. We are permanently on alert for the next economic crisis, earthquake, terrorist act, restructure or disaster. It's information overload coming at us from LED screens on our televisions, computers or phones; our poor bodies just can't cope and sustain this high level of stress any more. Good old-fashioned Prozac is just not cutting the mustard. It is only softening the edges of one's irritability, it is not getting to the root of why we are all feeling so stressed. It's this bloody technology – we are available twenty-four seven, there is no way of getting away from it all. I say it's time to look at other non-western ways of medicine and healing. I keep hearing about this Rongoā Māori, I heard the new coach Sven discussing it the other day in the Hauora meeting."

Melissa looks on bewildered, unsure of what she is meant to do or say about this latest statistic and trend, wishing it would just go away. She doesn't like the sound of it and so hurriedly palms her cigarette packet and lighter to calm her now heightened nerves. She tries to say the word 'Rongoā' and ends up pronouncing it 'Wrong Go A…' thinking it sounds like something out of India and fondly remembers her beach holiday smoking weed at Goa in the south of India.

"I'm going to attend the next lunch-time health and wellbeing hauora workshop Sven is running. I am not joining the queue for a prescription for Prozac, just to numb the pain. That seems to be the *'poison* du jour'*, not to be confused with *'poisson* du jour'. I hear Rongoā Māori gets to the root of the illness as opposed to putting Band-Aids over issues that become bigger if not addressed. It's a bit like this amazing counselling service all businesses have, EAP, you know – Employee Assistance Programme. All of us can tap into at least three free counselling sessions and I just received EAP's monthly invoice to sign off for payment and not one person used them. But our staff still stand around moaning about being stressed; I'm sure they prefer to moan and do the passive aggressive stance rather than go and download to a professional who is paid and qualified to listen to their issues. I will never be able to work out the human race."

Melissa has completely gone inside herself and her mind has left the conversation completely. Instead she distractedly wanders outside for yet another one of her half hourly cigarette rituals in solitude, before Shelley has even finished her story.

****

Looking down at the masses in the street from the BS office, there are screeds of figures dressed in black, standing around with their heads down, eyes glued to their ever-ready twenty-four seven devices, resembling a gathering of mourners at a stately funeral.

It could almost be mistaken for a Monday morning with people suffering from Mondayitis, due to the intense vibe on the street. Then Sven remembers it is still only Monday. *This must be the longest working day in history,* she thinks to herself.

Nothing has officially been announced to the masses, but something has happened. The energy is different, something is going down – made obvious with the heightened police presence. They are running around looking important with notepads and pens, a bit like a UK TV drama where it's up to the viewers, the audience at home, to work out the plot and subplots and wade through the red herrings to determine what is really going on.

The anxious black masses don't have to wait long, as the rescheduled, postponed, and rain checked HR meeting is about to take place, but with a twist, it has been upgraded in importance and is now an 'ALL of BS' Ministry meeting.

Finally, the announcement of all announcements is going to be made. The morning had dragged on and a few minutes before the stroke of eleven, hordes of personnel from all departments could be seen filing haphazardly into 101 for the rescheduled, rescheduled 'All BS stand-up of all times'. Never in the creation of BS, almost half a decade ago had there been a department-wide get-together, not even at Christmas due to the ongoing expenditure cuts. However, that did not stop the separate departments from having their own individual Christmas parties and spending extravagant amounts of the taxpayers' money, secretly under miscellaneous expenditure codes.

People may say they rebel against rules and structure, but deep down we all need structure, discipline, a set of rituals and some sort of agenda, even if it does mean meeting after meeting. This is evident today by the way the occupants of the BS building are milling around aimlessly, not knowing what to do next, besides wait and watch their screens.

You can't overestimate the beauty and relief a routine creates. It may feel restricting, boring and monotonous at times, but at least this gives one a framework to work within, a purpose, a *raison d'être* as the French would say – a reason for being.

Today at BS Castle nothing is structured, nothing is certain. Everyone as a result is feeling on edge as rooms and corridors are full of an atmosphere so thick it could be sliced with a knife.

The computer network is still playing up as everyone is sending and receiving far too many emails and attachments, and with their phones, texts, WhatsApps and Snapchats feeding their Twitter and Facebook accounts with useless speculation or what they had for breakfast, or the latest sales at Farmers Trading Company, the entire network is being used to full capacity. Everyone's brains, like Melissa's, and the internet waves are fried and filled to capacity. The masses of humans, like flocks of sheep, need to be herded together in one place and told what's going on.

Fiona, the receptionist down in the main foyer is a little flustered after her frisky first liaison with Security in her private boudoir, the chair cemetery. It has been a whole weekend since she last got it and she was gagging for it much to Dave's delight, and a very messy encounter ensued.

Feeling very flustered and on edge, as she too can't get hold of any Rescue Remedy, she uses the intercom, the old-fashioned paging system to speak to the masses as the modern day technology and equipment is operating so slowly.

"Good morning everyone – I mean tēnā koe whānau, sorry to interrupt your busy mornings but for those of you who are part of the HR team – I mean all BS staff, can you please start filing into 101 for the rescheduled 'All of BS' meeting. SMT will be attending and ELT, and it is compulsory that you all attend. An electronic roll call will be taken to ensure you have all attended. We do apologise for this inconvenience as we are aware that for some of you stalwarts this will be cutting into your lunch break, and we know you had to go without your morning tea break earlier. Again, if all concerned could start making their way in an orderly fashion to 101, it would be greatly appreciated." Fiona starts doing her nails before she snaps off the intercom and the sound of nail filing along with the clipping of her nails can be heard over the intercom waves. She starts to discard her nails, casually tossing them towards the waste paper basket under her desk, completely missing her target.

Hundreds of people start appearing on the ground floor, drifting in from all directions – the lifts, the front stairs, the back stairs, the front entrance, the back entrance, from the café and other meeting rooms. They sound like a herd of shuffling sloths, dragging their heels across the Italian marbled floors.

Perhaps the Incident Management training course has paid off after all, as temporary and permanent IM wardens are directing people to where they should be going in an orderly fashion and everyone is paying attention and following closely behind. It resembles an orderly evacuation procedure. Thank goodness the IM team have been called back into work, and are no longer working from home; even Brady the surfer is back as the waves at Lyall Bay just weren't pumping today.

Sven appears from the back door, relieved that at last there seems to be some methodical system in place and people know where they are going. When the next earthquake or tsunami hits, someone will step up and take on the role of Incident Controller and direct them on what to do. This is not as far-fetched as it may sound as most of the downtown offices, apartments and shops in the CBD are built on reclaimed land – in other words, where Papatūānuku, Mother Earth would prefer her harbour. Sven thinks about the fact that there is a highly likely chance that Wellington could flood. In fact, some buildings were always prone to flooding. Then being on the major fault line for earthquakes, it is highly likely that the city could 'rock and roll' at any time. This of course would then bring Civil Defence on high alert for a tsunami and send everyone off in a panic, up to the hills. It was like one incident could easily trigger another one. If they headed for high ground, they would be okay. After all, with the last earthquake, backpackers from the lowlands – the city level where most people worked – were directed up the hill to Parliament and suddenly backpackers from all corners of the globe found themselves up at the Beehive, sharing the facilities with the MPs of New Zealand. A wonderful way of getting to know people and the politicians where normally they wouldn't have a chance to rub shoulders with such esteemed (well, in their own minds) people.

Some enterprising backpackers were overheard talking their way into an extended visa rubber-stamped by the MPs they had been chatting up.

The phones and internet have gone into overload again, as colleagues contact their mates who have gone AWOL into the nearby Midland Park for a smoke, coffee and chat with fellow public servants from other nearby government departments giving them the rundown on the latest goings on in BS House.

It doesn't take a rocket scientist or Alex, the Head of Scientists for that matter, to put one and one together and come up with 917. Alex's mind does overtime. Something as sinister as a murder has taken place, he's sure of it – the talk on the street is that's pretty plausible. He doesn't usually buy into such rumours and idle gossip but Donna, his floor's Health and Safety rep is saying it's true, so it must be. She's from the same English town Alex spent his earlier years in, Winchcombe, so he knows he can trust her. Maybe something happened at BS House over the weekend or with some minister and they are now positioning themselves around the building to collect evidence and probe into people's personal lives to try and get to the bottom of the case. He nervously mutters to himself, like any mad scientist out of an Enid Blyton *Famous Five* novel would be portrayed to do. "Now if our Head of People and Performance were here she would be able to distinguish fact from gossip. Where is she? I haven't seen her all day. The place clearly can't operate without her."

That was one area where Cat did practise what she preached and that was to use one's sick leave sparingly. Very different to Sarita, the Head of L & D who promoted to her staff that 'sick leave is to be taken and if you don't use it you will lose it, no one will thank you for not taking it, so use it all, that's an order. Look, I won't even record it in your online leave entitlements, so that way it will appear that you are always in the black, with a minimum of ten sick days to use. Unlimited sick leave. Besides, we haven't got enough work to go around all of you, let alone desks to sit at so please use it, otherwise it will appear blatantly obvious we have nothing to do and my head will be on the chopping block'. That is if you are an anxious Indian immigrant with a bogus ten-rupee HR degree from the University of Calcutta trying to keep her job, extend her work visa and then get permanent residency before skipping through the back door to the lucky country of Australia, or further afield, Canada.

Sven realises HR are creatures of habit and that nine times out of ten most of the important HR stand-downs have always been booked in 101. The room number matches the level of intelligence and emotional intelligence that the HR crew manage to conjure up at the best of times. Maybe it's a cover-up. Maybe they are quite intelligent underneath, maybe it's just an act. Hard to tell when they are spouting off their acronyms and HR jargon in parrot fashion and difficult to determine what is actually being said.

Sven laughs to herself as the familiar words she has been listening to all day dance across her mind. 'Synergies, words on a page, pipeline, BAU, piece of work, capability, capacity, ELT, SLT'.

Standing around waiting can get a bit tedious as there is only so much people-watching you can do before her thoughts turn back to Charlie. Checking her phone, there is still no answer from Freya, Sven fires off another text, 'Charlie is in the BS building!' Then to distract herself,

Sven gets out her laptop and starts keying in her findings from the recently held quarterly HR stand-down meeting she had to attend as part of her professional development. She can't believe that the last HR stand-down conference was solely dedicated to collating the findings of the focus group that had been working for months on determining what type of personality the HR group wanted to exude, compared with the personality they currently had, and more importantly what type of personality did they want to portray?

Deciding on one's personality may sound a little strange as humans are usually born with one and a personality naturally evolves over time. But for this ministerial beast of an organisation, the HR group was tasked with establishing the BS personality. The reason, five government departments had merged resulting in the birth of the BS Ministry and they were still sailing through rough seas without a rudder (in an irreparable waka), and a personality had to be formed to give it some sense of purpose or direction. There had also been no time to create values or a culture, and these too had to be determined. One would have thought these types of basic foundations or philosophy would have naturally evolved or would have been stated by the Minister and his merry men whose bright idea it was to amalgamate five distinctly different departments into one. When people are involved, tribes and groups naturally or forcefully are created and a culture and personality develops, matures and evolves. However, this was something that had not yet been established and subsequently a regular half-day summit was being planned to figure out how they wanted to brand themselves. But first they had to work out who they were, what was important to them and how they wanted to be perceived, and then the BS Personality could be established. These essential half-day planning meetings for this purpose were being held twice weekly.

In HR speak, this collection of ideas would be written in the commonly over-used cluster of words such as 'synergies, strategies' and the end result would be the famously clichéd PS phrase of 'words on a page' that would eventuate as a 'piece of work'. Now with Cat at the helm of the HR ship, this 'personality piece of work' was finally going to be explored and it was so important that HR advisors, leaders, consultants, managers, supervisors and team leaders from all over New Zealand had been flown in at no expense spared to discuss this particular piece of work, even during these desperate cost-cutting times. Why? Cat's reasoning was if they got the personality of the group nailed, then they could use this language as part of the advertisements they would place when recruiting and enticing new people from afar into the organisation.

Sven has managed to type up most of the notes from the HR Personality planning meetings. Bernard had regretfully not been able to accept Cat's kind invitation to attend and speak and Sven had promised she would go and make notes and send the highlights to him. It had been so boring she had forgotten, until now, when the phrase 'HR Personality' had been triggered by watching a gaggle of the HR team congregating in the park for an offsite team meeting. And being void of personality, this had flashed her back to the cyclic meetings and she realised she hadn't written up the preliminary report as promised.

The next minute, Sven receives a text. Excitedly grabbing her phone thinking Freya has got back to her,

Sven's elation dramatically subsides as she reads, 'Big announcement all of BS to attend.' She closes her computer and heads back towards 101 for some more ground-breaking 101 scintillating Comms, yet again another announcement.

She is really getting sick of all these random, kneejerk announcements this morning. It seems like no one knows what's happening, and that they are just making it up as the morning progresses. She realises this is BAU, but it's not bloody BAU for her. Besides, she still needs to talk with the girls and find out what the heck Charlie is up to. Just thinking about him sets her pulse racing. *Why does he still make me feel this way? Geez, I need to get a grip on myself!*

Random announcements come and go regarding the rescheduled, rescheduled HR announcement. Depending on where people are in the building and which type of media they are relying on for communication, there are randomly inconsistent communications going out about the next meeting. Emails, instant messengers, texts, phone calls and people are informing one another about the rescheduled meeting.

Coming from the corporate world in Sweden, this endless haphazard merry-go-round dance of meetings and all back-to-back for the sake of filling the day with meetings in an Outlook calendar for big brother to examine as a 'time management' exercise is very tiresome. Sven feels like her soul is being sucked dry. She doesn't know if she can stay on; she is not feeding her soul, and she is definitely not fuelling her purpose. To quote Prince Harry's new bride's wise words, she thinks to herself, *Do I just have too high an expectation, should I just settle for less?*

Meeting after meeting whizzes by with no time to

actually be still, reflect and plan, let alone be creative, or do some actual work. Everything is too structured and yet so last minute; it is just an endless filing in and out of meeting rooms to listen to a bunch of people but ending up as fragments of time consumed by navel-gazing, white noise and nothing of true substance.

Sven hopes this announcement, as her colleagues would say, is seriously going to 'add value'. She is starting to wonder why she bothered catching the train today and wishes she had just worked from home.

Everyone noisily files into 101 and Andréa, the Deputy Chief Executive of the Finance, Admin Recruiting team, naturally titled with another acronym, 'FART', walks up to the podium and starts fiddling with the intercom, looking awfully serious. Everyone gets confused, understandably so, with the two similar names of Andréa and Adrienne as they both happen to be part of the ELT which also is interchangeably known as SMT. Some acronyms are so last century and others have been created to give the BS more of a modern feel and flavour attempting to keep up with the corporate sector and failing dismally.

The voices suddenly mute instantaneously as they watch this little red-faced rocket stamp her comfortable heel-less shoe to the wooden podium beneath her.

Some people have been waiting for almost half an hour while others, who have just got the news, traipse into the room with seconds to spare to hear the announcement.

Andréa, from ELT and FART, one of Bernard's faithful and loyal, eager-to-please Deputy Departmental Chief Executives clears her throat and begins proceedings. "Good morning, I won't waste time with the niceties today. I understand you are all under a lot of stress this morning and in hindsight, you should have probably been told this a lot earlier to stop the jungle wireless gossip getting to the stage it has. Unfortunately, I had to wait until our Internal Comms team gave me the green light to make this announcement and unfortunately due to most of them being away for assorted reasons on this Monday morning, we have had to deal with the issue with the limited resources we have. As a result, news has leaked out, yes, our greatest fear has become reality, the *Capital News* are releasing a story about us. Well, our people. And I owe it to you, as your safety and wellbeing is paramount, to share the news first-hand from the horse's mouth, so to speak, me." There is a pause as Stephanie starts ruffling her papers and starts making a beeline to the stage.

My god... Please woman, just get to the point! Sven says to herself. If, like most people here, she is incapable of presenting to an audience, she could at least tailor the conversation to suit the average person's IQ here, and just fast-forward the dramas and get to the point. Everybody knows Comms is useless and Sven wonders why is Stephanie taking the floor – is that the best they can do?

Sven's internal dialogue has taken on the bad habit of flashing to sarcastic extremes since being with the Ministry. To date she hasn't managed to find herself a trusted ally who speaks the same language as her, so she has started talking to herself about the goings-on around the place, storing it up all day and then letting it rip with the girls on the Kiwi Con journey home. Sometimes she manages to offload sooner over coffee with her mates or writing poetry in meetings. But even on the train, it is not the most conducive place of pulling fellow public servants to pieces, especially with most of Public Servantsville being on the same train. Sometimes the train resembles another large meeting room, the only difference being this one is on wheels and moving faster than the average public servant can make their jam and marmite sandwiches in the morning.

All 458 out of 3,500 employees, including backfills, are present. A representative from each department scurries around doing a headcount and entering the numbers into their digital devices. Most people are 'out of office' for various reasons: working from home; at meetings; any excuse that satisfies their respective bosses' checklists. It is a good wake-up call for Bernard to see how many people on a Monday are physically (not necessarily emotionally and mentally) at work.

Bernard sweeps past the masses of people. It isn't very often people get to see their leader and the room suddenly falls quiet except for one HR Advisor. "Now this has never happened before, the head honcho, what on earth is going on to bring him into the building? Another restructure that we have been kept in the dark about?" she rhetorically asks her colleague.

"And yes, an electronic roll call, what is the world coming to? Are we back at school again? That's how it feels! Also, I don't like how we are the last to know what is going on. Everyone, even the other floors are speculating and suddenly finding excuses to visit us on our floor. God, you put yourself out all year saying 'feel free to send us an email if there is any help you need with your team, whether it is performance appraisal, an updated JD, a communication or staff issue, a training need'. And suddenly this morning of all mornings, they are flying in with the most trivia of questions pretending they want to use our services. The cheek of it," an HR Consultant is heard ranting on to another.

Annette, another Senior Advisor can be heard saying a bit too loudly, "The cops are swarming, the journos are outside, what is so big this time? We haven't had this much publicity since Harold, the last CE was snapped naked in a nightclub in Hamburg with three leather-clad dominatrices. One of which looked suspiciously like his EA, a couple of years ago. And they never did get to the bottom of his expenses, did they?"

Helena replies, "Typically the Tories swept that well under the carpet as usual. Old Harold and his EA were rewarded by getting paid shitloads of money from their golden parachute clause, stepping down gracefully and moving onto more senior roles in the diplomatic core overseas to live the life of Riley."

Andréa has finished her bit and Stephanie hobbles to the front of the room and opens her mouth to squeak hesitantly, "Okay everyone, if I can get your attention please? We have a very important announcement to make, so I am going to pass you onto our Head of Communications, Sonya, thank you." Stephanie, no sooner has she stepped up, steps down and makes way for Sonya.

Bernard's phone rings; he glances at the screen. "It's the Minister. I'll be back in a minute," he mutters to Sonya as he turns and heads *tout de suite* back out of the room.

Stephanie shakily hands over the mic to Sonya. She has been flapping around all morning trying to persuade her staff to come back from sick leave as her team are short-staffed, but to no avail. Everyone's cell phones are either switched off or diverted to their soft phones, which are tied to the BS computer system which is overloaded and is being answered by the backup subcontractors in Mumbai.

Sonya, even though she is the Head of Department, is another backfill as the Communications team have gone through a huge shake-up this year. And last year too, in fact ever since it merged with Public Relations at the beginning of the formation of the BS Ministry. Internal Communications are, like the name implies, in charge of communicating to all the internal stakeholders, which is a posh way of referring to staff. It's just that the word 'stakeholders' makes the statement sound more impressive and it's always about perception.

The Comms team (when they are at work not writing reports to justify their existence) post stories on the intranet informing everyone of what is happening, what has happened and what is about to happen, which may never happen. The trouble is the stories are bland and boring and as there is too much mostly out-of-date information on the intranet, no one bothers to read it as they are 'terribly busy'. The stories are meant to celebrate successes, break down the silos and make everyone aware of what all the different teams and business units are doing within the Ministry. But what commonly happens is everyone gets insular and they are only interested in what their small neck of the woods is up to and are tied up in back-to-back meetings which of course are of little, if any, importance at all.

Glossy and glossier pictures and beautiful text gets published with a non-existent audience to 'ooh and aah' through it. The Comms team unfortunately comes across as highly unapproachable, which is not helped by a certain Bulgarian Rottweiler.

Sven experienced this first-hand and involuntarily shudders as she recalls the experience.

For Sonya to be pulled from whatever highly–important task she was doing to head up this meeting, and with Bernard making a rare appearance, something big had to have gone down.

Sonya begins. "Good morning, kia ora everyone. Listen up. Thank you all for attending today. We really appreciate your time during this unusually busy day. You will no doubt have noticed that our Home and Away café has been busier than usual; all the meeting rooms are full to capacity. There is no parking outside, and the park is full of neighbouring public servants and there are people out there with mics in their hands, not to mention the mobile television units that are circling the blocks like a school of sharks. I would be very, very surprised if anyone in the room hasn't noticed anything untoward today?" She pauses as she looks around the room for a response from anyone who has not noticed what is happening all around them, ready like a cat to pounce on them.

Sonya is a very good speaker – she appears to have captured everyone's attention, but she pauses and looks around the room just in case. Satisfied that everyone seems to be listening, she continues.

"Now, I would like everyone who hasn't already done so to switch off their phones as what I am about to say to you is highly confidential. It doesn't have ministerial sign-off to be released, so please now take the time to turn off your phones. Don't mute them or vibrate them, turn them off please." Again she pauses, but for considerably longer this time, to ensure everyone has followed her instructions.

Sven hastily texts the girls, 'Something BIG is going down here! Coffee & kōrero soon!' Before shutting her phone down.

"Okay, I appreciate you doing this. As I said, you would have noticed the paparazzi lurking around outside our building most of the morning. They are hungry for the official story and I have told them they can have one as soon as I have spoken to you. I am speaking to all the Ministry as this is of grave importance. I would appreciate when I have finished speaking, that you all walk out and go straight back upstairs in a professional, organised manner. Please do not leave the building and do not linger outside in the immediate foyer. In accordance with your contract, and as our privacy and confidential policy and code of conduct policy stipulates, I do not want anyone talking with the press. This is a breach of your contract and anyone who is caught disclosing this highly confidential material will be instantly dismissed and then prosecuted via the ERA. I do hope I make myself clear."

She pauses for what seems an age, and everyone is on tenterhooks for her to continue. It is like watching some bad reality TV show, where the time is up and the viewer is scared it is going to go to commercials for another week, just before the next contestant is eliminated.

Carmen is beside herself and yells out, "Please, can you just tell us why we are all here? We have been waiting a long time for this, so can you just tell us?"

Sonya smiles at Carmen and continues with a straight face, "It is with great regret that I must inform you our HR Director, Cathryn Tennyson, was found dead this morning."

The whole vibe in the room goes from one of suspense and impatience to sheer shock and surprise.

Sonya continues. "I am very sorry to be the one that had to bring this tragic news. I realise there have been rumours flying around for most of the morning and for some of you this will not be a great shock, but for most of you it will be. Please take a little time now for this to digest."

She looks at her notes, takes a few seconds and then continues. "However, I do hope I have made myself clear just how sensitive this matter is. This is considered highly confidential. You are not even at liberty to discuss this with your loved ones, family or unloved ones for that matter. I am almost done. So please be ready to file out of the room like I said in an orderly manner. It will be best to take the back stairs up to your respective floors. If you are unable to walk up the stairs then take one of the two back lifts, but please do not go into the café. It is a security risk with the press prowling, ready to pounce on any dirt they can dig up! Do not use the front lifts or the front entrance. Security are waiting outside and will escort you to the back of the building."

The stunned occupants of the room sit and stand in silence, mouths open, their brains doing overtime as they slowly process this surprising news. Then, like a silent school bell announcing lunch break, the chatter starts up again around the room. Carmen, not doing her career any favours is heard spouting off. "OMG! Okay, it's now official. Right now I just wish she would hurry up and finish. She's a bit too full of her own self-importance, bordering on being a drama queen." She takes a quick pause, coming up for a breath and then blurts out something just as career limiting but for a change too quietly for the outer circle to hear.

Sonya continues. "The reason why we are just telling you now is nothing had been confirmed until a few minutes before we called this urgent meeting. Those of you who commuted in on the Kiwi Con this morning were probably the first who got wind of what was happening…"

Bernard who unfortunately had to brief the Minister and left the room as quickly as he entered, left the announcement in the capable hands of Sonya. However, he comes running back in after taking the Minister's call. Two of the gophers run out to the chair cemetery room to collect the two remaining chairs still stored in there. They place the chairs helpfully next to Sonya and Bernard, for them to use once they have both finished talking.

Sonya, sitting, quickly alters her skirt for some unknown reason and much to the amazement of those sitting in the front row, a long globular mass of gluey substance gets flicked from her skirt onto Bernard's shoe. Suddenly it becomes obvious to them what this sticky substance is – the remains of a sexual encounter. A very pink-faced receptionist glances guiltily towards a certain Security officer standing near the door.

Bernard, who is standing, almost loses his balance and composure, but manages to say, "Apologies, ladies and gentlemen, we have a bit more to discuss and we would like you also to hear what the police have to say. Please be accommodating with the police as they will have to interview most of you, so keep your devices on you at all times. As such the police will be taking over most of our first and sixth floor meeting rooms for the interviews. We are also organising counselling services, so there will be access to EAP personnel here in 101, should anyone feel they need it."

The awkwardness of their situation heightens as Sonya and Bernard are now joined by a long trail of the sticky substance. Exchanging a look of sheer embarrassment, they realise exactly what the tacky material is that is now joining them both at the hip. Everybody looks mortified, while Fiona and Dave have turned a brighter shade of red.

Huge sighs, whispers and not so quietly raised voices can be heard going off in all directions around the room. The noise quietens down very quickly as Bernard tries to compose himself at this awkward moment and turns on the stage. "Ladies and gentlemen, as you have just heard from Sonya, this communication is of the highest security classification, meaning nothing on this matter is to be discussed verbally or in writing – emails, texts, twitter. This discussion finishes here. Thank you in advance for your co-operation."

A beetroot-faced Dave swings open the two large doors and two police officers enter the room. Loud whispers can be heard around the room, 'Shish. Look, it's the cops, oh my god, this is big. Shut up, listen up everyone…'

Oh my god it's Charlie! Sven's mind roars, her pulse racing, *What's he doing here?*

Confidently striding towards the front of the room, the hunky officers step up onto the podium, which Sonya and Bernard have now embarrassingly vacated.

"Kia ora, ladies and gentlemen. My name is DS Charlie Rogers. I apologise that you have had to be the recipients of such sad news; I will give you a bit of time to digest this in a moment, but for now, if you could just listen up to what I have to say. You will notice that there are quite a few of us from the Force here today and we will be here for as long as it takes. We are interviewing anyone who can help us with our inquiries into the death of Cathryn Tennyson. It has been confirmed her body was found on the commuting train, Kiwi Con this morning."

Charlie carries on, while Sven aghast at the news but can't help admiring him from the back row. *Shit, he is still incredibly good-looking and with that added tan. Clearly he has been out on the farm helping his dad, he can't have got that tan from walking the beat and streets of Wellington!* Charlie, being of Māori descent, already has a bit of tan, albeit diluted due to his dad being a Pākēha. He always looked good, but today he is particularly easy on the eye. Sven tries not to attract attention or look too interested and starts looking at others around the room, to show she is interested in everyone, not just him. Meanwhile her stomach feels like it has been invaded by a stampeding heard of butterflies.

Charlie continues. "The time of death has not yet been determined as the coroners are examining the body, but at this stage we would say it could have been anytime between Friday evening and Sunday evening, last night. No doubt some of you would have been the last to see her, so it is vitally important that we interview all of you and the priority is for anyone who spoke with her as late as Friday afternoon to please come forward. We have taken over the meeting rooms in the west wing of the building on the ground floor and most of the meeting rooms on your sixth floor. We want to do this as discreetly and as quickly as possible to save any further unnecessary disruption to your business. My colleagues and I will be staying behind, so if you have any information, any information at all, please come forward before you leave the room. If the rest of you, as Sonya said, could file out in an orderly manner and not draw any more undue attention from the reporters waiting outside. Please do not talk to anyone. If anyone does ask you any questions, just make it clear that it is now a police matter and you cannot help them," he finishes off in his serious tone.

The doors swing open again and a couple of officers bearing clipboards enter the room.

"Okay, everyone, thank you again and I am sorry for your loss. We are keen to get to the bottom of this matter as soon as possible. So please do come forward even if you believe that what you have got to say is of little importance. It could be vital. We really need to talk to anyone who may have dealt with Ms Tennyson over the last week, especially if you were on Friday evening's train and noticed if she was acting strangely or if any of her actions or behaviour were not in keeping. Thank you again."

He talks to his offsider Rex and then comes back to the microphone. "Oh, and your organisation, in the best interests of your safety and wellbeing, has organised a group of EAP counsellors. They are here already, downstairs, so if you need to see them and book a time, please do so through Reception."

The room falls into loud conversation again, amongst a lot of shocked, dazed and appalled faces. Some people are crying; some just look like they've seen a ghost. Most are completely stunned, shell-shocked and unable to utter anything. In a daze, like a bunch of sleepwalking zombies, they file out, turn right down the corridor and head for the back stairs and set of lifts. Stephanie drops her pile of papers as she enters the lift and some of the papers fall down the lift shaft, never to be retrieved again.

Sarita, the HOD of L & D, had been particularly close to Cat and had admired her a great deal. She had never hidden that fact and she is the one who appears to be the most visibly upset. "I just can't believe this, I don't care what people have to say about Cat, she was a great lady, she made a dramatic difference to our department and I admire her a lot." Voicing her opinion makes it more real, sending her off into more tears, and she detours briskly via the ladies' for some tissues.

Carmen, never one to mince her words, says far too loudly as usual, "Hmm, so finally she got what she deserved. What I don't understand about all of this is why it took so long for someone to do this. She really was the biggest bitch here. I can't say I will miss her. In fact, maybe this means her restructure is off the cards! That at least gives some of us some security and certainty in the future of our roles."

A group of HR advisors are now lingering outside the meeting room, looking like they have just had the stuffing taken completely out of them. "That's it, I'm over all these constant changes here. I think going back to a smaller ministry is the best way to go. At least there you get noticed and you are a person. Here you are just one of the many cogs in the big factory wheel."

Alex is not his usual cocky self and he is speechless. Sven goes up to him. "Alex, are you okay? You were both close, weren't you?"

"Of course, I don't know who to…" He walks off in a daze, mumbling to himself, *Should I approach the Minister direct?*

Then Sven realises what Charlie said and reading between the lines, the penny drops, *OMG, I'm a suspect!*

A few staff do stay behind though, and nervously start making their way towards the less populated corners of the room to talk with the police who have by now positioned themselves in the different areas of the room with clipboards and pens in hand.

A handful go off to book EAP appointments with Reception, while the rest make their way even more slowly than usual back to their podiums.

*****

PART 3

MONDAY AFTERNOON

Meetings and even more meetings

Chapter 11

There's been an 'Incident'

Oh my god, is this true? Kirsty voices to her team. No sooner has the HR sit-down finished, than the usual 'there has never been one like that before' comments around the departmental silos are made as they climb the stairs and settle back into their pods. But then the fire alarm goes off, and forgetting their evacuation training, everyone files out chaotically into the foyer looking for the fire exits. Everyone, to be fair, is in a state of shock.

Masses of people can be seen heading off in all sorts of directions like the usual flocks of sheep. However, against previous instructions, they are seen filing out of the main entrance as well as the back entrances.

"Where are we meant to be going? Is the assembly area at the back of the building or out the front?" one says alarmingly, rummaging in her bag for Rescue Remedy. It had been made quite clear that in the case of an emergency there was no time to pick up handbags and the like, but those instructions have gone out the window as well. Everyone is scurrying for their bags, devices and coats and then running for the door.

"No, it must be the back entrance. Surely that would be the obvious choice as that is by the park. If we go out the front then we will end up with all the other ministries, and besides, today that road is packed with journos and cops. Why doesn't the receptionist make an announcement and tell us where to go?" Kirsty demands. "I need some direction."

Sven comes out of the meeting room, red as a beetroot, her laptop tucked under her arm and animatedly talking into the phone to Freya. "Oh my god, Freya, where have you been? I've been trying to get you all morning! You'll never guess who is in town…No, not my parents, bloody Charlie, that's who! And now we've just been told that Cat is history…No, as in she's dead, probably murdered, and Charlie is heading the investigation…Oh, you know this place, there is the usual lack of communication, no systems in place, cops and journos swarming and now a fire alarm. Damn, he's still so hot! I just realised that we are all suspects, everyone that was on the Kiwi Con Friday night! But I mean for god's sake, what could possibly go wrong next? No one in this place knows what to do in an evacuation when there has been untold training for it and no doubt the Cap News gets to hear about our HR Director being murdered before our own Internal Comms, let alone HR team can notify us. I just can't believe this place, it is completely nonsensical, and I can't bear this pandemonium. Do you want a coffee? My treat, hey, hang on, the wardens are escorting us back into the building. It was a false alarm, but people are still piling out of every exit imaginable. Hey, I've got to go before someone hears me slagging off the place. Meet me in the park in half an hour. We just have to talk about Charlie, Oh why does he still make me feel this way?"

Sven is seen walking back into the building while the rest of her colleagues are scattering themselves thinly over three rows of streets that surround the BS building. There are many exits and entrance ways. The back door, the side door, the front door, and the basement car park entrance.

Meanwhile, inside the building, Sven can see that the police are filing in and out and around the building. Blue uniforms can be seen at every corner of the downstairs foyer and more officers are milling in and around the meeting rooms on the ground floor.

Sven finds it amazing that the police could get security access within an hour as it usually takes at least a fortnight of working in the building to receive security ID. And what's more, all the temporary visitor swipes went missing from the open box at Reception that morning. The receptionist had left the box of security cards on the desk when she went to have a howl in the ladies' earlier on when the pressure had got too much, and when she returned she found the box and the cards had gone. *Probably swiped by some journo, now that's never happened before,'* Sven jokes to cheer herself up.

People slowly start returning to the building and spreading out across the floors to their respective pods. There is no danger of things returning to normal today. Dismayed looks spread across people's faces as each cop knocks on the meeting room doors and enters. It's like one of those police check points out on the roads over the weekends and in the summer. They check out every meeting room and then another group can be seen heading up the front stairs, no doubt to flood the next floors' meeting rooms. As the cops take over staff are naturally piling further and further upstairs into any vacant meeting room or cupboard. Hopefully there won't be another earthquake as most of the staff are now congregating on the top floors, and would have to run down more flights of stairs in the case of an emergency and the higher up you go, the worse the earthquake feels.

The Internal Communications team are running around acting weirder than usual, with their phones glued to their ears, looking very concerned and secretive at the same time. A couple of them have bounded outside to check the lay of the land out there and all come racing back into the foyer once they espy the paparazzi circulating like vultures out on the side roads.

"Damn, word must've got out to the press and they are now hovering outside waiting to pester all and sundry as they leave the building," Eric from Comms says to his colleague, Petra.

"God, if only bloody HR had included us in what was going down sooner, we could have kept this under wraps and now Sonya wouldn't be running around flapping like a headless chicken."

Sonya is not impressed with the way everyone has failed to follow correct procedures today, and gossip, news – factual and non-factual – is leaking fast, a bit like the *Titanic. It's not a matter of IF we will sink, but just when,* she thinks to herself.

The Comms team are seriously stretched today, and the Head of Comms makes a call to the rest of her team who are away on sick leave, to entice them to come back into work. "We need you here, an incident of grave proportions has happened. I'm sorry, we need you back ASAP. I don't want us to make the front page of the paper, let alone the six o'clock news this evening." Sonya makes several phone calls and mostly gets diverted to the recipients' voicemail. Feeling frustrated she goes up to Rachel in Recruiting to ask her to put an order in for half a dozen backfills to cope with the workload.

To be fair, Rachel is on the case and within the hour, backfills are arriving like headless chooks without visitor security lanyards, as there are none left. Another breach of security.

Sven looks out the window. Which is a new experience as it is against the H & S rules to raise the blinds as the policy is to keep all windows completely covered in case of the heritage glass shattering, in the event of another earthquake. However, today, with all the action of paparazzi and the police, for the first time in a month the Department of Cultural Affairs across the road can see in through the BS's windows, and colleagues between the two departments are waving at each other from their respective meeting rooms across the street. Wellywood is a small city and everyone knows almost everyone.

Looking over the balustrade of the sixth-floor break out room, Sven gets a bird's eye view of the ground floor and the café. There is a small orange party hat haphazardly placed next to one part of the balustrade that is missing vital panes of glass, leaving the area dangerously open to a potential disaster. One false move and an innocent victim could slip through the gaping hole and end up as a late breakfast order, bordering on early lunch on one of the many tables below in the Home and Away café.

She avoids that part of the balustrade and peers down, her heart fluttering when she sees Charlie confidently striding from one meeting room to another, pausing only to have a brief word with a couple of uniformed officers. Closing her eyes briefly, her mind slips back to the past, remembering feeling so safe in his muscular embrace. Then slowly breathing through her tension, Sven knows she has to put her unresolved feelings to one side. Her inquisitive mind is hanging out for an update. She wants to see Charlie and talk to Bernard and see where she can help.

Sven flies downstairs again and heads towards Reception, where Fiona, the receptionist is sitting agitatedly at the front desk in the foyer. She has got her flaming red-haired head in an absolute spin. Her face is still the same colour as her hair, her brain has gone into overdrive and it hasn't taken long for her to reach boiling point, still feeling guilty that her Monica Lewinsky moment could be discovered after the public display of the remnants of her earlier tryst with Dave. She is over all the questions being asked by every Tom, Dick and Lars, and the untold people congregating around Reception gaping at everyone that comes and goes, blocking her view. She no longer has a clear view of what is going on outside as everyone is obstructing her line of vision, creating a huge hazard. She is not that concerned about the recent announcement about the HR Director. She is more concerned about her love life being exposed, and getting out of the building should another earthquake strike. There are far too many people in the building and she can't see how she could get past them quick enough to get to safety. Forget staying inside and doing the DCH (Drop, Cover, Hold). If the rumour is true about this earthquake coming, they will all be doomed as the complete downstairs foyer and coffee bar is packed, not to mention all the swarming groupies piling up outside to have a good look at what is going on.

Her colleague, Sally, comes back from her long over-extended break. "Wow, have you seen the crowds outside? I've just been talking to my mates from across the road at Māori Affairs. I don't think anyone at work today is actually working, let alone in the actual office as they are all too busy having a gander outside."

Fiona snaps at her. "So how long was your smoko today? I think we could proudly announce you the *Guinness Book of Records* winner for the longest smoko break ever. And I know us public servants specialise in having more extended breaks than doing actual work, but you are definitely taking the piss today. What about me? I haven't had a break since I got here at seven-thirty this morning, and it is now well after twelve."

"Well you did have a longish break yourself around eight when I first came in. That wouldn't have been to check the chair cemetery, would it? I thought I saw Barb…" Sally queries, jesting with her colleague. She is over Fiona's temper tantrums and having to cover for her every time she goes off with Dave. Sally has genuinely seen Barbara and that new backfill from Immigration going off to the same room with Dave at other times, and although she marvels at Dave's stamina, she suspects he is not just two-timing but possibly three or four-timing the lot of them.

Fiona in full rant carries on. "In my contract it says I am legally entitled to a ten-minute break and I am now off to have an extended, extended break. The phone hasn't stopped and the visitor enquiries have got pettier and pettier. Where is Barbara?"

Sally replies, "As I was trying to say, have you noticed that Dave the Security guy hasn't been around for the last hour?"

Fiona, already wound up, goes an even darker shade of crimson. "You are joking me! Is she getting it off with my man? I thought that was just a one-night stand at Friday drinks that time. Are they still banging each other? OMG, don't tell me, let me guess – you found them in the stationery cupboard again?"

"I just told Lewis, the Head of Security what he was up to," Sally gloats.

"You are joking me, what would he care? He's just as bad!" Fiona snaps back.

Sally retorts, "You know they are not only contracted to do work here, they don't care where. I saw Dave at a gig up the road the other week and he was doing those same chat-up lines over there with the ushers. It was at a concert. So obviously the same security company just contract themselves out all over town, bit like Dave with his body, he just contracts it out wherever there is someone keen and mean. Did you hear about the incident with the chairs in the HR stand-up this morning? You were there, weren't you?"

Trying to cover her embarrassment, Fiona blusters out, "What are you on about now?"

"Well you should know, you and your boyfriend have been leaving a bit of 'fluid' evidence around…the look on Sonya and Bernard's faces was priceless!"

Fiona storms off, mortified; she can't take any more. She is ashamed that anyone has put one and one together about the sticky substance discovered in the meeting of all meetings and pretends she is annoyed about other more important stuff. Today is the day she will hand in her notice, she will not be humiliated like this anymore.

Keeping her eye out for Charlie or Bernard, Sven passes through Reception on the way out; overhearing some of the conversation she is horrified when she suddenly realises what Bernard had hanging off his shoes while making the serious announcement about Cat.

Sven heads for the park, avoiding the paparazzi just as Dave comes flying back into the foyer with his fly halfway down. Sven has images in her head of David with his pants down and the 'flying semen' on Bernard's shoes. *Oh my god, just too much information!*

"Excuse me, madam," says one of the pushy journalists, "would you like to make a comment on the disappearance of your HR lady? We really are going to have to run this story, so if you don't help us fill in the gaps, we will just have to join the dots ourselves. You know how it works."

Sven responds, "Hello there, sorry, I didn't catch your name?" and stands there waiting for a response.

"Talia," replies the reporter.

"Great, thanks for that, Talia. I have no comment, but thanks for asking. I do hope you won't just fill in the gaps with anything. Look, couldn't you just be really creative instead of the usual twaddle you come up with, like 'MP has alien's baby'? Hey, I would love to stop and talk, but I've just seen someone who is more worthy of talking to." Sven points to the homeless man juggling a crushed cigarette packet and a lighter, an upturned beanie at his feet.

She then receives a text letting her know about the next Head of Science meeting and before rushing off turns to look back at the journalist. "Good luck with joining your dots and making your deadline."

Sven couldn't help herself. She knows it was a little nasty, but she didn't like the tone of the young, naive upstart of a journalist. Having a verbal with the journalist was exactly what she needed to release a bit of her increasingly pent-up tension. Texting an apology to Freya, Sven heads back for the upcoming meeting.

*****

Chapter 12

Head of Science calls a meeting

The day progresses on and for most of the building's inhabitants it is just BAU and meetings continue in their haphazard fashion, but more and more meetings are being held on the top floors which is a serious earthquake risk and concerns Alex, the Head of Science, greatly.

After the last earthquake, it was established that buildings seven floors or higher had more chance of being affected and it was advised to keep staff on the lower floors for meetings as much as possible.

However, with the police invading the BS's territory they have no other alternative but to search the upper floors for any meeting space that can be found. The Home and Away café (HAA) has been doing a roaring trade becoming the gossip hub-cum-drop-in centre where other public servants have decided to get in on the action and spend Monday morning people-watching and eavesdropping. In exchange for the cost of a mocha caramel latte or trim soy chai tea, they sit and stare at all the comings and goings of the police, EAP specialists, counsellors and psychologists. Some sit marvelling as the BS public servants tear in and out of the building every five seconds because of a false alarm, a designated rest break or simply to walk around the block to avoid attending another tedious meeting, wondering if they do less work than their other BS colleagues do.

Sven, having to be in multiple places at one time to attend most of her over-scheduled meetings, finds it difficult to keep up with everything that is evolving as the time ticks on by. She has talked with Bernard about this and he has said (off the record) that "sitting in on most of the meetings will be a waste of time and for you, it will do your head in. But I want you to please take special note of our unfortunately named SHIT department. I think they are talking a lot of their 'namesake' so keep a good eye on them, especially that new HOD, Alex, that Cat 'accidentally' dragged in and employed without consulting me first."

With the green light from Bernard, Sven has started covering more ground, gaining a better understanding of what is and is not happening within the BS and auditing how meetings are run.

However, having said that, there are always exceptions to the rule and the Science department is one of them.

She had been asked to attend this very important meeting about the startling test data Simon, Alex and the rest of the team had collected and were presenting. The chime from her calendar phone app reminds her of the upcoming meeting which she had forgotten about in all the mayhem of the day. She doesn't know if she can be bothered with making her way back to the office and ploughing her way through all those pushy paparazzi, including that idiot Talia, and risk bumping into Charlie. She's in two minds – she wants to see him but then the other part of her screams, NO!

Sven finds the older she gets, the less tolerant she becomes of people and their petty games and all the white noise and hot air they produce. The endless suffocating meetings where people attempt to do one better than each other, obstructing great ideas just because they weren't the one who came up with the idea first.

She has learnt with years of experience the hard way, that it's best for her to keep her mouth shut on most occasions unless she feels really passionate about a cause. She smiles sweetly, agrees, nods and does all the positive non-verbal gestures that are necessary and then goes and does her own thing anyway. In this pending Science meeting, there is no exception.

Sven hurries now to the rescheduled SHIT meeting, thinking about one of her favourite lines in meetings: 'Going forward it is business as usual...' In other words, we've done sweet fuck all and will continue to do so, but if we can continue to blind side you all on what we are really doing or more importantly not doing, we can pull in another year's salary, disguise our cruisy days with full Outlook calendar appointments...

Never one to give up transforming a challenge, problem, or headache into an opportunity and achieving something positive out of it, like an excuse to network, learn something new or find more contract work, she thinks better of skiving and makes her merry way to the Science Lab-cum-partitioned area.

Sven rethinks about catching one of those asbestos-filled Chinese trains now run by the French home and decides she would rather stay in town the night or wait for a ride home.

Sven arrives five minutes late to the meeting and being good Scientists, they haven't wasted time with small talk and finding out how everyone's weekends went or getting side-tracked on the latest recipes and department store summer sales, like HR do. Within five minutes a lot of ground has been covered and duly noted. Strangely enough, Sebastian, the Internal Comms guy for Science is there, busily scribbling down copious notes. Obviously something of interest has been said. The Ministry's intranet is usually sparse and void of anything interesting or newsy, as usually it consists of a great deal of same ol' same ol', so this is a good sign to Sven that something big has just been announced.

Sven's mind does overtime as she thinks back to Friday night and what she may have missed out on.

After all, it was Sven who had noticed, first-hand, when the decibels in the carriage on the way home on Friday evening had turned down a notch or ten. And why? Because the absence of Cat was very evident; but to be fair, it hadn't seemed too untoward at the time as Cat sometimes got off one stop early – in Paraparaumu to do her shopping. At least that's what Cat's friends Claudia and Debbie led everyone to believe, unless those two had had something to do with her suddenly suspicious disappearance... Sven speculates. After all, they were getting miffed that Cat hadn't yet offered them a role at BS Castle.

It was important that she reserved judgement on Alex, even though he was an arrogant Pom, and try to get alongside him. Sven rushes in looking more flummoxed than she actually is and apologises for her lateness, placing herself strategically by the door so she can make a quick exit if she needs to excuse herself suddenly.

"Apologies Simon, Alex, everyone, for my tardy arrival, I was at another HR meeting," Sven lies. "You know how it is – no one seems to be able to settle today after the shock announcement. Everyone is in such a state and having a pretty surreal day," she apologises.

Sven thinks about the fact that Bernard has invested a lot of money into this department of recent times on Cat's high recommendation, uncertain if he is getting bang for his buck.

She sits down and quietly observes the overly excited but anxious Alex who has been in a tizz running around the office, pulling his remaining hair out muttering something that no one can understand. He has been burning the midnight oil the last couple of weeks trying to calculate where and when the next big earthquake will strike and what size and impact it will have. Quickly recapping, Sven recalls that only a month previous in November, without warning, the big mother of all earthquakes hit. Because of this, Cat sacked Trusty Ted the old HOS and took Alex on as Head of Science almost immediately.

There is real fear within the capital city and surrounding areas after the huge unexpected earthquake of 7.8 on the scale in November. This one was centred out of Kaikōura, a popular whale spotting tourist destination in the top half of the South Island

Alex appears excited, nervous and is acting a little strangely. No one knows much about him, rumour has it he has either worked with Cat in a previous life, or they are getting it on; either way Cat had a soft spot for him and this was reciprocated.

However, being driven like she is – or *was,* and being awfully impatient, Cat has been seen having heated words with him. Clearly, to the outside observer, he has not been delivering as quickly as she had wanted. Or is the argument of a more personal nature, something to do with Cat? After this morning's revelations, nothing would shock Sven.

Nevertheless, Alex and Cat have been seen having a number of coffee rendezvous in a local café up the coast. Their little tête-à-têtes have been observed on more than one occasion. Alex, Cat and a second guy were spotted one particular day, all three so deep in conversation that they failed to notice Katarina (Bernard's secretary) walking past the café several times, trying to work out who the third character in the ménage à trois was.

For some reason, the mousey, tall, yet scrawny-looking guy seemed vaguely familiar, but Katarina couldn't place him. Had she seen him before? Or did he just have one of those common faces? Perhaps she could have mistaken him for someone else.

Katarina and Sven go way back, to Sweden days. They often meet for coffee and both are aware of the weird goings-on in the Science, Health and IT department, and take an extra special interest in them, on Bernard's behalf.

The SHIT team is pretty small, and it is not hard to summon them all into a meeting with very short notice. Being Scientists and Innovators, they work strange hours, as everything depends on when they get their ideas. Similar to most artistic types, a light bulb moment doesn't suddenly appear between the standard nine to five workday while sat in a sterile, open-plan office with deadly fluorescent light beaming down on them, frying their brains.

Alex is dribbling on about the science behind the simulations and the impressive calculations of this new piece of software and Sven finds herself drifting off to another not so similar time when another team member from Science was rambling on.

The best way to describe the current Science team is this: they are a group of half a dozen men dressed permanently in lab coats who work out of the basement floor, down where the unisex changing rooms are, next to the basement parking area opposite the secret tunnel entrance to the Beehive. No one knew they existed until recently when a 'Science talk' was organised. One of the Head Scientists was asked to present to whoever was interested in attending about their latest work on the New Zealand Space Agency. Having a space agency and here in New Zealand was very 'out there' and very innovative and Simon, the red-haired Scientist was pleasantly surprised, not to mention flattered with the number of people who turned up for the talk.

In fact, the double meeting room was extended by taking out the partitioned doors enabling seating in the three adjoining rooms. Even people from outside the Ministry attended.

This particular day, Simon was talking to an 'over' full house. Everyone had been waiting for a long time for him to start and they were getting bored and frustrated waiting for his arrival, the speech had been set for two-thirty on a Friday afternoon, a ridiculous day and time for any good public servant who had weekends on their mind and the thought of getting stuck in the north bound State Highways 1 and 2 traffic was enough to make anyone a little anxious.

There was a lot of wriggling of bums in comfortable seats, checking of phones for latest developments on weekend plans, and then at 2.45pm he waltzed unmindfully onto the stage to present the latest Space Agency findings.

It was one of those topics that had all the potential of being a really riveting, once-in-a-lifetime, jump-out-of-your-seats type of talk. However, sadly it was full of statistics, numbers and very, very dry data, sending most people into an uncomfortably sleepy why-am-I-here state of mind. No one wanted to be the first to jump up and walk past dozens of their colleagues and superiors and leave the hall before he had finished. There were no pretty pictures of spacecraft or planets at all. Even some appropriate space movie soundtrack as background music to jazz it all up and make it more enticing for the eager attendees would have been a great distraction. Alas, they were subjected to slide after slide of tables with data and Simon's monotone voice playing in the background on the same speed and pitch for over an hour, delivered from his boring bland face. It was the classic 'death by PowerPoint' delivery. At least if he had been good-looking, there would have been some eye candy to savour, but alas, it was a complete washout – the speech, delivery and deliverer.

Sven had weighed up whether to go or not as she had an important report to submit by close of business that Friday, but she wanted to learn more about New Zealand's 'one and only, and the first ever' Space Agency. The press had not got wind of the talk, and there weren't a lot of write-ups on it, which made attending it even more appealing. As BS workers would be the first to hear about it, it was like a special elite club, a preview 'one night only special' of what no one else in New Zealand was privy to. It was still quite top secret, so she decided to go, thinking it would be great to get the gen on it before the CN got the swoop and twisted it to their way of thinking.

Mistake, big mistake. Put public servant and Science in the same sentence, let alone rolled up in the same person, all in the same corner of the room and then add a bunch of non-Scientists and a Friday afternoon. Humid and hot due to the hot day along with no air conditioning and it is a sure recipe for disaster. Sven hung out for thirty minutes hoping it would get better, but found herself bucking the system yet again and starting a trend without intending to. She was the first one to get up and walk out, and once she made the big move, others started following suit like sheep.

Sven finishes daydreaming about her previous encounter with Simon and the Space Agency talk and looks up to find herself at the meeting table with the Scientists looking on anxiously at her. "I'm sorry, did I miss something?" she says, pinching herself, realising her mind had completely astral-travelled to another time, place and 'space' far away from the current boring meeting room.

"Yes, Samantha, we just asked you what brought you here today? Was there something you wanted to share?" Alex asks in his usual pompous English public-school way.

Needing a couple of seconds to bring herself back into the room and centre herself, she struggles to work out why she's there. Then she gets an idea. "Apologies gentlemen," she says, looking around, noticing there are no women in the room – a completely opposite scenario to the environment of HR where it is ninety-nine per cent women. "Good point Alex, thank you for raising that. As you will probably know I am working upstairs alongside our HR team. Has anyone in the room noticed anything different between HR and Science that they would like to share?"

A couple of the Scientists laugh but aren't up for sharing. Sven comes back to them with, "Yes, gentlemen, do share." They are still reluctant and keep their lips sealed. "Well, the obvious one is HR is strongly female-oriented whereas here in this room, it is male-dominated. In fact not one woman; why do you think that is?"

Alex has a lot to get through and isn't interested in this namby-pamby line of questioning. "Samantha, can you get to the point? Time is of the essence!" He loves saying this.

"Well it is quite obvious, isn't it? Why do some professions attract mainly women or mainly men?" She has opened herself up here.

One of them responds, "Because Science is a Science, a real profession, and you need to be very selective with who you bring on board; preferably someone with high intelligence, at least one university degree, a PHD. HR is everything we are not – it's just very flowery, in fact it's a step up from Floristry."

Alex shuts him down before he says anything else that will get the Scientists in the SHIT. He understands Sven has a close relationship with the DCE and does not want to get Sven off side and have the DCE breathing down his neck.

Also, knowing he didn't exactly land the job under ethical terms and with Cat now gone he may not be able to continue to get away with operating below the radar. With a lot of extra effort and charm, which he is capable of when he has to be, he responds to Sven. "Samantha, please ignore my colleague's words, it is just his sense of humour, he means nothing by it. The work you and your team do in

HR is incredible and we are all very appreciative of it. I'm sorry, but what was your point?"

Sven, composing herself and ignoring the sexist comments, replies, "I attend your meetings from time to time because 1. Your team add a lot of value to our Ministry and it is important to be across it, and 2. I want to learn more about the role of a Scientist as I do a lot of career vocational guidance and I would like to be able to recommend this line of work to women as there is definitely a shortage of them in your arena. Now I know you are all extremely busy; enough about me, gentlemen, please continue."

Phew, I got out of that one, Sven thinks to herself as she tries to look like she is engaged, at least for the next ten minutes. She wonders why she is really here again, and reminds herself that she needs to get the dirt on Alex for Bernard. She hears her name mentioned again, and pays full attention.

"Well, it's like this, Sven," says Alex as he launches into his well-rehearsed introduction. "You will recall that Cat employed me with one major task, and that was to be able to predict the next earthquake. If we could be the Super Super Ministry and be able to let Wellingtonians know in advance when the next big one was hitting, we would win the engagement survey this year for being the best and most caring little employer in town – in fact in the entire public service. Well, I think I have come up with just the formula to determine this."

Alex continues without taking so much of a pause, let alone a breath. "Unfortunately, something has got out to the press, as this morning the CN has already published something on their website to say the next earthquake is coming today. This has done nothing to alleviate the stress and the mood of our office, let alone the town. As there are no senior leaders in HR today and this is of a sensitive nature, I have asked Sebastian and Cecily from Comms to come down and take notes. That way they can get the real story and field all the calls that are coming through asking us what is fact and what is rumour. I have been working day and night along with one of our temps Chris to get these calculations accurate and I would have to say, within a degree or two, I think I have cracked it." He points towards a mousey, geekish-looking character. Sven realises she has seen him before and is trying to rack her brain on where. He nods to her and says, "Hi Samantha. I have heard so much about you, pleased to meet you."

"Interesting stuff Alex, you have been busy. Come on now, spill the beans, don't keep us in suspense longer than you have to." Sven encourages.

"Yes, yes, quite. I know you HR people have meetings to go to. Out of interest, when do you ever have time to do real work, like how do you ever get to action what you discuss in meetings? You spend all your life in meetings or having coffees, so when does the real work get done?" Alex sarcastically responds. It hadn't taken him long to forget to be on his best behaviour and slip back into his natural mode of operation.

"Hey Alex, you can't wind me up on this HR lark. I am not HR – my salary may come out of their budget, but don't taint me with the same paintbrush. That's like saying all Scientists are like IT boffins, a pack of geeks who forget to use deodorant, never venture outside and are pasty and gangly from never seeing the sun or the inside of a gym. And that they all wear starched white lab coats with plastic pen pocket protectors, have a pair of black horn-rimmed glasses and all suffer from receding hairlines, with overly pointed heads," she finishes off with a giggle to show she means nothing of it and she's just bantering back.

It must've hit a raw nerve as most of the meeting attendees are exactly as she described.

Well that worked, Sven says quietly to herself. "So, when is the next big earthquake coming? What does your new piece of software tell you? Do I need to be concerned and get the Incident Controllers on full alert now, or later?" she asks, thinking it is a load of crap.

"Well, madam, thanks for your comments and putting all us Scientists in the same square, compared to floristry graduates in HR. Touché!" Alex responds, covering his arse. "The earthquake is coming at five o'clock this evening actually, the precise reason why I have called the meeting. We have to start evacuating the buildings and ensuring KiwiRail or French Snail Rail or whatever you want to call them – Escargot Rail – have enough trains on and are working to time, because we have thousands of commuters we need to get out of town ASAP."

"Oh my god, are you joking me? No one seemed to know what they were doing when the last 7.8 earthquake hit. I don't think they have had time to learn from that event. How the hell will they know any better with this one? Anyhow, it won't be as big as that one or for as long, will it?" Sven says, finishing with a question, a very important one.

"Wrong, Ms Svensson, wrong. You are terribly wrong. This one is the Mother of all earthquakes. This will make San Fran, the Philippines, Christchurch look like a Sunday School picnic. This one will be huge, and it will be centred in Wellington, about 500 metres south of Pea Tony," Alex bites back.

The meeting continues, and Sven does a quick breathing exercise to calm herself down and not rise to the obvious mis-pronunciation of Petone, so she can take notes to pass onto Bernard, but then instinctively thinks she may remember where she first saw Chris. Like Alex, though, she's just not that sure of him. His voice is awfully familiar though, and her mind forms a quick ditty:

CHRIS

Chris appears to be a little weird

Geeky with glasses and a ginger beard

He really has a nerdy look

And by his side some sort of book

Oh my god, a Scandi thriller!

Could he perhaps be the killer?

Just then the boardroom table shakes. Being in such a tall building, and in Wellington, they are used to the building rocking and rolling and even though this meeting is only in the basement, the rooms, desks, and even the heritage glass windows shake every time a heavy truck rolls past. This isn't a big deal, well not to Sven once she remembers she is in the basement and not on the sixth floor.

Alex and Simon both speak up. "We do not have time to convince you of our findings. We know by close of business today or by midnight at the latest, the next huge earthquake will have hit and it is up to us to report this to the Minister and the relevant authorities immediately."

"Well," responds Sven, "you won't have to go too far – half the downtown cop shop are in this building, you can save yourself a phone call and just walk up one flight of stairs. They are completely over-resourced today and not getting very far with their enquiries, so I am sure they would really appreciate you giving them another reason for being here today."

Sven can't help but wonder why Alex is going straight to the Minister. Surely this needs to be escalated to ELT and Bernard firstly. Why does Alex think he has the authority to bypass senior management and go straight to the top?

Sebastian's phone chimes and he is called away to investigate another more pressing Comms issue, leaving his female colleague, Cecily, to continue writing. Alex is not happy with this, unconvinced that a female is up for the job, let alone has the appropriate technical knowledge like a male.

Nevertheless, Cecily writes down the latest announcement and then excuses herself from the meeting, knowing time is of the essence and it must get published immediately. She hasn't produced an article worthy of hitting the intranet let alone the front page of the CN since she started with the Ministry almost six months ago. She is another backfill, on a six-month fixed-term contract and needs to produce something so she can get her contract extended. She needs the regular fortnightly pay cheque, as she has a mortgage to pay and Christmas presents to buy and a credit card to pay off, after her last swanky holiday. She excuses herself, tipping over a chair in the flurry and leaves the room to type up her news.

Sven stays behind to talk to Alex. "What are you basing these predictions on? Have you got some amazing magical formula in your phone that spits out all this information, based on records of the last few earthquakes, density, and location? Or are you basing it on the full moon and these recent king tides?" she adds sarcastically.

Sven proceeds to deliberately bombard him with questions in an attempt to bait him and make him spill what he is really up to. "Oh, and by the way, who is that guy Chris I keep bumping in to when I do the odd overtime in the evening? He's always skulking around at night and I'm sure he doesn't need to be on the HR floor at night. Is he one of your team's old cronies from the DSIR days? You 'Sci' guys travel in packs, don't you? Don't you ever get sick of following each other from one company to another? I assume you came from the NZ DSIR equivalent back in the UK? Anyhow, don't you ever want to make a fresh start and have a new staff member with fresh eyes?" The Science team really needs shaking up, she decides – never mind the pun – and with some new fresh blood who would see things differently; someone a little more outgoing and someone who would not be afraid to challenge the status quo, with a personality and the ability to positively engage with others.

"Well if you would just pipe down for the first time in your life for at least just a few minutes, I will answer you." A seething Alex pauses momentarily and then continues talking through his teeth, almost hissing. "It is fact based on raw data, and I am not some astrologer or psychic here just predicting your love life based on where the sun and moon are right now and whether Jupiter and Saturn are aligned. This is the real deal. Take it as you wish, but I am warning you, if you don't get out of town tonight before the rush hour, we won't be having this conversation. This time tomorrow, Wellington and everyone in it will be history."

Sven smiles sweetly. "Sure, I will take your thoughts seriously and touch base with you later."

Sven knows she has seriously overstepped her mark and is off side with Alex having rattled him, but it didn't help having one of his team putting HR down as if they were a bunch of scatterbrain women who were continuously having tea parties and talking trivia and producing nothing of real importance, while men were the superior sex and doing real work. It was time to change the male dominated culture of that team and employ more women. She would suggest this to Bernard when she saw him next. She decided that would be the last Science, Health and IT meeting she would go to for a while; she just couldn't seem to stay engaged for long enough and it was getting obvious.

Sven looks at her Outlook calendar and Bernard's to see when he is next available, mindful that he is very busy with what is happening with the police and remembering that they still aren't on such favourable terms since she accused him of having an affair with Cat on the Friday train. She sends him a meeting invite and a smiley face in the message box, saying: 'My shout, coffee, sorry about my foot in mouth on Friday. It won't happen again (until next time).' She finishes off with another smiley face. Then after thinking about it, texts Bernard, 'Sorry B, but are you aware that Alex wants to tell the Minister directly about a huge Welly earthquake due in a few hours?' then copies Katarina in to follow up with Bernard to cover her own arse. It sounded like a lot of brown-nosing to her, and the sort of thing that Cat would get up to. Any excuse to get herself known with those who could directly influence and fast-forward her career-climbing, as she reaches the dizzying heights of yet another ivory tower detached from all of reality.

*****

Chapter 13

The BS's Coffee Shop, 'Home and Away'

The Ministry have their very own café, 'Home and Away' (HAA), obviously named after the very popular Australian soap opera *Home and Away,* and some of the conversations that can be heard in there could easily have been taken from a typical scene from that show. All conversations threaded with similar themes ranging from sexism, ageism, discrimination, bullying, divorce, burnouts and every mental health issue under the sun. Is there anyone today who is not suffering from some trauma and has some type of syndrome to prove it?

There are around fifty tables all crammed in together within at least an inch of each other in the rectangular space that takes up the rear area behind Reception. Each table has a clear view of what Reception is, or more succinctly is not doing, all the visitors and who is there to meet with them.

As Sven studies all the nooks and crannies around the

Reception area, she realises she is hoping to see Charlie. She can't help herself. She doesn't want to run into him, and yet here she is daring herself to bump into him.

Directly behind Reception is a little open-plan waiting room and this is where from time to time Sven sits and waits for her clients to come in, watching all the background scenes of Reception. Today, as she watches Reception like a hawk, waiting for Charlie, she notices more untoward behaviour than usual. Appallingly there never seems to be anyone in charge of this area. The receptionists are bickering as usual, oblivious that they are the front window to the Ministry.

One of the procurement guys, Winston, recognises Sven and wanders over with his coffee, "Hey, Sven, how are you?" he says as he plonks himself down beside her. "Sorry it's taken so long to get back to you regarding the great coaching you did for my team. I've been really busy. The team were always buzzing after your sessions. Would you be able to come back sometime and run a course on that 'Emotional Intelligence' piece you were talking about?"

"Hey Winston, great to see you. I would love to, that's right down my alley. However, I wonder if that falls under L & D. They would get upset if I took any work off them."

"I thought you said that they outsource all of L & D, therefore I wouldn't be taking it off them, would I? Besides, if you did it in-house it would save BS shitloads of money. You don't charge like a wounded bull, do you?" Winston innocently asks.

"You have a good memory, Winston. No, I'm sorry, it is not best practice to keep the training in-house – they prefer to give it to one of the All of Government's preferred suppliers. Now come on Winston, you are the Commercial

Procurement team, you know how it works," Sven replies jokingly.

Just then Dave the Security guy bursts out of the chair cemetery room and the door slams behind him. "Strange, what's with the door slamming off its hinges like that? What's Security doing in there? There's nothing too secure in there, is there?" asks Sven innocently, plugging Winston to see what he knows about the mysterious activities.

"No, just the horny receptionists; he has obviously been following his JD to a T. The last clause that says, 'And to do all other duties above and beyond, when required'. You've got to admire the guy, he's been getting down and dirty behind the old chair cemetery door since I've been here, and that's going back three years. The stamina of the man has to be admired, that's the third time I've seen him exit that room today!"

Sven and Winston have a laugh and then witness a very upset Fiona bounding out of the room with her buttons on her shirt done up in all the wrong places and her usually perfectly groomed hair out of place. Sven bursts into laughter yet again. "Oh my god Winston, that's the first time I have laughed all day. I must come down here more often. It's amazing what you see, and look – no one else in this huge 'Hall of Fame' has blinked an eyelid over it!"

Winston's client is late, clearly coming from the usual back-to-back meetings scenario. He's glad for the down time and continues to chew the fat with Sven and educate her with some more inside goings-on he has observed in the last few years at BS Castle, with reference to the ground floor personnel.

"Often the big burly Security guys get contracted to us at BS and even if they are not rostered on with us, they get full-time work elsewhere. They also work down the road at those big concerts and gigs, you know the outfit who runs those venues around town. Bit sad, most of their venues are lovely old buildings and have been yellow-stickered and we the patrons suffer as there are less and less events to go to now. Now the council is overcharging the rentals on the remaining venues to try and pay for the earthquake strengthening required and most of the gigs bypass us now and go straight to Auckland or Christchurch, and even Dunedin in the deep south."

Sven replies, "Sorry, I'm new, and just back into Wellington. I have no idea what you are talking about. However, I did go to a gig the other night and there was a showdown with the manager and a patron as the venue had not accommodated for people with wheelchairs coming in, so she was turned away. Ugly scene. It even hit the media."

"Yeah, those people, they wouldn't know how to run an orgy in a brothel, let alone a pop concert at an arena. We were trying to help them out with a tender the other day; the venues are run by the council and council being local government they can fall under our All of Government umbrella. We try to get good deals for any local and central government agency when they are purchasing. In fact, I am waiting for someone from the council now. They are shocking, they have signed up so many contracts with all these dodgy suppliers who are such cowboys that now no one is repairing let alone maintaining their buildings. These lovely old theatres – St James, Opera House, Town Hall, are just wasting away. My background is in quantity surveying, construction and architecture, and I appreciate lovely old buildings, but these ones won't be around in a few years' time due to the complete lack of maintenance."

Sven listens on but is starting to drift and Winston picks this up and gets back on target. "Reception, aye, and the characters that drive her. You know Reception has a great reputation?"

Sven replies, "No, I hadn't heard that one before," laughing at her own choice of words.

"Well they haven't got a great reputation, but they have for reducing the silo effect across departments, especially Security. They have put new meaning to the cliché 'cross-fertilizing' between teams. They used to be a bit more discreet, but now they 'pop it all about' in full view of everyone. However, it appears most people today are suffering from a big dose of distraction blindness, noticing nothing untoward. It's like passengers on the train, when someone talks loudly nonstop on their phone and everyone else continues as if it is not happening."

Winston is on a roll and continues, clearly finding Sven a breath of fresh air after all the stale clones in procurement he works with day in and day out. "It's not half obvious by the way the receptionists greet you on whether they have just got lucky in the stationery cupboard, or whether they are still nervously waiting for Security's arrival. Actions speak louder than words. But then you would know that, wouldn't you, being into coaching and non-verbal gestures and all that 'soft stuff'?"

Sven laughs, relieved she doesn't have to be in a meeting and continues to listen on with amusement. Winston continues. "Sometimes a man can feel like the invisible man, standing there at Reception waiting for someone to look up and acknowledge him, let alone check in his client. In fact, it was so bad some days, one particular receptionist would not bother looking up from the glossy pages of her magazine, no matter how many times I cleared my throat to get her attention."

Sven knows most of the receptionists now by face but not by name and listens on intently. Winston carries on describing two receptionists in particular. "There's the blonde, curly-haired ditzy one called Barbara, and the fiery one, Fiona, both competing for the same man. Real Jekyll and Hyde acts, where some days you get VIP treatment when one of them gets lucky and turns into the most vivacious, accommodating receptionist anyone could ever meet. To the other extreme, when Dave from Security hasn't called she is the complete opposite. Due to all the previous restructures, they have never got around to recruiting a new Head of Front Office and therefore the young girls are not accountable to anyone. And because no one takes responsibility for them they always miss out on each restructure round as no one ever thinks of including them."

Today, with all the goings-on, the receptionists are feeling ruffled and stressed. Sven can hear Fiona talking too loudly with her colleague. "Bugger Dave, if he can't be bothered in turning it up, I mean how could he not get hard being sandwiched between these beauties?" Fiona asks while pushing her ample cleavage together. "If he doesn't have the courtesy to tell me he's not interested then I'm going off sick on domestic leave… nothing like absence to make the heart grow fonder." She gets up and storms out to adjust her blouse and powder her nose.

Winston eventually catches up with his client and leaves Sven to it, who, intrigued by the receptionists, takes advantage of Fiona's abrupt departure and walks on up to Reception to have a chat with Aileen, the older receptionist.

Aileen on the other hand is refreshingly conscientious and has never taken a sick day off in her thirty years of service, and is of a different opinion to the other young receptionists. She is old school; she still has those good old-fashioned values of being loyal and trustworthy to her employer, sticking around for years, turning up every day at the same time, taking her breaks at the required times and having the 4.6 weeks' annual leave at the same time at the same place, with the same husband every year, year in year out. Not to mention the incredibly generous long service leave she acquired after clocking up so much time served as a public servant.

Part of Sven's brief from Bernard was to carry out a very intensive needs analysis, which involved getting around the key areas of the business and asking questions on how systems and jobs could be improved. Bernard's Swedish secretary, Katarina, and Sven's good mate had brought to Bernard's attention a summary version of what the receptionists were up to and suggested a thorough investigation of their activities would not go amiss. Sven, wanting to see more of what was happening from the ground up so to speak, and besides, any excuse to escape the predictability and boredom of HR or attending pointless meetings, approaches Aileen. "That didn't look like a very happy camper, is she okay?"

"Hmm, how the young people have changed so much, they just don't seem to care, this Gen Y/Millennials or whatever they call it, everything and everyone has to happen right now, but preferably yesterday and if they don't it's all one huge sulking fest. No, Barbara nor her so-called mate Fiona are not okay. They are both competing for the same men, often going off to different stationery cupboards at the same time and then when they get back, they swap men, trying to make each other jealous! Even though the men deny it, the irony of it is they are both already married. Where are these peoples' ethics or standards? These men are just lapping it up! Also, with all the dramas going on, Security has had to actually work today. There just hasn't been the usual time for them to hang around with their idle chatter and banter. It's all hands to the pump rather than 'on' the pump so to speak."

Sven bursts into laughter again as this older woman, who appears conservative at the best of times, refers to Dave's appendage. She has visions again of what his pump has been up to and leaving behind, almost grossing herself out and desperately tries to blank out that mental image.

Aileen continues, oblivious to Sven going red in the face. "Unfortunately the silly girl has taken it all rather personally and thinks the universe revolves solely around her, and one of her fan club hasn't been to visit because he is not interested in her anymore. Can't she see the place is swarming with police trying to get to the bottom of this very nasty business? Oh no, it's all about her."

Sven can't help laughing for the third time within the hour. She always laughed when older women and those who appeared so well-spoken or sweet and innocent spoke unexpectedly like that. However, Aileen was right, working with some of the younger generation could be a right pain, but then there was the fun side of working with young, fresh faces who brought in young, fresh ideas. The only problem was they wanted all the latest technology, phones, latest fashions and to be promoted and laid ASAP! Everything had this dire urgency; everything had to be delivered almost instantly so one could enjoy that adrenalin surge of instant gratification.

*****

Today, the Home and Away café is buzzing even more than usual and everyone who is anyone is queuing up waiting to order their coffees. The queues are so long they are snaking around past Reception and the eight sets of lifts all the way out onto the street. It is like queuing up for a concert hours before the venue has even opened let alone before the main stars arrive. Standing waiting in line is a good excuse to just stand and stare and take in all the movement and ambience. There are cops, public servants and paparazzi everywhere.

Dave appears from the mens' room and positions himself by Lift A and resumes duty. The Head of Security is nowhere to be found and Dave, as usual, is not accountable to anyone. Fiona leaves the powder room and as she makes her way back to Reception, she notices him there. Walking up to the café counter she picks up a full jug of iced water and makes it look like she is going back to her desk with it. She suddenly sidesteps and pours the complete contents of the jug over Dave who is left standing there saturated from top to toe.

"Take that, you big tosser, that will cool you down and stop you panting over your other girlfriend Barbara, you S.O.B.!"

Dave, completely losing it, goes to take a swing at her and at the last minute remembers where he is, right in the middle of a public place with half the café's patrons staring straight at him. He thinks first and then quietly says, "You'll keep. You weren't that good anyhow. Least Barb knows how to satisfy a man, more than what you can do, honey. I will leave it to you to clean up that little mess here, shall I?" He points to the water on the floor.

Fiona can't believe the words that are coming out of his mouth. "So that's why you couldn't get it up. Thanks for confirming my suspicion, I didn't know for sure. How dare you two-time me, and with Barbara Big Nose of all people, you two-timing S.O.B.!" she retorts, red-faced, and turns and runs back to the ladies', almost slipping in the puddle of water that has now spread out across Reception. Aileen calls Health and Safety as cones are needed to isolate the area to avoid any patrons or staff slipping unnecessarily.

With that drama well and truly over, not to mention that relationship, Dave's boss Lewis returns from the other side of the foyer, oblivious to what has just happened. He has bigger fish to fry. He has been watching the crowds snowballing all day in and out of the café.

The paparazzi who are playing undercover as patrons have now split from their crews and are trying to blend in more while standing in the queue, pretending that their sole purpose is to get a coffee. These paparazzi parasites are not sniffing out coffee beans, but sniffing out today's leading story hoping they will hear some juicy news and be the first to pounce on it.

As Wellington is so small, known as 'the village', many faces become readily recognisable. Hence it doesn't take long for Head of Security, Lewis, to take the familiar journo faces aside and question them for ID. Once he knows they are journos they are escorted out of the queues, although at the end of the day it is not illegal for a journalist to queue up for a coffee.

Home and Away (HAA) has been humming away and

takings have been healthy and high for four hours by the time the cops realise what they are dealing with and have it shut down. To be fair, a serious crime has just gone down and they need to interview the staff and look for evidence; they can't allow the downstairs café to be left open in one of the key crime scenes and risk letting any Tom, Dick and Lars waltz in.

Finally, Sven catches a glimpse of Charlie as he walks through, her heart skipping a beat. Her logical brain takes over; here is the opportunity to have a talk with him. She needs to know what progress is being made. Also, why has no one found her yet to interview her? She was probably one of the last people to see Cat on the train Friday evening and wants to clear her name. And there is the small matter of her and Charlie parting ways that still hasn't been resolved.

Decisively Sven plucks up enough courage – this is her chance, and walks confidently up to Charlie. She hears him talking to the manager of HAA. "Hi, Zelda, is it? Look, I'm very sorry Zelda, this is the centre of a crime scene and we need to collect evidence. I appreciate this is your busiest time, but we now need to shut the café down."

Charlie, not wanting to cause a scene, asks Reception to make an announcement. "Excuse me, ladies and gentlemen, I apologise in advance, but Home and Away café is now closing. Please finish up your refreshments and make your way through the front door. We do apologise for any inconvenience. Have a nice day."

A lot of high-pitched voices, especially from the inconvenienced women dressed in their matching power suits can be heard echoing all around the atrium.

No one seems to be going anywhere fast, so Charlie gets on the intercom. "Ladies and gentlemen, as you are aware the BS Building was yellow-stickered due to the recent earthquake. All those eight floors of pretty heritage glass windows you can see above you are considered severe hazards. If an earthquake hits us now, there is nothing protecting you from this glass. It could get messy. The engineers have instructed us to evacuate the café/conservatory area. It is in your best interests, ladies and gentlemen."

Charlie, like Sven, is very quick at thinking on his feet, sensibly refraining from alerting everyone to the real reason why they are evacuating the café.

It works a treat as people move a lot faster than they did following the receptionist's first message. "Now no one wants to see in Christmas Day in a hospital bed, do they? It's not a good look having shards of glass protruding out of our…" Charlie says quietly to his partner Rex, once the intercom is switched off. Charlie sometimes has the tendency to take advantage of his super good looks and add a load of sarcasm when dealing with the public. In the main he really enjoys working with people but sometimes they just act so dumb.

Sven watches on in amazement, before boldly marching up to Reception. "Well, Charlie Rogers, you haven't changed at all, have you? Have you got ten minutes? I think I have something you will be interested in hearing. Shall we?" She points to the seat she had been sitting in minutes earlier behind Reception. Sven does her best to remain cool and collected, she has had all morning to rehearse her lines and control her composure. Unbeknown to her, Charlie had clocked her earlier in the day and had been doing the same, rehearsing in his head how he would approach her.

Making a quick call as they walk towards the booth,

"Yes Bernard, I have her here," he says as he passes the phone to Sven.

"Sven, look I know this is unorthodox but the Minister is spitting fire and brimstone from the hospital, we need to help the police to get to the bottom of this ASAP! Can you…"

Within ten minutes all one hundred and ninety-eight Home and Away customers have evacuated the building. The café is closed and cordoned off with police tape and two ex-lovers have called a truce.

Outside BS the roads are pandemonium once again, with people and cars intertwined around all four roads surrounding the building. Complete mayhem. Security has called in their Traffic Management team in an attempt to manage the mess and keep it under control.

*****

Chapter 14

Interview with Veronica

Veronica is a long-standing member of HR; she has come up through the ranks alongside Stephanie, starting at the same time. However, she has made it to the dizzying heights of Senior Learning and Development Advisor as opposed to the Assistant HR Director. She is one of the people Rex and Charlie are interested in interviewing.

Charlie's offsider Rex starts the line of questioning. Rex is tall, slim, average weight, but very muscly in all the right places. Nothing to look at, but like all good coppers oozes that X-factor of 'Don't mess with me'. He's been in the police force for as long as Charlie and they have been working together as 'partners in crime' for a very long time; they are like a typical old married couple who finish each other's sentences. In his mid-forties, he is starting to go grey, but like most men has that distinguished salt and pepper look.

"So, Veronica, is it?" Rex confirms. "Can you please tell us about your interactions with Ms Tennyson last Friday?"

"Well, it's a bit like this." Veronica takes a deep breath and starts talking as only someone with ADHD and one too many coffees can. "You know I'm part of the L & D team and my boss Sarita has tasked me with the responsibility of spreading the news that the BS Ministry actually does have an L & D team and that they need to utilise our services, because if we don't have any internal clients we will be made redundant. Well of course I don't say that last part, but that's what my HOD Sarita says."

"Sorry, what's HOD? And how does this relate to Ms Tennyson's activities on Friday?" Charlie asks. He has been given an organisational chart which resembles that of an incestuous South Carolina redneck family tree, but he has been told it is out of date and therefore is not of much use. He scans the document all the same and is still none the wiser as to how Veronica fits into the big scheme of things.

Veronica glares at Charlie. "I'm getting there, okay? HOD is Head of Department, silly, and if you don't have the full picture to begin with, then you might think I have something to do with this mess!" Veronica explains impatiently. "Now, where was I? Oh yes, so that's why on Friday we were having a meeting about the L & D Approach, which we had just finished writing. It's only taken nine months and we had just got word that it had been approved by SLT! So, we were having a little celebration. Kirsty had brought in a yummy batch of her gluten-free, sugar-free, low-calorie vegan brownies. We had to celebrate as we are just so happy that we are now safe for another round. Safe as houses in fact – well, at least until the next restructure."

"Let me interrupt you there, Veronica, you are losing me. I am not sure again how this is relevant?" asks Rex. Charlie is in a state of shock about the sheer stupidity the girl is displaying and if this is the average IQ let alone EQ of the Ministry, then heaven help the country! Maybe he is just prejudging unfairly and putting all the BS employees in one box, when it is only L & D he should be labelling.

Veronica, oblivious to what Rex is saying and to what Charlie is not saying, continues on in her merry way. "So now we need to create a workshop to determine what actions need to be taken going forward. Because we still don't know what 'Approach' means, as in the 'L & D Approach' we have been working on. I mean we know what 'Strategy' means, but not 'Approach'. But we are not allowed to design our own workshops – that must be outsourced. I guess it's a bit like you guys, you know you are the subject matter experts in solving crimes, so we have indirectly outsourced you to come in. And you are a government department like us, so it's part of our AOG policy. We are all part of the same happy family." She stops talking and looks to the two men for some clarification.

"I'm sorry, Veronica, you have lost us again. What has the Assembly of God got to do with the police force?"

"Wow, you guys really are quite stupid, aren't you? I mean no offence – AOG – everyone knows what that means." She starts laughing. "Oh my god, I am so funny, I just said the word 'offence' and that is what has happened, an offence has been committed and that's why you guys are here to solve it!"

Charlie now speaks up. "Ah, yes, you are one smart cookie, or is that a gluten-free, vegan, sugar-free, chocolate-free, chocolate-coated brownie?" Charlie can no longer contain himself and part of his sarcastic defence mechanism kicks in. He can't work out if she is trying to wind them up or whether she is naturally thick, and if this is representative of the BS Ministry, then the interviews and investigation will take forever.

Veronica, with the emotional intelligence of a gnat, continues. "You see we don't really know what our jobs look like. Someone's 'piece of work' is doing a stocktake of what our jobs look like now, even though we have out-of-date job descriptions, then they will work out what the JDs should look like, and how many consultants need to be brought in to do the new stuff and so it then all becomes BAU."

Rex is still hanging in there as he is determined to crack this case – and this nutcase. "And BAU, is this another one of your fancy acronyms? Do you mind sharing with us AOG followers what that's about?" He's not sure whether to laugh, cry or just terminate this interview. It is one of his first with BS and he wants to believe this is just a small glitch and the calibre of interviewees are going to get better, like wine does with age.

"Well, it means 'business as usual'. Like 'AOG' is 'All of Government'. Anyhow, as we have had so many restructures and so many backfills, things are constantly changing, and no one really knows what their normal everyday job is. But having said that we are extremely busy and always running from one place to another getting our 'piece of work' done."

Charlie stops fiddling with his pen while looking out the window and wakes up to hear 'piece of work'.

"'Piece of work', Ms Jones, now would you consider

yourself to be a real 'piece of work'?"

Veronica completely misses his sarcastic sense of humour and his play on words. In Charlie's mind she is one painfully unaware piece of work who is clearly high maintenance and he realises he isn't going to get much more sense out of her. Changing his tone from being the good, patient guy, he finishes with repeating the question several times until she gets it. "Ms Jones, this is a very important case and we must get some answers. As you and your team are incredibly busy I don't want to take up much more of your time working out what it is you do. However, what I do need to get from you is what dealings did you have with Ms Tennyson on Friday?"

Veronica replies, "Well, why didn't you just ask that at the beginning? I would have told you."

"We did, it's just that you were too busy telling us about how you spend your Friday afternoons in the office. So once more, what dealings did you have with Ms Tennyson last Friday or any other day of the week that may help us find out what happened to her?"

"Well, nothing really, but I can tell you that every time we start a very important new 'piece of work' Cat cans it as the priorities and projects change again, or someone else comes in to do it. She does that with a few people, and people get upset. We are not allowed to ask her too many questions because she complains that we are 'doing her head in'. Sometimes she is quite rude, and fobs us off and says she needs to go and have a cup of coffee or must run to another meeting, telling us our time is up and she will get her EA to reschedule another meeting. But she never does. She reckons she's keeping the pharmacy across the road in business as she visits them often to get aspirins to get rid of her headaches. In fact, the other day I heard Elspeth, her EA say that the chemist had run out of both aspirins and paracetamol."

"Now that's interesting, you are saying Cat was taking a lot of OTC drugs?" asks Rex.

"What's OTC? I don't understand what you mean."

"Well that makes three of us, doesn't it? Don't you know what OTC means?" Charlie can't help dishing back some of Veronica's lines to her, but realises he can't go too far.

"Over-the-counter medicine, so you don't need a prescription."

"Oh no, she had a whole lot of prescription drugs as well. I sat quite close to Cat and Elspeth, so I used to hear Elspeth reminding Cat to take her medication and Cat used to refuse or forget and then suddenly down them all at once as she had forgotten to take them for days on end. She loved taking them with diet coke or that zero coke stuff, which I am sure wasn't that great – coke, coffee and… Also, she hardly ever ate. She never came to our free coffee and cake celebrations. She was always far too busy for that. She was so skinny; she got skinnier and skinnier and was proud of it, coming in with size eight dresses she had just purchased from David Jones, showing off her latest fashions for all to see. While the rest of the millennials around here were finding it hard enough to make ends meet by paying the landlord, or some lucky enough to be paying the bank directly with a mortgage."

"So, Ms Tennyson was taking a few drugs, OTC and prescription?" asks Rex.

"Yes, but who isn't nowadays? At least it was all legal. But Friday nights some of us would stay behind for a few wines on our floor and Cat would join us from time to time, but by the time she got there at five o'clock she was already high as a kite! Some of us suspect that Cat had been elsewhere for a wine or two and had a head start on the rest of us. Look, I feel I am saying too much now, I don't want to dob her in. If I had a high-powered job like that I would probably be running around on adrenalin and be self-medicating myself to get through the day. None of our HR Directors last very long. Well, that's not true – Stephanie was Acting HR Director for ages before Cat got here. In fact, we thought Stephanie would be the new HR Director. I know she went for the job, because Nigel in Recruiting told me. Whoops, I shouldn't have said that, should I? That was confidential."

Rex humours her as he has had time to anchor himself and feels he is starting to get some good information out of her. He decides it is worth persevering with her for a bit longer. "Look Veronica, you are doing an absolutely fabulous job, and we have almost finished. Just one more question. What can you tell us about Stephanie?"

"Oh, she's nice enough, she's been here for a long time, she leaves you alone mostly. Like Cat, she is too far up the chain for anyone to know her intimately. She keeps to herself. We did start at the same time together, but that's about all we have in common."

Rex questions her a bit more. "Why do you say the word 'intimately' and Stephanie in the same sentence?"

Veronica shuts down, looks incredibly guilty and focuses on the table to hide her face which is now a slight shade of red. "It was nothing – it was just a flyaway comment. I meant nothing by it. Look, gentlemen, if there is nothing else, I need to get back to doing my 'words on a page' as it's part of this HR Personality focus group I have been asked to come in and help with."

Rex has started nervously tapping the desk with his Bic Biro pen, and the tapping is becoming more and more intense. Silence swallows the room up and he realises she has stopped talking, thankfully. He fills the silence with, "Sounds interesting and an effective use of taxpayers' money. Okay. Well, Ms Jones, thanks very much for your time, we really appreciate it. If there is anything else, here is my number."

Charlie bounces in, "Look Veronica, I really appreciate you being so open with us today. If you would feel better talking to someone closer to home so to speak, you know there is always Samantha, who I know would be happy to have a chat. Thanks, Veronica," and he opens the door to lead her out.

He then gets straight on the phone to Sven. They had had a brief chat with introductions and small talk downstairs, breaking the ice after all those years, which made the call relatively easy. "Hey Sven, I have a potential client for you to talk to. Veronica Jones, from L & D, do you know her? Well, we got some interesting info. It would be good if we could catch up later, but basically, 1. Did you know Cat was on OTC drugs and prescription drugs? And 2. What do you know about Stephanie, in particular the intimate side of her life? Any love interests?"

"Hmm, no, I didn't know about the drug stuff," Sven replies, "but Stephanie, I think she has the hots for Bernard. I'm not so sure about her – maybe she bats both ways, who would know? I've tried to talk to her, but haven't got very far as she seems so touchy. I'm scared of tipping her over the edge. I think she is holding back on something. Do you want me to try again?"

"Yes, thanks, that would be great, *bra hej.*" Charlie tries to get clever; he had been looking up the meaning of a few commonly used Swedish words so he could impress Sven. He detected that she was still a bit cool towards him when they were chatting earlier and it was time bygones were bygones.

Rex looks at him sideways. "Mate, ease up, I know you two go way back, but less of the sexual connotations. Getting up close and personal by talking about her bra is probably not a good move and so not PC. Remember you are meant to be heading this investigation, so settle down boy."

"Mate, chill out, for your information – or FYI if I'm going to do the HR acronym thing, *bra* means good, and *hej* is goodbye, or hello, according to this Swedish language glossary app I downloaded, so all sweet."

"Yeah, right!" Rex mimics the Tui beer advertisement.

"What do you make of all that stuff? Let's get someone to go over to the pharmacy on the Quay and check out what drugs Cat had been prescribed. It will tell us who her specialist is, so that may lead to where those regular appointments were. Also, let's get someone to go and empty her desk again and see if there is anything else of interest. And take some fingerprints. I feel like we are actually getting somewhere. I think our Ms Tennyson wasn't as cocksure and confident as she made out to be. Perhaps another one of those suffering from the imposter syndrome," Charlie theorises.

"Oh god, you are losing me today mate, all this new corporate jargon, abbreviations, and now Swedish and a bit of psychology thrown in. Do I need to ask the boss for a bit of PD so I can catch up to you?" Rex queries with a grin.

"What PD, periodic detention?"

"No bro, professional development, get with the programme."

They both laugh. "Right, who is the next culprit?"

"God, I wish Forensics would hurry up and get back to us with the cause of death. These interviews are really taking it out of me. I thought some of the white tops down at the station were a bit past it and boring, but this lot here, they are a completely different kettle of fish. Maybe it's an age thing, but our lingo is so different to theirs, it's like being on assignment overseas, where English is their second language."

"Hey, Charlie, can't you pull some strings with Forensics? We need a better lead on this investigation. I don't know how many more Veronicas I can take!" Rex pleads.

"Yeah mate, under control. Now get someone to follow up with Cat's medical record and check out her desk again. Also, who is searching her house?"

"Oh, I forgot to tell you, Cat's neighbour has called in with some additional information. Evidently, no one has seen Cat since Friday morning, but some guy has been seen popping over there. To Bob the neighbour, it looked like some tradie fix-it guy as he had some gadget he was installing. He's been seen a couple of times during the day, when Cat was at work, and he was seen on Friday evening and then again, today."

"Okay, get Bob in for questioning as well, so we can get a description of the guy, maybe even an identikit picture of who he saw at Cat's."

"Hey, you know there is some truth behind this sun and

Swedish thing. When I was talking with Sven downstairs she was telling me about what she had been up to. She's been living in Sweden, and was telling me that a lot of people over there commit suicide over the winter because they are so deprived of sunshine and Vitamin D. Now with these window blinds permanently down due to safety issues, everyone is sitting in darkness for eight or nine hours a day. Have you also noticed that most people don't go outside for lunch, they just sit at their desk or in a break out room?"

"No wonder people go stir crazy; if you work all week, you miss any chance of getting some sunshine as you're too busy wasting away in a building all day and then commuting. The weekend comes and if it isn't fine, you could go for weeks missing sunshine and fresh air, and with no vitamin D your immune system is down and your feel-good chemicals are redundant. Which in turn leads people to grab a quick fix like a coffee, drink, smoke, prescription drugs, whatever their poison is and their body basically – like my car – is running on empty. You can only sustain it for so long but in the long-term your system is heading for a crash. I'm glad we do shift work and get to play when others are stuck inside."

"Yeah, and adding to a lack of vit D and feeling down, everyone in town is nervous about when the next earthquake is coming and being separated from their loved ones. With no public transport operating, they're cut off. It's a pretty depressing state of affairs, that's why I like living up the line. Palmy is just right for me, well away from all this drama and political BS," Charlie adds.

Rex interrupts. "Right, sermon over? I think that Swedish girl is getting to you, she was going on about the same stuff and now you're like a parrot, repeating it almost word for word."

Charlie shuts him down. "Right after that intense conversation I need to go and grab a coffee and have a smoke, and as you would say, go and self-medicate. I'm on the other end of the phone if you need me. Let me know who the next one is?"

Charlie walks off with the same thoughts as Sven. He needs to go and find her. They have unfinished business, and she can help them with their line of enquiries now that she has been seconded to the investigation.

*****

Chapter 15

HR meeting to determine the HR Personality

Sharon, Margot and Bernice file into the meeting room they book every week to determine what the HR Personality looks like, feels like and how to move forward by massaging and shaping it. Unfortunately, nothing has moved forward in weeks – in fact months, as they just can't agree on a 'personality' that fits all. Today is no different except Veronica has sent her apologies as she is traumatised after her police interview. They all look like stunned mullets with pen, paper and phone clutched to their sides, but all are expressionless. Sven constantly feels the same every time she psyches herself up to take on the next meeting of boredom.

The feeling on every floor has suddenly changed, you could cut the atmosphere with a knife. Even the IT geeks who are usually far too busy dealing with pressing computer and network issues can sense something is up.

Security and the fledgling Incident Management teams, HR, IT, Finance, Health and Safety, Comms, everyone except for Science can sense something is up.

"Everything okay?" Stephanie asks enquiringly as the HR advisors slink past. Sharon just stares back and doesn't answer as she continues walking towards the meeting room.

The three ladies plonk themselves down at the round table and collapse. "What on earth just happened? I am in a state of shock. I want to go home. I don't feel safe," says Bernice, sighing more than usual. Bernice is known for communicating solely through her constant sighs, although she is totally oblivious to the fact. Those who don't know her may take it personally, thinking she's bored with them.

"Hey," says Margot, yet another Senior HR Advisor, who realises she has to step up now as she is one of the advisors who has been around the longest. The label 'senior' implies she should be the wisest, however, the job descriptions read exactly the same for juniors and seniors. It appears discriminatory to call someone a junior, but it is okay to be called a senior. Staff members are either labelled an Advisor of some sort or a Senior Advisor. Margot continues after thinking carefully what she is going to say next. "Look, I am sure nothing untoward happened. You know Cat has been working really hard these last few weeks, and preparing for this stand-up today, I know she was really on edge. You know, in confidence, and I shouldn't really say anything, but she has been pushing herself to the max. I can't put my finger on it but there was something distracting her, and I can't work out if it was something good or bad, but Cat wasn't being her usual self."

Bernice finds her voice. "What do you mean? With all due respect, Cat was being her normal self, she was working us really hard and anyone who couldn't keep up she was dispensing with. You know how she works. Look what she did to Ted, down in Science. What do you mean she wasn't acting her normal self?"

"Look, everything isn't as it appears. Ted was happy to leave, he was nearing retirement and he struck a good deal, it was a win-win for everyone. Now, moving onto other more pressing and sensitive issues – and this is just between you two and mustn't go any further – I've been talking with Cat's EA Elspeth. I have had to get quite a few sign-offs recently from Cat and when I would look at her diary, it clearly stated that she was here, but when I went to her desk, she was never there. I double-checked with Elspeth who said according to her diary Cat should have been in the office. As it happened on one occasion, I had to shoot off across the park to score a pair of stockings from David Jones, and I saw her outside Dunbar Sloane's talking to someone."

"Hang on, slow down, nosey parker. Who is Mr Sloane when he's at home? Are you referring to some Sloane Ranger from London, is he royalty?"

"No, Dunbar Sloane's, it's the name of the auction rooms. You must know what I'm talking about, they've been there for yonks. They specialise in selling antique furniture, silver, paintings – you know, all the superior quality stuff that comes from deceased estates."

"Really? Wow, who knew. Anyhow, do go on."

"Well, with Cat, it seemed odd, seeing her having a serious meeting in the middle of the street of all places. I did think it was weird and she was talking to some slime ball, you know, not the sort of person our Cat would normally be seen dead with... Whoops, sorry about the pun, but..."

Sven is running late as usual – she is meant to be doing the 'guest speaker' stint at the Personality meeting. She really finds the girls that run this meeting ironically lacking in any resemblance of personality at all and is not sure why they out of everyone were chosen to determine 'personality' when they don't even have one between them. Perhaps she could give them some tips, so she takes along some definitions of 'personality' and a few of her personality tests.

Sven walks in and realises she has just walked into something pretty heavy as everyone looks more perplexed, if that's possible, than usual.

The more boring one of the three speaks up and says, "Margot, you need to tell the cops about this, this is not something we should be bantering about here."

Sven pipes up in her breezy manner, "Apologies ladies, for being late. It looks like I may have missed something big. Can you back up a bit so I can get the gist?"

The three are tight-lipped and there is no way they are letting some outsider barge in on their tight threesome and get the goss.

They pretend they are ever so interested in their neatly typed minutes and like synchronised swimmers, start ticking off the items on the agenda together, to give the impression they are already halfway through the formal side of their meeting.

Sven plays them at their own game. "Ladies, I just want to say I have been very impressed with the way you have run this project and the results so far speak for themselves. I don't know why Cat used to say what she did. I personally think you are doing an excellent job."

It works a little and one of them defending Cat to the bitter end thaws a bit and opens up. "No, I'm sure it was nothing. It wasn't a big deal, I just wanted to say our Cat was under a lot of pressure, wasn't she?"

Sven, repeating herself, says, "So what have I really missed, ladies?"

"WAIT! Just what is happening out there?" Bernice interrupts, pointing towards a commotion in the HR area.

"Who is that dressed as a latin ball room dancer?" Margot asks.

"No, freakin' way…that's Lloyd! From the mailroom." Sharon exclaims.

The meeting quite forgotten as all the women are riveted staring at the unfolding drama, as Lloyd dressed in pin-striped pants, black waistcoat with shiny lapels, a flowing red silken shirt with the collar turned up and a rose clamped firmly between his teeth, pushes the play button on a portable Bluetooth player and dances seductively towards a totally surprised Carmen.

The whole floor has stopped what they are doing, enraptured. Lloyd does a magnificent twirl as he reaches Carmen's desk, presents her with the rose and as she receives the offered flower, he takes her other hand, draws her to her feet and kisses her passionately, before taking her into his arms. Carmen hastily throws her handbag over her arm and Lloyd tango dances her towards the lifts, leaving the floor and everyone speechless.

"Well, I've never seen that before!" Sharon breaks the silence, picking up her files.

Margot closes the meeting and stays behind to catch Sven up. After listening intently, with this latest information

Sven feels a visit to Elspeth, Cat's EA is well in order. She puts that in her phone's calendar to follow up on, and sends Charlie a quick text, 'Following a lead, talk soon'.

Sven contemplates her recent findings. Cat has been seen around town and on the coast with a few different characters that no one seems to recognise. She wonders if she was doing her usual and recruiting on the side, missing out the middle man, the Recruiting team. Or was she into something else entirely? She wonders who these shady characters are Cat had been seeing.

*****

PART 4

LATE MONDAY AFTERNOON

All is revealed, or is it?

Chapter 16

Meeting with Jillian, Cat's consultant

After the meeting, it becomes clearly obvious to Sven that more than half the building is allergic to work. She can't believe that so many of the HR team are away. Why is this? It is also becoming clearer as the hours race by that most people who had last spoken with Cat on Friday are not at work today. Why is that? Is there a connection?

Most of those who did choose to turn up to work today in the old-fashioned way are subjected to being jammed away in interview rooms, leaving the remaining ones on the floor unsupervised and unmotivated, doing very little.

Sven is sitting at her desk, looking through her ipad and comes across a poem she had written about Cat when sitting in one of those long drawn-out tedious meetings with her. She reads the notes she had made on that particular day, and now feels guilty about writing it.

The meeting had been full of the usual trite and trivia, with most people communicating in their usual passive-aggressive way, getting their colleagues' backs up. Sven had decided she might as well join in and do her own character assassination, but from the safety of her own ipad.

CAT

Cat's short and a little wide

When HR see her they run and hide

Dark hair and piercing green eyes

She stretches the truth with her big, white lies

Our Cat has one of those unusual faces

Thinks she's Lady Muck with airs and graces

She loves to shriek at the top of her voice

Sporting everything top of the range like Rolls Royce

And ALL projects need to be finished like yesterday

No wonder staff never seem to stay

Results driven she's a real tough cookie

Off with her bosses having nookie

Only designer clothes will ever do

Empathy and kindness she hasn't a clue

Her tongue sharpened to a razor's edge

Are you part of her cult like Sister's Sledge?

With Cat she'll make you bow and sweat

She'll get her pound of flesh, you wanna bet?

However, when all is said and done

You'll learn a lot as she can be lots of fun

With a great sense of humour, very dry

But if not careful she'll make you cry

She does have her favourites so you could be in

She has the 'Shark with Lipstick' type of grin...

Nervous that someone may read over her shoulder, Sven snaps her ipad shut and looks around.

She does a quick scan of the sixth floor and all she can see is Stephanie shuffling through papers nervously on Cat's desk, and decides to see what's happening.

As Sven approaches Stephanie at Cat's desk, she notices the top desk drawer is slightly open and she can see a collection of what appears to be prescription packets strewn haphazardly throughout the drawer. Remembering her recent chat with Charlie about drugs, Sven positions herself closer. While pretending to jot down some notes on her ipad, she peers into the drawer. Frustratingly, the boxes and containers are overlapping each other and she can't see everything, but she does take note of the familiar packaging for Fluoxetine, Epilim and something else that is half concealed – Tetra-something. Not wanting to be too obvious, an anxious Stephanie startles as her private space is being invaded. Coming from large cities, one is used to people being so close due to being huddled on public transport together or walking down the street in clusters, whereas in New Zealand there is more room and the private space around people is a little larger.

Sven has carried out several personality profiles of

the different key players in HR, but not Stephanie, so she is keen to find out more about her. Stephanie had been with the organisation way before the merge and Sven is interested in finding what makes her tick.

"Hi Stephanie, I thought I would find you over here. At least someone took on board what Bernard had to say downstairs. It looks like most of your team has deserted you. I know it's a bit of a stupid question, but how is your day going? I bet you didn't expect it to turn out like it has?"

Stephanie nervously looks up and says nothing, looking even more gobsmacked than usual.

Sven tries again, this time a little more casually. "I'm sorry I couldn't attend the last-minute HRLT meeting on Friday. Did I miss anything?"

Stephanie is present, but no one is at home. Sven, seeing she is on edge, doesn't want to be the straw as usual that breaks the camel's back and cause Stephanie to lose the plot, especially today of all days. She finishes off by saying, "Hey listen, if you need to talk to anyone about anything, I am always here. Bernard speaks very highly of you and it would be great to be able to have a coffee with you sometime. Obviously not today as too much is happening, and you are thankfully holding the fort. By the way, you are doing a wonderful job, but I'm sure you know that." Sven for the first time feels sorry for Stephanie and she genuinely wants to help, but nothing she is saying seems to be making a difference.

She is just about to walk away when she sees Stephanie's eyes water up. "Hey, I'm sorry, I didn't want to upset you. We are all finding it really stressful and each of us is just trying to deal with it in the best way we know how. Hang in there and like I said, if you ever want to talk, you know where to find me."

She walks away and logs onto her computer to have a look at the minutes from last Friday's HRLT meeting. She had heard a little about what had happened and scribbled down some notes. She reflects on the reaction from Stephanie, certain she is at tipping point and hiding something. Usually Sven would persevere, but she doesn't believe that the time is quite right. She intends to try again soon, as she taps into her phone diary another follow-up reminder. She must talk to Bernard about Stephanie and find out what he knows about her. He must know heaps as they are almost weekend next-door neighbours at the bach. She makes another note to tell Charlie about the prescriptions in Cat's top drawer, if he hasn't already checked that out. Surely Cat's desk should be out of bounds.

Sven had heard on the grapevine that the Friday HRLT meeting had got a little overheated as the various managers could not agree on how many people from their respective teams should be shoulder-tapped to take voluntary redundancy, without leading to yet another personal grievance (PG). HRLT, the Human Resources Leadership Team comprising of all the senior leaders and acting leaders in the large, ever-expanding HR department meet monthly. They usually meet after the SLT have met, and the agenda covers what SLT is up to, staff changes and developments. It's usually to discuss another major 'piece of work' that has come up and how many backfills have been requested and approved to cover these last-minute projects, but Friday's agenda had been dominated by Cat's redundancy drive.

The Recruiting team naturally believed they didn't need to downsize but do the opposite, upsize the numbers on their team, and were happy to be team players as usual and compromise by settling for contractors versus permanent staff.

The Employment Relations team said with all the personal grievances they couldn't cope as it was, the result being their most trusted workers were having burnouts and had been signed off to have virtually unlimited sick leave until they were strong enough to come back.

The Learning and Development team (L & D) said they needed more time to formulate a strategy, or was it an approach? They get mixed up with the two. However, they need to come up with a plan for their future and due to last year's restructure they had not had time to get their feet back under the table and come up with a plan of attack, let alone implement it.

The Organisational Development team needed to rewrite an induction plan for managers coming on board, as the last lot of managers that had started complained there hadn't been a single introduction and no handover. They were unaware of how to do their jobs effectively and who the go-to people were to find out more about their job, and their job descriptions were either not finished or out of date and the go-to people had been made redundant in the last round of staff cutbacks.

The different HR sub departments all had their say and the two hours allocated for the meeting had not been long enough. They had run out of time and by the sounds of it had run out of steam. No one could agree to a) Who should, as Cat would say, 'be sliced' let alone b) Who of the remaining should then 'be diced'. It was a tall order expecting them to come up with these answers and especially on a Friday afternoon with just two weeks to go before Christmas.

The meeting had started at 1pm and was still going after 3pm. Sven had been booked out with one-to-one coaching sessions and only heard bits of what had happened when Carmen came storming over to the break out room where Sven was coaching.

Carmen had become quite upset and could be heard over the partition saying, "Damn that insensitive cruel woman! I could kill her for the way she spoke to us all! I am not going to tell my staff that they are surplus to requirement. I am not, especially at this time of the year, going to tell my staff that having been here the longest means that they are lucky because they are on the old employment agreement (IEA) and are still entitled to redundancy. Then go on about how fortunate they are as they will get a poxy four to six weeks' redundancy for the first year and two weeks for each year they have worked after that, and that means they are entitled to around six months' salary each! I mean to say where does six months' salary go nowadays, once you have paid a portion of your mortgage off and you still have at least fifteen years left until it is all paid off? Not to mention the growing epidemic discrimination called 'ageism' which is prevalent in the workforce, just where are they supposed to find work?"

"Oh, and then Madam's parting shot was, "I have noticed you are now in your late forties, early fifties so your use-by date has well and truly expired and no one will look at you twice for an office job now, so off you go to run a checkout counter at the local supermarket!"

Carmen was not particularly good at hiding her feelings and the look on her face said it all; she was highly embarrassed, her face had gone beetroot red and her bottom lip was quivering. People who knew her knew that when her bottom lip quivered it meant she was about to either break down in tears or get a grip and turn to that steely look of revenge best served cold.

If Sven had known Friday's session was going to be so interesting, she would have definitely made a point of gate-crashing the meeting.

Carmen was understandably upset as she was very loyal to her staff. She may have looked like the Wicked Witch from the West with that severely bleached hair, non-matching tattooed black eyebrows and serious layers of thick, black mascara and green eye shadow, not to mention the bright pink lipstick she had acquired back in the eighties when she joined the Civil Service gravy train. Maybe she had bought her life supply of lipstick at the same time Aileen in Reception had bought her orange supply. Maybe two for the price of one, as the department stores were so desperate to offload it all.

However, Carmen had a tendency to be quite hard underneath and she would bat through and through for her team. Originally when Cat had come on board, she and Carmen were as thick as thieves, but of recent times the expanding cracks, like the aftershocks of the recent earthquake or the cracks in the thick layers of foundation plastered on Carmen's face, were beginning to show.

Sven finishes jogging her memory and taking down notes and then looks through the intranet directories to find HRLT's folder labelled 'Minutes and Agendas'. There she finds an unfinished record of the minutes. Aghast, she reads on, horrified that Cat was able to go ahead with making those redundant when no one had seconded it. She wonders how she managed to bypass Bernard, the ELT, SLT and the HRLT with this, and makes a note of it. She knows someone who will be able to confirm if this was approved or not…Elspeth.

Sven suddenly remembers to check the Outlook calendar for appointments, and as Bernard has given her full unrestricted access to the Outlook calendar system, she can check Cat's diary. She starts with what she had on today and more importantly what she had on last Friday. Sven notices that there are a lot of 'private' appointments, but knows who will be able to unlock them and see where she had been. She will text Elspeth to find out more, but first she needs to have a chat with someone who Sven considers was probably Cat's closest, if not only ally, Jillian, who also started at the same time as Cat. She is on contract as a 'Consultant' and no one really knows what her 'Consultant' role entails.

First she texts Elspeth and then Jillian, asking her to meet her downstairs in the hope that she will be able to shed some off-the-record light on what Cat has been up to.

*****

Now Home and Away is well and truly closed, much to Zelda's disappointment, seeing a once-in-a-lifetime opportunity to cream it on sales go down the tube thanks to some incredibly hot-looking copper. If he wasn't so good-looking, she would have given him her ten cents worth, but he was so charming, and it was difficult not to fall deep into those big brown eyes and get swept away.

Jillian and Sven meet out on the David Jones side of Midland Park, well away from prying eyes. It wouldn't do anything to improve morale if suddenly HR saw Cat's private consultant in deep conversation with the CEO's flavour of the month, Samantha Svensson. They can't go far as both need to keep nearby or onsite in case Bernard, Comms, the police, or any of a whole array of people need to talk with them at a second's notice.

They pop down the stairs to a basement café that the masses don't really know about; well, the public servants at least don't.

"Jillian, how's it going today for you? Are you holding up with all this suddenly extra special attention to HR?"

"Well, Sven, under the circumstances, yes I am. In fact, I can't say any of my roles have ever been this exciting. Suddenly I feel like you, a bit of a movie star, everyone suddenly needs to talk to me about Cat, the last meeting, the last few weeks – I am being pulled in all directions. And by a couple of cute police detectives too! God knows what Comms are doing, but somehow the journos have got hold of my direct line AND my cell phone so my softphone is going nonstop! I've put my cell on silent and have changed my message, thank god for softphones, aye? My little laptop is ringing herself silly as each call comes through to it. I have taken my earphones off, so I can no longer hear it. What about you?"

"Well, I am lucky. No one is pestering me because basically no one knows I exist, and if they do, they don't know my contact numbers."

"What do you mean by that?"

"Well, I'm still waiting for my official contact numbers to be connected to my devices. They've been allocated and they're on the intranet, but unfortunately I'm at the bottom of the list as the IT team are so focused on the earthquake prediction piece of work."

Sven carries on. "I must admit, nothing like this has

happened since the Swedish minister was taken out when I was living and working over there back in 2003. It wasn't the first time that had happened, but the first assassination was way before my time, back in the late eighties, I think around '86 or something like that."

Jillian is hanging onto the edge of her seat, taking in every word. "Oh Sven, spill, what, where, when, how, who? Remember I have lived a sheltered life compared to you. You know NZ doesn't get too much overseas news, but I do remember a female Swedish minister being killed. Can you elaborate?"

Sven comes back with, "I will give you the bullet points – whoops, that's bad taste, mentioning bullets when talking about assassinations! But on the understanding you give me a rundown on your leader and what she has been up to the last few weeks, especially about that overheated meeting that Cat chaired on Friday. Okay?"

"Yes, it's a deal."

"Okay, well as you know I was working in Stockholm off and on from 2003 until recently. While I was working at Handelsbanken at the bottom of town, near the popular department store NK (Nordiska Kompaniet), like our David Jones (ex Kirkcaldies), one of the female Swedish ministers was attacked, Anna Lindh. I had only just got back to work from a little shopping trip at NK, when it happened, it was late afternoon and she had gone into the department store without her bodyguards to grab some clothes for an interview. She was knifed everywhere – chest, arms, stomach, the works. We could see the emergency services from our office windows, it was so crazy and there were flashing lights and hundreds of armed police everywhere. She didn't die straight away though; the scary thing was she died on 9/11.”

“You mean the 11th of September like when those towers went down in the US?” Jillian asks.

“Yes. The thing is, the current Prime Minister at the time, Göran Persson, had made her Minister of Foreign Affairs and she was tipped to be the next Prime Minister, the first female one. And even further back in ‘86, the Swedish Prime Minister was assassinated. I wasn’t around for that one, but my granddad was in Sweden at the time. So, you can imagine, that’s all the journos reported for weeks on end. Anyhow, our little mystery murder down the road pales in comparison, but still for dear little Wellywood I suppose it is big-time. Okay, your turn. What’s the dirt, what’s been going on in Cat’s neck of the woods? Tell me about her recent behaviour, meetings, anything odd?”

“Okay, well as you know, Cat and I have had a bit of a bumpy relationship. Sometimes I’m not sure what I was being brought in for. It was to work on a project, but I feel like I’ve been a glorified Agony Aunt-cum-sweep-under-the-carpet-this-and-that. She doesn’t do herself any favours the way she acts like the Iron Lady.”

Sven laughs. “Yes, well that’s apt as we are talking about Prime Ministers. From Olaf Palme to Anna Lindh to Maggie Thatcher. I think Cat would love it if she knew we had just compared her to old Mags. Yes, do go on.”

“Well, I actually began to feel sorry for her. I wouldn’t say I liked the woman or even respected her, but I got to find out a little about what made her tick. Now I know everyone has a story to tell, of how they were this and that when they were younger, and so forth. But Cat did have quite a tearful childhood and home life. Her mum died young of a heart attack, and she basically had to play mother and do everything around the house. It was just her, some loser brother or brothers who were always scrounging for money to feed their habits, and her dad. He was – or is – an alcoholic, so he drank himself into a coma most of the time I believe, and bullied Cat. Basically, he took everything out on her, and blamed Cat for her mother's death. I am assuming he is still alive. She of course ended up carrying on the family cycle of being a bully like her dad, and it's no secret she likes a glass or five."

"How did you find out all of this? Cat wouldn't have opened up about all of that?" asks Sven.

"Well, from a mixture of sources. Firstly, Cat has been going to see a doctor and some days she would come back to work in quite a state. I don't like seeing anyone upset, so I took her offsite a few times for a coffee or something stronger in most cases. She had no one to talk to so would slowly over time let a few things about her past slip. Plus, I used to overhear some of her phone conversations. Look, the way she treats some people is inexcusable but you kinda get why she does; she had one fucked up childhood. No wonder she escaped Auckland to start afresh down here."

"And the other sources you got this information from?" Sven asks rather brusquely, wanting to get to the crux of the matter.

Jillian has also learnt by attending a few coaching sessions that when Sven lets her professional guard down she is quite a straight shooter and likes to get to the point, instead of dancing around the matter when the elephant is sitting right in the middle of the room, as is the Kiwi way. She is guessing this is her Swedish side coming out in her, where they don't make small talk like the English do far too well – they get right to the point.

"Have you met that guy Chris who has come into IT?" asks Jillian.

Sven thinks for a moment. "Yes, I did meet Chris in a SHIT meeting earlier today."

"I beg your pardon, a SHIT meeting? Which SHIT meeting are you referring to? They are all shit aren't they, can you be a bit more specific?" asks Jilly with a twinkle in her eye.

"Oh, you know how this place has acronyms and abbreviations for Africa? Well, I have made up some of my own. You know how they have merged Science with Health and IT? Well that's the SHIT team, but ironically enough also because they mostly talk a load of shit. Anyhow, at today's meeting one of them spouted off that HR are a pack of ditzy females who do 'flowery' work. So, I basically told them they are seen as a pack of geeks, lacking in all emotional intelligence (EQ), something they all fear, so they make up for it by overcompensating with their intellectual intelligence (IQ). They are just not that flash in imparting their information in a friendly, communicative, Plain English way. They expect all their audiences to be mini Einsteins and if you are not, then too bad. Whoops, sorry, I got sidetracked."

She takes a breath and continues. "Yes, I know who you mean. Chris, I met him in their meeting. Oh my god, I've just clicked where I last saw him. He was on the train last Friday night." *Shit, shit he was the one that spoke to me briefly in the bar on Kiwi Con,* Sven thinks to herself. *Oh shit, he was also the one I think I saw in our carriage talking to...and in Cat's office that night I worked late. Oh...*

"Are you okay, Sven?" Jillian asks.

"Oh my god, I have to see Charlie, as soon as," she spouts out.

"Charlie? Not that adorable Detective Charlie Rogers?"

Sven recomposes herself. This is not the time to wear all her emotions on her shoulder. "So why was Cat seeing a doctor?"

"Because she's been having anxiety attacks lately, and getting stressed by burning the candle at both ends. She has taken on a huge job here, and I think it just all got too much. So, the doctor has been trialling her on different drugs in order to get her stress levels down, get rid of those anxiety attacks she's been having, and get her sleeping again."

"Wow, I had no idea. I just thought she was permanently hyper, that it was just her personality. Do you know if she has a man or not? What's the crack with her and others at BS? Is she shagging anyone?"

Jillian appears speechless; there is something she wants to say, but doesn't feel right about it, especially talking ill of the dead. "Look, Sven, I think I have probably said enough. Time is ticking on, and my phone hasn't stopped vibrating since we've been in here."

Sven slows down the momentum. "Hey Jill, you know that anything you say to me I will keep in confidence, unless it is something that I believe needs to be shared with those who need to hear it, like the police. Look, I don't know what to think about how Cat died. I just know that nothing is as it seems sometimes. If Cat did have a troubled childhood and was running away from something, do you think she did herself in? Did something happen on Friday or the weeks leading up to that night, to make her even contemplate that?"

"I don't know. I just know she wasn't happy, and yes,

she was seeing someone. I have had to cover for her several times when she was meant to be in offsite meetings with the Minister. Cat was a complex creature. I just know that she thrived on adrenalin – that's what made her tick and if she was the centre of attention on some huge project, at some networking function, she loved it. I know she has been to many functions lately and has probably been drinking too much."

"Shit, we've been here over half an hour. I'm so sorry Jillian, look, we'd better call this meeting a day. I don't want HR, Bernard, Charlie or Comms on your case. Let's get back to work, but thanks for helping me out. I just needed to know what Cat had been up to the last few weeks. Did Friday's HRLT meeting finish badly?"

"Yes, Nigel from Recruiting walked out after he made his case of keeping his current staff and employing more. He had a go about all the backfills that keep coming in and how half of them he had no idea about so who was employing them, let alone security checking them. He asked about you, Alex and…"

"Who else was angry on Friday?" asks Sven.

"Put it this way, who was *not* angry when they left the meeting? You should have seen Carmen…"

"What about Stephanie, how was she? What's her relationship like with Cat? Is it a happy one?"

"Look Sven, I've really got to get back to my desk and at least look like I am steering the ship on Stephanie's and Cat's behalf. Being out for so long today is really taking the piss. Look, are you free later? I am happy to continue this conversation later. You?"

"Yep, sweet as Jillian. Thanks a lot for your time, I really appreciate you opening up to me and being so honest.

I wouldn't want you to be disloyal to Cat. Like I said, I don't think things are as they appear to be on the surface. There is something going on here, and I can't put my finger on it yet. Catch you later, have a good afternoon."

They dart off in different directions so it doesn't look obvious that they have just met up. Everyone is self-absorbed in their own lives, but currently, rumours are flying around like wildfire and for once Sven doesn't want to be the main character in their speculations or gossip.

She needs fresh air and time to percolate over her new findings and does the circuit around the block several times. She can't help herself and walks back via the railway station to see what's going down. She needs to talk with a few others, but most of all with Charlie. *Bygones need to be bygones, life is too short. I mean look at Cat's, cut down in her prime,* Sven thinks to herself as she heads off to look for Charlie to update him with the latest.

She reflects on her lengthy discussion with Jillian and the revelations about Cat seeing a doctor on a regular basis, being on prescription drugs and mixing with booze at all the pre-Christmas functions. She starts feeling sorry for her and wishes Cat had used her as a resource, a sounding board. Why didn't she come to her and have a bit of a download and admit the job was getting on top of her? Women, why do they always have to overcompensate and be superwoman? Why do they have to be everything to everyone: super wife, super mum, super daughter, super sister? Her thoughts then progress to Chris from IT, and she marks in her diary: 'Yet another person I need to catch up with, Chris'.

With no sign of Charlie or Bernard, she goes back to the office and plonks herself down in a break out area and opens her laptop, mindful that she has a few spare moments before meeting with Elspeth.

She wishes she'd gone to Police College with Charlie when he went; it's just that she needed to do other things and it would've been 'Cringeville' being the 'his and her' Ken and Barbie number in uniform together, like something out of a Mills and Boon novel. She tells herself she did the right thing – if she had gone to Police College she would never have got the opportunity to travel and flit between London and Stockholm. Thinking about it now, she wouldn't have changed it for the world.

Her mind goes off on a tangent while she thinks about Jillian's words and starts doing some more detective work in and around the appropriate document folders and Outlook calendar appointments. Jillian said she would do the same, and try to unlock the private appointments on Cat's Outlook calendar. At the same time, unaware of each other's findings, both ladies come up with a lot more information than they bargained for.

Sven stares wide-eyed, unable to stop her mouth from opening in shock when she starts delving into the recent folders Cat has been creating. Thinking that she could have been a bit more original with the naming of some of them – although to be fair Cat wouldn't have suspected that they would be looking through her private directory – she comes across folder names such as 'Restructure Round 1, Round 2 and Round 3', 'Voluntary Redundancy', 'Redundancy Payouts', 'Redundancy No Payouts', 'Slice and Dice Presentation Part 1, Part 2' and then folders for each department that would be affected, such as 'ER', 'OD', 'LD', and the like. She can't get into any of them, but she can see when they have last been accessed. Strangely enough, the 'Presentation Part 1' folder has been accessed recently, but after the close of business last Friday. It had been accessed on Saturday and Sunday.

Sven's mind races. Who would have been in the office or had access to Cat's private files over the weekend? She's certain it has something to do with IT, as they would be the only other people, besides possibly Bernard or Stephanie who might have access to these highly confidential files.

She gets up from her desk and decides it's time to pay Chris a visit – she may just be able to give him a little project he will enjoy getting his teeth into. Evidently, when someone deletes something, it is only temporarily deleted. It appears deleted to the naked eye, but like a footprint or DNA, the evidence still remains there; it just can't be seen. However, IT experts can recover just about anything.

Sven had bumped into Chris earlier in the day at the SHIT meeting and had had a good chat with him afterwards. He was actually quite a nice guy, and approachable too; just very shy and it took a bit of work to build a rapport with him, but surprisingly enough the two of them had a little in common, a love of Van Morrison.

*****

Chapter 17

Meeting with Cat's EA, Elspeth

Sven prepares to meet up with the other half of the equation, Cat's EA, the adorable Elspeth.

Sven has been standing nervously at the shared printer, used by half the floor, making sure it doesn't jam as she prints off all of Cat's confidential movements over the last few weeks. She wants to avoid the scenario when someone sends a private, long-winded, confidential print job off to the shared printer and Murphy's Law the printer jams or runs out of toner just at the crucial time. Suddenly, everyone in the office needs their printed reports immediately. Everything goes wrong, there is no paper or toner anywhere, and they don't want to leave the printer to get someone in to fix it in case in their absence the printer starts off again merrily printing their private material in full view of all the wrong people who would love to report their wrongdoings to someone to get them into trouble.

Phew, good printer, I owe you one. Thanks for being

on your best behaviour. Sven hurries off to meet Elspeth with the ream of Outlook calendar posts. They meet in the nearby coffee bar upstairs, across the road from the Ministry. A great meeting place with a bird's eye view out over the Quay, and with the windows tinted you can see out, but no one can see in. This has become Elspeth's office away from the office. It's quiet, like a library and not a voice can be heard across the length of the floor. Elspeth finds it easier to work in this more conducive atmosphere, and takes her laptop and phone and gets a whole day's work done in a couple of hours. With Cat attending meetings all over town, as long as Elspeth is contactable by phone she is happy for her EA to work offsite.

Sven rushes over to the Tiger Café and plonks herself down next to Elspeth. Elspeth is one of a kind. Charming and lively, with plenty of energy, incredibly generous, exuding confidence, very experienced, she makes you feel like you are in safe hands. Heaven knows why Cat didn't make the most of her. Clearly too full of her own self-importance and playing the busy game, she never took the time to notice that she could have a great ally.

"Hey Elspeth, what a wonderful place. I love this retro furniture, very Josef Frank, very Scandinavian – I feel like I am back in Sweden. I am sure over there that's IKEA furniture – the material looks very funky too. Hey, thanks for meeting up with me. How long have you been coming here? What a great hideaway!"

"More Danish in here I think, could be either Arne Jacobsen or Poul Henningsen perhaps? What about those groovy catlike vases? Kosta Boda I think, so there's your Swedish influence. Where were we? Well, once Cat forgot she had an EA with a brain and started spending most of her time out and about, I realised there was no point in me being in the office. It got awfully embarrassing having to find a hotspot desk after Cat gave mine away to Jillian. And as for not keeping me in the loop, you can imagine the looks and responses I got, especially being her EA – shouldn't I, out of everybody, be in the know? Well clearly not!" Elspeth responds infuriatingly.

"Well, it's funny you should say that. Look, I won't pretend I liked Cat, or should I say 'respected' Cat, nor admired the way she treated people, but I do feel bad – the last time I saw her I was quite rude to her. I had no idea that would be the last time I would see her though. I just thought she was indestructible, invincible, and like Celine Dion when belting out lyrics in her famous song, 'my heart will go on and on' and Cat would too. But I couldn't help myself, and as the day has developed I have got more and more curious about where she's been and what has actually happened to her. Look, I can mention a handful of people who would like to see the back of her, but I can't imagine anyone wanting to go through with it. Can you? You are the one who knew her the best. What was going on in Cathryn Ann Tennyson's life?"

Elspeth takes one last gulp of her mochaccino and sits back in her IKEA Poäng chair. "That's the sixty-four thousand-dollar question, isn't it? I don't think we should speculate, and just leave it up to the police. I mean that's what they get paid for. Thinking outside the square is not part of a public servant's portfolio. Well, so I keep hearing whenever I ask someone for something."

"I admire that you want to stay loyal to your boss, Elspeth, but she didn't exactly treat you like royalty, did she? I couldn't help watching you guys from afar. It's not so much what was said, it was just the body language and probably what you didn't say to each other. Never any pleasantries or small talk on how your evening or weekends had gone, and I know she started excluding you a lot from meetings and seemed to give more and more of her work to Jillian, her consultant. In fact, looking at these emails, your name doesn't appear on any of them. She excluded you from her email distribution list. She wasn't going to make you redundant on this next round, was she? Is that what the heated argument was partly about last week?"

Elspeth opens up. "How do you know that? How did you know my job was on the chopping block? I thought it was confidential."

"Just a guess. However, what clinched it was seeing she had already taken you off her email distribution list. I mean how can you include a consultant but not your permanent, full-time, loyal EA? I mean how did Jillian and you fit into the equation, both at the same time? Two's company, three's a crowd, and like the Bermuda Triangle – someone or something had to disappear eventually."

Elspeth laughs. "I love your way with words – the Bermuda Triangle, the mysterious triangle where people and planes go missing. Now that's a real synergy, isn't it? First Cat disappearing and now me, well should I say my role, is disappearing. That just leaves one out of the three left. Jillian, the consultant, is she disappearing anytime soon?"

Sven replies, "I don't know about that. I just know, like I keep saying to people who get precious about their job, we all have our use-by date. I have one, Jillian has one, and more than half of the sixth floor have a use-by date. No, seriously E, I didn't know your role was history, but I do now. I've seen how Cat likes to surround herself with 'yes' people, preferably people that know less than her so she shines. She's not very good at inheriting staff, and with no disrespect, you were too nice, too honest and far to intelligent to want to last that long in her shadow. Listen Elspeth, would you mind opening up your Outlook calendar and telling me what these appointments were all about?"

Sven, respecting what Jillian had to say was confidential, does not let Elspeth in on her findings from the last meeting.

Having access to Cat's private appointments and meetings, Elspeth reluctantly looks up her diary to see what Cat's movements were over the last few weeks. To their astonishment they stumble across a pattern of similar appointments. The last thing either of them suspected – clearly typed 'CP' for a weekly meeting followed by 'Chemist, collect new prescription'.

Jillian had let on that Cat had been seeing a doctor and was trialling a mixture of prescription drugs to reduce anxiety, stress, depression, and to get to sleep. But they didn't know the extent of it, until now. Just what was she on?

"Elspeth, in your opinion, had Cat been acting strangely? Or should I say more strangely than usual? She never came to see me, and I know she had a lot on her plate."

They both focus intently on the screen in front of them – Cat's Outlook calendar for the last six months along with personal notes.

"Who is this Dubravka she keeps referring to? Not the one in Comms, is it? No, surely not. Suddenly this name is very popular. And why has she got every Thursday at 10am blocked out with this person? Where is she from? Is she a fellow HR Director in another government department?" As she looks over Elspeth's shoulder, Sven notes that this appointment is a regular occurrence.

"All I can say is that Cat used to leave the building at 9.30am every Thursday and return at 11.30am. At a guess she was going somewhere half an hour away from work, so it obviously wasn't a local government department. Maybe she was having an affair?" Elspeth speculates. "She did seem overly friendly with a number of men…"

"Yes, and who would they be?" asks Sven, keeping her suspicions to herself.

"Well, there is a whole list of them, like Bernard, she's pretty close to him. I'm not sure how close, but I don't believe it's a purely platonic relationship."

Sven flashes back to her argument with Bernard on the train on Friday when she started having him on about his affair with Cat. She wonders if Bernard is up to his old tricks again. She had thought that was why he brought Katarina out here as his EA. That way he could keep the relationship going but keep his wife happy at the same time by returning to New Zealand. Margaret, keen to get back on the career ladder, was more than happy if she could be 1. Close to family and 2. Be playing Iron Lady at the top of certain government departments and on the board here, there and everywhere. It would be fair to say Bernard and Margaret had an agreement and it worked well for both parties.

"Okay, fair cop about Bernard. Who else?"

Sven isn't committing herself to a yes or no, and knows Elspeth is fishing for dirt. Wouldn't anybody, if they had suddenly heard that they were going to be made unemployed just before Christmas? Sven would give her ten out of ten for showing up today after being given her marching orders on Friday – now that's loyalty. It's a shame that loyalty and passion don't go towards keeping a job nowadays.

Elspeth continues. "Now Alex, he's an interesting character. Cat brought him in from god knows where and she's been having a few too many coffee meetings with him. Those two are – or 'were' I should say – up to something. He's playing with some experiment downstairs locked away in his basement. Hmm, experiment, or possibly Cat was the experiment he was playing with; the cat who had the mouse, who would know? Anyhow, he used to come up quite a bit to the sixth floor in the evening, always talking very quietly. A few times Bernard walked in on those two having their serious meetings and papers were quickly shuffled under piles of other papers, and voices were muted. Something was going down that Bernard knew nothing about. You know, I think Bernard put up with a lot for a while, but I think he was cottoning onto Cat towards the end. In fact, I think Cat's days were numbered here and Bernard was going to give Cat her marching orders after she had finished off her big 'slice and dice' project. She possibly had another job lined up and that was also the reason for all her disappearances. Look at the number of meetings with other government departments, I recognise the names of a few of the HR managers and DCEs – she was obviously networking and planning her next escape route and choosing her new torture chamber."

"Really? Cat was formulating her exit strategy?"

"Probably, she was always very sneaky, and this week

was the week to implement her plan, put it into action. You know how it works, you hand in your notice just on Christmas, then take off and get paid stat days and annual leave, and TOIL on the company over the summer months. Then come back for a few days in late January to hand in your tools of the trade, collect your last pay cheque and bugger off to your new employer, all refreshed and ready to do it all again. Now that's business as usual these days!"

Sven is not surprised with what she is hearing but is loving how with just a couple of questions Elspeth is off, spilling everything and more.

"Wow, go on, Elspeth," Sven says encouragingly.

"I think Cat and Alex were working on something to do with this earthquake thing; they were definitely bypassing Bernard on this and going straight to the Minister with their findings in a neat little report. I mean look at the timing of these meetings with Alex and then followed by a meeting with either the Minister or his secretary Ernest Ragbottom. Those two would do anything to claw their way to the top. Cat definitely would, and I think Alex, like a typical bloke, was sucked in and going along for the ride. Oh, and watch that Ragbottom fellow like a hawk, he's always been a shifty character!"

"Elspeth, you are fabulous, nothing gets past you. Go on, what else have you got? Oh, and how is Ragbottom after being rear-ended today in the ministerial car?" Sven wants to keep pumping Elspeth while she's on a roll. She has had to be discreet and keep her mouth shut for such a long time, Elspeth obviously needs to talk; she is gutted, she is hurting, feeling rejected, and knows a lot. It is important for her to get it all out before she leaves. There is nothing worse than taking your baggage from one place to another and landing with it at the next. Best to offload it, get it all out and walk free.

"Don't know about Ragbottom's demise. Not interested, but on a more exciting note, there's one other lad I'm not sure about and he has been skulking about our floor, to be precise in and around Cat's desk far too many times to be a coincidence, and at strange times of the night. Let me explain myself. You may not know that I live in an apartment in town, in fact just down the road. Because I've been working away from the office a lot, which is great and a pain at the same time, I have to keep coming back to the office to pick up files. On my pathetic salary I'm certainly not going to use my home printer and use up expensive ink cartridges and paper, so I've been coming in on the odd evening to get access to the shared G drive to print off minutes, agendas, that sort of thing. Well, a couple of times I've caught that new guy, Chris at Cat's desk. He always has an impressive set of excuses."

Sven, hanging onto every word, says, "Really? And what sort of excuses has our 'Creative Chris' the IT genius, and Alex's best friend, been coming up with?"

"Well, firstly, Alex and Cat are not best friends. He plays at being Cat's best friend, hence him getting the HOD role so quickly while he plays with his fancy science equipment on that ridiculous earthquake prediction project, while dodging the immigration visa requirements. Cat brought Alex in, but Chris came in from the temp agency, and he's definitely not one of Cat's worshippers! His brief is to get our five differing departmental software systems and hardware talking and playing nicely with each other – yes, after all these years. As you know, the system has been down more than it's been up and trying to cross-reference information from one system to another can take an absolute age."

"Yes, do go on," Sven pleads, not sure where this next piece of information is going to lead to.

"Well, one night Chris was sitting at Cat's desk and when he saw me, he jumped out of his pale little IT skin and pretended he was just doing a backup for her at her request. It sounded plausible at first, because as you know it's now policy – yes, I know! Yet another policy, that we do not save anything on our desktops, everything must be on one of the intranet's drives so everyone can have twenty-four seven access to these drives, folders, documents subject to relevant permission, or an OIA (Official Information Act) request. He reckoned Cat had asked him to come in and back up her files from her desktop."

"And did you follow up with Cat, was this true?" asks Sven.

Elspeth goes red in the face and looks away.

"Look Elspeth, I completely understand if it slipped your mind, or you just omitted it from your overly-stretched to-do list," Sven says, winking and moving on swiftly as she doesn't want Elspeth closing up.

"Put it this way, I got side-tracked on other more pressing issues. But the answer to your question is yes, Cat has been acting more weirdly than usual. Is it stress, with a combination of new drugs mixed in for good measure with pre-Christmas silliness? I'm not sure. Was she seeing someone else? Well I think she was seeing a whole array of people, both men and women who were serving her different needs. I can't pinpoint one person. Oh, and I almost forgot, I have seen her outside the back entrance several times talking to some waste of space guy. They did look similar, you know, similar facial features, and I wondered if it was some brother of hers. Anyhow, he looked a creep and it did look like he wanted something, and she wasn't delivering. He was probably on the take and thought he could get some money out of her as he clearly didn't look like he was working. She was really embarrassed as I made a point of going up to her and talking to her which forced her into introducing me to him. He looked like one of those guys you would pay money to if you wanted someone kneecapped, you know what I mean?"

Sven is a little shocked yet again with Elspeth talking like that and wonders when Elspeth would ever be in the market to hire such a person. Clearly she's been watching too much UK prime time crime drama.

"Hmm, very interesting. Did you catch her brother's name?"

"Yes, I did, something unusual like Ree… Reagan, yes, as in the American president's name back in the day."

Sven senses Elspeth is almost done, and revisits safer ground, the locked private appointments for specialists and the reoccurring appointments. "I think you are pretty much on the money, E. These appointments appear very damning. Cat was clearly playing many an office political game as well while ignoring her health issues which started piling up. Is there nothing else to give us a clue? How long have these appointments been going on for?"

"Since…" Just then Charlie comes in for a coffee and spots Sven straight away.

He tries to act casual and pretend that they have just met for the first time in a while. "Hey, Sven, good to see you, long time no see. I thought I saw you across a crowded room this morning."

Charlie is always very good at trying to keep anything low key, and especially with Cat's EA present, he doesn't want to let onto her that he knows Sven as well as he does.

Sven nervously gets up and thanks Elspeth for her time and in a very matter-of-fact, almost sterile tone, says, "Charlie, Bernard was hoping to catch up with you. Have you seen him?" and leads him away from the table.

Charlie continues with his conversation. "Sven, still the diverter, aye? Leading people off down the garden path, exactly where you want to take them. I am talking about conversation-wise here, not physically. I know you would never take any Tom Dick or Lars down the garden path. I wish you had kept taking me down that garden path all those years ago, but que será, será, aye? How can a little Kāi Tahu Māori boy from the mainland compete with a stocky tall Viking from the bright lights of downtown Stockholm?"

Sven scowls at him and they are both aware Elspeth's eyes and ears are still very much on them. Charlie leads her out of the coffee bar and over to the park.

"What brings you to these parts of the woods? How long are you in town for before heading back to Europe?" Charlie quizzes her with a huge grin on his handsome face. He always loved making Sven squirm and still has that amazing ability to do so.

Sven, going red at being sprung and knowing this would cause Elspeth's mind and possibly vocal cords to do overtime, tries hard to cover up her embarrassment. "Yes, we must do coffee sometime, but I have a back-to-back meeting right now so I've got to fly." Then she adds quietly, "But we must talk soon, okay? I've just got to check out a couple of things, have you checked Cat's desk? See you soon," Sven gives Charlie's arm a little squeeze and then hurriedly runs off back to work. Her heart is pulling her back, but her head is pushing her away from him.

Charlie, grabbing his coffee, and one for Rex, races after Sven. *Hmm, still as stubborn a wahine as ever and hard to pin down as usual, but I've missed that touch of hers,* he says to himself. "Hey, Sven, wait up, what's the rush?" Charlie says to thin air as he tries and fails to catch up with her, as Sven disappears into the mass of onlookers surrounding the BS Ministry.

Sven gets back to the office after texting Katarina, her next port of call. What light can Katarina shed on the situation?

*****

Charlie returns to his makeshift office at BS. He and Rex are working between KiwiRail House and the BS Ministry. They have interviewed quite a few people, and they are making progress. He feels they have reached a turning point in their investigations. However, something is not making sense; he can't put his finger on it, but his gut is leading him off into another direction.

*****

Sven is feeling the same. She needs some fresh air, well away from Charlie and work; she needs time to think. Her emotions are up and down like a roller coaster. She takes out her pen and paper and starts scribbling on a page, toying with each character, and jotting down notes by each one.

Alex – possibly manipulated, probably shagging C?

Bernard – Shagging??? Surely not, but definitely getting shafted one way or the other.

Chris – mystery boy, up to something…

Reagan – Shady, hitman??

Stephanie – motive, but really??

Nigel – recently crowned the Queen of tantrums and tiaras, but…?

Carmen…the suspect list is getting longer.

While thinking about each suspect and their motive, she continues to fabricate, starting with her favourite old-time boss, Bernard. Henpecked to return home, but not a bad thing – it's a slower pace of life, the money is not nearly as good, the job satisfaction almost nil, but he gets to be on the beach a few nights a week with weather like this and fewer crowds to compete with.

BERNARD

Bernard, middle-aged, now what does that mean?

A gym junkie, slim and lean

Made his $ while in foreign waters

Now back home at Head Quarters

Accountable now to the Minister

His relationship with Cat, a little sinister?

(A relationship with one short spinster!)

Sven can't finish the poem as her thoughts keep going back and forth to Charlie.

She wonders why Charlie Rogers, of all coppers, is heading up this case. What are the chances of both of them ending up in Wellington again all these years later, at the same time and in the same building? Is fate playing tricks on her? She doesn't understand her depth of feelings for him after all these years. Not a suspect, but can't stop thinking of him.

CHARLIE

The best-looking man without a doubt

I'm such a mess, when you're about

Your Māori complexion, that permanent tan

Back in the day, you were my man

Now in charge and on the case

With time ticking, we've gotta crack this case.

Now Stephanie, she just can't work out.

STEPHANIE

Short and dumpy with mousey hair

Very quiet with that unusual stare

Very plain and very shy

Nondescript, I do not lie

Oversized clothes far too big

Always eating like a pig

Cat and you hardly speak

You really are just mild and meek.

Just one more suspect – dear Carmen. Now she really despised Cat.

Sven reflects on this 'real piece of work' who thinks she's God's gift to mankind, but has really passed her use-by date in all areas. Thinking of Carmen's ability to do a mean sheep whistle Sven wonders if she has had 'fashionable and frivolous' added to her CV under 'skills and attributes'.

CARMEN
Carmen, now she's a real 'piece of work'
Her favourite line, once upon a time an office clerk
Famous for her leopard skin
Her delicate skin, paper thin
Highly sensitive in every way
You have to be careful what you say
Comes across really strong
In a flap when things go wrong
But is it all just for show
With Lloyd and her departing Tango?

Sven shuts her ipad full of suspects, leaving a space to write more about Alex and Nigel, and heads back.

*****

Charlie and Rex are waiting on an update from Forensics, but have met with Cat's neighbour Bob and looked at the identikit sketch the officers came up with after listening to Bob's description. They have also interviewed most of HR and the passengers from carriage four on Friday evening, as well as most of the people identified as being on Friday night's fateful train journey. Charlie thinks about the one person he hasn't interviewed thoroughly yet

– Sven. All roads keep leading to Sven. She's from HR, was on the train, lives up the coast, didn't particularly like Cat and now according to recent IT records, he can see she has been delving into Cat's private files and calendar. Is she covering her tracks or is that part of her brief?

Just then the expected call comes in from Forensics. "Kia ora Marama, how can I help you on this bright Monday afternoon in downtown Wellington? Thanks for organising the sunshine while I'm in town, I really appreciate it. Wow, almost a reason to move back down here, aye, cuz? You would love it if we were both working in the same patch again, nei?"

Marama laughs. "You never change, do you? You sweet-talker. Have you got all those chicks circling you like a pack of hungry sharks up your way?"

"No Ra, I'm still waiting for the right one."

"I thought you had found the right one but let her go," she responds, thinking of the cute blonde he had had back in the day when they were at Police College together.

"Hmm, funny you should say that, Ra. One thing about this case, it's bringing lots of people back from the past. Something bigger than meets the eye is going on here." He looks at Rex who is looking at him strangely and realises he has said too much. He shuts that part of the conversation down and moves on. "So, on more important issues, Project M – ha, do you like it? What can I do for you?"

"Well, it's the results from the girl on the train. They are taking a bit longer. We have had a few complications down here at the lab. Whoever moved the body from the train has contaminated the scene by moving her without our permission. Not to mention her personal belongings that they also picked up and spilled all over the platform, idiots! It's slowed us down. However, all good; I'm still running the autopsy. Interesting contents. I think our cold case loved a drink or two, she…what's that? Aroha mai, but I've got to go, some more data has just come in. This is an interesting one. Okay, stand by. Catch you soon, I hope." Marama rings off.

"What was all that about?" asks Rex.

"Just what we suspected." There's a knock on the door. "Okay, we're on, here's the next culprit. Let her in, mate. Hopefully this one isn't a replica of Veronica. Like you, I don't think I could take more of that. Mind you, she was really helpful and gave us a few leads, albeit unintentional."

The boys settle down for the next interview.

*****

Chapter 18

Sven meets with Katarina, Bernard's EA

Sven and Katarina, Bernard's EA go way back to when they used to work hard and party hard in Stockholm, with Freya, Clara and the gang. Sven reflects on the good old days. It was always a riot and she does miss those times. She hopes that perhaps the good times can continue to roll here, with BJ in party mood like last Friday until she dropped the 'Cat' clanger. Surely he's not still screwing Katarina on the side, Sven muses, plus Cat, and going home faithfully to his wife Margaret, who's no saint herself. She never did understand their arrangement.

Sven knows she can trust Katarina, but isn't overly excited about the awkward position she finds herself in. She wonders how a DCE whose main focus is to pick this Ministry up by the boot straps and soldier on to bigger and better places can be in this predicament. She feels torn. She likes and respects both Katarina and Bernard, but she has been hearing all sorts of rumours.

Determined to get to the bottom of this, Sven races up

to her old mate Katarina and they give each other a hug and the traditional European peck on each cheek. "Hey, you, thanks for meeting up with me. I know you are running around like a blue-arse fly with all of this carry-on today, but I need some off-the-record information and I believe you can help."

Getting straight to the point in true Swedish style, Sven goes on. "I have just been looking at Cat's Outlook calendar, and there appears to be a regular appointment she has been attending every Thursday, and there are some other appointments that just don't match with her physical whereabouts. Can you shed any light from your perspective and distinguish between the facts and fiction?"

Katarina nudges her mate and laughs. "*Ja ha,* always the *utredare,* the investigator, you should be the Kiwi version of Detective Kurt Wallander, *nej?* You are wasted as a coach. You know Kiwi businesses are not ready for your interrogation and deep delving questions – you scare them off. They may get to fathom out after all these years who they really are. You could completely fast-forward everyone's lives and they wouldn't need to hold onto all those burdens and busy minds for many decades if you could actually do your job and help them out. So as a result, you are now busy-bodying in other people's areas like your *polis pojkvän Char-lie."* Katarina smiles cheekily as she emphasises his name in her cute Swedish accent.

Katarina's English is remarkably fluent given it is her second language, "I assume you will have bumped into him by now? After all, he and his team are questioning all the Kiwi Con passengers from Friday and Monday. And we know you were on the train and in the same carriage with her, so Miss prime suspect, what's the *skvaller?"*

They have no sooner started talking than Charlie finds them and trying to get Sven's attention, swaggers up to the pair of funkily dressed ladies, thinking to himself, *Man there are some perks to this job!*

Katarina, like Sven, is always brightly dressed and today has a floral number on – a sundress with splashes of pink, turquoise and blue. Sven is normally in a similar dress code, but today she wears a tie-dyed dressy top she picked up in the Cook Islands, to go with her cute white skirt.

With these two women looking like real South Pacific flowers, how could someone not notice them, especially a detective, and one on a mission? Charlie looks at them both and can't help breaking into a smile. "Sven, why is it that everywhere I go I see you, and when I do, you are deep in conversation with someone I need to talk to or have been talking with? Are you trying to do me out of a job?" he asks with a glint in his eye.

Katarina goes red with embarrassment. Being a highly sensitive person she can feel the intense chemistry between the two, the unresolved passion is almost unbearable.

"Hey guys, I can leave if you have more important business to explore?" she volunteers.

Sven responds, looking at Charlie. "Hey Charlie, I just need to have a small chat with Katarina here, so how about we meet up after? There are a few things I need to get off my chest. Give me your card and I promise I will call you when we're finished here." Sven is always good at diverting people and with Charlie she has managed to do that one time too many today.

It's Charlie's turn now not to look embarrassed, but he composes himself; after all, that's what cops do – keep that straight face while interrogating or being abused. "Sure Sven, you get whatever you need off your *chest,*" he replies, exaggerating the word chest as he grins. "I will look forward to your call," he adds as he jots down his details on the back of a coffee receipt. "Cops don't have a big enough budget for flashy corporate business cards. But hey, Sven, you have fobbed me off three times today, you won't be getting away with this again. I seriously do need to talk to you, okay?"

Katarina jumps up as her phone rings. "Hey guys, I am really sorry but Bernard is calling. I do need to take this one. It's my turn to exit. I will call you Sven, gotta go, *hej da. Puss och Kram.*" She kisses and hugs her old chum and flies off.

Charlie takes Katarina's seat. There's a bit of catching up to do, even though right now is not the time or place.

"You and Katarina obviously know each other really well. She has an accent and I know I am assuming, but she's blonde and gorgeous, she's obviously Swedish? What's the crack with you and her?" he starts out with small talk.

"Yes, I met her while working with a bank in Stockholm and again in London. She is Bernard's EA. Now you didn't stop me to talk about her, did you?" Sven smiles, putting a little dig in. "What is it you really want to talk to me about after all these years?"

"Hej Sven, I am glad I can make you smile again, that was a long time coming. Look, I know this is an old adage, but what happened in the past, can we leave it in the past? Look, to use your favourite expression, things aren't what they appear to be. You can't keep putting me off, Rex is starting to get suspicious that you have something to hide.

He stares into her big brown eyes. "Look, I am on the

clock and there is a lot of shit going down. I am getting pressure from the Commissioner to shut down this case, and I know you know more than you probably should. Can you help me? Can we let bygones be bygones?"

Sven responds. "Look, I don't want to ruin your career, and you know I will help you in any way I can. Okay, let's put our differences and past behind us. But Charlie, I saw what I saw that night in Courtenay Place, while you were celebrating. But you're right, that's for another time. Okay, what do you need from me?"

As hard as it is, Sven knows she has to park that and move on. Time is against Charlie.

"Thanks Sven, I knew I could rely on you. Look, I'm getting grief from the Commissioner and your Minister. Yes, your Minister is now on the case, better late than never. I need to get a result, the right result, not any result like the Commissioner wants or some cover-up that the Minister is pushing for. I know you have inside knowledge which can help me fast-track my enquiries. This is unethical and not by the book, and I know my wingman Rex is not on board with this, but Bernard gave you the green light earlier today as a quasi-deputy investigator. This is your calling, Detective Svensson, you know you want it! Bernard wants the press, the Minister, the matter, everything to go away. But you know me, I won't rest until I get the right answers and verdict!"

Looking deeply into his dark brown eyes, Sven almost loses control, she takes a deep breath and centres herself, "Charlie Rogers, you of all people should know I will always be there for you. But I've got lots of conflicting information, can you give me half an hour? There are a few other things I need to finish off."

"For you Sven, anything. I've waited a lifetime for you, I can surely wait another half an hour," he replies, thinking how good it is to be back in her company. He didn't realise how much he had missed her. It must be fate that brought them back together today and no coincidence that Marama is part of this case as well. He knows if he can get the three of them in the same room they will be able to resolve everything. It's like this case; it's not how it appears.

Katarina has returned from talking with Bernard and hears the last bit of the conversation. Facing them both, she says, "Yes Sven, I have just got off the phone from Bernard and he was wanting to know how your enquires are going? Are you being, how do you say – 'an open book' – for Charlie, did I get that right? Bernard gives me such a hard time with your English phrases."

Charlie leaves the girls to get his coffee. Now it's Sven's turn to compose herself, but not before Katarina gets in with, "You know that guy is still in love with you, don't you?"

Sven tries to shut her down. "What do you mean? We are not an item!"

"Hey Sven, don't lie to me. Remember it's Katarina here, *hello,* I've seen you in action, remember? I know when you fancy someone – remember that Lars guy at Handelsbanken? You had everyone else convinced that he was just your boss, but it stood out like Moose's balls, it was so much more."

Apart from a slight trace of a Swedish accent, most people wouldn't know that English is Katarina's second language. However, she often gets colloquialisms mixed up, with a rather comical outcome.

Sven corrects her friend's English. "Darling, it's

nothing to do with moose balls. Besides, we don't have moose over here walking down Lambton Quay; it's *dog's balls*. But K, on a serious note, I have been collecting all sorts of information and I'm sharing it with Charlie; it appears events are getting right out of hand. And that's not including this impending earthquake announcement going public soon. I can't make head or tail out of it all just yet. We are seriously running out of time!"

"I agree. Bernard is pretty cut up about this and the pressure from the Minister and that weasel secretary Ragbottom with the long nose hair, you wouldn't believe. You would think his lover would pluck it out, it is so unbecoming. Anyhow, yes, time is something we don't have a lot of, the day is quickly passing us by, so don't waste your time with me – you need to be somewhere else," she winks.

"Yes, we must speak to Bernard immediately. If I was running this show, I would be getting every single suspect in one room together without raising their suspicions, so that Charlie can finally arrest the criminal. A special 'meeting' in the executive boardroom with Bernard, no one will be able to refuse that, especially with a police escort! Can you perhaps have a talk with Bernard? I've still got a few people to see."

"Ja ha, I agree, Detective Wallander," Katarina half jokes, *"Lycka till, sköt om dig..."*

Charlie walks back swapping hands with the hot takeaway coffee and blowing on the top of the cup to cool it down. He takes a gulp and faces Sven. "That's good, man I needed that! Now Sven, I need to catch up with you before the next meeting, Rex is insisting that we get your 'interview' done ASAP."

"If you insist. Bernard is calling us all into another meeting now, and then I'm catching up with IT, so we can meet after that as I have a plan I want to discuss with you," Sven suggests.

"I'll stall Rex for as long as I can, now get on the case. Welcome to investigations, Deputy Svensson!" Charlie jokes.

The three walk off in different directions. Sven, for the first time since starting at BS, is on a real mission. She is finally getting to put her journalistic and coaching questions into practice and this time no one is holding her back.

Charlie takes another call; it's from Stuart, one of his colleagues. The lengthy list of prescriptive drugs has come through. "What a cocktail, everything from the commonly over-prescribed Prozac or Fluoxetine, Lithium, Epilim, Quetiapine and a range of sleeping pills. All prescribed at different times, in different dosages. Clearly she's been trialling a different combination for several months at a time and then the drug or the dosage has changed."

*****

Chapter 19

The Announcement and the Red Folder

Sven is in demand, everywhere. Rex and Charlie need to see her, Bernard wants to see her, but she is on a mission, heading downstairs to the basement to talk with Chris.

She had recognised him a couple of evenings ago, when she had stayed late, burning the midnight oil. Thinking it was just her and the cleaners in the office, she was surprised to look up from her pod to see someone going through Cat's desk. She hadn't thought it was anything at the time. Just an IT guy fixing Cat's computer as usual, as she was always downloading so many documents at a time that the poor computer couldn't cope and would go into a tailspin, a bit like the user. Cat also had the habit of opening documents on the shared directory and leaving them open, which meant the document was locked and no one else could get into it. This caused problems as only IT could close the document, but because Cat was so high up the ladder, they needed her permission before they could do this. All other frustrated users had to wait patiently to get access to the document again. With Cat going AWOL and according to her Outlook calendar, being offsite at a meeting or a private appointment, it would take a while to track her down and get her permission. Meanwhile, everyone else could not access the documents and would need to wait until she was found. Sven recalls the evening she spotted Chris and sat back quietly watching, hoping she wouldn't get sprung.

Time is ticking, and Monday afternoon is well underway. There are many people Sven needs to see but Chris will have to come first, even before Charlie and Bernard.

*****

Bernard is stuck in his office, with the door shut. He doesn't feel like the cheery DCE today with the open-door policy. He needs time to think.

He knows people are pointing the finger at him asking, 'What is with Bernard?' He has noticed that people are treating him differently, even Sven. He is certain he has lost her respect. People have seen him talking with Cat more than usual lately and if Sven saw him in the boardroom that night, who else had seen him? He decides that he needs to come clean, to break confidences. But who can he trust, who can he go to?

*****

Katarina had texted Sven, updating her on the rumour of a whistle-blower in the SHIT team. With this in mind she questions Alex, "So, Alex, how is your research going? Have you reported it to the Minister yet?" giving the impression that she doesn't know about the leaked information to the Minister's secretary and that an OIA probably isn't far behind with questions in a Red Folder that would land on Bernard's desk to give him another stomach ulcer.

Alex looks up suspiciously at Sven. "And why are you suddenly interested in what I am up to? Have you got nothing else better to do? Besides, I've already talked to that copper friend of yours about everything."

Sven, a little startled about the 'copper friend' line, continues as if she hasn't heard that personal dig. "Now that's unfair, Alex, I've always been interested in what you are doing, especially when it involves my livelihood: my safety and wellbeing. I take safety and wellbeing very seriously. Why do you think I organised the Incident Management training? It was in the event that something like what you have predicted would happen and we had the right resources and tools to handle it. Aren't you glad I did that?"

Alex calms down and is about to speak up when Chris, looking completely stressed, flies in at a hundred miles an hour carrying what looks like quite a heavy load, physically and mentally.

"Hey Chris, what's up? You sounded pretty stressed on the phone. What's in the bag?"

Chris turns to see Sven in the room and tries to compose himself, but very unsuccessfully. Not being the type who is great at conversation at the best of times let alone under stressful situations, he freezes like a stunned mullet.

Alex is on a mission – he has his prediction and testing

to further back it up, to finish – he has no time for some backfill and his ongoing erratic behaviour, and returns to his work. He's been interrupted enough today.

Sven takes her opportunity and steps in. "Hey Chris, how are you? I thought I recognised you the other day in the meeting. You were on the train with me the other night, on Friday?"

Chris almost wets himself, looking so obviously guilty that even Alex would have noticed if he had been looking. That's the last thing he wants anyone to know, let alone his boss Alex, and now Sven. His mind races into overdrive as he frantically tries to figure out how to get her off his scent.

Chris has just returned from the locker room with the last of the surveillance gear he had readjusted on Friday night. Hoping to return the surveillance gear before anyone notices it has gone missing, and stay under the radar but everything has backfired because some nosey neighbour came out and saw him leaving the property after the dog went off next door. He is panicking because the guy may have seen him. *Shit, shit,* he says to himself. This is not how it was meant to unfold. He needs to share the footage he's got, but he can't because then the truth will come out and the finger will point at him. He collapses into a chair, suddenly overwhelmed.

Sven, seeing Chris is anxious, goes over and sits down beside him. "Hey, are you okay? You look like you've seen a ghost."

"Yeah, I think I have, he replies.

Alex looks up. Sven quickly butts in before he has a chance to talk. "Hey guys, it's been a long day, how about I get some coffees in. Alex, what do you drink? Chris, come on, let's go and get some coffee and bring it back down here. Sometimes coffee is exactly what the doctor has ordered. My shout." She knows the HAA café is closed so it's a good excuse to walk and talk and find out this piece of the puzzle.

Chris doesn't need much persuading and follows Sven upstairs. They both pass Rex heading down.

*****

Alex has cracked it, well almost. He is seconds away from discovering how to predict the exact time of the next supersized earthquake. He is beside himself. He needs to report this, but now with Cat gone, who does he go to? He can't go to Bernard as he has no idea what he is up to. He can't go to the Minister. No one can find the Minister. He can't go to the Minister's Secretary as he took himself out in the car today, being rear-ended and is now confined to an even bigger and better wheelchair and can't get around as freely. He has this amazing information, he needs to tell someone. He needs to warn the people, but how can he do that? He can't go to Comms.

He suddenly has a light bulb moment as he tries to think where to go to spread news as quickly as possible. Not the Minister, and not the Comms team, they are too slow and will twist it to their way of thinking. Of course, the *Capital News*. The CN, and they are all still upstairs circling the building. His decision is already made – he'll go straight to the press.

Just as he gets up to go, Rex pops in. "Gidday mate, you're on. How about a word?"

*****

Not wasting any time, Sven leads Chris over to Midland Park to grab some coffees.

"Hey Chris, honestly, it's all going to be okay," she says. "I know things aren't as they seem. I know Cat is – or should I say was *high* maintenance. I'm with you. Look, you have obviously got something you need to download and better out than in.

Chris looks at her. "Look, I think I need to talk to my lawyer."

"Do you have one?" Sven asks.

"No, I don't, but isn't that what they say in films when the heat gets too much, and you need to spill, but you want a lawyer beside you in case you say the wrong things to the cops?"

"Why do you think the cops want to talk to you?"

"Because an unknown number has been ringing my cell all day, and I have heard the rumour about that HR lady, Cat is curtains, isn't she?"

"Hey, listen, let's have this coffee, and how about I contact the cop who oversees this case, he is actually in the building. It may be better if you have a chat with him and I am happy to be here with you?"

Chris, realising there is no way out of this, agrees. Sven seems nice enough, but he is a little untrusting of females after what's happened in his past, with Cat, his mum, past relationships and he would prefer to speak to a male.

Sven is about to call Charlie when both of their phones chime in unison. They look at each other, slightly bewildered, and Chris says, "Well that's never happened before..."

"An 'All of BS' meeting in five minutes' time in room 101! What's going on now?" Sven ponders aloud.

"Well, let's find out. Hey, thanks for the coffee, Sven," Chris replies as they head back to BS Castle.

*****

As everyone files into Room 101, Bernard is up on the podium along with Charlie, looking very grim. *Oh god, what on earth are they going to say?* Sven wonders.

Sven's mind hasn't stopped doing overtime all day and neither have the rest of the occupants in the BS building. On a completely different track to others in the building, Sven is starting to wonder if it was murder or something else entirely.

*****

Carmen is watching Sven from afar. The feeling is mutual, she doesn't particularly like Sven and she knows Sven is doing her own little investigations. She wishes the woman would back off and mind her own business. Every time she turns around she has her nose in something else. Next she will have it up that cute-looking copper.

Unbeknown to Sven, Carmen is jotting away as a wannabe writer, composing poetry. Carmen has come to the realisation that if she can't get a job elsewhere, let alone a promotion here at BS, she might as well follow her heart and passion and take up her life-long hobby, writing. She has done a variety of correspondence courses in writing and if she hadn't married so young she would have gone on to university. Instead, she got married to a man twenty years older and had the usual 2.5 kids. Her man, Ron, died several years ago and left a very generous life insurance policy behind and now she no longer needs to work. With the lovable Lloyd declaring his intentions so flamboyantly, she is seriously considering taking up writing full time. While Carmen writes away, another woman is doing exactly the same on the other side of the floor. Carmen writes about this very subject, Sven:

SVEN

Sven is a very different kettle of fish

Every man's kind of wish

I believe very intelligent and very astute

Blonde with brown eyes, hmm very cute

Olive skin that easily tans

Back in Sweden, heaps of fans

NZ Māori with a touch of Swede

Always working at top speed

She loves playing that detective role

But too much of the 'superwoman' will take its toll

Rumour has it, that copper Māori lad

Did the dirty on her, back in the day, really bad

So she escaped to a land faraway

For a decade or more she was there to stay

Now these are the kind of rumours I cannot ignore

Because this today is the talk on the floor.

*****

Sven doesn't want to believe her old boss Bernard was having an affair with Cat. She understands he has an open arrangement with his wife that works both ways, but he wouldn't…or would he? Brushing the idea aside, she wonders if it's that sleazy new HOD for Science, the arrogant Pom, Alex. Or what about Ted, who lost his job to Alex, could it be him?

*****

Ted had been with the Ministry since it was created. He was one of the few originals; well he *was* until a few weeks ago. Without any warning, Cat had him carted off like a redundant third wheel and put out to pasture. At fifty-five, in the eyes of the beholder, the nappies in recruiting throughout town believe he has passed his use-by date. He has a wealth of knowledge with double master's science degrees, and has thirty years' experience, but no, he is 'not quite the right fit – charming, clever, confident, all the c's but no, no longer required, surplus to requirements. Another case of ageism, bitten by the same bug as Carmen.

Ted remembers how Cat had set him up. What made it worse was he was passed over for a young, upstart foreigner who didn't have residency, or a visa, was half his age and no doubt double the price.

Ted is at home licking his wounds. This side of Christmas and the wrong side of fifty, no one wants to employ him. Even his wife is not interested in him. His children have left home; they are busy working and no one has time for him.

*****

Sven continues to go through the list of suspects, discounting some as she goes. She stops at Ted.

Trusty Ted, was he trusty, good old Ted? She wonders if Ted would go off and get revenge for losing his job that quickly and being dispensed of like that after all those years of loyalty.

She goes through her other list, and finding no other obvious suspects, is about to give up. But then she thinks about Stephanie.

*****

Stephanie is still bouncing around amongst the paperwork upstairs. She has gone around and around in circles, getting nowhere except getting herself into more of a state, torturing herself, wishing she hadn't made that pass at Cat that time. She feels such a fool and wonders why she didn't just stick to Ollie, her loyal, affectionate dog – always there for her, no matter what. She wishes that woman hadn't come into her life and turned it upside down; she was happy being alone before she came crashing in. She deserved the job as she had put in the years, done the time and as a result, she deserves better treatment. She needs to tell someone the truth, but who?

*****

Another highly important meeting has been called. Everyone is feeling uneasy as they all huddle together – there are more in the meeting room this afternoon as a lot of the permanent staff have been asked to come back in off sick leave for this urgent, out-of-the-ordinary meeting.

Everyone has been told under no uncertain terms that this time a Skype call or an email just won't cut it. The communication needs to be made face to face.

Sven looks around the room to see how everyone is bearing up. A couple of the senior managers from this morning aren't there, and where is Stephanie? Shouldn't she as Acting HR Director be there to talk to her people? Stephanie is third in line, so who would step in, in her place?

Bernard gets up on the raised platform with Sonya. "Good afternoon, ladies and gentlemen, thank you very much for staying later than usual to attend this meeting. It is of the utmost importance and you deserve to hear it from me directly as opposed to hearing it through the CN. You know how important it is that we communicate with our staff first-hand so that you hear the news – the real news – from us and not twisted from another unreliable source.

"Now those few who attended the earlier meeting will have already heard some of this, so please bear with me. However, now we have almost everyone here, I can make this additional announcement. I am very surprised that the grapevine hasn't worked as well as it usually does, let alone the captive ears of the Capital News. For once, I am grateful for this.

"The first item of news I have, which the HR team were made aware of earlier today, is very sad and to save any more speculation and unnecessary suspense from the rest of the teams, here are the facts. Due to a misadventure our Cathryn Tennyson, dearly known to us in the room as Cat, was taken from us over the weekend. Her death is being treated as suspicious and she may have been involved in some foul play, which explains the additional police presence on site today. Please extend your full co-operation with them during their investigations. As soon as we have more news, we will let you know.

"The next news item is in regard to the studies carried out by Alex and his Science team, who have been…who the hell is that…?" Bernard stops awkwardly as his mobile rings. He glances at the screen, and seeing the caller ID he apologises to the meeting room. "Sorry, but it's the Minister."

Abandoning the announcement, he turns his back on the audience to answer his phone and all the staff can hear is, "Yes, yes, of course, yes I understand. Fuck, no, oh my god!" He then realises he has just said this out loud on the mic, in front of the whole meeting room, and pauses, composes himself and then readdresses the audience.

"Apologies for that announcement, ladies and gentlemen. Something of grave importance has just come up, so I need to finish this meeting now. I will ensure Katarina reschedules this essential meeting, however, as a Red Folder is coming over from the Minister's office, we need all hands on deck to provide the official information so that the Minister can answer the questions in the House of Representatives. Please carry on with the important work you do and be prepared to assist immediately when asked. Thanking you in advance."

He leaves the stage, returning to his office, and those outside in the hallway can hear him saying to Katarina, "Who does that upstart little weed of a man think he is? What's his name? Ernest Ragbottom, what a useless excuse for a man. That is the last time I am going to be talked to like that. He has never shown me any respect and all because I come from a corporate background rather than up through the public service ranks. All in all, he is a jumped-up, brown-nosing, pen pushing little secretary."

Katarina responds quite harshly. "With all due veneration, Bernard, who do you think I am? I am a secretary and very proud of it, so please don't put all us secretaries in the same carton." Katarina is now starting to feel the stress from the day's events and getting her English mixed up.

"I'm sorry if I offended you, Katarina, but you are not a secretary, you are a highly effective and efficient Executive Assistant! There is an enormous difference, and besides, it's just that Ragbum really gets up my nose."

"Bernard, I think it would be greatest if you got his surname right, for beginners, it is Ernest Rotherbottom."

Bernard suddenly bursts out laughing. "Katarina, what would I do without you? I love the way you pronounce these stupid names and mix your metaphors! You are such a breath of fresh air. Alright then, in future I will call him Roastbottom. Right, now what does that little toe-rag want? Let's put personalities aside and get to the matter in hand, as no one will be letting the Minister down on my watch!"

Some days Katarina's English is almost impeccable, but others, especially when she is tired and under stress, her conversational English goes backwards and as the day progresses, it becomes increasingly obvious. She still makes perfect sense but does tend to get the social slang mixed up. Katarina comes up with a funny response; she is getting the hang of this dry Kiwi quick-witted humour.

"Well, I got Mr Roastbottom," Katarina has a little laugh and continues, "to let me in on the folder's contents before it gets here, and somehow the news on the earthquake prediction has been leaked and CN have got hold of it. If no one gets back to them to confirm or deny this allegation, they are going to take the matter into their own hands and release this information to the public. They have already leaked the news to the Opposition MPs and they are threatening to ask an official question in this afternoon's session in the House. And Sir, you might want to take it easy on Roastbottom, he now has a brand-new wheelchair since this morning – some reporter rear-ended him in the Minister's flash new car."

Bernard laughs. "Did you say rear-ended? Now that's apt." Realising he is being highly inappropriate and there's no time for snide remarks, he gets back to the matter in hand. "Oh shit, well that explains why Ernie Roastbottom was at his very weasel best. This has come somehow from that team of mad Scientists that I have asked Sven to keep an eye on. That is probably one of the reasons why Sven has been trying to get hold of me. She was going to report back to me on her findings after attending yet another 'urgent' Science meeting. Do you know anything about this, Katarina?"

"I do actually, as I met up with Sven not so long ago. Your Cat brought in Alex after chopping off Ted, so he could work on predicting when the next earthquake is going to strike, and according to Alex it will be by the shutting of business today. Seeing at your clock, that means we have a few more hours before all hell is going to break unfastened! But Bernard, can they be correct?"

Bernard is struggling a little to understand what Katarina is trying to say through her outburst, but manages to get the gist of it. "We will need more information. Right Katarina, can you get Sven to come and see me? I just want to get a few more facts before I do anything. And I need to put a call into CN."

Katarina, not wanting him to get into any more trouble than he already has, says, "No, you don't, that's up to Comms via the Minister's office to contact CN. Just because you are DCE doesn't mean you can go off and talk to the paper directly. You will put your feet in it."

Bernard laughs again. "I love how you bastardise our sayings here. It's 'put your foot in it'. Anyhow, we are well overstaffed with Comms, and if anyone should be 'sliced and diced', to use Cat's terminology, it should be them.

"Right, so this Red Folder, let me have a look at it as soon as it arrives. How long do I have to respond to this Roastbottom whatever his name is? Why would the Minister have such an imbecile as his secretary? Is there such a shortage of competent secretaries? Well, I should know, that's why I brought you over from Sweden. Katarina, can you get me an espresso please? My energy is flagging."

"The café is now closed downstairs, but I'll go over to Tiger and get one. Hmm, make that two. One double shot coming up. I'll phone Sven to come and see you while I'm on the coffee jog."

"Coffee *run,* Katarina, that's coffee *run...*" Bernard says, laughing again.

✶✶✶✶✶

Chapter 20

Sven meets with Charlie

Sven, while touching base with Bernard, pops her head over the partition to have a quick download with Katarina. They have been texting each other back and forth getting straight down to the case in hand.

"Yes, you too? I'm just a little confused as well. I don't know who murdered her, there are so many suspects and I think she fell into the trap of allowing her past to catch up with her. Like those coincidences up in Auckland. She may have got away with stuff up there as it is so big, but our little Wellington is only a village and we don't take kindly to outsiders, especially playing that kind of game."

"I know. Wellington is much smaller than Stockholm or London for that matter. You do have to be careful – you don't want to piss too many people off here, as word gets around, and fast."

Sven butts in. "Have you had much to do with those guys in SH...?" They both burst into laughter knowing she's referring to the SHIT team.

"Apologies, how highly inappropriate of me, let me start again." Sven winks. "Have you had much to do with those gentlemen in Science Health and IT?"

Katarina shakes her head. "No, just that odd meeting that Bernard drags me into."

"Do you seriously think it was murder – with a capital M?" Sven loves exaggerating to make a point and rolls the 'r' in murder to sound like some Scottish detective. "I'm just not sure about these Thursday regular weekly meetings. I thought she was having an affair during office hours, but even I have noticed she has been looking tired and a little on edge of recent times."

Katarina replies to her friend. "I'm sure it's just the usual stress of balancing a high-flying corporate job. I think you are letting your imagination run away with itself. Hey, listen, I do have to get back to this Red Folder saga, to get the papers organised for Bernard's meeting with the Minister. The appointment has been postponed a couple of times and between you and me, the Minister has gone AWOL and no one seems to be able to locate him. His secretary has gone AWOL as well, and no one else is privy to his diary, so god knows where he is," Katarina explains. "Something to do with the *sjukhus,* whoops, I mean hospital, but even the public health system doesn't take all day to produce another wheelchair, a couple of paracetamol and discharge you. Or is that the New Zealand public health system? It wouldn't happen in Sweden."

Sven rushes off to her next meeting with the IT guys. She can't keep up with who is who in that department; there has been an influx of backfills but now she has broken the ice with Chris, she feels she can make more inroads with the team. She originally thought he was quiet and a little offhand, but after talking with him, she has changed her opinion of him. Now she has found out a bit more about him, she wants to ask him some questions face to face and watch his reaction and body language.

The meeting, like all meetings, has been postponed. Alex is in a mixture of moods, from having meltdowns every couple of minutes when the computer crashes again with all his hard facts to jumping for joy when he makes another revelation.

Sven, completely over meetings today, is glad of another lucky escape. She bumps into Chris while in the SHIT dungeon-cum-office-space-cum-lab and gets ten minutes with him where she finds out more about his background and what brings him to BS. As Katarina said, New Zealand is a small place and Wellington is like a village – everyone is connected to someone who is connected to someone, and Chris, coming from Auckland, is no exception.

Sven puts on the blonde image and doesn't let on what she's recently learnt, allowing Chris to volunteer what he wants to. The ice has been broken after their last meeting, and he is a lot more trusting and animated. He has also been to see Charlie and looks like he has got a bit off his chest.

Chris let's Sven know that he had been working with Cat up in Auckland. It also transpires that he happened to get his current job at BS without having to go through HR's so-called robust reference and security checking process as they incorrectly assumed that the agency he had come through had done the necessary checks.

Sven, reflecting as usual, thinks the place is like a disaster zone ready to go off at any minute, and isn't surprised that Nigel keeps having kittens. They just have no idea who is walking around here, what their background is, nor what their purpose is. And with all the important ministers that walk through here for meetings, she finds it alarming to know that there are no proper security measures in place. It's just like down at the State Services Commission, the same thing is happening there. As Freya had said, helping out on their huge transformation project with overloaded, antiquated computers not wanting to play nicely with each other, there has been a huge demand to get in contractors to deal with the workload and fill in for all the people who were made redundant, a little too prematurely. In haste, the security and reference checking went out the window as they had outsourced the reference checking to an employment agency across the ditch in Australia. And due to the time differences, and someone transposing the numbers in the referee's phone numbers, often the agent never ended up reference checking. In frustration, they just ticked the boxes saying that they had checked the referees, and completed the police and security checks, signed off the forms and collected their commission.

Sven's thoughts are interrupted when she comes across Chris.

"Hey Chris, glad I found you. Isn't it great when meetings are postponed? Look, we might have a few minutes before it gets rescheduled. Sorry, I know before was a bit intense. I didn't ask you, how are you settling into Wellington life? Missing the big smoke of Auckland?"

Chris looks up from his computer sheepishly, as if he was working on something on the screen that she shouldn't have seen. "Oh, good, Samantha."

"Please, Chris, you can call me Sven. Only my mother

calls me Samantha, so when I hear that name I feel like I am being told off, if you know what I mean?"

That was the right answer as Chris is beaming now with his barriers down; they have something else in common. "I so know what you mean! When my mum calls me Christopher, I know I am about to get a right bollocking, even at this stage in my life. No, I'm not missing Auckland too much – of course the weather and the beaches, but I sure as hell don't miss the traffic jams, the crowding…"

"So how do we down here in the Public Servant city of windy Wellington get lucky enough to snap up an IT whizz kid like you from the big flashing lights of Auckland?" asks Sven in her serious, yet curious way.

Chris temporarily gets a little on edge again, but then, looking at Sven's earnest expression and not sensing any animosity, the filters start coming down again. "Oh, let's say someone owed me a favour and I heard through the grapevine that the Ministry was crying out for people with skills like mine. And let's face it, who wants to give up their evenings and basically their life to commit themselves to working down in the cold basement here to nut out IT solutions all night long?"

"I can't think of too many; maybe some university leavers would love a job like that? Just to make some 'readies' and to learn more at the same time, network with new people, and hey, to get the privilege of working for the biggest Ministry in Australasia. Who gets to put that on their CV? But yes, you're right, young sparks like you want to be out and about in the evening, spending all their money. It would seem you are wiser than that. I'm picking that evenings are a fantastic way of getting stuff done without all the interruptions and a big bonus is you miss out on all those tedious meetings, and you get to save because you are not out and about," she qualifies.

"True, Sven. No, seriously," he says, backtracking, aware he may have come across a bit sinister and offhand, and knowing that Sven only means well. Besides, she was the first person who had bothered to take the time to talk to him. To most people he was invisible but Sven had bothered to come and introduce herself and let him know if he needed to talk about anything to drop her a line. The only other person who ever spoke to him was his boss Alex and that was only to skite about how clever he was and how great his job was and how wonderful Cat was.

He was so deep in thought he had forgotten what the question was. "Sorry, what was the question again? Sorry, I remember now. I needed to get out of Auckland for a bit and I heard good things about Wellington. It's arty, lots of job opportunities and it takes no time at all to commute – well, unless you live way out like you do, Sven."

"I don't know why, but I thought you lived in town, in Miramar? Why would you be living way up the coast? The coast is usually reserved for retirees and of course people like me, whatever that means?" Sven ponders.

"No, I have been staying at the backpackers around the corner, the Waterloo, and thanks to my Auckland connections, I am now living out in Porirua."

"The old Waterloo, eh? I remember when it was one of *the* hotels in town, like the Midland, and had a couple of cool bars. I'm biased – I used to work in the house bar serving all those Auckland businessmen who were down in the capital on business. And of course local lawyers who had just spent their day in court. So, it's a backpackers' palace nowadays. Lucky your mates saw the light and moved down here. Excellent choice. It's always good to have mates in a new city, aye?"

"Yes, I am very lucky, I worked with them at a factory up in South Auckland. In fact, one of my mate's aunties works here. You may know her – she's Head of Pasifika and Māori?"

"Not Julia? Is she your mates auntie?" replies Sven excitedly. "She is lovely, so down-to-earth. I've been working with her and her team. Real salt of the earth woman. You are lucky to know such lovely people and in such high places, those two qualities don't usually go hand in hand."

"Yes, I know what you mean," laughs Chris, thinking about Cat.

Sven feels a little guilty about where that conversation could go, and not wanting to speak too ill of the dead, she responds with, "Hey, gotta get out and pound that pavement and clock up some steps before I chicken out. It was great chatting. Have a nice day – well, what's left of it," and she races off.

Sven looks at her Fitbit. It is now reading 23,500 steps so far today, and there are only two hours left in her working day to co-ordinate with when the Kiwi Con or some other mode of transport for today, whisks her away homeward-bound. But will it go tonight, she wonders? Surely they will need to keep it in overnight… No Comms update on that yet either.

She decides a change of scene will be good, and not wanting to make small talk with anyone or get stuck in the mass hysteria of 'she says, he says, and what do you think' she goes down to the basement to her locker and jumps into her running gear. Sven has definitely become a sports junkie and enjoys getting out on the streets of Wellington, as running gives her a chance to clear her mind and suss out different parts of town.

As she runs down the waterfront quay, the whole goings-on from the day, the conversations with Charlie, Chris, her last one with Cat on the KC last Friday, Jillian, Elspeth and Katarina, not forgetting Bernard, all race through her head. Was this a murder, or just Cat's time? What was it? She decides to slow down on her way back up the wharf and takes a walk alongside the Cake Tin – Westpac Stadium, the biggest stadium in town, to have a glimpse of the dear old Kiwi Con and see what's happening to her; she may bump into Bert and Ernie and find out what's happening in their neck of the woods.

She stops jogging and walks slowly along the platforms and up the ramps that lead to the stadium. She looks down on the yard and sees the Kiwi Con, all on her lonesome, parked up. There are a number of people dressed in either blue uniforms or white disposable SOCO suits hovering around outside one of the carriages and from where she is standing she can see people walking up and down the corridors inside. She wonders if she'll be on the commuter train tonight, dragging out over all twenty stops, and groans inwardly at the prospect of a long journey home.

She starts walking back down the ramps towards platform one and two when, as luck would have it, she sees Ernie, one of the cleaning supervisors from this morning striding towards her. He doesn't recognise Sven as she is in her jogging gear, with cap and sunnies covering most of her face, hair tied back in a ponytail. She slows down to a standstill when she sees him in deep conversation with someone she doesn't recognise. Clearly another workmate from KiwiRail. She bends down as if to tie up her shoelace and overhears the tail end of a potentially interesting conversation.

"Oh my god, what a sight, not something I want to repeat in a hurry. Bert made me open up the door, it took a bit of force as the body was stuck, pinned up against it. I haven't seen a dead body before and it wasn't a pretty sight, especially the gash on her head. She was all made up with full lipstick and gunk plastered all over her face, looking like a doll. Nothing but a rag doll, just hanging there so to speak; so sad. I can't believe she had been there in that position all weekend. And no one had noticed her missing. How sad is that? You would hope if you or I had gone missing for a night or two, let alone *three* nights, that at least our wives would contact the cops and raise the alarm. This woman had no one – well so it would seem," Ernie exclaims. He wells up and gets quite emotional just reliving the trauma all over again. He shouldn't really be talking like that to Stan, but Stan is one of the old-timers who has been working with him for decades. *Stuff Comms,* he thinks. He owes them nothing. Besides, he needs to talk about it, and by the time they organise their 'best practice' this and that and so-called counselling services, it will be Christmas next year.

"Well, who was she? And what's all this fuss, was she a celebrity or something? If she was a celebrity, what was she doing on a commuter train? I mean to say, celebrities don't catch trains do they, so who was she?" asks Stan.

"Some bigwig from across the road, over at the Big Super Ministry. I heard she wasn't too popular as she was in charge of a lot of people and rumour has it she was about to make most of them redundant. Just before Christmas, so they wouldn't have a job to come back to. No pay packet, no dignity, no nothing," explains Ernie.

"Well I'm afraid, young man, that's the way of the world today, nothing is secure. The only constant out there is change. Besides, KiwiRail did the same thing to us this time last year, so how do we know it won't happen all over again for us? You just don't know who you can trust. Best to keep it to yourself, what you are really thinking. I've learnt not to share too much and when I'm not busy, I just look busy – no point bringing attention to oneself. I say stick beneath the radar and you'll be fine. Oh, and belonging to the union always helps."

*****

Sven, meanwhile, has progressed from tying her shoelaces – one job that can't be drawn out for too long – to doing some serious stretches, starting with her calves and then thighs, and swigging back mouthfuls of water from her drink bottle. It's a sunny December day and with her cap and sunnies on, she's hoping Ernie won't recognise her from the train this morning. Fortunately, like most human beings, he is far too involved in his own micro world.

Hearing enough she starts jogging off back towards the showers in the basement at BS Headquarters. She showers, changes and walks up the stairs. Everyone is still rushing around like headless chickens, but she hears that an announcement is going to be made and just HR are being called back into the ground floor meeting room. It's going on for four o'clock and a lot of the early starters, the ones who clock in at 7am are angry that they have to stay beyond their 7.35 to 8.0 hours (depending on what contract they are on) and should have all been gone at 3.30pm, by 3.31pm at the very latest.

Rumour has it that possibly the murderer is in the office; or is that a rumour as well? It has got to the stage where no one can siphon fact from fiction.

Sven hooks up with Katarina. Sven is buzzing on a mixture of adrenalin and all the caffeine her body has been pumping for most of the day. Not to mention the endorphins from all the exercise. She is aware she is heading for 'top gear' and doesn't want to spiral out of control with everything she has buzzing around in her head. She knows too much, as usual, and needs to download. But first she must collect a bit more information, and make sure she has her facts right. The last thing she wants to do is make a fool of herself, especially in front of Charlie. Still on a high from their last talk, she tries to suppress the excitement.

However, her heart is trying to rule her head, and she has to take a couple of deep breaths and get through this.

Charlie hunts Sven down and finds her emerging from the changing room downstairs – the beauty of having unisex facilities.

"Hey girl, I thought I would find you here. Good timing, glad you are changed and all ready to rock and roll. I need you in this meeting. Come with me please."

Sven, for the first time all day, obediently follows Charlie up the stairs. It is now her turn to be questioned and Charlie is not letting her get out of this. "Sven, I know I keep repeating myself, but it is good to see you again, I mean that. How have you *really* been? I've missed you."

"Great, I'm really enjoying working for such an interesting ministry and working back in New Zealand again."

"Don't lie, Sven, you are bored shitless, I can tell by the way you walk around. And that look on your face, remember you taught me that, Sven. Actions speak louder than words and if I'm not wrong, I would say you are still just in first gear. Possibly second gear on good days. Am I right?"

Sven can't make eye contact with him. She remembers how much she used to get lost in his big brown eyes and how she used to sit there for hours hanging onto his every word, but she will not get lost in them again. Besides, being single is much more fun and that's how she wants to stay, doesn't she? They need to catch the lift and stand waiting for it. As they enter, her heel gets momentarily stuck in the lift shaft and as she frees herself, stumbles into Charlie's willing and waiting arms. The silence is deathly as Sven realises that there was never anyone else for her, Charlie has always been the one. Eventually she looks up and responds…

*****

In the meeting room, behind closed doors, she shares the information he needs from the train ride home on Friday and the train back into town on Monday. She reveals the brief conversation with Chris in the buffet car, dancing in the aisles with Bernard – everything she recalls, right down to the cleaners getting the WC door open on the train this morning. She recounts the whole uproar in and around the building since she got to work only eight hours earlier, her findings and observations over the last few weeks, the revelations with the Outlook calendars, and the recently overheard conversation down at the railway station.

Sven is getting a little frustrated with the repetitive questioning and is feeling guilty even though she has nothing to feel guilty about. She is a bit over Rex's line of questioning and wants to tell him where he can stick it, but thinks better of it. "Like I told you before, all I can tell you from Friday is I got a second round of drinks in and I noticed it went quiet after that, so I assumed Cat had got off the train or had gone and annoyed others with her self-importance in another carriage. I noticed a few people were congregating out between carriage three and four, by the loos, having a chat about something. It was like a Sunday market, there was a constant flow of people going through and talking out there. I don't know who they were talking to, or what they were talking about."

"Okay, great, Samantha, you're doing good. Remember, any finer detail, anything is good," Charlie says, gauging she is getting a little pissed.

"At one stage Bernard was out there, then Stephanie, and then Chris, from IT. It was like a mini BS meeting, except it was being held offsite from BS Castle. I just wondered what it was all about, and being like I am, I had to walk out there to see who they were talking to. I pretended to go to the bog and pushed past and saw it was Cat who seemed to be the centre of attention. Knowing she loves that sort of thing, I just moved on, leaving her to it."

"Why didn't you like Ms Tennyson? Had she done something wrong?" Rex asks.

"I don't like or dislike Ms Tennyson. She is who she is. I just don't admire her behaviour. One must separate the behaviour from the person. Anyhow, god knows why they all had to have a kōrero out there. I came back to my seat, had another drink and then needed to visit the little ladies' room yet again, after downing my drinks and plenty of water."

Rex, ignoring some of Sven's sarcasm, proceeds with his line of questioning. "How much longer after you saw her the first time, until you went out to the loo?"

"Ah, probably about fifteen minutes or so. When I went back out, the clearway was empty of all people. That's when I noticed the loo door was shut. Not engaged, but I couldn't push it open. Someone or something was behind it. I swore and cursed and then went to another carriage. By the time I got back the toilet door was completely shut and it said 'engaged'." She volunteers this information quite briskly.

"Sven, we're almost done, this is great," chips in Charlie, the peacemaker.

"I didn't see Cat again after that. In hindsight, maybe it was her that was in the loo. We hadn't got into Paraparaumu at that stage. She had made a lot of people very unhappy, especially on Friday at the HRLT, stringing everyone along with all this restructure business. She had had all week to rub it in people's faces and then dropping loud hints on the train, she had to go on and on as well. Sometimes she never knows when to stop."

Rex speaks up. "Well now she has stopped."

Charlie cuts in. "Sven, I can't really disclose too much yet, but yes, what I have gathered today from various sources is that Bernard and Cat have been burning the candle at both ends with many an evening meeting. They have both been clocking up quite a bit of glide time and I know they haven't been seeing eye to eye. Again, to use your phrase, don't jump to conclusions – things are not how they appear to be."

"Yes, I caught them in the boardroom one night, far too close for my liking and..."

"Yes, go on, Ms Svensson, and…?" prompts Rex.

"It was nothing. I misinterpreted their actions. I have spoken to Bernard and he was consoling her. She had got very upset of recent times, working too hard, and he was just comforting her."

Charlie stands up and leads her to the door. He shuts the door behind him and in the hallway says to her quietly, "Sven, you really are wasted here, working in such a rigid, suffocating environment. I bet you were a huge hit overseas. How long are you thinking of sticking around down under this time? How long is this gig? Another fixed-term or is this more of a permanent nature? Don't tell me you are grown up now and have come home to settle down. Is there someone you have come home to settle down with?"

Sven looks up, feeling quite relieved she can talk to someone for a change instead of listening, and Charlie isn't just 'someone'. He was her ex-fiancé and the best listener she had ever come across. He was everything packed into one package, an incredibly good-looking package; a great listener, a confidante, her best friend, lover, her soul mate. Why had she been so insistent on breaking up with him just because of what she saw that night? She did have a tendency when emotions were on high alert to misjudge events. She had covered it up by saying she was putting her career first.

Answering part of his question, she responds. "What's with the ninety-eight questions? This gig is for six months, but who knows what will happen with all this mess? I was meant to be reporting to Cat and Bernard this week with my findings and ideas going forward. My needs analysis is almost complete, but then with the last few weeks' courageous conversations staff have been having in my coaching sessions they have been really revealing all sorts. So now with all this new evidence – I mean information, it's like we need to wipe the last few months and start again. Nothing like opening a can of worms and then all sorts of shite comes to the surface and just keeps coming."

"You see, you were born to be a cop – you just said the 'evidence' you have collected; that's hilarious. Anyhow, on a serious note Sven, I would appreciate if you could keep everything that was discussed today confidential. You haven't gone and shared your 'evidence' and thoughts with anyone else, have you?" he asks, looking suspiciously at Sven. He knows from experience how passionate Sven can get and once she has a theory, it's like a bee in her bonnet and very hard for Sven to ride beneath the radar.

"Ah, I did say a bit to Elspeth and Katarina, the two EAs, and maybe a few flyaway comments to Flat White and Freya, but besides that, no, not really...was that wrong of me?" she asks Charlie innocently, fluttering her eyelids to imitate the much over-used blonde bimbo image.

"Well put it is this way, we have enough speculation going on at the moment within the BS and surrounding public service that the rumour mills are doing overtime! KiwiRail has been coming up with theories all day, a lot of hearsay and nothing too concrete as clearly nothing like this has happened in most of the youngish, current staff's lifetime. So of course, it is 'dead' exciting for them. Sven, if anything else comes up please ring me. Have you put my number into your contacts on your phone yet? Or better still, under your favourites – that way if any more useful information comes up you can readily text me. You know

I am available for you anytime, Sven. I must go, my cell phone is vibrating itself off the table and I am needed downstairs. I have the Commissioner breathing down my neck and after all, its taxpayers' money and we wouldn't want to take any longer than we need to on this. I also don't want to get stuck in that Wellington traffic, I want to be back in Palmy sooner rather than later." Charlie throws one of his jaw-dropping smiles Sven's way.

"Hang on a minute, Charlie. I know you are in a hurry, but I have an idea to fast-track the case. I've already talked with Katarina and we know we can make it happen with your help.

Sven repeats her conversation with Katarina earlier about getting everyone in the same room. He agrees. "Great idea, Sven. You are right, it's very old school, but what the heck. Get your mate Katarina to contact the suspects, find out where they are and she, as his EA, can tell them all that Bernard has called a meeting urgently in his boardroom, okay? I will round up the necessary police escorts to take them up there," he says and swiftly leaves the room.

Sven is left sitting in the hallway feeling a mixture of excitement, sadness and a little flustered. She can't believe how he has that amazing ability to make her feel so much lighter, like she's just had the best downloading session ever, but on the other hand, seriously frustrated at how his good Kiwi 'she'll be right' bloke accent and good-looking boy charms can woo women left right and centre in a room. Most women react to his charm like a storm in a tea cup has just whistled through and they have no idea why they are suddenly feeling weak at the knees and so out of kilter.

*****

PART 5

NEWS FLASH, THE BS HAS HIT THE HEADLINES

At last!

Chapter 21

The Murderer is in the Office?

Within thirty minutes, Katarina and Bernard are strategically placed in Bernard's private boardroom with Rex sitting at the top of the table. Several chairs are still sitting empty.

Alex has made his 'announcement of all announcements' informing everyone that an earthquake of great magnitude will be hitting in and around close of business, at 1700 if not earlier. With time rapidly approaching that golden hour, most people are beside themselves. The occupants of the boardroom would sooner be somewhere else rather than stuck in this room.

They continue to make small talk about the earthquake announcement and Bernard and Katarina are at the other end of the table, devising a strategy for advising the Minister while waiting patiently for their guests to arrive.

As the suspects enter the room, Sven shows them to the empty chairs while Bernard is pacing up and down in front of the whiteboard finishing off the strategy, which in his opinion is of equal importance, the welfare and safety of his staff. However, he also wants this murder inquiry to be done and dusted and to go away. And then there's the matter of the Red Folder and the disappearing and reappearing Minister and his PA or his secretary, something to do with the hospital. He's had his wife, Margaret, on the line, asking when he can take leave as she wants to attend some niece's wedding in Melbourne, and he can't even remember which niece it is.

Really, I could do well without Mondays like this, he thinks to himself.

He looks up at his whiteboard which is now covered in illegible writing scripted in an assortment of colours. From orange, to the standard blue, green, black and red. There are words written strategically inside and outside of the drawn-up boxes with arrows between them. Each arrow haphazardly points in a variety of directions with a timeline scribbled down the left-hand margin of the whiteboard. And what looks like initials are sprawled over the x axis, horizontally across the board.

Bernard is tired of waiting and is ready to say something when his phone goes, and all that can be heard is, "As I was recalling to one of our HODs, Alex here who is new to the public service, it's not the Minister you have to watch out for, but his weasel-faced secretary. That jumped-up little poo…"

Katarina to the rescue as always leaps in and shrieks, "Bernard! You can't say that! That he is a *bög* is irrelevant. However much he is a conniving, back-stabbing, brown-nosing, butt-covering, nasty piece of work with extra-long nasal hair who can't stand anyone who encroaches on his lofty domain and will shaft anyone with his petty little power games…"

Everyone turns and stares at the Swedish EA, jaws dropping and mouths gaping, a newfound respect at her insight – most of the attendees in the room had thought she was just a pretty blonde accessory that Bernard had collected from some disestablished ABBA fan club from long ago.

"Go you good thing!" Sven cheers, turning to Bernard and winking. "No mixed metaphors that time, was there, Bernard? My English lesson coaching days are complete, Katarina has just graduated."

She then continues on a more serious note. "However, with all due respect, ladies and gentlemen, it has been brought to my attention today that the Minister's flamboyant secretary has unfortunately suffered some quite nasty injuries from a car accident earlier on in the day. The Minister and his secretary were en route to our offices when one of the paparazzi who were following too closely tail-ended the Minister's brand-new car."

She tries not to laugh, knowing she got the giggles at the worst times possible. She had one of those uncontrollable, contagious laughs – something between a pig snorting and a hyena laughing, and whether the content was funny or not, those surrounding her, especially Katarina, would burst into hysterics.

Bernard looks at Sven. "What unfortunate accident? What happened? Is the Minister okay?" He was hoping that he may have been detained, not a nice thought, but at least honest. That way it would stop the Red Folders coming over thick and fast and he could get back to some more serious work like running the business without the constant political interference.

Sven, having had time to control herself, comes back and replies, "Yes, Minister, I mean, yes, the Minister is fine. It was Ernest who took most of the impact. He was in the back on the side the car drove into. He is unable to walk. In fact, A & E has just released him, in a wheelchair. I believe he is on his way over."

"Well that will slow the …" Bernard thinks out loud.

Nothing like a bit of an icebreaker or two to keep the attendees distracted from the pending matters in hand – the murder inquiry and the predicted earthquake.

*****

The remaining guests are escorted in and take their allocated seats in the executive wood-panelled boardroom. It almost resembles a scene out of a Miss Marple Murder Mystery, where the designated murder suspects all line up with ghastly green velvet curtains acting as a backdrop, ready for the inquisition and process of elimination.

Sven, keen to get this meeting underway, looks a little too hard at Bernard in an attempt to work out what's really going on with him. She is in two minds; she wants to think good of her boss and believes he is purely innocent, but she can't ignore the hearsay that's out on the floor and she hears the verdict in her mind: 'Guilty, guilty as charged'. Bernard and Cat have been acting very strangely and if she's not mistaken they have become more than friends. She knows how intoxicating Cat can be with men; they can't seem to resist her. Bernard has had to attend a number of seminars and heated meetings lately with the Minister and he has taken Cat along to most of them, as she is the 'people' person and networks with all and sundry. She is very crafty, and it is quite a show watching her 'do' the room… Sven's thoughts are interrupted by Charlie's formal opening of the meeting.

"Tēnā koe. Thank you everyone for coming, apologies for the short notice of this very important and urgent meeting. As you know we have been running investigations for most of the day and it is nearing the end of the working day and we have to bring this matter to a head. We have been doing our due diligence and we just have a few more t's to cross and i's to dot and then I think we can wrap it up for the day." Charlie looks at Alex.

"I understand, to use your phrase Alex, that 'time is of the essence' and there is a high possibility that an earthquake is heading our way soon, so I will ensure we have this finished up and we have all left the building, one way or the other by that time. We have the luxury of…" he pauses to look at his watch "…just under an hour and we know we won't be kicked out of this boardroom. This is only for VIPs," he jokes, to add light to the atmosphere.

All eyes are fixed on Alex.

"Alex, thank you for joining us here today, I appreciate it and will make this quick, in order for you to get back to your investigations. I understand from my notes that you were not brought into the Ministry in the usual, or should I say *official* way. How did you get your role here? Can I remind you that it is in your best interests to give accurate, succinct answers; that way, everyone else can get through quickly and you can get back to your important work."

Alex, who feels he is above having to be interrogated, responds. "My god, man, do you not realise how vital my calculations are? Nothing like this would happen back home in Mother England. At the end of the day, it was your lot who were the exiled prisoners." Turning to Bernard he adds, "Are you going to allow this jumped-up colonial bobby to publicly humiliate me?"

Bernard, his face turning an angry shade of purple, controls himself enough to respond. "Just answer the man's questions, you condescending, stuck-up…"

Charlie leaps in to stop Bernard mid-sentence. "I realise that this interrogation is not good timing. However, despite the pathetic grasp of your own history, let us get back to the question in hand…one might think you were trying to hide something…are you?"

Alex, realising that he might have just met his match and that 'time is of the essence', meekly answers. "I worked with Cat previously and through a mutual colleague of ours, she contacted me with an offer I couldn't refuse, solely to do one 'piece of work' – to predict the next earthquake. I admit we have been a little unethical in the way we have been conducting this earthquake investigation and should have been more upfront with Bernard here about it. And I must apologise, Bernard; we have been in touch directly with the Minister's secretary about our earthquake predictions. However, I can safely say I never intentionally leaked this to the newspaper or the TV station." Then, weaselling up a gear, "Like you, Bernard, the safety and welfare of our staff is of utmost importance and I believe they are in grave danger. Hence we pushed along with this project, and with such tight deadlines and with your busy schedule, we felt it was best to deal directly with the Minister and not worry you with this matter."

Bernard wants to explode, yet again, but Katarina kicks him under the table to centre him and mouths two words:

'Big picture'.

Charlie looks at Alex and asks, "You have also been seen on a number of occasions after hours and during hours meeting Ms Tennyson. As it is a purely professional relationship, can you tell me why you and Ms Tennyson felt it necessary to meet as far away north as the Kapiti Coast and on weekends? Were you having an extracurricular liaison with Ms Tennyson?"

"I most certainly was not! Cat is not like that. She is highly professional; she would never mix business with pleasure."

Sven, meanwhile, is watching Bernard's body language very closely to see if he flinches at the possibility of another man having an affair with his calculating Cat. Bernard is unable to sustain the poker face at the best of times, she remembers from Sweden days.

The conversation continues a little longer and Charlie is satisfied with his results. Rex helps him along the way but is mainly taking notes as well as recording the conversation. Due to cost cutting they have an old tape recording machine and the batteries have not been recharged as it was in no one's job description to use their initiative to do this. Charlie has, however, plugged the machine into the power point at the far end of the room. When Rex plays back the tape through his headphones, the voices are distorted and muffled in places.

"Please people, speak up in a nice, clear loud voice, we are experiencing technical problems, and this machine is not good at picking up voices. I am also recharging the batteries and we need to use the power socket in the meantime. Please bear with us folks."

"Okay, Chris, would you like to go next?" Rex asks.

Sven notices that Stephanie is fidgeting even more than usual and is using her asthma inhaler intermittently. She feels sorry for her. "Stephanie, are you okay, would you like some water?"

Stephanie nods to indicate she is okay; she does not like the attention focused on her. "I do have a very important meeting I should be at right now. Is this really so important that all of us need to be here at the same time? It really seems to be a highly ineffective use of time." Sven thinks that maybe they will get to see what Stephanie Welsh is made of today, and she wonders if any latent talents will be revealed.

*****

All eyes are now on Chris, who is incredibly nervous as he hates being in a room with so many people. He detests being confined and feels if he doesn't watch his breathing inhalations he will start to hyperventilate and bring on a panic attack. This is why he prefers his night shift gig.

He used to think he was quite unique with his set of mental health issues, but since visiting Cat's sixth floor he has witnessed more than a few suffering from panic attacks. He remembers what his psychologist taught him: just remove yourself from the room if you are feeling an attack or outburst coming on. Go to the toilet and breathe into your paper bag – always have one in your pocket. Also count your breaths like counting sheep, and focus on your breathing and not what is happening all around you. He is now counting and watching his breath – in one, out two, while he works out what he is going to say to Charlie.

"Yes, here to help." Chris looks at Sven who he has

built quite a good relationship with over the last few hours. She smiles back and gives him the thumbs up, which reassures him.

"Can you tell me what your relationship is with Ms Tennyson?"

"I don't have a relationship with Cat. I'm not sure what you mean?"

"Okay, shall I put it another way? How were you introduced to Cathryn and when and where was this?" asks Rex.

Now feeling even more uncomfortable, if that is possible, Chris breathes calmly again, looking at Sven for reassurance and says, "No matter what I say, I know it is going to be twisted and will all be taken out of context. This is not fair. You want the truth and nothing but the truth, I will give it to you, but please let me finish first. I am not good in social situations and I don't come across as professional and polished as the rest of you. I'm not used to crowds or working in offices, especially this size, that's why I am happy working the late shifts."

"It's okay, Chris. Remember our conversation from before. Just take your time," Sven says.

Chris continues. "I have told Samantha here a bit about my past, but for the record, yes, Cat and I go way back. My relationship, or should I say 'meeting her' goes back to when we were kids growing up in Auckland. We lived in the same street, knew each other's families."

Charlie goes to butt in and decides against it. However, Alex can't help himself and says, "So, childhood sweethearts?"

No one laughs, and Charlie speaks up. "Alex, you seem to have the habit of speaking up when it's not your turn or where you can't add value. Now time is of the essence, so let's move this along, shall we?"

Too late, Chris has lost it and decides to go off on a more sarcastic tangent, which doesn't do him any favours.

"Yes, that's right, the all-American dream, me and Cat. And we have been inseparable ever since, hence why I followed her down to Wellington. Bit like you, Alex, I couldn't get enough of her."

It had been organised that should Chris require assistance, Sven would speak on his behalf. He nods to her and Sven cuts in and gets them all back on track. "The 'childhood dream' from hell, the type you want to forget about as soon as you can. However, that is neither here nor there. What's important is Chris *did* bump into Cat again and she offered him a full time role to come into the Auckland company she was working for to fix the computer system. He did as she asked but unfortunately, Cat was in the middle of her restructuring proposal which would mean Chris's new workmates would lose their jobs and just before Christmas. Chris confronted Cat on this as he felt it was unfair and as a result, he lost his job."

"Is this right?" Rex asks. "And are you happy for Samantha to talk on your behalf? I will need you to sign this statement at the end."

"Yes, I am happy for Sven to do this for me, she's doing a better job than I could. Like I said, I'm not great with talking with people, especially in this confined space."

Sven continues. "The bottom line is yes, Chris was very angry with her and he wanted revenge, but not the type of revenge you think. He wanted to get even for all the harm she caused to so many innocent people's lives. He borrowed the camera surveillance gear from work, always with the intention of returning it. The purpose being to record what Cat was up to with her extracurricular activities after hours at home. He did adjust the step on Kiwi Con's carriage four with the intention of holding up the train at the first station, Paraparaumu, so he could get to Cat's home during the train delay to pick up the week's camera coverage and replace it with a new tape for the weekend. The idea was to humiliate her and insert certain parts of the film coverage into her PowerPoint slide show at the big HR announcement she had scheduled today. Yes, he had also been lurking around her desk and looking at her files, especially the ones she was using to justify yet another restructure. It went horribly wrong when Cat's neighbour, Bob, saw Chris making several trips to and from Cat's property and called the police."

Sven continues. "After collecting the weekend's camera footage today, there was nothing of Cat on the tape, which seemed weird as the last time he saw her was Friday night on the train, just before it had pulled into Paraparaumu. Yes, he had had an argument with her on the train on Friday night, but then who didn't? He was just one of the many who were questioning her on her integrity and actions that night."

Sven finishes off her detailed speech and sits back in her chair with a huge sigh of relief. Everyone in the room looks at her and Chris, some distraught and some confused. Suddenly a lot has been revealed, and in a meeting of all places. Now that's never happened before!

Charlie gives her time to compose herself. "Samantha, have you finished? Is there anything else you would like to add?" And looking at Chris, "Is this the truth and the whole truth, will you attest to this?"

"Yes, I most certainly will, I couldn't have said that better myself. I will sign on the dotted line for that." Then, looking at Sven, he adds, "Thank you so much, I really appreciate everything you have done for me. You are seriously one in a million – every company needs someone like you. Why don't we have more coaches that we and the boys can go to instead of this HR lot, who are so up themselves they can't see up their…"

Stephanie looks like it's her turn to explode.

Charlie quickly intervenes. "Okay Chris, I think we gave you plenty of opportunity to talk. Right, next on the list is Bernard. Would you like to tell us about your relationship with Cat?"

Bernard is checking his phone and responding to emails. He finds it very difficult to slow down and do nothing. All the same, this meeting is a great inconvenience and he is not sure why he has to be present.

"Bernard…?" Rex asks.

"Right, so I am on. Very well then." Bernard begins as he reluctantly puts his phone down, "Ms Tennyson and I met each other at a conference recently in Rotorua. It was the annual leadership conference where key people from HR and training backgrounds come in to talk to us about how we can improve our businesses and put them into the twenty-first century. I was very impressed with the way she presented her piece and the content was clearly very professional. As my brief is to cut costs and improve the reputation of our business it was an obvious choice to employ Ms Tennyson. She has an impeccable reputation for being a 'mover and shaker' and our government department is sadly lacking in this area. She was between jobs and it was very timely."

Katarina looks at Stephanie, who looks like she has just been kicked in the face. "Nice one Bernard, we could have done without that comment. Do you want to make Stephanie feel even more second-rate than she already does?"

Ignoring Katarina's comment, Charlie summarises. "So Ms Tennyson's professional background is impeccable. What about her personal reputation, can you comment on that?"

Bernard, not liking the tone in his voice, stares back at Mr Rogers with a blank expression and Katarina comes to Bernard's defence immediately. "I don't like your tone and I certainly didn't like your attitude towards others in this room," she says in her best English.

Rex and Charlie work well together; having an excellent reputation of solving the tricky cases, they often play the good and bad cop duo well. Today, each of them is playing both depending on who they are talking to. Charlie usually comes across the laid-back one, but at times can't help himself with his sarcasm and they swap roles, depending on the audience, their mood, and time constraints. He seems to enjoy playing these long-winded games, unnecessarily winding people up like some absurd cat and mouse game in the interim to keep him occupied. It is reminiscent of a theatrical production, where he has already come to the conclusion, but is going through due process.

Charlie apologises almost convincingly and continues on. "I'm sorry, Mr Johnson, if that is what you felt. I promise I will do everything I can to speed up this process and make it as pain free as possible. Nevertheless, these questions must be asked; however, I will rephrase it. What do you consider your professional relationship to be like with Ms Tennyson?'"

Bernard responds. "I think we had a very good relationship, professionally. Each time we would meet, Cat and I got on very well. She knew what her brief was, and she was carrying it out very effectively."

Katarina coughs. Rex, on cue, realises it's time for him to cut in and smooth the waters. "Katarina, is everything okay? Would you like some water or other refreshment?"

"I'm fine, thank you."

Stephanie takes over even though it's not her turn.

"With all due respect, Bernard, I do need to interject here. Relations with you and Ms Tennyson have not been going smoothly of recent times and she has been doing a bit behind your back. Today, right now, I believe you got proof of this. She's been off scheming as usual and previously had gone straight to the Minister with this earthquake prediction nonsense. She may be following your 'brief' but she's also following her own modus operandi along with our other so called impeccable HOD here, Alexander. Do you not think I haven't noticed your heated tête-à-têtes of recent times?"

Charlie goes to butt in, but is enjoying this suddenly surprising display Ms Welsh is putting on and making up for lost time. He has been quiet for a few minutes and besides, something else has popped up on the radar he hadn't noticed – extracurricular activities with the CE and yet another woman besides the infamous Ms Tennyson. Had he been blind, or worse still, why hadn't his new trusty assistant, Sven told him about this?

Charlie asks, "Excuse me, Ms Welsh. Could you please tell me about Mr Johnson and Ms Tennyson's relationship and distinguish between the personal and professional if you would like, for better clarification? It's always good to nip these sorts of misunderstandings in the bud. Please continue, take your time."

Sven looks at him twice, thinking he can be very diplomatic and tactful when he chooses. She wonders why Stephanie is suddenly so anti with Bernard; she seems to have flicked a switch and flipped her lid all of a sudden.

Stephanie continues. "Look, I have met women like Cat all my professional life. They are charming to their male bosses and give them all the persuasive lines along with empty promises they never keep, both in the boardroom and in the bedroom. I can see through those lines and Cat was no exception. She played Bernard all the way, saying the words he wanted to hear. I can't say I ever saw them actually getting down, but I wouldn't be surprised."

Bernard has finally found his voice. "Excuse me, Stephanie. It's not what it appears. Sven also accused me on Friday night of having an affair with Cat. Yes, I agree, Cat is one very persuasive lady, but it's not what it appeared…"

Rex chimes in. "Well, as time is of the essence, could you perhaps tell us once and for all what all this 'it isn't how it appears to be' stuff is in fact all about?"

Bernard continues. "Cat was sick – very sick. She had been suffering for some time from I'm not sure exactly what, as I am not a doctor or a specialist. But she was stressed and in a few recent meetings she had had to walk out. I didn't know what was happening at first. I just thought she didn't like what was being said, and was leaving the room to calm down. I had confronted her several times and it appears she was starting to suffer from anxiety and panic attacks again. She had evidently had them previously, but they had temporarily gone away. I had suggested she see a doctor here in Wellington and get some advice."

Bernard pauses and then continues. "Against her better judgement, she finally gave in and went to see a doctor who referred her to a specialist. Sven, that night you saw me with my arms around her, it was not what you thought. We were not having an affair – she looked up to me as the father figure she had never had. Not that this is anyone's business, but I will tell you all anyway. While my wife and I were in Sweden, Margaret had suffered from panic attacks. I could see the same patterns with Cat; the hyperventilation, the shortness of breath and the huge overwhelming feeling."

Charlie looks at Bernard. "Do go on."

"With this pre-Christmas drinking fest that happens in NZ, she had been burning the candle at both ends and getting stuck into alcohol while the doctors were testing her on different medication and varying dosages. Friday night, after just a couple of wines, she was as high as a kite and was speaking out of turn, revealing classified ministry information in a public place, so of course I spoke severely to her. That was why I was seen having an argument with her outside of carriage four. Sadly, that was the last time I saw her. I had arranged to catch up with her over the weekend, to rehearse a bit of the big announcement today and she didn't answer her phone all weekend. I thought this was really strange and that is why I was late in this morning. I had gone around to her house this morning, but there was no one there. So, I guess we all look guilty as charged, but I can assure you I am not!"

"Thank you for your full and frank conversation. It has all been duly noted and yes, that does fill in some of the missing pieces," Charlie continues. "Right, I believe it could be your 'official' turn now, Ms Welsh.''

Stephanie has calmed down a bit since her sudden outburst. However, she looks like she is about to burst into tears as usual. Clearly she is not coping with this situation at all. Sven sits next to her. "Stephanie, would you like a glass of water or something? I know this is a highly stressful time, none of us are having much fun at the moment and we can't wait until it is all over. Can I help at all?''

This makes Stephanie feel even worse, someone being kind to her, and she bursts into tears. Sven consoles her with tissues and grabs a glass of water.

Rex steps in. "Miss Welsh, we just have a couple of questions and we are in the home straight. It's just the usual set of questions we have been asking everyone. I apologise that you are the last. It's not nice being the last person in the room to get up and speak – the suspense and the waiting is worse. So, this is the easy part. Okay, are you ready? Do you need a couple more minutes perhaps?''

"No, I'm fine,'' Stephanie replies, even though she clearly isn't. "I want to get this over and done with. So, what is the question again, would you mind repeating it?''

Rex repeats the question. "What was your relationship with Cat?''

Stephanie looks incredibly nervous and says defensively, "What do you mean, what was my relationship with Cat? What has that got to do with anything? There wasn't a relationship.''

Everyone looks at each other, clearly thinking the same thing. Her response to a pretty fair and not unexpected question is most unusual, especially given that she did have a long time to formulate her answer.

Rex keeps his eyes on Stephanie. "Oh, I'm sorry,

I'm a little confused. You are saying you didn't have a relationship with Ms Tennyson?"

"No, I didn't. I don't know what people have been saying, but I never had a relationship with that woman. And really, what I do in my private life is none of your business. And for the records, I'm Ms Welsh, not Mrs or Miss."

Sven suddenly clicks, thinking back to the uncomfortable exchange she overheard between Cat and Stephanie. Were they lesbian lovers? She certainly never picked that. Surely she's mistaken.

Sven had walked over to their desks one day to ask something and Cat was just finishing snapping at Stephanie for doing something wrong. It didn't seem out of character on Cat's part, but what was weird was Stephanie looked like someone had just kicked her in the face. Stephanie had apologised to Cat and hurriedly walked out towards the ladies' room. Cat was left muttering under her breath, 'Really, what did I do to give that impression?'

Sven had been in the middle of something important at the time and had forgotten about it. But now, recalling that day, it all comes back to her.

Sven and Katarina exchange knowing looks; it is all starting to make sense. No wonder Stephanie had been in a bit of a mess in recent times – it looked like she was just under a lot of stress, but she was also finding it difficult to have a professional relationship with her boss when she was really in love with her. Most people had put the friction down to Stephanie being upset about being passed over for the top dog job. Stephanie didn't fancy Bernard after all. Now it was making sense that 'things are not what they seem'.

Rex clears his throat, pours himself some more water, thankful that his time working with these weird and wonderful people is almost over, and proceeds. "Stephanie, is there something you would like to tell us about your personal relationship with Cat? It's out now, so to speak, so you might as well finish what you have started, to speed up this process. You know you were the last person seen talking to her on the train on Friday evening; well, should I say the last one to have been arguing with her. Would you like to clarify with us what was the nature of the argument?"

Stephanie looks at the others around the table who now have all eyes on her. The room is so silent one could hear a pin drop. "I know what you are all thinking, your minds are always doing overtime, but like with Bernard you have got it all wrong. I was not seeing Cat. Yes, I did fancy her, but it was not reciprocated. Cat was in love, but not with me."

The room remains silent; even Rex and Charlie look gobsmacked, wondering what on earth is going to be revealed next. How had they had missed a lot of the finer points of who was doing what and with whom?

"So who was Cat in love with?" Rex asks.

"You men really think you have it sussed, don't you? Coming in being the big policemen, and you have no idea. No, Cat wasn't in love with another woman and she certainly wasn't in love with the pathetic opposite sex. She was in love with her job, that's what got her going. That's where she got her kicks, the thrill and buzz of her job, the power, the games, the corruption. She was so in love with her job she got sick over it. Bernard is right, she was not her normal self. She was tired, stressed and busily burning herself out, but you couldn't tell her. I tried to help her, but Cat was her own worst enemy. And yes, we did argue on Friday night, about her working too hard, and I offered to help her out with the announcement on Monday. She was so infuriating, frustrating and god damn independent, she would not take help from anyone. There you go, I'm not guilty. You are pretty desperate and clutching at straws if you think it was me. Haven't you got something better to base your accusations on?" Stephanie throws back at Charlie and Rex.

Stephanie has certainly come out of her shell, firing on all cylinders. Rex checks his vibrating phone, and whispers in Charlie's ear before leaving the room. Seconds later he returns with a Māori policewoman by his side. Sven recognises her straight away from that evening in the pub all those years ago, when she had sprung Charlie with his mates and another woman drinking away to their heart's content in a Courtenay Place bar. Feeling defensive and confused, like the rest of the room's occupants, she wonders why on earth this woman is back in her life again. How could Charlie, in the middle of this serious interrogation, bring her in? Is he trying to rub something in her face for effect? Just when she started thinking she could trust him again.

With no more time to think or speculate, Charlie stands up nervously as the policewoman walks over to him and he offers her the seat right next to Sven, to add insult to injury. "Everyone, this is Detective Mason, she is doing the Forensics on this case and has an update for us."

"Kia ora everyone, you can call me Marama. Thanks cuz, but first can I have a quick word outside with you both?" she says, looking at Charlie and Rex.

The clock in the boardroom strikes 4.30pm. It's one of those old-fashioned ones, antique imitation with a special chime like a grandfather clock, chiming on the hour and the half hour.

A few minutes later they all return to the room. Something has obviously gone down. A few words are spoken and then Charlie makes an announcement. "Ladies and gentlemen, thank you very much for your time. Something has come up and we need to pop down to HQ."

Rex turns to Charlie summing up, "Now with the autopsy report being finalised and everything out in the open, the truth has been revealed. What a relief!"

Everyone looks on expectantly, "Well don't keep us all waiting, man!" Alex angrily asks on behalf of the assembled, "Who is the murderer?"

Charlie responds. "Please continue about your business and can I ask that you all remain contactable by phone." Charlie looks pointedly at Alex. "Oh, and no one is to leave the country. Because of the extreme media interest in the case, the Police Commissioner will be holding a press conference to reveal the outcome of our investigation at 5.55pm tonight."

"A shrewd move, just in time for the 6pm News," Bernard articulates. "So we are free to go then…"

"Absolutely, thank you all again for your time," Charlie expands. "Sven, can I see you for a moment?"

Sven catches up with Charlie as they walk down the corridor. "So, don't make me ask…whodunnit?"

"Now, now, Sven, that would be telling," Charlie teases. "Besides, I was going to offer you a ride home, once I finish briefing the Commissioner, around 4.50pm? I still have a security pass card, so shall I pick you up in the car park downstairs?"

"That would be great, thanks," she says. Plucking

up her courage she adds, "And you can tell me all about Marama – your *cousin?*"

"Oh, the stories I could tell. She takes after her father, Uncle Wiremu – man that side of the family can put a drink or two away…"

Sven is in a state of shock to learn that the attractive Māori woman is in fact Charlie's close cousin, and nothing else.

****

Chapter 22

Unofficial Announcement – 8.1 earthquake

The headlines flash across the TV screens throughout New Zealand as the 6pm News begins. "Wellington has fallen victim to the biggest earthquake this century, bigger than the last 7.8 one on November 5th. Measuring 8.1 it struck just before 5pm and many public servants were either still at work inside the tall downtown buildings of the CBD or on their commute home. The extent of damage and the toll has not yet been released. The Incident Management team at BS Ministry have not been located, so we are unable to release what the official course of events are...We cross to the BS Minister..."

A picture of the harried BS Minister flicks up on the screen and it looks like he is being filmed exiting the A & E entrance at Wellington Hospital with a very attractive blonde.

A raucous chorus of "Minister, Minister, do you have

any comment…" emanates from the media pack.

"Look, I can't answer that yet, I don't even know where the Incident Management team is! Where's my secretary, Ernest, he will know their location, Emily can you find out where that damn ministerial car is…"

Back to the news desk where the 'Aunt of the Nation' TV anchor chimes in, "If anyone can shed any light on the whereabouts of the BS Ministry's Incident Management team, please ring this number immediately."

Her offsider, Dwayne, a young weasel-faced career climber who recently dodged a very public court case involving lap dancers and illegal substances, interrupts in a nasal twang. "In the greater Wellington region, news to hand. Trains are not going as there has been severe damage caused on the tracks; the electrics are out so all electric trains are not running. As the earthquake struck at peak commuting hour, a number of commuter trains were on the tracks and many trains have come to a standstill in the middle of their journeys to and from Wellington. There are many trains unaccounted for although some are believed to be stuck inside tunnels. With no cell phone coverage in the tunnels, we are out of touch with the passengers of these trains and again are unable to determine just what the extent of the fatalities and damage actually is."

'Aunt of the Nation' Jenny cuts in with, "We now have some CCTV camera footage which shows the extensive damage to buildings in the CBD." The camera crosses to a sea of glass on the pavements and roads with crumbling masonry scattered haphazardly among the debris. Some brave souls stagger about dazed and confused, while others try to help people from damaged vehicles. "Oh my god…" she exclaims.

Dwayne, seizing the moment, announces, "This next footage is from the rescue helicopter from Paraparaumu Airport, responding to a call to Miramar." The camera pans out over the suburbs as he continues. "The Wellington hill suburbs being hit with the combination of the latest earthquake and recent torrential rain, have resulted in a large number of slips and small landslides. Please, if you are driving or walking home, god forbid, take care, as a number of the roads are impassable due to the high volume of rubble and rocks on the road.

"State Highway One, the main route north out of Wellington is experiencing huge delays due to the massive landslide in the Ngauranga Gorge which is blocking the southbound traffic. Some northbound lanes are open at this stage. However, motorists, please take extra care.

"The Minister of Transport has strongly advised that those heading out of town please take the alternative route of State Highway 2 via Lower Hutt, or better still, please do not travel. Wait until further reports come to hand and the peak hour traffic has died down."

Aunt Jenny interrupts,"We cross live to the Civil Defence headquarters for an announcement," as the camera shows a balding thin man in his sixties. The shaken Civil Defence National Controller pleads, "Please everyone, for you and your fellow citizens' safety please stay inside and unless you have to please do not go out onto the street. The CBD is currently suffering from flying debris coming from broken panes of glass from tall buildings. We are declaring a state of emergency. Please stay inside the office or if at home, please stay at home.

We have no idea if or when there may be aftershocks or how strong they will be, so please stay where you are. Help where you can and check your emergency preparation kits are intact, and remember most phone coverage is down. We do have an 0800 number you can ring. The Big Super Ministry's Incident Management team have their work cut out for them this evening, so please be patient with them. We will get back to you once more information comes to hand."

Photos and video coverage come in thick and fast as two of the rescue choppers fly over the city taking up-to-date camera footage of the downtown area, surrounding suburbs and main arterial routes in and out of town, on their way to their medical emergency calls.

Another newsflash comes in. "There are also tsunami warnings but at this stage they are reported to be quite small. However, in the Nelson, Golden Bay regions, residents be aware they will be larger, with possible pockets of swamped areas.

"All Cook Strait ferries have been cancelled. Unfortunately, the capital is experiencing their usual high winds, and this has created a huge swirl out in the Cook Strait making it too rough for the sailings. This is causing extra pressure to the peak hour traffic as school holidays are beginning for some schools and there is a backlog of traffic queued up waiting to board the newly cancelled ferries. The backlog of trucks, campervans and cars are spilling out from the ferry terminals onto the motorway near Aotea Quay.

Anyone wishing to head southbound into Wellington, please delay your journey into town as there are backlogs of unhappy travellers parked along the quays," Dwayne quips.

Aunt Jenny, glaring at Dwayne, continues. "It is too

rough for the ferries to be berthed in at the port and one ferry has broken away from the wharf. Two ferries are anchored out in the harbour. The local commuter ferry to and from Eastbourne has been cancelled. Extra Eastbourne buses are running. However, with high tide fast approaching, and the small harbour tsunami that struck immediately after the earthquake, it is suspected that the narrow road in and out of Eastbourne and Lowry Bay will be flooded with high tide waves. Therefore, we urge you, if you want to get home tonight please make the journey now or stay in town with friends and family."

Again, the Civil Defence words flash across the screen:

'Earthquake 8.1 hits the capital at 4.55pm. Electric commuter trains unable to run due to power cut and outages over the city. Cook Strait ferries cancelled. Traffic jams in and out of Wellington due to huge slippages on two of the main gorges. Flying panes of windows falling from high rise buildings. Panes of shattered heritage glass continue to fall, along with crumbling masonry from the damaged buildings. Please stay inside the buildings. Internet and phone coverage down due to increased demand of usage on the remaining undamaged cell towers and the overloaded network. Please stay indoors if possible.'

More footage comes to hand of a second huge slip on Ngauranga Gorge and traffic piling up along State Highway 2.

"More helicopter coverage is coming to hand soon, as our Auckland-based news helicopter was in Taupō on another story. It has refuelled and is already en route…" Aunt Jenny announces.

Dwayne interrupts with, "We have just received some horrifying news about the new Chinese trains run by the

French transport company, from an employee who was recently dismissed for raising safety concerns with the new trains. We cross live to him now…"

Paul, an angry ex KiwiRail engineer stares into the camera. "Would they listen to me? Oh no, they wouldn't, they bloody well fired me instead, and why? Because that bloody frog sitting in Melbourne, Jean-Marie Leclerc wanted to cut costs…"

The reporter interrupts with, "So tell me, what safety features are you talking about, Paul…?"

"Well the bloody Chinese first up lined every carriage with asbestos, and said it would be fine as long as the carriages weren't put under structural stress, but we know that asbestos breaks down over time and the resultant dust is highly carcinogenic! But the worst was when they cut out the manual emergency door release, because the Chinese didn't have one and had to import a system from Germany which cost so much that they wouldn't have got the transport contract from KiwiRail!"

"So, you are telling me that all those passengers can't get out of the carriages? They are now in fact stuck within the train with no way out?" the reporter asks in disbelief.

"Not unless the driver or ticket conductor can use their lock and key system to open the door from the inside, but with most ticket conductors made redundant as soon as the frogs took over, that leaves the driver, and if he's injured or not in that particular carriage, all those passengers are trapped!" Paul explains. "And don't start me on the windows…"

Jenny is now glaring even more at Dwayne as these interviews are live and no one is controlling or editing what he is saying. It is not appropriate to be talking about the French or the Chinese in this way, but no one is there to stop Paul's free flowing unaudited words coming through. TVNZ had been cutting costs as well.

*****

Family members, knowing that their loved ones are creatures of habit, know that they will be on certain trains; the 4.55 out to Johnsonville, the 4.42 to Waikanae, the 4.57 to Porirua, and all these routes mean going through tunnels. They know exactly what time these trains are due in to their destination stations and hurriedly rush down there hoping like hell that they see these tiny commuter trains pulling up to the platforms. Their worst fear comes true. The trains never arrive. Does that mean they are stuck on the line somewhere, on a hill exposed to potentially more landslips, or worst still, stuck in tunnels without phone coverage and no way of disembarking from the train?

Passengers inside the trains are starting to panic and some hyperventilate. One particular passenger is having an anxiety attack and has thrown herself on the floor, clutching at her heart, screaming, "I'm having serious heart palpitations, I am going to have a heart attack. Oh my god, I knew this day would come, I am going to die of claustrophobia. I need to get out of here, now!"

Most of the passengers are in automatic 'public transport' mode and are either staring ahead blankly or pretending to be engrossed with the content on their phones that are no longer working, trying to ignore the woman's cry for help.

However, there are the trusty few who are looking on empathetically and wanting to help. Another woman screams out with the classic line, "Is there a doctor in the house? I mean a doctor on the train? We need a doctor NOW!" She is rummaging through the girl's handbag to see if she has any medication and finds her security badge, labelled 'Veronica, Occupation L & D Advisor, BS Ministry'. It's ADHD Veronica, who is allergic to confined spaces. She can hardly take the lift from the first floor to the sixth floor, let alone take a train, but she can't drive, and going by commuter train was the only way she was going to get to her friend's dinner party out in Paekakariki. It was only a forty-five-minute ride, and what could possibly go wrong, escaping town before the five o'clock rush hour?

The train to the coast has stopped bang in the middle of the tunnel, and it is not going anywhere.

*****

A few of the public servants still at work inside the BS building are starting to stir. A lot of them have taken note of the earthquake instructions that have been drilled into them: 'Drop, Cover, Hold', and most have dutifully followed the directions. There is a bit of a roar and hiss down in the basement car park; obviously someone is still trying to escape and has revved up their car beneath the BS building.

Wellingtonians are getting more and more worked up. Those in the streets are unable to do a lot either, except run for cover from falling debris and in the case of BS, run from flying heritage glass. The blinds protecting the windows have reduced the amount of flying glass within the building, but the glass has shattered outwards and like hail, is falling to streets and pavements beneath.

The one good thing is there is a series of underground tunnels running between the main ministries and the Beehive, and it is believed that some of the respective Incident Management Controllers have managed to get some of their staff down below to the inner sanctuary and safety of these tunnels. Comms managed to release this vital information to the Incident Controllers, and just before the earthquake struck.

Unbeknown to the outside world, everyone is feeling incredibly vulnerable and helpless, completely disempowered by Mother Nature's latest display of displeasure. What is the Incident Management team doing? Bernard, who delegated the Incident Management Control team to his second in command, Adrienne, cannot raise her on the phone. He cannot get an outside line…

Where is Sven? She was last seen returning to her pod on the sixth floor to pick up her handbag and laptop and take Charlie up on his offer, a ride home up the coast, supposedly away from all the chaos of today's developments.

Charlie had filed his report with HQ and was last seen heading for his car, parked down in the basement.

*****

Another newsflash and the announcers are interrupted as breaking news from a reporter live outside Police HQ comes onto the screen. "Juliette, Talia, what news have you got to report? You are on, live now…"

"The Police Commissioner has just announced that the Forensics report has been released regarding this morning's mysterious death on the Kiwi Con. The HR Director, who was found dead this morning on the Wellington train, died of natural causes, the homicide inquiry has been concluded. More details coming to hand. The name cannot be released yet, as next of kin cannot be located. Stay tuned, we will have more news once it comes to hand. All our CN reporters are out here. Most of them have been in and around the BS Ministry most of the day; we are attempting to make contact with the BS Ministry's Incident Management team..."

*****

Epilogue

Blood dripping from a nasty gash across her forehead, the woman slips in and out of consciousness as images, events and conversations flash through her mind. She can see them as vivid as life and she asks herself, *is this series of events what you see before or after death?* Am I already dead?

Amazed at what she sees and hears, the fear of rejection and abandonment along with reconnection and hope are the themes that flash across her mind.

The woman sees these images along with the sound of loud, shouting voices in the background. They are coming from a mixture of people from her life; previous friends, colleagues, and family. It is too much for her and she blacks out, her head dropping back into the headrest of the car seat.

Beside her, a man stirs and wrestles his way back to consciousness. "Sven, what the…" he manages to get out before his brain registers that he is now experiencing the aftermath of the earthquake and the situation he finds himself in. Automatically his hand reaches across to Sven to check her pulse. "Thank God, you're alive," says Charlie with a huge sigh of relief. Then seconds later, "What a mess," as he looks through the underground car park of fallen masonry and beams that are now partly crushing the parked cars. "Let's try and get out of here, Sven, and alive. I am not losing you ever again!"

*****

The End
Ka Kite Anō

GLOSSARY

Acronyms

There are far too many to mention here but enough to give the general gist:

ABBA Swedish pop band in the 1970s
AOG All of Government – tendering process (or Assembly of God)
ASS Aluminium Smelting Systems (Auckland company)
BAU Business as Usual
BO Burn Out, formerly known as Body Odour
BS Big Super Ministry or Bull Shit Ministry
B-52 Pop band in the 1980s
CAT Cathryn Ann Tennyson
CCE Chinese Capability Engagement
CD Constructive Dismissal
CEO Chief Executive Officer
CN Capital News (TV and Wellington's paper)
DCE Departmental Chief Executive
DCH Drop, Cover, Hold (earthquake preparation mantra)
DCM Don't Come Monday
DDCE Deputy Departmental Chief Executive
DIC Drunk In Charge of a motor vehicle (traffic offence)
DIC New Zealand department store Drapery Importing Company
DSIR Department of Scientific and Industrial Research
DSM-5 Psychiatrist's bible for labelling one's mental health deficiency
EA Executive Assistant
EAP Employee Assistance Programme
EEO Equal Employment Opportunities commission

ELT	Executive Leadership Team (aka SMT, Senior Management Team)
ER	Employment Relations
ERA	Employment Relations Authority
GETS	Government Electronic Tenders Service
HAA	Home and Away Café (In-house café)
HOD	Head of Department, the boss
HR	Human Resources, aka Personnel Management
HRLT	Human Resources Leadership Team
IKEA	Popular Swedish stores, similar to NZ's Warehouse
IP	Intellectual Property
JAFA	Just Another Fucking Aucklander – person from Auckland city
KC	Kiwi Connection commuter train from Wellington to Palmerston North
MOS	Meeting Overload Syndrome
OCD	Obsessive Compulsive Disorder
OIA	Official Information Act (request)
PC	Politically Correct or personal computer
PD	Professional Development
PG	Personal Grievance, a legal claim you can bring against your employer
PO	Purchase Order number needed for invoicing
PR	Public Relations or Permanent Residency (visa)
PS	Public Servant, paid by the taxpayer, you and me
PTSD	Post-Traumatic Stress Disorder
SAD	Seasonal Attention Deficit
SHIT	Science, Health and Information Technology team
SMT	Senior Management Team
SOCO	Scene of the Crime (suit) – white suit
TMI	Too Much Information
TOIL	Time Off in Lieu (take time off instead of getting paid)
VIP	Very Important Person
WFH	Working from Home (not really skiving)

Phrases and words

Bach	A very modest Kiwi holiday home, or crib (South Island)
Backfill	Filling in for someone, a contractor
Blue-sky thinking	Big picture, thinking outside the square or circle
Business as usual	Normal everyday work (BAU)
Consultant	An outside person who provides a service to a business
Chair Cemetery	Where all redundant chairs go, when dispensed with
Fitbit	21st century wearable device, fitness activity tracker for steps
Focus Group	Another excuse for a meeting
Hi-Vis	High Visibility vests and clothing
Open door policy	You can interrupt your boss at any time
Piece of work	A project
Podder	Desks set up in clusters, like pods, looking the same, like a PS
Stand-down	A long drawn-out, old-fashioned, sit-down meeting
Stand-up	A 'quickie' meeting, on the fly
Transvestic disorder	An excessive interest in cross-dressing
Words on a page	An old-fashioned page with words on it, like this one
.4	You are just 4/10, 40% of a person
.6	You are 60% of a human
.8	You are at the dizzying heights of 80% of a person
1.0	You work full-time but do very little. The backfills do it for you
101	Level 1 (elementary study) aptly named for HR meeting room

Māori Dictionary

Aotearoa	Land of the Long White Cloud: New Zealand
Aroha mai	Sorry, my apologies
E mōhio ana koe?	Do you understand?
Hapū	Clan, tribe, sub-tribe
Hauora	To be fit, well, healthy
Hīkoi	Journey
Hui	Social gathering, meeting
Iwi	Tribe, people
Iwi matakite	Tribal Seer
Kāi Tahu	The South Island tribe (Ngāi Tahu dialect)
Ka kite	See you again
Ka kite anō au i a koe	See you again soon
Kai	Food
Karakia	Chant, prayer
Kaumātua	Elder, person of status within the tribe
Kauri	Largest forest tree in NZ
Kete	Basket
Kia ora	Hello, be well, good luck, best wishes, cheers
Kōrero	Talk, chat, dialogue, conversation
Mahi	Work
Māori	Native, belonging to Aotearoa
Manuhiri	Visitor, guest
Marae	Māori meeting place, courtyard
Ngāi Tahu/Kāi Tahu	Māori tribe from the South Island, Sven belongs to
Pākēha	New Zealander of European descent
Papatūānuku	Earth, Earth mother
Rimu	NZ red pine
Rongoā Māori	Māori medicine, all four areas of health
Tangata whenua	Local people
Tangi	Tangihanga – funeral
Tapu	Sacred, forbidden
Tātou tātou e	Everyone

Te aroha	The love
Te rangimārie	The peace
Te whakapono	The trust
Tēnā koe	Hello, thank you
Te reo Māori	The Māori language
Te Whare Tapa Whā	Māori (holistic) health model, all four cornerstones: tinana (physical), hinengaro (mental/emotional), wairua (spiritual), and whānau (family)
Tohunga whakairo	Master carver
Tiriti O Waitangi	Treaty of Waitangi one of New Zealand's founding documents
Tui	Song bird, and brand for a NZ beer with cheeky advertising
Wahine	Female, also name of a famous shipwreck
Waka	Canoe or vehicle
Whakapapa	Lineage, descent, family tree
Whānau	Family, extended family, friends

New Zealand Places (Māori names)

Aotea (Quay)	A main road, off-ramp in Wellington
Horowhenua	An area north of Wellington and Kapiti Coast
Kaikōura	South Island town, whale watching
Kapiti	Coastal region north of Wellington
Ngauranga (Gorge)	The main route out of Wellington
Ōtāhuhu	South Auckland
Ōtaki	Most northern town of Kapiti
Paekakariki	Coastal town, Kapiti Coast
Paraparaumu	Coastal town, Kapiti Coast
Porirua	First large city north of Wellington
Rotorua	Central North Island, tourist and geyser (hot pools) area
Te Waipounamu	South Island (The Greenstone Waters)
Wairarapa	Region northeast of Wellington
Waikanae	Coastal town, Kapiti Coast
Waiheke Island	An island within the Auckland commuting belt
Waitarere Beach	A west coast beach in Horowhenua

Swedish Dictionary

Bög	Gay
Bra	Good
Dagens Nyheter	The Daily News, Swedish newspaper
Handelsbanken	Scandinavian bank
Hej	Hello or goodbye
Kosta Boda	Swedish glassmaker
Lycka Till	Good luck
Mäster Samuelsgatan	A main road in the CBD of Stockholm
Nordia Kompaniet (NK)	Department store Sweden
Personalchef	Director – HR
Polis Pojkvän	Police boyfriend
Sjukhus	Hospital
Skvaller	Gossip
Skeppsvik	A bay, holiday destination out of Umeå, Sweden
Smörgåsbord	Buffet, choice of food
Sköt om dig	Take care
Svenska Dagabladet	The Swedish Daily newspaper
Umeå	Town in Northern Sweden
Utredare	Detective
Wallander	Swedish Detective (TV programme) starring Kurt Wallander

French Dictionary

Beau	Man, boyfriend
Boudoir	Bedroom
Crème de la crème	The best, top class
Escargot	Snail
Ménage à trois	Threesome
Poisson du jour	Fish of the day
Raison d'etre	Reason to be, purpose
Rendezvous	Meeting place
Tête-à-tête	Face to face
Tout de suite	Immediately
Touché	Someone who has made a good point against you in a discussion or argument

Main Characters

HR TEAM

Cathryn Ann Tennyson	HR Director
Stephanie Welsh	2IC HR director
Carmen	Senior HR Advisor
Samantha Ann Svensson	Lifestyle Coach contractor
Elspeth	Cat's EA
Jillian	Cat's Consultant

SVEN'S MATES

Clara (Flat White)	Sven's school and workmate
Freya	Sven's school and workmate

RECRUITING TEAM

Nigel	Recruiting Manager

LEARNING & DEVELOPMENT TEAM

Sarita	Learning and Development Manager
Veronica	Learning and Development Advisor
Kirsty	Learning and Development Advisor

SCIENCE TEAM (SHIT)

Alex Goldsworthy	Science (SHIT) Manager
Chris	Science and IT contractor
Ted	Ex-Science (SHIT) Manager

RECEPTIONIST TEAM

Aileen	Receptionist, longest standing
Sally	Receptionist
Fiona	Receptionist
Barbara	Receptionist

SENIOR LEADERSHIP TEAM

Bernard	Department Chief Executive (DCE)
Katarina	Bernard's Swedish Executive Assistant
Sonja	Communications HOD
Winston	Procurement HOD
Andrea	DCE Finance, Admin, Recruiting Team
Julia	Pasifika and Māori HOD

SECURITY TEAM

Lewis	Security Manager HOD
Dave	Contractor Security Officer/Gigolo

POLICE TEAM

Charlie Rogers	Detective Sergeant, Head of Investigations
Rex Croft	Charlie's Police partner